SILKEN PREY

SILKEN PREY

JOHN SANDFORD

G. P. Putnam's Sons | New York

PUTNAM

G. P. PUTNAM'S SONS
Publishers Since 1838
Published by the Penguin Group
Penguin Group (USA) Inc., 375 Hudson Street,
New York, New York 10014, USA

USA · Canada · UK · Ireland · Australia
New Zealand · India · South Africa · China

Penguin Books Ltd, Registered Offices: 80 Strand, London WC2R 0RL, England
For more information about the Penguin Group visit penguin.com

ISBN 978-0-399-15931-2

Printed in the United States of America
1   3   5   7   9   10   8   6   4   2

Book design by Gretchen Achilles

This is a work of fiction. Names, characters, places, and incidents either are the product of the
author's imagination or are used fictitiously, and any resemblance to actual persons, living or dead,
businesses, companies, events, or locales is entirely coincidental.

For Summer, Colin, Mac, and Gus

SILKEN PREY

CHAPTER 1

S*queak.*
Tubbs was half-asleep on the couch, his face covered with an unfolded *Star Tribune*. The overhead light was still on, and when he'd collapsed on the couch, he'd been too tired to get up and turn it off. The squeak wasn't so much consciously felt, as *understood*: he had a visitor. But nobody knocked.

TUBBS WAS A POLITICAL.

In his case, political wasn't an adjective, but a noun. He didn't have a particular job, most of the time, though sometimes he did: an aide to this state senator or that one, a lobbyist for the Minnesota Association of Whatever, a staffer for so-and-so's campaign. So-and-so was almost always a Democrat.

He'd started with Jimmy Carter in '76, when he was eighteen, stayed pure until he jumped to the Jesse Ventura gubernatorial revolt in '98, and then it was back to the Democrats. He'd never done anything else.

He was a political; and frequently, a fixer.

Occasionally, a bagman.

Several times—like just now—a nervous, semi-competent black-mailer.

TUBBS SLEPT, USUALLY, in the smaller of his two bedrooms. The other was a chaotic office, the floor stacked with position papers and reports and magazines, with four overflowing file cabinets against one wall. An Apple iMac sat in the middle of his desk, sur-rounded by more stacks of paper. A disassembled Mac Pro body and a cinema screen hunkered on the floor to one side of the desk, along with an abandoned Sony desktop. Boxes of old three-and-a-half-inch computer disks sat on bookshelves over the radia-tor. They'd been saved by simple negligence: he no longer knew what was on any of them.

The desk had four drawers. One was taken up with current employment and tax files, and the others were occupied by office junk: envelopes, stationery, yellow legal pads, staplers, rubber bands, thumb drives, Post-it notes, scissors, several pairs of finger-nail clippers, Sharpies, business cards, dozens of ballpoints, five or six coffee cups from political campaigns and lobbyist groups, tangles of computer connectors.

He had two printers, one a heavy-duty Canon office machine, the other a Brother multiple-use copy / fax / scan / print model.

There were three small thirty-inch televisions in his office, all fastened to the wall above the desk, so he could work on the iMac and watch C-SPAN, Fox, and CNN all at once. A sixty-inch LED screen hung on the living room wall opposite the couch where he'd been napping.

———

Squeak.

This time he opened his eyes.

TUBBS REACHED OUT for his cell phone, punched the button on top, checked the time: three-fifteen in the morning. He'd had any number of visitors at three-fifteen, but to get through the apartment house's front door, they had to buzz him. He frowned, sat up, listening, smacked his lips; his mouth tasted like a chicken had been roosting in it, and the room smelled of cold chili.

Then his doorbell blipped: a quiet *ding-dong*. Not the buzzer from outside, which was a raucous ZZZZTTT, but the doorbell. Tubbs dropped his feet off the couch, thinking, *Neighbor*. Had to be Mrs. Thomas R. Jefferson. She sometimes got disoriented at night, out looking for her deceased husband, and several times had locked herself out of her own apartment.

Tubbs padded across the floor in his stocking feet. There was nothing tubby about Tubbs: he was a tall man, and thin. Though he'd lived a life of fund-raising dinners and high-stress campaigns, he'd ignored the proffered sheet cake, Ding Dongs, Pepsi, Mr. Goodbars, and even the odd moon pies, as well as the stacks of Hungry-Man microwave meals found in campaign refrigerators. A vegetarian, he went instead for the soy-based proteins, the non-fat cereals, and the celery sticks. If he found himself cornered at a church-basement dinner, he looked for the Jell-O with shredded carrots and onions, and those little pink marshmallows.

Tubbs had blond hair, still thick as he pushed into his fifties, a neatly cropped mustache, and a flat belly. Given his habits and his diet, he figured his life expectancy was about ninety-six. Maybe ninety-nine.

One big deficit: he hadn't had a regular woman since his third wife departed five years earlier. On the other hand, the irregular women came along often enough—campaign volunteers, legislative staff, the occasional lobbyist. He had always been a popular man, a man with political stories that were funny, generally absurd, and sometimes terrifying. He told them well.

As he walked toward the door, he scratched his crotch. His dick felt sort of . . . bent. Chafed. A little swollen.

The latest irregular woman was more irregular than most. They'd had a strenuous workout earlier that evening, a day that had left Tubbs exhausted. Hours of cruising the media outlets, talking to other operators all over the state, assessing the damage; a tumultuous sexual encounter; and finally, the biggest blackmail effort of his life, the biggest potential payoff . . .

He was beat, which was why, perhaps, he wasn't more suspicious.

Tubbs checked the peephole. Nobody there. *Probably Mrs. Jefferson,* he thought, who hadn't been five-two on her tallest day, and now was severely bent by osteoporosis.

He popped open the door, and,

Surprise!

TUBBS REGAINED CONSCIOUSNESS on the floor of a moving car, an SUV. He was terribly injured, and knew it. He no longer knew exactly how it had happened, if he ever had, but there was something awfully wrong with his head, his skull. His face and hands were wet with blood, and he could taste blood in his mouth and his nose was stuffed with it. He would have gagged if he had the strength.

He could move his hands, but not his feet, and with a little clarity that came after a while, he knew something else: he was lying on a plastic sheet. And he knew why: so the floor of the car wouldn't get blood on it.

The images in his mind were confused, but deep down, in a part that hadn't been impacted, he knew who his attackers must be, and he knew what the end would be. He'd be killed. And he was so hurt that he wouldn't be able to fight it.

Tubbs was dying. There wasn't much in the way of pain, because he was too badly injured for that. Nothing to do about it but wait until the darkness came.

The car was traveling on a smooth road, and its gentle motion nevertheless suggested speed. A highway, headed out of St. Paul. Going to a burial ground, or maybe to the Mississippi. He had no preference. A few minutes after he regained consciousness, he slipped away again.

Then he resurfaced, and deep down in the lizard part of his brain, a spark of anger burned. Nothing he could do? A plan formed, not a good one, but something. Something he could actually do. His hands were damp with blood. With much of his remaining life force, he pushed one wet hand across the plastic sheet, and tried as best he could to form the letters *TG*.

That was it. That was all he had. A scrawl of blood on the underside of a car seat, where the owner wouldn't see it, but where a crime-scene technician might.

He pulled his hand back and then felt his tongue crawl out of his mouth, beyond his will, the muscles of his face relaxing toward death.

He was still alive when the car slowed, and then turned. Still alive when it slowed again, and this time, traveled down a rougher road. Felt the final turn, and the car rocking to a stop. Car doors opening.

His killers pulled him out of the backseat by pulling and lifting the plastic tarp on which he lay. One of them said, "Skinny fuck is heavy."

The other answered, "Hey. I think he's breathing."

"Yeah? Give me the bat."

Just before the darkness came, Tubbs sensed the fetid wetness of a swamp; an odor, a softness in the soil beneath his body. He never heard or felt the crunch of his skull shattering under the bat.

Nothingness.

CHAPTER 2

Lucas Davenport was having his hockey nightmare, the one where he is about to take the ice in an NCAA championship game, but can't find his skates. He knows where they are—locker 120—but the locker numbers end at 110 down one aisle, and pick up at 140 on the next one.

He knows 120 is somewhere in the vast locker room, and as the time ticks down to the beginning of the match, and the fan-chants start from the bleachers overhead, he runs frantically barefoot up and down the rows of lockers, scanning the number plates. . . .

He knew he was dreaming even as he did it. He wanted nothing more than to end it, which was why he was struggling toward consciousness at eight o'clock on a Sunday morning and heard Weather chortling in the bathroom.

Weather, his wife, was a surgeon, and on working days was always out of the house by six-thirty. Even on sleep-in days, she hardly ever slept until eight. Lucas, on the other hand, was a night owl. He was rarely in bed before two o'clock, except for recreational purposes, and he was content to sleep until nine o'clock, or later.

This morning, he could hear her laughing in the bathroom, and realized that she was watching the built-in bathroom TV as she put on her makeup. She'd resisted the idea of a bathroom television, but Lucas had installed one anyway, claiming that it would increase their efficiency—get the local news out of the way, so they could start their days.

In reality, it had more to do with shaving. He'd started shaving when he was fifteen, and had never had a two-week beard. Even counting the rare days when he hadn't shaved for one reason or another, he'd still gone through the ritual at least twelve thousand times, and he enjoyed it. Took his time with it. Found that the television added to the whole ceremony.

Now, as he struggled to the surface, and out of the hockey arena, he called, "What?"

She called back, "More on Smalls. The guy is truly fucked."

Lucas said, "Have a good day," and rolled over and tried to find a better dream, preferably involving twin blondes with long plaited hair and really tight, round . . . ZZZ.

Just before he went back to dreamland, he thought about Weather's choice of words. She didn't use obscenity lightly, but in this case, she was correct: Smalls was really, truly fucked.

LUCAS DAVENPORT WAS TALL, heavy-shouldered, and hawk-faced, and, at the end of the first full month of autumn, still well-tanned, which made his blue eyes seem bluer yet, and made a couple of white scars stand out on his face and neck. The facial scar was thin, like a piece of pale fishing line strung down over his eyebrow and onto one cheek. The neck scar, centered on his throat, was circular with a vertical slash through it. Not one he liked to remember: the young girl had pulled the piece-of-crap .22 out of nowhere and shot him and would have killed him if Weather hadn't been there with a jackknife. The vertical slash was the result of the tracheotomy that had saved his life. The slug had barely missed his spinal cord.

The tan would be fading over the next few months, and the scars would become almost invisible until, in March, he'd be as pale as a piece of typing paper.

LUCAS ROLLED OUT OF bed at nine o'clock, spent some time with himself in the bathroom, and caught a little more about Porter Smalls.

Smalls was a conservative Republican politician. Lucas generally didn't like right-wingers, finding them generally to be self-righteous and uncompromising. Smalls was more relaxed than that. He was conservative, especially on the abortion issue, and he was death on taxes; on the other hand, he had a Clintonesque attitude about women, and even a sense of humor about his own peccadilloes. Minnesotans went for his whole bad-boy act, especially in comparison to the stiffs who usually got elected to high office.

Smalls was rich. As someone at the Capitol once told Lucas, he'd started out selling apples. The first one he bought for a nickel, and sold for a quarter. With the quarter, he bought five more apples, and sold them for a dollar. Then he inherited twenty million dollars from his father, and became an overnight success.

Weather loathed Smalls because he advocated Medicaid cuts as a way to balance the state budget. He was also virulently pro-life, and Weather was strongly pro-choice. He was also anti-union, and wanted to eliminate all public employee unions with a federal law. "Conflict of interest," he said. "Payoffs with taxpayer money."

Lucas paid little attention to it. He generally voted for Democrats, but not always. He'd voted for a nominally Republican governor, not once but twice. Whatever happened, he figured he could live with it.

ANYWAY, SMALLS HAD LOOKED like he was headed for reelection over an attractive young Minnesota heiress, though it was going to be close. Her qualifications for office were actually better than Smalls's; she looked terrific, and had an ocean of money. If she had a problem, it was that she carried with her a whiff of arrogance and entitlement, and maybe more than a whiff.

Then, on the Friday before, a dewy young volunteer, as conservative as Smalls himself, and with the confidence that comes from being both dewy and affluent—it seemed like everybody involved in the election had money—had gone into Smalls's campaign office to drop off some numbers on federal aid to Minnesota for bridge construction, also known as U.S. Government Certified A-1 Pork.

She told the cops that Smalls's computer screen was blanked out when she walked into the office. She wanted him to see the bridge files as soon as he came in, so she put them on his keyboard.

When the packets hit the keyboard, the screen lit up . . . with a kind of child porn so ugly that the young woman hardly knew what she was seeing for the first few seconds. Then she did what any dewy Young Republican would have done: she called her father. He told her to stay where she was: he'd call the police.

When the cops arrived, they took one look, and seized the computer.

And somebody, maybe everybody, blabbed to the media.

Porter Smalls was in the shit.

———

SUNDAY MORNING, A TIME for newspapers and kids: Lucas pulled on a pair of blue jeans, a black shirt, and low-cut black boots. When he was done, he admired himself in Weather's full-length admiring mirror, brushed an imaginary flake from his shoulder, and went down to French toast and bacon, which he could smell sizzling on the griddle even on the second floor.

The housekeeper, Helen, was passing it all around when he sat down. His son, Sam, a toddler, was babbling about trucks, and had three of them on the table; Letty was talking about a fashion-forward girl who'd worn a tiara to high school, in a kind of make-or-break status move; Weather was reading a *Times* review about some artist who'd spent five years doing a time-lapse movie of grass growing and dying; and Baby Gabrielle was throwing oatmeal at the refrigerator.

There were end-of-the-world headlines about Smalls, in both the Minneapolis and New York papers. The *Times*, whose editorial portentousness approached traumatic constipation, tried to suppress its glee under the bushel basket of feigned sadness that another civil servant had been caught in a sexual misadventure; they hadn't even bothered to use the word "alleged."

Lucas was halfway through the *Star Tribune*'s comics when his cell phone buzzed. He took it out of his pocket, looked at the caller ID, clicked it, and said, "Good morning, Neil. I assume you're calling from the Cathedral."

Neil Mitford, chief weasel for the governor of Minnesota, ignored the comment. "The guy needs to see you this morning. He should be out of church and down at his office by ten-thirty or so. He's got to talk to a guy at ten-forty-five, more or less, until eleven-thirty or so. He'd like to see you either at ten-thirty or eleven-thirty."

"I could make the ten-thirty," Lucas said. "Is this about Tubbs?"

"Tubbs? No, Tubbs is just off on a bender somewhere. This is about Smalls."

"What about Smalls? That's being handled by St. Paul."

"He'll tell you. Come in the back," Mitford said. "We'll have a guard down at the door for you."

LUCAS CHECKED HIS WATCH and saw that he would make it to the Capitol right on time, if he left in the next few minutes, and drove slowly enough.

"Wait," Weather said. "We were all going shopping."

"It's hard to tell the governor to piss up a rope," Lucas said. "Even on a Sunday."

"But we were going to pick out Halloween costumes . . ."

"I'd just be bored and in your way, and you wouldn't let me choose, anyway," Lucas said. "You and Letty will be fine."

Letty shrugged and said to Weather, "That's all true."

SO LUCAS IDLED UP Mississippi River Boulevard, top down on the Porsche 911, to Summit Avenue, then along Summit with its grand houses, and over to the Capitol.

The Minnesota Capitol is sited on a hill overlooking St. Paul, and because of the expanse of the hill, looks taller and wider than the U.S. Capitol. Also, whiter.

Lucas left the car a block away, and strolled through the cheerful morning, stopping to look at a late-season butterfly that was perched on a zinnia, looking for something to eat. The big change-of-season cold front had come through the week before, but, weirdly, there hadn't yet been a killing frost, and there were still butterflies and flowers all over the place.

At the Capitol, an overweight guard was waiting for him at a back door. He and the guard had once worked patrol together on the Minneapolis police force—the guard was double-dipping—and they chatted for a few minutes, and then Lucas climbed some stairs and walked down to the governor's office.

The governor, or somebody, had left a newspaper blocking the doorjamb, and Lucas pushed open the door, picked up the paper, and let the door lock behind him. He was standing in a darkened outer office and the governor called, "Lucas? Come on in."

THE GOVERNOR WAS A tall, slender blond named Elmer Henderson, who might, in four years, be a viable candidate for vice president of the United States on the Democratic ticket. The media said he'd nail down the left-wingers for a presidential candidate who might prefer to run a little closer to the middle.

Henderson might himself have been a candidate for the top job, if he had not been, in his younger years, quite so fond of women in pairs and trios, known at Harvard as the "Henderson Hoagie," and cocaine. He certainly had the right pedigree: Ivy League undergraduate and law, flawless if slightly robotic wife and children, perhaps a half billion dollars from his share of the 3M inheritance.

He was standing behind his desk, wearing a dark going-to-church suit, open at the throat, the tie curled on his desktop. He had a sheaf of papers in his hands, thumbing them, when Lucas walked in. He looked over his glasses and said, "Lucas. Sit. Sorry to bother you on a Sunday morning."

"It's okay." Lucas took a chair. "You need somebody killed?"

"Several people, but I'd hesitate to ask, at least here in the office, on the Lord's Day," the governor said. He gave the papers a last shuffle, set them aside, pressed a button on a box on his desk, and said, "Get in here," and asked Lucas, "You've been reading about Porter Smalls?"

"Yeah. You guys must be dancing in the aisles," Lucas said.

"Should be," said a voice from behind Lucas. Lucas turned his head as Mitford came through a side door, which led into his compact, paper-littered office. "This is one of the better political moments of my life. Porter Smalls takes it between the cheeks."

"What an unhappy expression," the governor said. He dropped into his chair, sighed, and put his stocking feet on the desktop. "But appropriate, I suppose. He's certainly being screwed by all and sundry."

"And it kills the Medicaid nonsense," Mitford said, as he took another chair. "He was carrying that on his back, and anything he was carrying is tainted. *You want to pass a bill sponsored by a kiddie-porn addict? What kind of human being are you?*"

"Grossly unfair," the governor said. He didn't seem particularly worried about the unfairness of it. He'd been looking at Mitford, but now turned to Lucas. "You know what the problem is?"

"What?"

"He didn't do it. Wasn't his child porn," the governor said. "I talked to him yesterday afternoon, over at his house, for a long time. He didn't do it."

"I thought you guys were blood enemies," Lucas said.

"Political enemies. I went to kindergarten with him, and knew him before that. Went to the same prep school, he went to Yale and I went to Harvard. His sister was a good friend of mine, for a while." He paused, looked up at the ceiling, and smiled a private smile, then recovered. "I tell you, from the bottom of my little liberal heart, Porter didn't do it."

"He could've gone off the rails somewhere," Lucas suggested.

The governor shook his head. "No. He doesn't have it in him, to look at kiddie porn. I know the kind of women he looks at. I can describe them in minute detail, and nobody would call them kiddies: he likes them big-titted, big-assed, and blond. He liked them that way in kindergarten and he still likes them that way. Go look at his staff, you'll see what I mean."

"Can't always tell . . ." Lucas began, but the governor held up a finger.

"Another thing," he said. "This volunteer said she walked into his office and put some papers on his keyboard and up popped the porn. If it really happened like that, it means that he had a screen of kiddie porn up on his computer, and walked away from it to a campaign finance meeting, leaving the door unlocked and the kiddie porn on the screen. The screen blanked for a while, but was still there, waiting to be found. Vile stuff, I'm told. Vile. Anyway, that's the only way her story works: the screen was blanked when she walked in, and popped back up when she put the papers on the keyboard. Porter was near the top of his class at Yale Law. He's not stupid, he's not a huge risk-taker. Do you really believe he would do that?"

"Even smart people—"

"Oh, horseshit," the governor said, waving him off.

"Suicidal . . ."

"Porter goes to the emergency room if the barber cuts his hair too short," the governor said. "He wants and expects to live forever, preferably with a big-titted, big-assed blonde sitting on his face."

Lucas thought for a moment, then conceded the point: "That thing about the volunteer—it worries me."

"It should," the governor said. He kicked his feet off the desktop and said, "I want you to look into this, Lucas. But quietly. I don't want to disturb anybody without . . . without there being something worthwhile to disturb them with."

"One more question," Lucas said. "This guy is a major pain in your party's ass. Why . . . ?"

"Because it's the right thing to do, mostly," the governor said. "There's something else, too. This sort of shit is going too far. Way too far. Most Republicans aren't nuts. They're perfectly good people. So are most of us Democrats. But this kind of thing, if it's deliberate—it's a threat to everybody. All you have to do is *say* 'kiddie porn' and a guy's career is over. Doesn't make any difference what he's done, what his character is like, how hard he's worked, it doesn't even matter if there's proof—once it gets out in the media, they'll repeat it endlessly, and there's no calling it back. You could have the Archbishop of Canterbury go on TV tomorrow and say he has absolute proof that Porter Smalls is innocent, and fifty other bloggers would be sneering at him in two minutes and CNN would be calling the bishop a liar. So we're talking about dangerous, immoral, antidemocratic stuff."

"You're saying the media is dangerous, immoral, and antidemocratic?"

"Well . . . yes," Henderson said. "They don't recognize it in themselves, but they're basically criminals. In the classic sense of that word."

"All right," Lucas said.

"And, of course, there's the other thing," the governor said. "The less righteous thing."

Lucas said, "Uh-oh."

Mitford said, "We're already hearing rumors that he was framed. That there were hints *before* anyone found the porn that something was coming on Smalls. If it turns out that some over-zealous young Democratic hacker did it, if this is a campaign dirty trick . . . then there could be a lot more trouble. If that's what happened, we need to know it first. The election's too close to be screwing around."

The governor added, "But the preliminary investigation has to be quiet. Invisible might be a better word."

Mitford said, "Totally quiet. That fuckin' tool over in the attorney general's office wants to move into this office. He thinks prosecuting Smalls is one way to do it. If he finds out that you're digging around, he'll paper your ass so fast you'd think you were a new country kitchen. You'll be working for him."

"You don't sound as *offended* as the governor," Lucas said to Mitford. "About Smalls being framed."

"I'm paid to keep my eye on the ball, so that's what I do," Mitford said. "Short term, there's no benefit to us, saving an asshole like Smalls. If we get a reward, it's gonna have to be in heaven, because we sure as shit won't get it now. If the party found out we were trying to help Smalls, then . . . well, you know, we're thinking about the vice presidency. On the other hand, if *we* did this, meaning *we* in the all-inclusive sense, and if that comes out, say, the Friday before the election . . ."

"I can't afford to lose the state House," Henderson said. He wasn't running. He still had two years to go on his second term.

"But Smalls is in the U.S. Senate," Lucas said. "How could that affect the state House?"

"Because our majority is too narrow. If it turns out that we tried to sabotage a U.S. Senate race, with child porn, Smalls will eat us alive in the last few days before the election. He could pump up the Republican turnout just enough that we could lose those extra three or four close-run seats. If we lose the House, and the Senate stays Republican, which it will, they'll spend the next two years dreaming up ways to embarrass me."

"We can't have that," Mitford said. "I mean, really."

"But. If Smalls owes us, even under the rose, he'll pay up," the governor said. "He's that kind of guy. He won't go after us . . . if he owes us."

"ALL RIGHT," LUCAS SAID. He stood up. "I'll do it."

"Excellent," the governor said. "Call me every day."

"But what if he did it?" Lucas asked.

"He didn't," the governor said.

Lucas said, "I'm going to tell Rose Marie about it. I can't . . . not do that." Rose Marie was the public safety commissioner and an old friend.

The governor was exasperated: "Jesus Christ, Lucas . . ."

"I can't not do that," Lucas insisted.

The governor threw up his hands. "All right. When you tell her, you tell her to call me. I'll need . . . Wait. Hell no. I'll call her right now. You get going on this. I'd like to get something pretty definitive in, say, mmm, three days. Two would be better."

"Man . . ."

"Go." Henderson waved him away.

———

ROSE MARIE ROUX HAD been a cop, then a lawyer and prosecutor, then a state senator, then the Minneapolis chief of police, and finally, the commissioner of public safety under Henderson. She had jurisdiction over a number of law enforcement agencies, including the Bureau of Criminal Apprehension. She viewed Lucas as both a friend and an effective tool for achieving her policy goals, not all of them involving crime-fighting. She'd gotten him his job at the BCA.

Rose Marie's husband was ten years older than she was, and when he'd retired, he talked her into dumping the suburban Minneapolis house in favor of a sprawling co-op apartment in downtown St. Paul. Lucas gave the governor a few minutes to talk to her, and then, as he walked back to his car, called her himself.

"You at home?"

"Yeah, come on down. I'll buzz you into the garage."

LUCAS HAD BEEN TO the apartment often enough that he knew the routine; buzzed into the garage, he parked in one of the visitors' slots and took the elevator to the top floor. Rose Marie's husband opened the door; he was holding the *Times* in one hand and a piece of jelly toast in the other. "She's out on the deck," he said.

"You raked the leaves off the deck yet?"

"Thank God for the penthouse—not a leaf to be seen," he said.

Rose Marie, wrapped in a wool shawl, was sitting on a lounge chair, smoking a cigarette; nicotine gum, she said, was for pussies. She was a short woman, going to weight, with an ever-changing hair color. Lucas liked her a lot.

When Lucas stepped out on the deck, she said, "I appreciate what you did, bringing me into it. This will be interesting, all the way around. Although it has a downside, of course."

She crushed the cigarette out on a ceramic saucer by the side of the chair. As Lucas sat down facing her, she asked, "How much do you like your job?"

"It's okay. Been doing it for a while," Lucas said.

"If this kind of thing happens too often, you'll get pushed out," Rose Marie said. "It's inevitable."

Lucas shrugged. "I do it because it's interesting. This assignment's interesting. If I wasn't doing this, I'd be chasing chicken thieves in Black Duck."

Rose Marie said, "I keep thinking about what I'm going to do when this job is over. If Elmer makes vice president, he'll take care of both of us. If he doesn't, then I'm unemployed, and you probably will be, too."

"That's a cheerful thought," Lucas said.

"Gotta face facts," Rose Marie said. "We've both had a good run. But I don't feel like retiring, and you're way too young to retire. We're both financially fine, but what the fuck do we do? Become consultants? I don't feel like running for anything."

"I haven't spent a lot of time worrying about it," Lucas said.

"You should," Rose Marie said. "Even if Elmer makes vice president, I'm not sure you'd want what he could get you. I'd be fine, because I'm basically a politician, I could work in D.C., or for his office here. But you . . . I don't know what you'd do. I don't think you'd want to wind up as some FBI functionary. Or Elmer's valet."

"No."

"Well. Sooner or later, your name will be connected to this job," Rose Marie said. "Whether or not it pans out. If the attorney general doesn't jump you for the prosecution, Porter Smalls will come after you for the defense. A lot of people in the Department of Public Safety and over at the BCA don't like this kind of thing, the political stuff. And you've been doing a lot of it. When I'm not here to protect you, when Elmer's not here . . ."

"Ah, it's all right, Rose Marie," Lucas said. "I've been fired before. Stop worrying about it."

"Yeah." She peered at him for a moment, then asked, "What are you going to do? About Smalls?"

"Try to keep it quiet, as long as I can," Lucas said.

"How are you going to do that?" she asked.

"Haven't worked it out yet. I've got a few ideas, but you wouldn't want to hear them."

"No. Actually, I wouldn't."

"So. Moving right along . . ." Lucas stood up.

Rose Marie said, "I'll talk to Henry. Make sure he has a feel for the situation." Henry Sands was director of the BCA and had been appointed by Henderson. If he knew Henderson was behind Lucas's investigation, he'd keep his mouth shut. Unless, of course, he could see some profit in slipping a word to a reporter. He didn't much like Lucas, which was okay, because Lucas didn't much like him back.

"Good," Lucas said. "And hey—relax. Gonna be all right."

"No, it won't," she said. "I can almost guarantee that whatever it is, it won't be all right."

LUCAS STARTED BACK DOWN to the car, still thinking it over. Rose Marie was probably right about the political stuff. Even if you were on the side of the Lord, the politics could taint you. Which created a specific problem: there was at least one man at the BCA who'd be invaluable to Lucas's investigation—Del Capslock. Del had contacts everywhere, on both sides of the law, and knew the local porn industry inside out.

The problem was, Del depended on his BCA salary, and all the benefits, for his livelihood. He had a wife and kid, and was probably fifteen years from retirement. Everybody in the BCA knew that he and Lucas had a special relationship, but that was okay . . . as long as Lucas didn't drag him down.

Lucas didn't particularly worry about himself. Back in the nineties, he'd been kicked out of the Minneapolis Police Department and had gone looking for something to do. He'd long had a mildly profitable sideline as a designer of pen-and-paper role-playing games, which had gone back to his days at the university. After he left the MPD, he'd gotten together with a computer guy from the university's Institute of Technology. Together they created a piece of software that could be plugged into 911 computer systems, to run simulations of high-stress law-enforcement problems.

Davenport Simulations—the company still existed, though he no longer had a part of it—had done very well through the nineties, and even better after the September 11 attacks on the World Trade Center. Instead of one simulation aimed at police departments, they now produced dozens of simulations for everything from bodyguard training to aircraft gunfight situations. When the management bought Lucas out, he walked away with enough money to last several lifetimes.

He was rich. Porter Smalls was rich. The governor was *really* rich, and for that matter, so was Porter Smalls's opponent; even the volunteer who'd started the trouble was rich, or would be. Rich people all over the place; gunfight at the one-percent corral.

Anyway, he was good, whatever happened. If the Porter Smalls assignment turned into a political quagmire, he could always . . . putter in the garden.

Del couldn't.

Lucas popped the doors on the 911 and stood beside the open door for a minute, working through it.

Del was out of it. So were his other friends with the BCA.

Which left the question, who was in, and where would he get the intelligence he would need? He had to smile at the governor's presumption: get it done, he'd said, in a day or two, and keep it absolutely private. He didn't care how, or who, or what. He just expected it to be done, and probably wouldn't even think about it again until Lucas called him.

CHAPTER 3

Lucas decided to go right to the heart of the problem and start with Porter Smalls. He called the number given him by Mitford, and was invited over. Smalls lived forty-five minutes from downtown St. Paul, on the east side of Lake Minnetonka.

His house was a glass-and-stone mid-century, built atop what might have been an Indian burial mound, though the land was far too expensive for anyone to look into that possibility. In any case, the house was raised slightly above the lake, with a grassy backyard, spotted with old oak and linden trees.

Lucas was met at the door by a young woman who said she was Smalls's daughter, Monica. "Dad's up on the sunporch," she said. "This way."

Lucas followed her through a quiet living room and down a hall, then up a narrow, twisting stairway. Lucas noted, purely as a matter of verifying previous information, that she was both big-titted and big-assed, as well as blond, so Henderson's description of Smalls's sexual preferences were showing some genetic support.

At the top of the stairs, she said, "Dad's out there," nodding toward an open door, and asked if Lucas would like something to drink.

Lucas said, "Anything cold and diet?"

"Diet Coke," she said.

"Excellent."

"Is Mrs. Smalls around?" Lucas asked.

"If by 'around' you mean the Minneapolis loft district with her Lithuanian lover, then yes."

"Maybe I shouldn't have asked," Lucas said.

"No, that's all right," she said cheerfully. "It's been in the papers."

SMALLS WAS SITTING ON a draftsman's stool on the open sun-porch, looking out over the lake through a four-foot-long brass telescope. He was wearing faded jeans and an olive-drab, long-sleeved linen shirt under an open wool vest.

Lucas thought he looked less like a right-wing politician than like a professor of economics, maybe, or a poet. He was a small man, five-seven or five-eight, slender—no more than a hundred and fifty pounds—and tough-looking, like an aging French bicycle racer. He wore his white hair long, with tortoiseshell glasses over crystalline blue eyes.

Lucas knocked on the doorjamb and said, "Hello," and Smalls turned and said, "There you are," and stood to shake Lucas's hand. "Elmer said you'd be coming around."

"You want me?" Lucas asked.

"I'll take anything I can get, at this point," Smalls said. He pointed at a couple of wooden deck chairs, and they sat down, facing each other. Before going to the telescope, Smalls had apparently been reading newspapers, which were stacked around the feet of his chair. "What do you think? How fucked am I?"

Lucas thought about Weather and said, "My wife was watching TV this morning, as she was getting ready to go out, and the story came up, and she said, 'Smalls is truly fucked.'"

Smalls nodded. "She may be right. She would be right, if I were guilty. . . . Your wife works?"

"She's a surgeon," Lucas said.

"And you made a couple of bucks in software," Smalls said.

"Yes, I did. You've been looking me up?"

"Just what I can get through the Internet," Smalls said. He reached down, picked up an iPad, flashed it at Lucas, dropped it again on the pile of paper. "You think you can do me any good?"

"If I proved you were innocent, *would* it do you any good?" Lucas asked.

Smalls considered for a moment, staring over the lake, pulling at his lower lip. Then he looked up and said, "Have to be fast. Nine days to the election. If you don't find anything before the weekend, I couldn't get the word out quickly enough to make a difference. I need to be at the top of the Sunday paper, at the latest. My opponent has more money than Jesus, Mary, and Joseph put together, along with a body that . . . never mind. Of course, even if I lose, it'd be nice if I weren't indicted and sent to prison. But I don't want to lose. I don't deserve to lose, because I'm being framed."

"The governor tells me you didn't do it," Lucas said.

"Of course I didn't," Smalls snapped, his glasses glittering in the sun. "For one thing, I'm not damn fool enough to leave a bunch of kiddie porn on an office computer, with all kinds of people walking in and out. The idea that I'd do that . . . that's *insulting.*"

"We talked about that," Lucas said. "The governor and I."

"And that rattlesnake Mitford, no doubt," Smalls said.

Monica came out with a bottle of Diet Coke and a glass with ice. She'd overheard the last part of the conversation, and said, "I promise you, Mr. Davenport, Dad's *not* a damn fool."

Lucas poured some Coke, took a sip, said "Thanks" to Monica and asked Smalls, "What do you know about this volunteer? Has she got anything against you? Did you have any kind of personal involvement with her?"

"No. That's another thing I'm not damn fool enough to do. Not since Clinton. If I were going to play around, there are lots of good-looking, smart, discreet adult women available. I really wouldn't have a problem."

"People sometimes get entangled—"

"Not me," Smalls said. He started to say something more, but then looked up at his daughter and grinned and said, "Monica, could you get me a beer? Or wait, no. I don't want a beer. This talk could get embarrassing, so . . . sweetie . . . could you just go away?"

"You sure you want to be by yourself, with a cop?" Monica asked.

"I think I can handle it," Smalls said. She patted him on the shoulder and walked back into his house, and down the stairs. When she was gone, Smalls said, "She's a lawyer, too. A pretty good one, actually." They both thought about that for a second, then Smalls said, "Look: I've done some fooling around. Got caught, too. Not by the morality police. It was worse than that: the old lady walked in on me."

"Ouch."

"Twice. The last time, she had her lawyer with her."

"Ahh . . ."

"So I *can* be a fool, but not the kind of damn fool I'd have to be if I were guilty of this kiddie porn stuff," Smalls said. "I think before I jump. The women I've been involved with, they're pretty good gals, for the most part. They knew what they were getting into, and so did I. That sort of thing, for a guy at my level, is okay. Elmer couldn't get away with it, anymore, but I'm not quite as visible as the governor. The other thing is, political people are pretty social, and they knew what the situation was between Brenda and me. So, looking outside was considered okay, as long as it was discreet."

"I get that," Lucas said. "I guess."

"But some things are not okay," Smalls said. "Going after volunteers—the young ones—is not okay. A relationship with a lobbyist is not okay. I wouldn't look at kiddie porn, even if I were bent that way, which I'm not. If I were interested in drugs, which I'm not, I wouldn't snort cocaine or smoke pot around witnesses, at a party. I wouldn't chisel money from my expense accounts. You know why I wouldn't do any of that? Because I'm not stupid. I'm not stupid, and I've seen all that stuff done by people who were supposedly smart, and they got caught, and some of them even went to jail. If I were to do any of that, and get caught, I'd feel like an absolute moron. That's one thing I won't tolerate in myself. Moronic behavior."

"All right," Lucas said. "So this volunteer . . ."

"To tell you the truth . . ." Smalls was already shaking his head. "I believe her. I think she's telling the truth."

"Yes?"

"Yup. It sort of baffles me, but I believe her," Smalls said. "I'm not a hundred percent sure of her, but mostly, I think somebody planted that porn on my computer. People are always going in and out of my office. I think somebody went in there, called it up, and walked back out. Then she walked in . . ."

"But how'd they know she'd toss the files on the keyboard?"

"How do we know this was the only time they tried it?" Smalls asked. "Maybe they did this ten times, just waiting for somebody to touch the keyboard. But the thing is, her story is too stupid. I keep coming back to stupidity, and whoever did this to me isn't entirely stupid. But the way *she* says it happened, this volunteer, this girl . . . it's too stupid. If *she's* the one who did it, I'd think she would have made up a better story."

Lucas shook his head. "Unless your office is a lot more public than I think it is—"

Smalls held up a hand: "Stop right there. Wrong thinking. The thing is, it *is* public," he said. "It's a temporary campaign office, full of rented chairs and desks and office equipment. I hardly ever go there, but technically, it's mine. I have another office, the Senate office. In that office, my secretary would monitor people coming and going. Nobody would get in the private office without her knowing, and watching them every minute. There's classified stuff in there. In the campaign office, there are staff people going in and out all the time."

"You think a staff person might have been involved?" Lucas asked.

"Had to be. There are undoubtedly a couple of devoted Democrats around—just as . . . and this is off the record . . . just as there are a couple of pretty devoted Republicans over in Taryn Grant's campaign staff."

"Spies."

"If you want to be rude about it," Smalls said. "So you get a couple of young people as spies, and some of them are a little fanatical about their status, and about helping one party or the other win. So, yeah, somebody on the staff. That's a good possibility. A probability."

"The computer didn't have any password protection?"

"Yes, of course it did. Want to know what it was? It was 'Smallscampaign.'"

"Great."

"Yeah."

Lucas asked, "Do you know what happened to it? Your computer?"

"The St. Paul police have it," Smalls said.

"You think you could get access to it?" Lucas asked.

"Maybe. Probably. I don't know if I could get to the computer itself, but we should be able to get a duplicate of the hard drive, which would give you everything relevant," Smalls said.

Lucas nodded. "Okay. You're innocent, right?"

"Yes."

"So: call your attorney," Lucas said. "Today. Right now, on Sunday. Tell him that you want to duplicate the hard drive to start preparing a defense. Take it to court if you have to, but get the hard drive for me. If you have to go to court, you argue that you will be irreparably harmed, with only a week to the election, if you're not allowed to see what you're accused of. You'll get it. When they give you access, call me, and I'll send somebody down to monitor the copy process."

"Somebody from your company?"

"No. It'll be a computer expert named Ingrid Caroline Eccols—everybody calls her ICE, for her initials," Lucas said. "She's an independent contractor, and she knows this kind of thing, inside and out."

"A hacker?"

"Not exactly," Lucas said. "She does a little bit of everything. She's worked for law enforcement agencies, from time to time, and the St. Paul crime lab folks know her. I think she may have worked on the other side, too. I do trust her, when she says she'll take a job. The key thing is, when it comes to copying the drive, she won't miss anything. There won't be any games. She'll get everything there is to get."

"John Shelton is my attorney," Smalls said. "I'll get him going. You get this ICE."

"Another thing: I need a list of everybody who works for and around the committee. Send it to my personal e-mail." Lucas took out a business card and a pen, wrote his e-mail address on the back of it, and handed it to Smalls.

"I'll do it this afternoon," Smalls said.

"Do it right away," Lucas said. "I need all the help I can get from you, or I'll spend a lot of time sitting on my ass."

"Let me tell you another little political thing," Smalls said. "The Democrats have me right where they want me. My opponent is young, good-looking, about a hundred times richer than I am, and is running a good campaign. Her problem was, I was going to beat her by six points, 53 to 47 or thereabouts, before the child porn thing happened. She might have cut a point off that. Now, she's going to take me down, probably 52 or 53 to 48 or 47. My core constituency will sit on its hands if they think I'm guilty of this child porn thing. I'm already hearing that."

"I knew some of that," Lucas said.

"But here's the thing," Smalls said, leaning toward Lucas: "The Democrats don't need to get me indicted, or to be guilty. They just need the accusation out there, with the attorney general running around, looking under rocks. If I'm innocent, they'll be perfectly happy to apologize for all of this, about an hour after I lose the election. 'That really wasn't right about old Porter Smalls. . . .' So to do me any good, you pretty much have to find out what happened. Not just that I'm probably innocent. 'Probably' won't cut it. We need to hang somebody, and in the next five days or so."

Lucas didn't say that his mission wasn't to save Smalls's career; he just said, "Okay."

"Damn. I'll tell you what, Davenport, you may have done the worst possible thing here," Smalls said.

"Hmm?"

"Elmer says you're really, really good. You've given me a little hope. Now I've got further to fall."

ALTHOUGH IT WAS SUNDAY, Lucas decided to stop back at the BCA headquarters, on his way home. He walked through the mostly empty building up to his office, where he found an e-mail from Smalls, saying that he'd talked to his attorney, who would go after the hard drive that afternoon. He asked Lucas to put ICE in touch with the attorney. Lucas called ICE, who said she'd take the job, "though I don't like working for a wing-nut."

"You're not working for a wing-nut," Lucas said. "You're working for democracy in America."

"For two hundred dollars an hour. Let's not forget that."

LUCAS SPENT AN HOUR at BCA headquarters, looking at e-mailed reports on investigations that his people were running, but nothing was pressing. Del, Shrake, and Jenkins were trying to find a designer drug lab believed to be in the Anoka area, and Virgil Flowers was seeking the Ape-Man Rapist of Rochester. Lucas wrote notes to them all that he'd be working an individual op for a couple of weeks, but he'd be in touch daily.

While he was doing that, an e-mail came in from Smalls, saying that he wouldn't have the list of campaign employees and volunteers until late in the day. Lucas then tried to call the young woman who'd discovered the porn, and was told by her mother that she was at a friend's house at Cross Lake, and wouldn't be back before midnight. Lucas arranged to meet her the next morning at her home in Edina.

That done, he made a call to the St. Paul cops, got shifted around to the home phone of a cop named Larry Whidden, of the narcotics and vice unit. Whidden was out in his backyard, scraping down the barbecue as an end-of-season chore. Lucas asked to see his investigative reports, and Whidden said, "As far as I'm concerned, you can look at everything we got, if the chief says okay. It's pretty political, so I want to keep all the authorizations very clear."

Lucas called the chief, who wanted to know why Lucas was interested. "Rose Marie asked me to take a look," Lucas said. "To monitor it, more or less. No big deal, but she wants to stay informed."

"Politics," the chief said.

"Tell you what, Rick," Lucas said, "how did you get appointed?"

"What's that supposed to mean?"

"Politics," Lucas said. "It is what it is."

"Funny. Okay. But I'll tell you what, this whole thing ranks really high on my badshitometer. If Smalls is guilty, he could still do a lot of damage thrashing around. If he's innocent, he's gonna be looking for revenge, and he's in exactly the right spot to get it."

"All the more reason for somebody like yourself to spread the responsibility around," Lucas said.

"I'd already thought of that," the chief said. "I'll call Whidden."

Whidden called Lucas five minutes later and said, "I can go in later and Xerox the book for you, but you're gonna have to wait awhile. I got my in-laws coming over. Why don't you come by at six? You want to look at the porn, I can have Jim Reynolds come in."

So Lucas had run out of stuff to do. He tried to think about it for a while, but didn't have enough material to think about. He called home, and nobody answered—they were still out shopping for superhero costumes for Sam. He left a message that he'd probably be home at seven o'clock. That done, he went out to a divorced guys' matinee, to catch the Three Stooges movie he'd missed when it came by in the spring. The divorced guys were scattered around the theater as always, single guys with popcorn, carefully spaced apart from each other, emitting clouds of depression like smoke from eighties' Volkswagen diesel.

Despite that, Lucas laughed at the movie from the moment a nun got poked in the eyes and fell on her ass; took him back to his childhood, with the ancient movies on the obscure TV channels. And Jesus, nuns getting poked in the eye? You'd have to have a heart of pure ice not to laugh at that.

He was out of the movie at five-thirty, called ahead to St. Paul, and at five-forty-five, he parked at the St. Paul Police Department, in the guest lot. He walked inside, had a friendly chat with the policewoman in the glass cage, and was buzzed through to the back, where he found Whidden leaning against the wall, sucking on a Tootsie Pop.

Whidden said, "This way," and led him down to Vice, where he took a fat file off an unoccupied desk and said, "Copy of what we got. Want to look at the porn?"

"Maybe take a peek," Lucas said.

He followed Whidden down to the lab, where Jim Reynolds, a very thin man in a cowboy shirt, was looking at a spreadsheet. He saw Lucas and Whidden, stood up and said, "Over here," and to Lucas, "Thanks for the overtime."

"No problem. Christmas is coming."

Reynolds took them to a gray Dell desktop computer. "Smalls is getting a court order for a copy of the hard drive," he told them. "It'll be here first thing tomorrow."

"He's denying any knowledge," Lucas said. "What do you think?"

"I've usually got an opinion," Reynolds said. "But this thing is a little funky. I don't know."

"Funky, how?"

"The circumstances of the discovery," Reynolds said. "When you get into it, you'll see."

Whidden said, "I'm sixty-five percent that he's guilty. But, if I was on the jury . . . I don't think I'd convict him."

Reynolds brought up the porn file: the usual stuff, for kiddie porn: young boys and girls having sex with each other, young boys and girls with adults. Nothing new there, as kiddie porn went.

Lucas asked, "How much is there?"

"Several hundred individual images and thirty-eight video clips," Reynolds said. "Some European—we've seen them before—and some, we don't know where it comes from. We haven't looked at it all, but what we've seen, it's pretty bad stuff."

"What about this volunteer, the whole thing about throwing some papers on the keyboard?" Lucas asked.

"We've tested that, and that's the way it works," Reynolds said. "You're looking at the porn, you walk away. In two minutes, the screen blanks. Touch a key, and it comes back up with whatever was on the screen. In this case, the porn file."

THERE WASN'T MUCH TO talk about, so Lucas thanked Whidden for the file, and Reynolds for the demonstration, and drove home. He arrived twenty minutes before dinner would be ready, and when Weather asked him if there was anything new, he said, "Yeah. I've been asked to prove that Porter Smalls is innocent."

"Shut up," she said.

PORTER SMALLS'S LIST OF campaign staff members came in, more than forty of them, both paid and volunteer. After dinner, Lucas spent a while digging around on the Internet, looking for background on them. He found a few things on Facebook, but quickly realized that nobody was going to post "Guess who I framed?"

He'd just given up when ICE called. "I talked to your wing-nut's lawyer, and he says we'll get a copy of the hard drive tomorrow, around ten-thirty, eleven o'clock," she said.

"I was told you'd get it first thing," Lucas said.

"Well, I was told that the attorney general's office wants a representative there, and they're bringing along their own computer guy. They couldn't get him there any sooner."

"I need to talk to you as soon as you've got it, but don't tell anybody you're bringing it to me. Let them think it's for Smalls's attorney and nobody else," Lucas said. "Could you bring the stuff here, to my place?"

"I'll have to see what the attorney says, but I don't see why not."

"Call me, then," Lucas said. "One other thing: I'm researching a bunch of people, I really need to get background on them. But all I get from Google is a lot of shit."

"You know that old thing about 'Garbage in, garbage out'?" ICE asked.

"Yeah?"

"Google is now the biggest pile of garbage ever assembled on earth," ICE said. "Give it a couple more years, and you won't be able to find anything in it. But, hate to tell you, I don't do databases. I do coding and decoding and some hardware. But I don't do messaging or databases. I don't even Tweet."

"You got anybody who's good at databases?" Lucas asked. "I really need to get some research done."

"Yeah. I do know someone. So do you. He probably knows more about databases than anybody in the world. Literally."

"Who's that?" Lucas asked.

"Kidd."

"What kid?"

"Kidd the artist," ICE said.

"Kidd? The artist?" Lucas knew Kidd fairly well, and knew he did something with computers, in addition to his painting. They'd been jocks at the University of Minnesota around the same time, Lucas in hockey and Kidd as a wrestler. Weather owned one of Kidd's riverscapes, and had paid dearly for it—a price Lucas would have considered ridiculous, except that Weather had been offered three times what she'd paid, and had been told by an art dealer that the offer wasn't nearly good enough.

ICE said, "Yeah. Believe me, he does databases."

"He's really good?"

"Lucas, the guy's a legend," ICE said. "He not only does databases, he does everything. There's a story—it might not be true—that Steve Jobs was afraid that Microsoft's new operating system would crush the life out of Apple. This was back in the late nineties, or maybe 2000. So Jobs asked Kidd to help out, and Kidd supposedly said he'd see what he could do. The next Microsoft release . . . well, you've heard of Windows ME?"

"Sort of."

"It did more damage to Windows' reputation among consumers than anything before or since," ICE said. "It sucked. It worse than sucked. Supposedly, Kidd had a finger deep in its suckedness." She hesitated, then said, "Of course, that might all be a fairy tale."

Lucas said, "Well, I guess I'll give him a call."

"Say hello for me," ICE said. "Tell him if he ever ditches his wife, I'm around."

"That way, huh?"

"He is *so* hot . . . don't even get me started."

HOT? KIDD?

Lucas had never thought of Kidd as hot, or even particularly good-looking. He certainly didn't know anything about fashion— Lucas had never seen him in anything but jeans and tennis shoes and T-shirts or sweatshirts, sometimes with the sleeves cut off. Weather gave money to the Minneapolis Institute of Art, quite a lot of money, and they'd once gone to a function that specified business casual dress, and Kidd was there . . . in jeans, running shoes, and a sweatshirt, but with the sleeves intact. He said it was casual, for his business.

Still, in regard to his hotness . . . Weather seemed to enjoy Kidd's company. A lot. Sort of like she enjoyed the company of Virgil Flowers, another predator, in Lucas's opinion. And Kidd had a wife who was herself so hot, in Lucas's view, that she was either far too good for the likes of Kidd, or . . .

Kidd had something that Lucas didn't recognize. Not that there was anything wrong with that, Lucas thought.

LUCAS DUG KIDD'S PHONE number out of his desk and called him. Kidd picked up: "Hey, Davenport," he said. "Wasn't there, didn't do it."

"How's Lauren?" Lucas asked.

"Who wants to know? And why?"

"Just making small talk," Lucas said. "I need to talk to you . . . about computers. A friend told me that you understand databases."

"What friend?"

"Ingrid Caroline Eccols." There followed a silence so long that Lucas finally asked, "You still there?"

"Thinking about ICE," Kidd said. "So, what's the situation?"

"I'd rather explain it in person," Lucas said. "But time is short. Would you be around tomorrow, early afternoon?"

"Yeah, but ICE isn't invited."

"She's a problem?"

"I couldn't even begin to explain the many ways in which she could be a problem," Kidd said.

"Okay. She's not invited," Lucas said.

"Can Lauren sit in?"

Lucas hesitated, then said, "It's a very confidential matter."

"She's a very confidential woman," Kidd said. "And if it's that confidential, I'd rather she hear about it. You know, in case I need a witness at some later date."

"Then fine, she's invited, if she wants to be there."

"Oh, she'll be there," Kidd said. "She thinks you're totally hot."

TOTALLY HOT.

Everybody was hot, everybody was rich. Better than chasing chicken thieves in Black Duck, Lucas thought, as he settled at his desk with the file from Whidden.

The file looked pretty good, until he opened it. Once opened, half of it turned out to be printouts of 911 conversations, repetitive reports on the seizing of the computer from the campaign offices, and reports of conversations and interviews with office personnel, most of whom knew nothing whatever, and an interview with Brittany Hunt, the volunteer who found the pictures.

Hunt was twenty and had been working as a volunteer since June, and would return to college—Sarah Lawrence—the following winter, having spent half a year working on the campaign.

She knew only slightly more than the completely ignorant office employees. She'd had a report on the ten-year cost of proposed bridge repairs, for which Smalls had gotten appropriations from the feds. She'd walked into his office a little after ten o'clock in the morning, and since Smalls himself had ordered the report, she'd placed it where he'd be sure to see it, and know that she'd fulfilled his request: she dropped it on his keyboard.

Instantly, she said, a picture flashed up, and she'd reflexively looked at it: at first it seemed like a jumble of dead people, and then she realized that it was a group sex photo, and that two of the people in the photo were children.

She called Dad, and Dad dialed 911. The rest was history. Lucas learned almost nothing from the report that he hadn't gotten from Smalls, except that Sarah Lawrence women freely used sexual references that Lucas heretofore thought confined to pornographic films.

He finished the file, and went into the kitchen in search of orange juice. Weather and Letty were leaning on the kitchen breakfast bar, programming something into Weather's cell phone. Weather looked up and asked, "Well? What was in the file? Did he do it?"

Lucas got a bottle of orange juice from the refrigerator and twisted its cap off. "File was useless. One good thing: I'm not far behind the St. Paul cops."

"I'm shocked that you're behind at all," Weather said.

"Me too," said Letty. "Shame."

"Thank you for your support," Lucas said. "You'll find me in the garage, sharpening my lawn mower blade."

Letty looked at Weather and asked, "Is that a euphemism?"

"I hope not."

Lucas ignored them, finished the orange juice, put the bottle in the recyclables, and went off to the garage.

They could taunt him all they wished; but Kidd's scorchingly good-looking wife, Lauren, thought he was totally hot.

CHAPTER 4

Taryn Grant came back from a campaign loop through Rochester, Wabasha, and Red Wing, and found Doug Dannon, her security coordinator, waiting inside the door from the garage. Her two German shepherds, Hansel and Gretel, whimpered with joy when she walked in, and she knelt and gave them a good scratch and got a kiss from each of them, and then Dannon said, "I've got some news. Where's Green?"

Alice Green was a former Secret Service agent. She was not in the loop on the shadow campaign. Taryn said, "Alice is with the car. . . . What happened?"

"The word around the Smalls campaign is that there's a new state investigator looking into the porn scandal," Dannon said. "I don't know if they've taken it away from St. Paul, but Smalls is pretty happy about it. He thinks something's gonna get done. There are rumors that Smalls talked to the governor, but nobody knows what was said."

"The governor? He's supposed to be on our side." Taryn bent sideways and gave Gretel another scratch on the head.

"Don't know—don't know what's happening. Maybe Connie can get something."

Connie Schiffer was Taryn's campaign manager.

"What about the investigator, the new guy?" Taryn asked.

"I've been looking him up on the Internet. He's a killer. His name is Lucas Davenport, he's been around a long time," Dannon said. "Works for the Bureau of Criminal Apprehension. There's a ton of newspaper clips. He's killed a bunch of people in shoot-outs. He seems to be the guy they go to, when they need somebody really smart, or really mean."

"But what could he find out?"

"Worst case, he could find the thread that leads from Tubbs to Smalls," Dannon said. "Everybody's looking for Tubbs, but they don't know about the connection. We can't do anything about it. They'll probably come and talk to you, Taryn. If they think there's something fishy about the porn, this campaign is where they'll look. If they find out that Tubbs is connected, and Tubbs never shows up . . . then they'll be asking about murder."

"But Tubbs will never show up," she said.

"No. No chance of that," Dannon said.

TARYN GRANT, DEMOCRATIC CANDIDATE for the U.S. Senate, suffered from narcissistic personality disorder, or so she'd been told by a psychologist in her third year at the Wharton School. He'd added, "I wouldn't worry too much about it, as long as you don't go into a life of crime. Half the people here are narcissists. The other half are psychopaths. Well, except for Roland Shafer. He's normal enough."

Taryn didn't know Roland Shafer, but all these years later, she sometimes thought about him, and wondered what happened to him, being . . . "normal."

The shrink had explained the disorder to her, in sketchy terms, perhaps trying to be kind. When she left his office, she'd gone straight to the library and looked it up, because she knew in her heart that she was far too perfect to have any kind of disorder.

NARCISSISTIC PERSONALITY DISORDER:
- Has excessive feelings of self-importance.
- Reacts to criticism with rage.
- Takes advantage of other people.
- Disregards the feelings of others.
- Preoccupied with fantasies of success, power, beauty, and intelligence.

EXCESSIVE FEELINGS OF SELF-IMPORTANCE? Did that idiot shrink know she'd inherit the better part of a billion dollars, that she already had enough money to buy an entire *industry*? She *was* important.

Reacts to criticism with rage? Well, what do you do when you're mistreated? Shy away from conflict and go snuffle into a Kleenex? Hell no: you get up in their face, straighten them out.

Takes advantage of other people? You don't get anywhere in this world by being a cupcake, cupcake.

Disregards the feelings of others? Look: half the people in the world were below average, and "average" isn't anything to brag about. We should pay attention to the dumbasses in life?

How about, "Preoccupied with fantasies of success, power,

beauty, and intelligence"? Hey, had he taken a good look at her and her CV? She was in the running for class valedictorian; she looked like Marilyn Monroe, without the black spot on her cheek; and she had, at age twenty-two, thirty million dollars of her own, with twenty or thirty times more than that, yet to come. What fantasies? Welcome to my world, bub.

THAT HAD BEEN more than a decade ago.

Taryn was now thirty-four. She still had those major assets—she was blond, good-looking, with interesting places in all the interesting places. She'd graduated from Wharton in Entrepreneurial Management, and then from the London School of Economics in finance. Until four years earlier, she'd worked in the finance department at Grant Mills, the family's much-diversified agricultural products business, the fifth largest closely held company in the U.S.

She'd spent six years with Grant Mills, six years of snarling combat with a list of parents, uncles, and cousins, about who was going to run what. She might have won that fight, eventually, but she'd opted out. There was a lot of money there, but she couldn't see spending her life with corn, wheat, beans, and rice.

She'd quit to start Digital Pen LLC, which wrote apps for smartphones and tablets. She employed two hundred people in Minneapolis, and another hundred out on the Coast, and had stacked up a few more tens of millions, on top of the three-quarters of a billion in the Grant Mills trust.

But even with Digital Pen, she'd grown bored. She'd turned the company over to a hired CEO, told him not to screw it up, and turned her eyes to politics.

Taryn had watched the incumbent U.S. senator, a Republican

named Porter Smalls, stepping on his political dick for five consecutive years. She thought, *Hmmm.* She had an interest in the Senate, as a stepping-stone, and it was clear from early on that the main Democratic candidates would be the usual bunch of stooges, clowns, buffoons, apparatchiks, and small-town wannabees—and a witch—who couldn't have found Washington, D.C., with a Cadillac's navigation system and a Seeing Eye dog.

Taryn had everything she needed to buy a good, solid Senate seat, and start looking to move up. She'd pounded the field in the Democratic primary, taking fifty-one percent of the vote in a four-way race; the witch had finished third. She'd been a weekly visitor on both local and national talk shows, was good at it, and people started referring to her as a "rising star."

She liked that. A lot. As anyone with narcissistic personality disorder would.

There was one large, juicy fly in the ointment. Three weeks before the election, she was losing. The thing about Smalls was, he was *likable.* Okay, he'd screw anything that moved, and in one case, allegedly, a woman who said she'd been too drunk to move. But then, what did that mean, anymore?

So Taryn, working anonymously through the shadow campaign, had hired Bob Tubbs to do his thing, to win the election for her. Tubbs didn't know the man who passed him the 100K in twenties and fifties.

But Tubbs was a political, and had been around a long time, and knew how to follow a trail. It took a while, but he eventually followed it back to Dannon and thus to Taryn.

He showed up at her house at midnight.

He wanted more money.

Like this:

DOUG DANNON WAS A sandy-haired man of medium height with a trim, sandy mustache and a wedge-shaped body, marked with a few shrapnel scars from nearby explosions. On the particular night that Tubbs showed up at the door, he was sitting on a twenty-thousand-dollar German woven-leather couch that was soft as merino wool, his feet on a seventy-five-thousand-dollar Persian carpet as delicately brilliant as a French cathedral's stained-glass window. He looked out through the faintly green, curved-glass porch windows at the billion-dollar woman, who looked like a million bucks.

She was topless, and the bottom of her bathing suit was not larger than a child's hand. She'd just pulled herself out of the deep end of the heated pool, after forty laps, and stood shaking off the water. Tall and blond and tanned, she had muscular thighs and small breasts tipped with erect pinkish-brown nipples.

Hansel and Gretel sat on the pool's flagstone deck, watching everything. The dogs made people a little nervous. Agitated, they could tear a rhinoceros apart, and they loved Taryn more than life itself.

Taryn knew Dannon was there behind the glass, watching, and that Ron Carver was someplace in the house, but paid no attention to that set of facts. Carver, who worked security with Dannon, was also part of the shadow campaign. Carver had suggested to Dannon that she could do this—swim topless, and occasionally nude, while they were in the house—because she was an exhibitionist.

Dannon thought that was probably true.

He was wrong.

She did it because, in the larger scheme of things, Dannon and Carver were irrelevant. The fact that they'd seen her nude meant nothing, because they meant nothing. They were tools; it was like being seen by a hammer and chisel.

TARYN HAD BEGUN TOWELING off when Carver came into the living room carrying a glass of bourbon; in fact, a glass of A.H. Hirsch Reserve, Dannon knew, which Carver had been regularly pouring from Taryn Grant's liquor closet. Carver had a deal going with the housekeeper, who would order additional bottles as necessary. Taryn need not know.

Dannon disapproved: but Carver had told him that he needed a bit of booze on a daily basis to keep his head straight and the Reserve was what he'd chosen.

"If she smells that on your breath, when you're working, she could fire you," Dannon said.

"Ah, she's so loaded she couldn't tell that she wasn't smelling her own breath," Carver said. He was a large man, thick through the chest and hips. A small head, with closely cropped brown hair, made his shoulders look especially wide. He had a 9mm Glock tucked into a belt holster in the small of his back, and, because he was slightly psycho, a little .380 auto in an ankle holster.

Dannon was less psycho, and carried only a single gun, a .40-caliber Heckler & Koch, butt-backwards in a cross-draw holster on his left hip. Of course, he also carried a Bratton fighting knife with a seven-inch serrated blade guaranteed to cut through bone, tendon, and ligament, on the theory that you should never bring a fist to a knife fight.

"Look at the ass on that bitch," Carver said, sipping at the Reserve.

"I don't want to hear that," Dannon said.

"'Cause you're totally pussy-whipped," Carver said, watching the billion-dollar woman arching her back, thrusting her breasts toward them, as she pulled the blue-striped pool towel across her back. "Though it is a pretty sweet billet. Kinda boring, though. Other than the fact we get to watch her rubbing her tits."

"Plenty of jobs outta Lagos," Dannon said, watching Taryn through the glass.

"Fuck Lagos. The goddamn Africans got gun guys coming out of their ass. They don't need me around."

"I knew this guy from Angola, black as a lump of coal," Dannon said. "Smart guy. Hired into the Bubble as a security guard. The first day he's there, some asshole raghead points his taxi at the Haleb gate . . ."

More been-there-done-that Baghdad bullshit, but Carver listened closely, because he liked war stories. In this job, so far, there hadn't been much to do but remember the Glory Days and collect the paycheck. Before he'd gotten kicked out of the army, he got to carry the SAW, the squad automatic weapon. It was twenty-two pounds of black death, loaded, and took a horse to carry. He was the horse, and happy about it.

OUT IN THE ENCLOSED pool, Taryn Grant finished drying herself and pulled on a robe. Carver was right: she was drunk, Dannon thought. She'd always taken a drink, and this night, at a campaign stop in a Minneapolis penthouse, she'd taken at least three, and maybe more, and two more back at the house, before she went for her swim; and she'd taken a drink with her, to the pool.

He'd talked to her about it, and she'd told him to shut up. She could handle it, she said. Maybe she could. In Dannon's experience, alcoholism was the easiest of the addictions to control. Look at Carver, for example.

TARYN WAS PICKING UP a pack of magazines when the front gate dinged at them, then a quick, more urgent *buzzzzz*. Somebody had hopped the gate.

Dannon snapped at Carver, "Get the camera. I'm on the door."

He started toward the front door, and as he went, pushed the walkie-talkie function on his phone. Taryn's phone buzzed at her and didn't stop, a deliberately annoying noise, impossible to ignore. She picked it up and asked, "What?"

"Somebody's inside, on the lawn, hopped the gate," Dannon said. He pulled his gun. "Get in here with the dogs and stay on the phone."

"I'm coming," she said. This is why she had security.

Carver was on the same walkie-talkie system, and said, looking at the video displays in the monitoring room, "Okay, one guy, big guy, coming up the walk. He's not lost, he's walking fast. Wearing a suit and tie. Hands are empty."

"I'm inside, locking the doors," Taryn said.

"Guy's at the door," Carver said. "I don't know him."

The doorbell rang and Dannon popped the door, gun in his hand; looked at the man's face and said, "Ah, shit."

"Hello, mystery man."

TARYN HAD BEGUN DOING research for her Senate run two years earlier. She did the research herself—narcissistic personality disorder aside, she was a brilliant researcher, both by training and inclination. Much of the research involved selection of campaign staff, from campaign manager on down. She shared the research with Dannon, whose personal loyalty she trusted, because Dannon was in love with her.

Because of that loyalty, and because of his history as an intelligence officer, she'd had him set up the shadow campaign staff—spies—to keep an eye on her opponent, Smalls. He'd also identified other possible assets: among them, Bob Tubbs.

Tubbs was a longtime Democratic political operative, and had been considered for a staff job with the regular campaign, to be eventually rejected. "He's been involved in some unsavory election stuff, so I want to keep our distance," Taryn told Dannon. "But also, it's good to keep him on the outside, in case we need somebody on the outside . . . somebody who could handle something unsavory."

The regular campaign staff, including the regular campaign manager, had no idea that the shadow staff existed.

When it had appeared that Taryn would lose despite a good, solid campaign, Dannon had met with Tubbs to discuss other possibilities. He hadn't identified himself, except as "Mr. Smith . . . or Jones, take your pick."

Tubbs probably wouldn't have talked to him, if it hadn't been for the 25K in the paper bag, and the promise of another twenty-five thousand dollars if Tubbs found a solution to the problem.

Tubbs hadn't even needed time to think about it. "Porter Smalls has a history of sexual entanglements," he'd told Dannon at that first meeting. Then he'd told him how that might be exploited. And that he'd need a hundred thousand dollars to pull it off. "It's dangerous. People have to be paid," Tubbs had said.

They met twice more: Dannon had demanded details, and

names. At the last meeting, he'd handed over the other seventy-five thousand.

"Time is getting short," he'd told Tubbs. "By the way—we expect results. We are not people to be fucked with."

"You'll get them," Tubbs had said. "We're already rolling."

TUBBS WAS A POLITICAL.

And this one time, a blackmailer.

As he walked toward Taryn Grant's door, a rippling chill crawled up Tubbs's back. He was about to commit a felony, blackmail, *real blackmail*, not for the first time in his life, but never before like this: the payout would be life-changing. A man had to take care of his own retirement funding, these days. Not that another felony would be a problem, if he got caught. He was already in it, up to his ears.

He reached out and rang Taryn Grant's doorbell. He knew she was home, because he knew her schedule.

The door popped open, and,

Surprise!

"Ah, shit," said the man inside.

"Hello, mystery man," Tubbs said.

TARYN GRANT WAS THERE with her two security men, in a robe, her hair still damp from the swim.

Tubbs said, "Look, I'll tell you right up front. You saw what happened this morning. And I realized, my political life could be over. They could figure this out. I'm willing to go down for it and to keep my mouth shut, but I need a little more cash. I need to fund my retirement."

Taryn asked, through gritted teeth, "How much?"

"You've got more money than Jesus Christ," Tubbs said. "I'd like . . . a million. That's what I want. I swear to you, if there's a fall coming, I'll take it. And I'll never come back for another nickel."

"Fuck you," Taryn said. The snap in her voice caught the attention of the dogs, whose ears came forward, their noses pointed at Tubbs.

"Miz Grant—" Tubbs began.

Dannon cut him off, and said to Taryn, "Let's take this out to the pool."

"What are we talking about here?" Tubbs asked, looking from one of them to the other.

"We're talking cameras," Dannon said to him. "There aren't any cameras around the pool."

Tubbs nodded, and they trooped through the house, into the pool enclosure, Hansel leading, Gretel following. The pool had a wide deck with grow lights around the edges, shining sixteen hours a day on orchids, bromeliads, and palms; a tropical jungle in Minnesota. Tubbs looked around and said, "Nice."

Taryn didn't want to hear *nice*. She said, "You motherfucker. You've been well paid."

Tubbs said, "Not well paid for what's happening. There'll be cops all over the place. I've got another person I've got to pay off, and this is like . . . this is a political Armageddon."

Taryn had left an unfinished drink next to the pool, a screwdriver, half vodka and half orange juice, and she picked it up and threw back the rest of it, then said, "You don't know what you're messing with. You don't do this: you get bought and you stay bought."

"I just put you in the U.S. Senate, and I know you're already thinking about moving up from that, *and I did it,*" Tubbs said, his voice climbing into the alto range. "You're losing. You'd be a loser if it weren't for me. You'd just be—"

"Shut up," Taryn shouted.

Dannon realized that she was drunker than he thought. He wrapped an arm around her and said, "Come talk to me for a minute."

She didn't want to go. She wanted to stay in Tubbs's face. But Dannon pulled her along, and halfway down the pool said to her quietly, "If you give it to him, he'll be back for more."

"So . . . what?"

"So, slow him down," Dannon said, leaning close to her, close enough to smell the chlorine. "Tell him you'll work something out. We need to get him out of the house so we can talk, come up with an action plan."

"He's not going away, he's never going away," she said. "God-damnit, how'd he track us down?"

"Well, there was really only one place that money could have come from, ultimately. Maybe he saw me in the background on one of the TV shots, or at a rally," Dannon said, glancing back at Tubbs. "Doesn't make any difference: he knows."

"I'm going to tell him to fuck himself," Taryn said.

Dannon hooked her arm as she started away. "Don't do that. Just delay, buy some time. Buy some time . . ."

Taryn pulled free, strode back down the pool, reaching for control.

As she came up, Tubbs said, "Don't try to screw me over. Don't try. Just give me the money, and it's done with. Don't drag your feet. You guys scare me a little, so I'm going to hide out somewhere, until the election's over. My offer here has a time limit: I want a million in a week, or I'm going to have to make an offer to the Smalls campaign."

"I need more than a week, it takes a while to round up that much cash," Taryn said, and despised herself for the begging tone in her voice.

"But that's what you've got," Tubbs said. "A week. I don't care how you get it. I'm sure you could fix something up in Vegas, through one of the casinos. Just get the fuckin' money, girlie, and get it to me."

It was the *girlie* that did it.

She turned to Dannon, now with an icy grip on herself, and said, "We'll get the money somehow. Get him out of here."

THEY GOT HIM OUT of there, with the promise of the money inside a week. When he was gone, Taryn had turned to the two security men and said, "This won't work."

Carver drawled, "No shit, Ms. Grant. He'll be back in your face like a rat. Even if you lose, he'll be back. If you win, it'll be five million, ten million, he'll be coming back forever. There's not enough money to fill that black hole."

Dannon said, "But if he talks . . . if he tries to turn us in, he'll implicate himself. He'll be right there in prison with us."

Taryn shook her head. "No. I'll tell you how this would go down. We refuse to pay, he goes to Smalls and says, 'I can get you your Senate seat back. I want a million dollars and immunity, or I never say a thing.' So Smalls takes it: he's got the cash, he could fix things with the prosecutors. Tubbs gets the money up front, then he confesses, points the finger, cries for the TV cameras. He does the right thing, says his conscience couldn't handle it. And we're done. The prosecutors won't care about Tubbs—he's small change. We're the ones they'd come for."

They all chewed on that for a while, then Dannon looked at Carver and said, "What do you think?"

Carver said, "You *know* what I think, Doug. He isn't going away, so I think we make him go away. If we're careful, we can pull it off—but I'd like a little appreciation for doing it."

Taryn looked at him: "How much appreciation?"

Carver shrugged and said, "Whatever you think."

She touched her lip, half turned away, considering: even rich people hate to give away money. Then she turned back and said, "A hundred thousand each. All cash. As soon as it's done."

Carver said, "Hooah!"

Dannon was less enthusiastic: "We'll need to do some recon. We'll need to fix it so that we've got alibis."

"You know about those things," Taryn said. "I'm out of it. If you get caught, I'll say I had no idea."

The two men nodded. Dannon said, "If we get caught, there's no reason to drag you into it. You could help us more from the outside, than if you were inside with us."

"I hope that's clear," she said, looking at Carver.

He said, "Clear."

"Then kill him," she said.

DANNON AND CARVER HAD buried Tubbs north of the Cities, in a marsh along the Mississippi. Taryn had helped: they'd put Tubbs's body in the back of Carver's SUV, and drove to the town house complex where both men were living. They parked in back, and Carver called Dannon, and then Dannon called Taryn, and a few minutes later, Taryn called Dannon back. They then went on to bury the body, while Taryn drove to their apartments and sent e-mails to herself and to a friend of Carver's, from their laptops in their respective apartments. All of that could be time-checked, if it ever came to that.

Then . . . nothing much had happened until the St. Paul papers reported that the police were looking for Tubbs, and feared foul play. And now the report that a new investigator was on the job.

When Dannon broke that news—that the new guy, Davenport, was a killer—she said, "Ah, God," and "Let's talk later. I need to go for a swim, and Alice'll be here in a minute. Let's talk tonight."

"I'm not sure we should talk later," Dannon said. "I think we ought to *stop* talking about it and focus on our ignorance. We don't know what happened with the porn, we don't know what happened with Tubbs, we don't know anything. If you can convince yourself of that, that you don't know anything . . . it'll be much easier to sell it to the cops."

"Focus on our ignorance." She didn't quite grasp the concept. She'd never been ignorant.

"Yeah. Just rewind back before we talked to Tubbs and think what your head was like," Dannon said. "Then think about the newspaper stories and think about your reaction to them. What you would have thought about them, if you didn't know what really happened. Then, when the cops come, if they come, you're confused about it all. A little scared. You ask questions, you suggest answers, you're all over the place. But basically, ignorant. Just delete Tubbs from your mind. You don't know him. You never knew him."

"I'll have to think about it, but I can do that," Taryn said.

"Of course you can," Dannon said. "But don't think about ways to trick them or outsmart them. Just focus on your ignorance. You don't *know* anything, but you're willing to speculate, and you'd like some information from them—to hear what they think."

"What about you and Carver?"

"We can handle it," Dannon said. "We've spent half our lives lying to cops, of one kind or another. Nobody else on the staff knows. Might not be a bad idea for us to stay away completely . . . unless they ask for us."

"Let's do that," Taryn said. "Maybe you two could start doing some advance security work."

"I'll talk to Ron," Dannon said. He heard high heels, and said, "Here comes Alice."

TWENTY MINUTES LATER, TARYN was sitting on the edge of the pool, wearing a conservative one-piece bathing suit. Alice Green, a lithe, handsome woman in her late thirties, relaxed in a chaise, reading the *Star Tribune*, while the dogs sat at her feet. The dogs were the world's most efficient burglar alarm. If anyone tried to enter the pool area, the dogs would be looking at them. If Taryn told them to attack, they'd tear that person apart, no questions asked.

Taryn slipped into the water, shivered, and started swimming laps. The exercise blanked her mind for the first two hundred yards, but after she got into the rhythm of it, she began reliving Tubbs's visit, and what happened next: not to obsess about it, but to cultivate her ignorance, as Dannon called it.

The two men had been gone for four hours, altogether, and when they'd come back, muddy and tired, they told a sleepless Taryn that they'd gone way up the Mississippi toward St. Cloud, found a fisherman's track that led to the river, and carried the body well off the track and buried it deep.

"Just about killed ourselves out there in the dark," Carver said. "He's gone. Put a few concrete blocks on top of him, just in case."

"In case of *what?*" Taryn asked, fascinated in spite of herself.

"Well . . . body gases," Carver said. "The ground was a little wet, you wouldn't want him popping up."

A few miles back toward the Twin Cities, they'd detoured down a side road, and threw Carver's carefully cleaned baseball bat into the roadside ditch. "Couldn't find it again ourselves, even if we had to," Dannon said, as they drove away in the dark.

TARYN KEPT SWIMMING, TWENTY laps, thirty, touching the lap counter at the west end of the pool after every second turn.

She had to think seriously about Carver and Dannon. Dannon was well under control—he'd been her security man for four years, and for all four years had hungered for her. Not just for sex. He was in love with her. That was useful. Carver was cruder. He didn't want her total being, he just wanted to fuck her. If she wasn't available, somebody else would do. So her grip on him was more precarious.

And the problem with Carver was, he was more of an adventurer than Dannon.

Dannon was happy to handle her security, and was good at it. He read about it, he knew about alarms and randomizing patrols and evasive driving, and all the rest. He took courses. She'd had a lover, a semi-dumb guy as anxious to get into her money as into her pants, and when she was done with him, he wouldn't go away.

Dannon had talked to him, and the guy had moved to Des Moines. No muss, no fuss.

On the night Tubbs was killed, Taryn had given each of the men a hundred thousand dollars in cash and gold, as a "thank you."

Dannon had carefully stashed his in a safe-deposit box. Carver, on the other hand, had asked for a day off. "The money just burns a hole in my pocket," he confessed. "I'd like to hop a plane for Vegas, if you don't mind."

That had been a Friday night. He'd left Saturday morning and had gotten back Sunday night, most of the money gone. Dannon said later he'd blown it on hookers, cocaine, and craps and felt that he'd gotten his money's worth.

So Carver sought risk, while Dannon tried to minimize risk. That made Carver a loose cannon, and given her involvement, she didn't need any cannons to be loose.

She thought for a few minutes about what would happen if, for example, Carver tried to squeeze her for money, as Tubbs had. He might suspect that Dannon would come after him, because Dannon was in love with her. But would that frighten him? Could Dannon take him? And if it got all bloody, and somebody tried to make a deal with the police, to trade her in . . . what would happen?

She had to think about it. Was Dannon loyal enough to take out Carver if she asked him to? Was Carver smart enough to set up a booby trap that would snap on them, if they took him out? Might he already have done so?

But thinking about it was hard. Ever since Tubbs had gone away, she'd had trouble tracking. But she had to track.

Because now, she was winning the election, up three points and climbing.

SHE HIT THE COUNTER at the end of the pool, and a big red LED "40" popped up. Forty laps, a thousand yards, a little more than half a mile.

She climbed out of the pool, and Alice, who'd been watching the counter, was waiting with a towel.

"You'd have been a good agent," Alice said. "Smart, terrific condition."

"Thank you," Taryn said. "I'm not sure I could handle the guns. I don't like guns."

"We had a saying in the service," Alice said. "Guns don't kill people, people kill people. Guns just make it really, really easy."

"Too easy, if you ask me," Taryn said. "When I get to the Senate, I'll try to do something about that. I always feel bad when I read about people being killed. It's usually so senseless. You know, 'The bell tolls for thee,' or whatever."

CHAPTER 5

When Lucas woke Monday morning, the first thing he did was check the window: blue sky. Excellent. Another good day. People had been talking about bad weather coming in, but he didn't know when it was supposed to arrive.

And, thank God, they were through the weekend. Working on a Sunday was a pain in the ass, with everybody gone. Today, there'd be a lot going on: no more matinee movies.

He'd start with the volunteer who found the porn, he thought as he got dressed. He picked out a medium-blue wool suit that he'd thought would look awful at the time the salesman suggested it, but that had become one of his cool-weather favorites. He tried several ties, finally choosing a red-and-blue check with a turquoise thread in it, which went nicely with his eyes. Black lace-up shoes from Cleverley of London, for which he'd been measured during a European trip two years earlier, finished the ensemble.

The volunteer's family, the Hunts, lived in Edina, an affluent Minneapolis suburb. Lucas took the Porsche, because it would feel at home there. He took ten minutes driving across town, and after a few minutes of confusion caused by the Porsche's outdated navigation system, found the Hunts' home: another sprawling brick ranch, at the end of a woody cul-de-sac.

BRITTANY HUNT MET LUCAS at the door, her mother a step behind. Lucas was amazed: they looked almost exactly alike, and that was like Doris Day in 1960. Lucas hadn't yet been born in 1960 to get the full Doris Day effect, but he'd seen her often enough on late-night television. . . .

"I'm Brittany," Brittany said, offering her hand in a firm shake. "I'm the one who outed him."

"I'm her mother, Tammy," her mother said. "Friends call me Tam." She had perfect white teeth and sparkled at Lucas, and she smelled of Chanel on a Monday morning at home.

They led the way inside and a sliding door banged shut in the back. A man in an open-necked white shirt and khakis padded through the living room and thrust out his hand and said, "Jeff Hunt."

They wound up seated on a semicircular couch in a conversation pit in front of a flagstone fireplace. Lucas said, "So tell me what happened."

Brittany told him, and it was exactly what she'd told the St. Paul cops. When she finished—she'd stood by the computer until the cops got there—Lucas turned to Jeff and said, "You called the cops right away?"

"Instantly," he said. "First of all, you can't let people get away with this kind of stuff. Second of all, I was worried about Brit. What if he'd come back and found her standing there, with that stuff on the screen? I mean, this is the end of everything for him. What if he'd gotten violent?"

"I don't understand why they haven't arrested him yet," Tam said. "He's such a monster. I mean, children."

"There are some questions," Lucas said. "But unless something changes, it looks like the Hennepin County attorney is planning to take it to the grand jury next week, unless the attorney general takes it away."

"The AG is gonna run for governor, and he'd love to bag Smalls, so I bet he takes it," Jeff said. Jeff was yet another attorney. "If he does, it'll go to a grand jury for sure. If he loses the case, he can blame the grand jury for the indictment. If he wins, who cares about the grand jury?"

Lucas said, "Well . . ."

THEN BRITTANY CHANGED EVERYTHING.

"What a weird summer," she said. "Child porn on Porter's computer and then Bob Tubbs vanishes."

Lucas looked at her for a moment, then said, "Bob Tubbs? What did Bob Tubbs have to do with this?"

"Well, nothing," she said. "But, you know, he was around. You ever met him? Big tall blond guy? He used to call me *chica*, like the Mexicans do."

"He worked for Smalls?" Lucas asked.

She shook her head. "I don't know the details, exactly, but he was a lobbyist for the Minnesota Apiary Association."

"You mean, archery?" Jeff asked.

"No, *apiary*, Daddy. You know, honey bees. There was some kind of licensing thing going on," Brittany said. "The state was going to put on a fee, and some of the bee guys said they wouldn't bring their hives into Minnesota if that happened, and Tubbs thought that the bees were interstate commerce and so only the feds were allowed to regulate it. Or something like that. I don't know. I wasn't interested enough to follow it. But Bob was around."

"What about Bob?" Tam asked Lucas.

Lucas said, "He's one of our local political operators. He disappeared . . . what, it must have been Friday night?"

"Same day the porn file popped up," Jeff said.

"I'm not sure that's right, though," Lucas said. "I just heard about it from a St. Paul cop. Tubbs's mother claims he's been kidnapped. A couple people have said he might be on a bender somewhere. He did that once before—vanished, and turned up a week later in Cancún, dead drunk in a hotel room. But, I guess he hasn't been using his credit cards, doesn't answer his cell phone, his passport was in his desk, and his car is sitting in his parking garage."

"Boy, that doesn't sound good," Jeff said.

Lucas looked at Brittany. "How'd you even know about him?"

"It was in the paper," she said. "This morning. People are looking all over for him."

Tam's hand went to her throat: "You think . . . dead?"

"Don't know," Lucas said. "My agency isn't involved. It's just, you know, what I hear."

WHEN LUCAS LEFT, ten minutes later, Brit, Tam, and Jeff came out on the porch to wave good-bye. He waved, and sped back to St. Paul.

As Lucas was on the way to his office, ICE called and told him that she had the copy of Smalls's hard drive. "Got everything, gonna take you six months to read it. There's about a million e-mails. And old albums. He's got every Bowie album ever made."

"Let's try not to judge," Lucas said. "Anyway, I'm not going home, I'm coming there. Wait for me."

When Lucas got to the St. Paul police parking lot, he found her waiting in a black six-series BMW convertible. She handed Lucas a hard drive about the size of a paperback and said, "Who do I bill?"

"Send it to me personally," Lucas said. "I'll get it back later. Anything happen out of the ordinary?"

"Purely routine," she said. "Tell Kidd that it was Windows 7 . . . not that he won't know."

She didn't ask if she could come along, to visit with Kidd.

WHEN SHE WAS GONE, Lucas went inside, badged his way back to the homicide unit, and found Roger Morris peering at a brown paper bag with a small grease stain at one end.

"Is that a clue?" Lucas asked.

"It's my lunch," Morris said. "I'm thinking about eating it early."

"Why?"

"Because I'm starving to death, that's why," Morris said. "My wife's got me on a food-free diet."

"You *are* looking pretty trim," Lucas lied, since he needed a favor.

"Bullshit. I only started yesterday," Morris said. Then his brow beetled, and he said, "Say, you don't work here."

"I need to see the Tubbs file."

"Ah, man," Morris said. "Of the twelve million things I didn't need to hear this morning, that is number one. Davenport wants to see the Tubbs file."

"You're working it?"

"Nothing to work."

"So let me see the file," Lucas said. "I may have some suggestions."

"That's my greatest fear," Morris said. "After the contents of my lunch bag, of course."

LUCAS PAGED THROUGH the thin file, sitting at Morris's desk, peering at his computer. Tubbs hadn't been seen after Friday evening. Tubbs's mother had called St. Paul on Saturday afternoon to report him missing. Not much had been done—a couple cops went around and knocked on his apartment door, and asked a few questions of his neighbors, who hadn't seen him. His mother had shifted into high hysteria on Sunday, complaining to St. Paul that her son must have been kidnapped.

According to Mrs. Tubbs, Tubbs was supposed to pick her up and go shopping on Saturday, but hadn't shown, and hadn't called to say he wouldn't make it. Mom said he'd never done that in his life. On Sunday, he was supposed to take her to Mass, but hadn't shown up then, either. She couldn't get him at home or on either of his two cell phones, and she'd been trying since Saturday morning.

The cops checked with AT&T and found that he hadn't used either his home or his cell phones, nor had he used his credit cards, which was when they began to take the old woman's complaints seriously: Tubbs had never, in a credit card record going back ten years, gone two days without using one. He paid for everything with a card, his mother said. He hardly used cash at all, because you couldn't deduct invisible business expenses, and almost all of Tubbs's expenses were business.

On Sunday afternoon, Tubbs's mother let the cops into his apartment for a look around. One of the cops said that it was apparent that he'd recently been sexually involved, as there were stains on the bedsheets. Samples had been taken. There was no sign of forced entry, or violence.

On Monday morning, there were a couple of stories in the local newspapers, based on calls by Tubbs's mother. The stories hadn't shaken him loose, nor had he begun to use his credit cards.

"You think he's dead?" Lucas asked Morris.

"That's what I think," Morris said.

"What about his apartment?"

"What about it?"

"Close it out yet?" Lucas asked.

"Not yet," Morris said. "You want to look around?"

"Yes."

"You'd have to get an okay from Tubbs's mother, but you'll get it. She's frantic," Morris said. "Why are you interested?"

"If I told you, you'd have to change your name and move to New Zealand," Lucas said.

"Seriously . . ."

"I'm a little serious," Lucas said. "I'm doing a political thing and you really don't want to know about it. And it probably has nothing to do with Tubbs. If it does, I'll tell you, first thing."

"First thing?"

"Absolutely," Lucas said.

Morris reached out and touched his lunch sack, and said, "She made me a BLT. With motherfuckin' soy bacon."

"Jesus, that's not good," Lucas said. "Motherfuckin' soy bacon?"

"That's the way us black people talk," Morris said.

"What about Tubbs's apartment?" Lucas asked.

"I've got a key," Morris said. "Let's call the old lady. If you find anything . . ."

"First thing," Lucas said.

Morris called Tubbs's mother, explained that a high-ranking agent from the state Bureau of Criminal Apprehension would like to check out the apartment, and was immediately given an okay. Morris gave him the key, said, "Use it wisely," and agreed to send an electronic copy of the Tubbs file to the BCA, where Lucas could look at it.

Lucas thanked him, and headed across town to the river, not to Tubbs's apartment but to Kidd's.

KIDD OWNED HALF A FLOOR in a redbrick restoration condo over-looking the Mississippi. Lucas had visited him a few times, and had watched the condo grow. Kidd had started with a single large unit, added a second one a few years later, and finally, during the great real estate crash, picked up a third unit for nearly nothing. He also owned a piece of the underground parking garage, where he kept a couple of cars and a boat.

Lucas rode up to Kidd's floor in a freight elevator that smelled of oranges and bananas and paint and maybe oil, walked down the hall and knocked on Kidd's hand-carved walnut door, which Kidd said he'd copied from some Gauguin carvings. Lucas wouldn't have known a Gauguin carving if one had bit him on the ass, so when told about it, he'd just said, "Hey, that's great," and felt like an idiot.

LAUREN OPENED THE DOOR, a slender woman, not tall, with red hair and high cheekbones and a big smile: "Lucas, damnit, you need to come around more often. Why don't you jack up Weather and let's go to dinner? I need to get out. So does she."

She pecked him on the cheek and then Kidd came up, chewing on a hot dog bun with no dog. He was wearing jeans and a paint-flecked military-gray T-shirt stretched tight across his shoulders. And gold-rimmed glasses.

"New glasses," Lucas said.

"Yeah. When I'm working, I walk away from the painting, then I walk right up close, and then I walk away again," Kidd said. "You know, figuring it out. I began to realize I wasn't seeing the close-up stuff so well."

"Getting old," Lucas said.

"I'm a year older than you," Kidd said. "I just turned fifty."

"Yeah . . . I'm not looking forward to it."

Kidd shrugged. "Forty-five was a little tough. Fifty, I didn't notice."

"Didn't even remember," Lauren said, nudging Kidd with her elbow. "Jackson and I popped a surprise party on him, and he didn't even know what it was for, at first."

Jackson was their son, who was five, named after some dead New York painter. They drifted into the living room, and Lucas told them about Letty and Sam and the baby, and they talked about schools and other domestic matters. Then Kidd asked, "So what's up?"

Lucas: "You've read about Porter Smalls?"

Kidd: "Yeah. Good riddance."

Lucas: "He might be innocent."

Lauren: "Oh, please."

Kidd: "Huh. Tell me about it."

LUCAS TOLD HIM ABOUT the computer, and Kidd listened carefully, eyes fixed on Lucas's face. Kidd was a couple of inches shorter than Lucas, but was wider across the shoulders, and narrower through the hips: a wrestler. He'd lost an athletic scholarship when he'd dragged an abusive coach out of his office and forced his head through the bars of a railing around the field house balcony. They'd had to call the fire department to get the coach free, and around the field house, Kidd had been both a hero and a persona non grata. Not that it mattered much: the Institute of Technology hired him as a teaching assistant, and paid him more than he'd gotten from the scholarship.

When Lucas finished with what he knew about Porter Smalls, Kidd said, "I need to see the hard drive."

Lucas took it out of his jacket pocket and handed it to him.

Kidd said, "Mmm. How long did she have it before she gave it to you?"

"Half an hour," Lucas said. "Maybe a little more."

Kidd turned the drive in his hands, then said, "She could have done anything to it."

"She didn't mess with it," Lucas said. "She'd understand the consequences."

"Which would be?"

"She'd make an enemy out of me," Lucas said. "She wouldn't want that. And she knows what's at stake here."

Kidd thought for a couple seconds, then nodded, a quick jerk of the head. "Okay," and then, "Come on back to the shop."

Lucas asked, "So you're in?"

"We're in," Kidd said.

KIDD, LAUREN, AND JACKSON lived in the original oversized unit, which had a long living room overlooking the river and the Port of St. Paul, and a couple of bedrooms and bathrooms; and Kidd used the other two units as studio and computer work space. He still did some computer-related consulting, he said, as Lucas followed him back to the computer space, though ninety percent of his time was now spent painting.

Lucas stuck his head into the studio—Kidd had three landscapes under way—and then asked, "Lauren doesn't work?"

"Not so much, anymore," Kidd said. "Pretty much a full-time mom."

"What'd she do when she was working?"

"Insurance adjuster," Kidd said.

His computer desk was an old oaken library table, ten or twelve feet long, with a half-dozen computers scattered down its length. Three printers sat on an adjacent table, and a heap of cameras sat next to them. He said, "Let's see what we've got here."

LUCAS CONSIDERED HIMSELF computer literate in the sense that he could hook up computers and printers and Wi-Fi systems, and that he could use Microsoft Word, Excel, and Access, and Google and a few other programs; and he'd once owned a software company, though he had nothing to do with coding the software.

But he had no idea what Kidd was doing, other than whistling while he worked. Kidd started by plugging ICE's hard drive into an unbranded desktop computer. He brought the system up, poked at some keys, looked at some numbers, then wandered across the workshop to a bin full of DVDs, flipped through them, chose one, brought it back, and loaded it into the computer.

"What's that?" Lucas asked.

"It's an inventory program. It searches for certain kinds of apps and . . . whoops. There we are."

"What?"

"I don't know. Let's look at it."

Kidd's fingers rattled on his keyboard, and a program popped up in reader form. Lauren came in, looked at Lucas, and raised an eyebrow, and he shrugged. Lucas knew nothing about the program, except that it wasn't very long.

After reading through it, Kidd said, "If this is what it looks like, you're right—Smalls didn't do it."

It was too fast. Lucas was astonished: "What is it?"

"Watch." Kidd pulled the DVD out of the computer, restarted the machine, and when it was up, rattled his fingers across the keyboard again. The screen instantly went blank.

"Good work," Lauren said.

They looked at the blank screen for a moment, then Kidd reached out, picked up a computer manual, and dropped it on the keyboard. A pornographic picture popped up.

"Aw, that's rotten," Lauren said. "Kids."

"That's the file," Lucas said. "How'd you do that?"

"Somebody wrote a little script—"

"A script?"

"Not even a program," Kidd said. "Just a few lines of shell commands." He paused. "How technical do you want this?"

"Just tell me what it does," Lucas said.

"What it does is, it tells the computer, 'If someone presses these keys all at the same time, show these photos.' It's more complicated than that, but it's not . . . mmm . . . complex."

"Show me."

"Well, first, you have to get the script and the porn file—it's actually a bunch of files, but they're stored in a wrapper format—on the computer. That's the tricky bit. You have to run the script once—just type the name or double-click it—and it installs itself so it starts on bootup."

"Like a virus," said Lucas.

"Not really. You have to do it intentionally. A virus would do it by itself. Anyway, if the script is running, it's just waiting for you to press four keys: QW with one hand, and OP with the other. If you do that, it sends the porn file to the default photo viewer—that's actually *called* Photo Viewer in this case. It also activates the screensaver. The next person who touches the keyboard or the mouse cancels the screensaver and, *presto*. Porn right in your face."

Kidd held the four keys and the screen blacked out. "The porn is floating under there. If I hit anything to cancel it, the porn's right there. But. If I hit the escape key, and only the escape key . . ."

He did it, and they were back at the Windows home screen. He tapped on the keyboard, and nothing more happened.

"What you have is a script that will take you right to the porn, blank the screen, and set it up for instant retrieval," Kidd said. "But if you need to ditch the program, you hit the escape key— specifically the escape key and nothing else. I can think of no earthly reason to set that up, if you were just looking at the porn. The only reason to do it . . ."

"Would be to set up a booby trap," Lucas finished. "But— wouldn't any computer investigator find that? The script? I mean, as soon as that turned up . . ."

Kidd looked at him and said, "No."

"No?"

"No, they wouldn't find it. My tool here chased it down. The script itself is actually fairly well hidden. My tool found it because it's not part of any standard Windows boot protocol," he said. "Here's another thought. Whoever did this, whoever wrote and installed this script, knows his or *her* way around coding. This is a very tight little piece of work. I don't think it's something a politician would write, unless he came out of the computer industry."

"You said his or *her*. You italicized the *her*."

"ICE could do it—she could write this in four minutes," Kidd said.

Lucas thought about it for a second, then said, "Nah."

"Okay."

LAUREN SAID, "WAIT A MINUTE. You're moving too fast. If this guy is like a . . . thrill freak . . . then he might get off looking at porn while there are other people across the desk. Then if he needed to dump it really fast, he could do it. One touch . . ."

Kidd shook his head. "I see what you're saying, but it doesn't feel like that to me. That feels backwards. He's got this complicated four-key press to get the file up . . . but he doesn't need to do that. If you know the file is there, you can bring it up fast enough. Just like any work file. But the script is designed to bring it up and simultaneously hide it. Why is that?"

Lucas and Lauren both shrugged, and Kidd said, "Because it was designed so that somebody could go into his office for a few seconds and bring it up as a booby trap."

Kidd continued: "If he was only out for thrills, he'd probably just bring it up the regular way. No reason not to. Then he'd write the script so that *any key would kill it*. If he was getting his thrills by looking at it in his office, with other people present, and then somebody unexpectedly stepped behind his desk, he'd want to kill it with any key. Now, you kill it with the escape key. But if you needed to kill it in a big hurry, you wouldn't want to have to reach out and hit the escape key—specifically the escape key—and nothing else, to kill it. You could fumble that."

They all thought about that for a while, then Lauren said, "Maybe."

"Find something else," Lucas said, flicking his fingers at the computer.

"That'll take a little longer," Kidd said. "I suspected something like this script was there. Anything else . . . I'll have to dig into the file."

"How long will that take?"

"Dunno," Kidd said.

"Gotta be fast," Lucas said.

"I'll make it a priority," Kidd said.

"THERE'S ONE OTHER THING," Kidd said. "Do you have any idea *how* this was put in there?"

"Not yet."

"That's gonna be a problem. If the machine is on the Internet, it's theoretically vulnerable. Even if it's on a local network. It's not likely, but it's possible. But if it's not that, and it doesn't look like it, you've got a different problem. To install this quickly, you'd have to know the machine's password. Just to run something the first time, nowadays, you need to do that."

"That's not a problem. Apparently everybody in the office knew it. It's 'Smallscampaign.'"

Kidd shook his head: "People never learn."

Lucas had another thought: "Can you tell me if the script was written at the same time the porn file was created?"

"Good thought," Kidd said. He rattled the keys for a while, peered at the screen, and said, "Yeah. They were. And . . . uh-oh."

"What?"

"Interesting." He said it like computer freaks do when they're preoccupied.

"What?" Lucas asked.

He got a minute of silence, then:

"This is an unusual collection," Kidd said. "When people create a porn collection, they almost always collect the pieces separately, because everybody's tastes are different. But here, every file was downloaded all at once. That's unusual."

"But what does that mean?"

"Don't know. It's possible that he made the collection on a different computer, put it on a thumb drive, and carried it over to his office, but it's also possible . . ."

"That somebody brought it to his office and loaded them all at once," Lucas said.

"Man, it feels like something dirty happened here," Kidd said. "This is just not right."

"Keep pushing," Lucas said.

"I'll call you," Kidd said.

Lucas took Smalls's employee list out of his pocket. "When you get tired of checking out the porn thing, could you look up some people for me? I don't know how to do this, and ICE said you're really good at databases."

WHEN LUCAS LEFT KIDD'S apartment, he called the governor: "We have some early indications that Smalls was set up."

"Could you prove it in court?"

"No. Couldn't prove he was set up, but we might get him acquitted . . . but that's purely a negative thing. Doesn't say he's innocent."

"Keep working," Henderson said, and he was gone.

LUCAS HEADED BACK to the BCA building to look at the St. Paul homicide file on Tubbs. That done, he'd go over to Tubbs's apartment. Then he'd harass the hell out of Kidd until he'd unwrapped the hard drive from top to bottom.

The case was getting interesting.

Eight days to the election, and counting.

CHAPTER 6

The St. Paul file on the Tubbs disappearance didn't quite convince Lucas that Tubbs had been murdered, but he thought it probable. The physical evidence was nonexistent, and the circumstantial evidence ambiguous, although the longer Tubbs remained missing, the more likely it was that he was dead.

The circumstantial evidence included the fact that Tubbs called his mother on an almost daily basis, and hadn't called her since he disappeared; that his credit cards hadn't been used, and that he used the cards for even the most minor purchases, including daily bagel breakfasts at a Bruegger's bagel bakery on Grand Avenue; and that he'd missed a number of appointments that would have been important to him.

On the other hand, he'd disappeared once before, so completely that he'd made the newspapers. Ten years earlier, he'd flown to Cancún for a wedding, intending to come back two days later. Instead, he'd apparently gone on an alcoholic bender and had not surfaced for a week. Before he showed up, it had been widely speculated that he'd gone swimming alone and had been eaten by a shark.

He'd never disappeared again, and after that alcoholic epi-
sode, he'd signed up with Alcoholics Anonymous. Abstinence only
lasted a few weeks before he'd started drinking again, but he'd controlled it, as far as anyone knew.

Still, there was the possibility that he was facedown in a motel
room somewhere.

Lucas didn't believe that, but it was possible.

WHEN HE'D FINISHED READING the file, Lucas put on his jacket,
got his keys, stopped at a candy machine for a pack of Oreos, then
drove south to University Avenue, and over to Tubbs's apartment
building.

He'd just found a parking spot when his cell phone rang. He
looked at the screen: Kidd.

"Yeah?"

"How bad do you cops hate Smalls?" Kidd asked.

"I don't hate him at all," Lucas said. "I didn't vote for him, but
there was nothing personal about it."

Kidd said, "When I started looking him up, I found out that he
doesn't like public employee unions. Any public employee unions,
including police unions. He wants to outlaw them. He debated the
head of the Minneapolis union on public television, the *Almanac*
program."

"He's a right-winger," Lucas said. "This is a surprise?"

"No, what's a surprise is, I think the porn file might have come
out of a police department," Kidd said.

Lucas wasn't sure he'd heard that right: "What are you talking
about?"

"A part of it may have come out of evidentiary files. There's some text with most of the photos, the usual pedophile bullshit. Then there's one says, 'Left to right, unknown adult male, unknown adult male, Mark James Trebuchet, thirteen, unknown female, Sandra Mae Otis, fifteen.' That's the only one with text, but there are about five photos related to that one. I looked them up, those kids—I had to do a little excavating in the juvenile files—and found out that both of them were involved in a prostitution ring busted three years ago by the Minneapolis cops. I assume evidentiary photos wouldn't just be turned loose on the Internet."

"Ah, fuck me," Lucas said.

"I thought you'd be pleased," Kidd said.

"Fuck me. I gotta think about this," Lucas said. "If anybody—anybody—got wind of this, the whole goddamn state would blow up."

"No, it wouldn't. The whole goddamn media-political complex would get its knickers in a twist, and then, after a lot of screaming and slander, life would go on," Kidd said. "You gotta keep some perspective."

"I'll tell you something, Kidd—that might be true if you're an artist," Lucas said. "But if you're a cop, what you see is endless finger-pointing, investigative commissions, legislative inquiries, accusations of obstruction of justice, perjury . . ."

". . . misfeasance with a corncob . . ."

"Yeah, go ahead and laugh," Lucas said. "Listen, keep working this. You think the Smalls file came out of Minneapolis?"

"I have no idea—but those two kids were involved with Minneapolis police. I could dig out the complete juvenile files, if you need them."

"Do that. Uh, how do you do that? I thought they were sealed."

Kidd slid past the question: "Oh, you know. Anyway, what I can't figure out is why the photos of these kids would be inserted in the middle of a child-porn file . . . unless maybe the cops got the file when they busted the prostitution ring. And then annotated it? I don't know, that sounds weird."

Lucas thought for a moment, then asked, "This girl in the picture, Sandra, you said she was fifteen? And this was three years ago?"

"Sandra Mae Otis, and yeah, the caption says she was fifteen," Kidd said.

"Huh. Look, I'm in my car. Are you in a place where you could look up her birth date? Like in the DMV files? See if she's eighteen yet?"

"Wait one," Kidd said. Lucas heard his keyboard rattling, and ten seconds later Kidd said, "She's eighteen . . . as of last March. March tenth."

"What's her address?"

Kidd read it off, then said, "I'm checking that address on a satellite photo. . . . Hold on a second . . . it looks like a trailer park."

"I know the place," Lucas said. Then, "All right. I don't know what access you have to Minneapolis police files, and I won't ask, but if you should stumble over what looks like the Smalls file . . . let me know."

"I'll do that," Kidd said. "Why was Sandra's age important?"

"Think about it for one second," Lucas said.

Kidd thought about it for one second, then said, "Ah. She's an adult now. You can twist her arm until it falls off, and nobody can tell you to quit."

"Perzactly," Lucas said. "And that's what I'm going to do . . . if that's what it takes."

———

Tubbs lived in a prosperous-looking, two-story redbrick apartment building, set up above the street. Still thinking about the porn file, Lucas let himself in with the keys he'd gotten from Morris, skipped the elevator for a flight of carpeted stairs, and let himself into Tubbs's apartment. The living room and bedroom were acceptably neat, for a bachelor who lived alone, and smelled faintly of food that was made in cans and cooked in pots, and also of scented candles. The office was a mess, with stacks of paper everywhere.

Lucas spent only a few minutes in the living room, bedroom, and the two bathrooms, because they'd have been gone through by St. Paul detectives and the crime-scene crew, and they wouldn't have missed anything significant. The office would be where the action was at, because Lucas knew something the St. Paul cops hadn't known: a possible connection to the Smalls problem.

St. Paul had taken out Tubbs's computers, so there wasn't anything to work with but paper. He skipped everything that looked like a report, and started shuffling through individual pieces of paper.

A half hour in, he found a Republican Senate campaign schedule, a half-dozen sheets stapled at the corner and folded in thirds—the right size to be stuck in the breast pocket of a sport coat. The outside sheet was crumpled and then resmoothed, and the whole pack of paper had been folded and refolded, so Tubbs had carried it for a while. There was no equivalent schedule for the Democrats, although Tubbs had been one.

Lucas carried the schedule to a window for the better light and peered at the sheets: there were penciled tick marks against a half-dozen scheduled appearances by Smalls. Interesting, but not definitive. Tubbs had been following Smalls's campaign.

He called Smalls:

"What was your relationship with Bob Tubbs?"

"Tubbs?" Smalls asked. "What're you doing?"

"Trying to figure out why he was tracking your campaign."

"Tracking . . . Well, I don't think you could draw any conclusions from that," Smalls said. "That's what he did for a living."

Lucas read off the list of the appearances Tubbs had been tracking. "Any reason why he'd pick those four?"

After a moment of silence, Smalls said, "The only thing I can think of is that I was out of town on all of them."

"Of course," Lucas said. He should have seen it.

"My God, Davenport, the papers say Tubbs has disappeared," Smalls said. "What does this have to do with the porn thing?"

"I don't know—but I was told that he went through your campaign office from time to time," Lucas said.

"Not while I was there," Smalls said. "But, you know . . . political people hang out."

"What about Tubbs? Did he hate you?"

"Oh, not really. We didn't particularly care for each other," Smalls said. "He was pretty much a standard Democrat operator. He also lobbied some, so he had to suck up to Republicans as well. He was just one of those guys doing a little here, a little there. He was supposedly a bagman for one of our less revered St. Paul state senators. Don't know if that's true or not, but I suspect it was."

"Did he do dirty tricks? Could he have come up with this porn idea?"

"Well, you know, yeah, probably," Smalls said. "He'd do opposition research, try to find a picture of you picking your nose, or wav-

ing your arm so that if it was cropped right, you looked like you
were doing a Hitler salute."

They talked for a few more minutes, and when Lucas got off the
phone, he started taking the apartment apart. It hadn't occurred to
him until Smalls mentioned the possibility that Tubbs had been a
bagman, and that he might have been involved in dirty tricks, but
the fact was, nothing the least bit discreditable had been found in
the apartment by either the St. Paul cops or the crime-scene people.
No porn, no cash . . . and looking around, Lucas hadn't found any
employment contracts, no car titles, no leases, no legal papers of
any kind.

Tubbs might well have a safe-deposit box somewhere, but Lucas
thought there was a good chance that he'd have a hidey-hole somewhere in the apartment, somewhere he could get at important
papers quickly. After a quick survey, in which he didn't spot anything in particular, he unplugged a lamp and carried it around the
apartment, testing all the outlets. Fake electric outlets, though
opening to small caches, were both innocuous-looking and easy to
get at. In this case, all the outlets worked.

He rapped on the wooden floor and got a hard return: the building was a steel-reinforced concrete structure, so there were no
holes in either the floor or the ceiling, which looked like genuine plaster. An access panel on the back wall of the bathroom
looked promising, because it appeared to have been removed a few
times—probably at least once by the crime-scene crew. He found a
screwdriver in a tool kit that he'd seen in the kitchen, and removed
the panel, and found sewer pipes and the usual inter-wall dust and
grime. He put the panel back on and moved to the closets, checking
for fake side panels.

Lucas had designed his own home, and worked daily with the

contractor who built it, almost inch by inch. He was standing in a closet when he thought, *Sewer pipes?* He went back to the bathroom and took the panel off again. Two white six-inch PVC sewer pipes were coming down from above—but Tubbs's apartment was on the second floor of a two-story building. Where were the pipes coming from? Couldn't be Tubbs's own bathroom because, unless there are big pumps involved, sewage flows *down*, not up.

He sat on the toilet seat, looking at the two large pipes, and it occurred to him that the access panel didn't give access to anything. You couldn't do anything except look at the pipes. He reached out and shook one of them: solid. Shook the other: also solid.

But when he tried twisting one of them, it turned, and quite easily.

THE PIPES WERE ABOUT fourteen inches long, with screw-in caps. He unscrewed the cap on the first pipe, and there it all was: the personal papers that had been missing, along with a gun—an old revolver with fake pearl stocks—and three thumb drives. The second pipe contained more paper, all curled to fit in the pipe, the kind of thing that Lucas might have been looking at in a corruption investigation. There were tax records, testimony clipped from lawsuits, bills of sale, corporate records, and $23,000 in stacks of fifty-dollar bills, held together by rubber bands.

He put back the gun and all the personal papers, and the money. He took everything else, and called Kidd.

"I've got three thumb drives and I need a quick survey, just to find out what's on them."

"How big are they?" Kidd asked.

Lucas looked at the drives and said, "Two two-gig, one four-gig."

"You could put the equivalent of several thousand books on those things, so the survey might not be quick," Kidd said.

"I just need an idea—and I need to know if that porn file is on one of them," Lucas said. "I doubt that there are several thousand books on them."

"Well, shoot, look . . . I guess. We could check for the porn fairly quickly. Come over in an hour. I'll put a little search program together."

"Would two or three hours be better? I've got something else I could do."

"Two hours would be better," Kidd said. "We're expecting some guests and I'm in the kitchen, being a scullery maid."

"See you then: two hours."

Lucas put the pipes back together and screwed the panel back on, walked back to the car, and headed north up I-35.

SANDRA MAE OTIS LIVED in a manufactured home in a manufactured home park off I-494 north of St. Paul. She also ran an illegal daycare center.

Otis was sitting on the stoop smoking when Lucas pulled into the driveway: she had bleached-blond hair, black eyebrows, and small metallic eyes like the buttons on 501 jeans. She regarded him with a certain resignation as he got out of the car, flicked the butt-end of the smoke off into the weeds, turned and shouted, "Carl, knock it the fuck off," and looked back at Lucas.

As Lucas walked up, a little boy, maybe three, dressed in a Kool-Aid-spotted T-shirt and shorts, and crying, came out and said, "Carl hit me, really hard."

Otis said, "I know, Spud, we'll get him later. You go on back in there and tell him that if he hits you again, I'll put him in the garbage can and let you beat on it." Back to Lucas: "How long have cops been driving Porsches?"

"Personal car," Lucas said. The musky odor of weed hung around her head.

She looked at him for a minute, then said, "So give me some money if you're so rich."

Lucas opened his mouth to say something when another small boy, a couple years older than the first, came out crying, rubbing an eye with his fist, and said, "Spud says you're gonna put me in the garbage can again."

"Yeah, well, don't hit him," Otis told the kid.

The kid said, "Sometimes Spud really pisses me off."

"But don't hit him," Otis said. "You see this guy? He's a cop and he's got a big gun. If you hit Spud again, he's going to shoot you."

The kid stepped back, his mouth open in fear. Lucas blurted, "No, I won't."

But the kid backed away, still scared, and vanished inside. Otis said, "So what do you want? I'm not responsible for Dick's debts. We're all over with."

Lucas looked around for something to sit on: the stoop would never touch the seat of his Salvatore Ferragamo slacks. There was nothing, so he stood, looming over her. "Three years ago, you were picked up and taken to juvie court as part of a prostitution ring that was busted over in Minneapolis."

"That's juvenile and it doesn't count," Otis said.

"It does count, because it's probably messed up your head, but that's not exactly what I want to talk about," Lucas said. "Sometime in there, when these people were running you, they took pictures of you and Mark Trebuchet and three adults in a sex thing. Did they sell those pictures?"

"I don't know if they had time, before they were busted," Otis said. "They were busted, like, two days after the photo shoot. I think the photographer bragged to the wrong guy about it."

"Now, who was this? Who's 'they'?" Lucas asked.

"The Pattersons. Irma and Bjorn."

"The Pattersons ran the business?"

"Yeah. They're doing fifteen years. They got twelve to go. And if you're a cop, how come you didn't know that?"

"Because I'm operating off a telephone," Lucas said. "Our guys just found the pictures . . . but the pictures were in court? You, and the two men and the woman and Mark?"

"Yup."

"Did the cops get them off the Internet? The evidence photos?"

"I don't think so. The Internet was already getting too dangerous, with cops all over the place. The Pattersons were really scared about that, telling their clients to stay away from the 'net. They mostly printed them out and sent them around that way," Otis said. "They said they were for my *portfolio*. They said I was going to be a movie star. Like that was going to happen, the big fat liars."

"So what happened in court?"

"Well, I had to testify about what we did. The sex and all. And about the pictures. They wanted us to identify the adults, but, you know, we didn't know who they were," she said. "I'd seen them around, but I didn't know their names. I think they took off when the Pattersons got busted."

"Were there a lot of other pictures put in at the same time? In court? Of you?"

She frowned. "No. When the Pattersons took the pictures, they took a lot of them. I can remember that flash going off over and over and really frying my eyeballs. And this guy I was blowing, he had like a soft-on all the time, I had to keep pumping him up. But the cops had, I don't know, four or five pictures. Or six or seven. Like that. I think all they had were like these paper pictures, and they took them right off the Pattersons' desk."

A little girl, maybe Spud's sister, came out of the house and looked at Lucas and then at Otis and said, "I pooped."

"Ah, Jesus Christ, you little shit machine," Otis said. "All right. You go back in, and I'll come and change you."

The girl went back in and Otis asked, "You done?"

"Yeah, but don't go anywhere, okay?" Lucas said.

"Where in the fuck would I go?" Otis asked. "I'm living in an old fuckin' trailer. My next stop is a park bench."

Lucas turned away, then back and said, "This place can't be licensed."

"Are you kidding me?" she asked. "I'm working for minimum-wage dumbasses who either leave the kids with me or lock them in a car. I'm all they can afford, and I'm better than a car. Maybe."

Lucas said, "All right, but don't put Carl in the garbage can anymore, okay?"

"Carl gets what Carl deserves," she said. "But they all like chocolate ice cream. I could get some for tomorrow, Porsche cop, if I had an extra twenty bucks."

"How many kids are in there?"

"Seven," she said. "Unless one of them has killed another one."

Lucas took a twenty out of his wallet. "Get them the ice cream," he said. "You spend it on dope, I'll put you in something worse than a garbage can."

BACK DOWN I-35 TO Kidd's place.

Lauren came to the door, said, "Hi," and then, as Lucas followed her inside, said, "We've got a couple of friends staying with us for a few days, with their kids. It could be a little noisy."

"I just need Kidd to take a look and give me an estimate on what's inside these things," Lucas said, showing her the thumb drives.

Kidd was sitting in the front room with a black couple, and Kidd said, "Hey, Lucas," and to the couple, "This is Lucas Davenport, he's a cop. Lucas, John and Marvel Smith, from down in Longstreet, Arkansas. John's a sculptor, Marvel's a politician. John does some stuff that you and Weather ought to look at."

"I'll do that," Lucas said. He shook hands with John Smith, an athletic guy with some boxer's scars around his eyes, and smiled at Marvel, a beautiful long-legged woman with a reserved smile; like she might be wary of cops.

Kidd said, "So let's see what you got. . . . Back in a couple of minutes, guys."

On the way back, Lucas gave Kidd a thirty-second summary of how he'd gotten the drives. "This Tubbs guy—I believe he's dead. Murdered. I mean, we all thought so, but now I'm pretty sure of it."

"That's disturbing," Kidd said.

In the computer lab, Kidd plugged in all three thumb drives at the same time, quickly figured out that one set had been formatted under an Apple OSX operating system, and the other two with different versions of Windows.

He put in a piece of his own software and tapped some keys,

and a file popped up. "There it is," he said. He opened it, and they saw the first photos of the Smalls porn files.

"How'd you do that?" Lucas asked.

"I've got the number of bytes from the file off the Smalls machine, and looked for a file of close to the same length. This one was exact, which is a rare thing."

"Goddamnit—Smalls is clear."

"Not necessarily," Kidd said. "Remember—the file could have gone the other way, too. From Smalls to Tubbs. Maybe Tubbs stole it, and was blackmailing Smalls."

"You sound like a defense lawyer," Lucas said.

"Thanks." Kidd did some other computer stuff, popping up files with all kinds of various corporate papers, real estate records, legislative committee meeting transcripts, court records.

"Cover-your-ass files," Lucas said.

"Might be more complicated than that," Kidd said. He went to the door and called, "Hey, Marvel? You got a minute?" And he said to Lucas, "Marvel's okay."

MARVEL CAME DOWN THE HALL, and Kidd showed her into the lab and said, "Look at this file. It's from here in Minnesota. Do you see anything?"

Lucas was a little nervous having the woman looking at the file, but she was from Arkansas, and Kidd probably wouldn't have asked her to look at it if she might become a problem. He kept his mouth shut.

The file Marvel was examining was one of the smaller ones, fifteen or twenty pieces of paper that had been scanned into PDF files, as well as three or four fine-resolution JPEG photos. Using a mouse, Marvel clicked back and forth between the images. John and Lauren came into the lab, leaned against a wall to watch.

Marvel took five minutes; at one point, the kids made a noise that sounded like they'd killed a chicken, and Lauren ran off to see what it was. She'd just come back when Marvel tapped the computer screen and said, "See, what happened was, this guy, Representative Diller, got the licensing fees on semi-trailers reduced by about half, so they'd supposedly be in line with what they were in the surrounding states. He said he wanted to do that so the trucking companies wouldn't move out of Minnesota. But what you see over here is a bunch of 1099 forms that were sent by trucking companies to Sisseton High-Line Consulting, LLC, of Sisseton, South Dakota. Over here is the South Dakota LLC form and we find out that a Cheryl Diller is the president of Sisseton High-Line Consulting. And we see that she got, mmm, fifty-five thousand dollars for consulting work that year, from trucking companies."

"So if these two Dillers are related . . ." Lucas began.

"I promise you, they are," Marvel said.

Kidd said, "Marvel's a state senator. In Arkansas."

Marvel added, "This shit goes on all the time. On everything you can think of, and probably a lot you can't think of."

Lucas said to Kidd, "So what these are, are blackmail files."

"Or protection files, if they're all the same kind of thing," Marvel said. "Whoever owned these files might have been involved in these deals, and kept the evidence in case he ever got in trouble and needed help."

Lucas looked at the computer screen for a moment and then said, "All right. Give me the drives back, Kidd. You guys don't want to know anything about this."

Kidd pulled the drives out, handed them to Lucas, and said, "You are *so* right. Do not mention my name in any of this."

"I won't," Lucas promised. "Can I print these out on my home printer?"

"Probably," Kidd said. "What kind of computer are you running?"

"Macs," Lucas said.

"Most of the files are on government machines, Windows," Kidd said. "I'll loan you a Windows laptop, a cleaned-up Sony. If anyone asks, you paid cash at Best Buy a couple years ago."

BACK IN THE CAR, the laptop on the passenger seat, Lucas called the governor and said, "I need to talk to you alone, tonight. Without Mitford or anybody else around."

"That bad?"

"Worse than you could have imagined," Lucas said. "The problem is, I can't get out of it now."

"I've got a cabin on the Wisconsin side of the St. Croix, north of St. Croix falls. I could be there at six, if it's that bad."

"Tell me where," Lucas said.

He got directions to the cabin, again told the governor to come alone, then went home, said hello to the housekeeper, who said that Letty wouldn't be back until six o'clock, that Weather had been called to do emergency work on a woman whose face had been cut in an auto accident, and she'd be late, and that the kids were fine.

Lucas took the thumb drives back to his den, hooked the Sony up to his printer, then had to download some printer software that matched the Sony to his printer. He took a few more minutes to re-familiarize himself with Windows, and started printing. There were thirty-four files on the three drives, not nearly filling them, but it took two hours to get them all printed out.

He didn't print the porn file.

While the printing was going on, he paged through the porn file, image by image, and found the photos that Kidd thought came from police files. He looked at the captions, which had apparently been printed onto sheets of paper that had been attached to the bottom of paper photos—the kind of photos you would give to a jury. Kidd was right, he thought: they were evidentiary photos.

When the printing was done, he used a three-hole punch to put binder holes in Tubbs's files, and bound them book-style between cardboard covers. Then he started annotating them, figuring out who was who, and trying to figure out what was going on in each file. Virtually all of them were evidence of payoffs to state legislators and a variety of state bureaucrats.

Some of the evidence was explicit, some of it was simply suggestive. Some of it would have led to criminal charges, or to clawback civil suits. Almost all of it would have ended careers.

A LITTLE AFTER FIVE, he went out to the Lexus SUV that he drove outside the Cities, and took off for Wisconsin. He was not in a mood for the scenic tour, so he went straight up I-35 to Highway 8, then east through Chisago City and Lindstrom and past Center City to Taylors Falls, then across the St. Croix into Wisconsin, north on Highway 82, off on River Road and finally, down a dirt lane lined with beech and oak trees to a redwood house perched on a bluff over the river. The front door was propped open with a river rock.

The governor was sitting on a four-season porch, already closed in for the winter, that looked over the river valley. When Lucas banged on the screen door, he called, "Straight through to the porch. Get a beer out of the kitchen, or make yourself a drink."

The kitchen was compact: Lucas snagged a Leinie's from the refrigerator, popped the top with a church key hung on the refrigerator with a magnet, and walked through the house to the porch. The house was larger than it looked from the outside, and elegant, and smelled lightly of cigar smoke. A side hallway led toward what must've been two or three bedrooms. A library featured pop fiction and a big octagonal poker table with a green baize surface; the living room was cluttered with couches and chairs and small tables. An oversized television hung from one wall.

Henderson was wearing soft tan slacks and a white shirt with the sleeves rolled to the elbow, and boat shoes. He said, "Give me one sentence to crank up my enthusiasm for being here."

Lucas sat on a wooden chaise with waterproof cushions, took a sip of the beer, thought for a few seconds, then said, "Bob Tubbs had the porn before it was unloaded on Smalls, and was probably murdered to shut him up."

The governor stared at him for a few seconds, then said, "Oh, shit."

Lucas pushed on: "I went into Tubbs's apartment, legally, with the approval of Tubbs's mother and the investigator from the St. Paul Police Department. I searched the place, and pretty much because of my superior intelligence . . ."

". . . goes without saying . . ."

". . . I found Tubbs's hideout cache, which St. Paul hadn't found," Lucas said.

"Why didn't they find it?" Henderson asked.

"Because he hid it in a weird place, and when they opened it up, they found just what they expected to find." He told Henderson about the pipes, and how he belatedly realized that they'd hardly be draining upward.

"And in the pipes . . ." Henderson prompted.

"I found a gun, a wad of papers, plus some money, cash, and three thumb drives. I opened the thumb drives and found exactly the same porn file—exactly the same—as the one the cops found on Smalls's computer. There's a remote possibility—remote in my mind, anyway—that the file went from Smalls to Tubbs. That Tubbs found out that there was a porn file on Smalls's computer, went in, stole it, and is, or was planning to, blackmail Smalls. So Smalls, or one of his henchmen, killed him. There's a much better possibility that it went the other way—from Tubbs to Smalls's computer. We know that Tubbs occasionally dropped by Smalls's campaign office."

"Let's look at the first possibility," Henderson said; he was a lawyer. "Why don't you think Tubbs was blackmailing Smalls?"

"Because there's nothing on the file, or in the other documents on the thumb drives, that mentions the porn or Smalls. He'd have no way to tie it to Smalls—all he had was the file itself. Why would anyone believe it came from Smalls, or anyone else, for that matter? If he tried to go public with it, Smalls would just blow it off as an egregiously vicious smear by a Democratic operative who'd been involved in other dirty tricks."

"Is there any reason to think it *could* be a blackmail file?"

"Only one that I could think of," Lucas said. He patted his bound copies: "Because it seems likely that Tubbs may have been involved in other blackmail operations. Maybe not for money, maybe for influence. So he might have been a practiced blackmailer."

Henderson nodded: "So what's the other side? Why do you think it went Tubbs to Smalls, that Tubbs planted it on Smalls's computer?"

"Couple of reasons," Lucas said. "If it had really been Smalls's file, he probably would have paid Tubbs off. He'd have done it in a way that Tubbs couldn't come back on him—filmed it, or done it with trusted witnesses. That way, if the file ever showed up again, Tubbs at least would go down for blackmail."

He continued: "The other reason is, just look what happened. A guy who does dirty tricks is involved, somehow, with a really dirty trick, which could change an important election. He might have been paid for it. Maybe a lot. So if you take the simplest, straightforward answer to a complicated question . . ."

"Occam's razor . . ."

Lucas nodded. ". . . the file was going from Tubbs to Smalls. A straightforward political hit."

"So, what you're saying is, Tubbs probably took the thumb drive to Smalls's office, and when Smalls was gone, inserted the file."

"Yes. Or more likely, an associate of his did. Whatever happened, for either side, Tubbs was probably murdered to shut him up. Neither one of us is going to be able to avoid that . . . fact," Lucas said.

"I wouldn't avoid the fact," Henderson said, "but that doesn't mean that I don't think it could use some management."

"I agree," Lucas said. He added, "The thumb drives included a lot of other stuff. I printed it out—it's all documents, with a few photos. I annotated them, best I could, and bound it up."

HE HANDED THE BOOK to Henderson, who weighed it in his hands and then turned to the first page. He thumbed through it for a few minutes, then, in a distracted voice, asked, "You know how to make a G-and-T?"

"Sure."

"Could you get me another? Lean hard on the G."

Lucas went and made the drink, and then brought it back, and the governor took it without looking up, and Lucas pulled off his shoes and leaned back on the chaise and drank his beer and stared out into the dark over the river valley. He could see stars through a break in the trees: winter could arrive any second, although there was no sign of it.

A minute or so later, Henderson chuckled and said, "Jean Coutee . . . I wondered where she got that Jaguar. Poor as a church mouse, all workingman's rights and anti-this-and-that . . . and she took the money and bought a fuckin' Jag."

And fifteen minutes after that, Henderson sighed and shut the book, and handed it back to Lucas. "Am I in there . . . anywhere?"

"No."

"I don't mean as a crook, because I'm not. But am I mentioned? Am I going to court?"

"You're not even mentioned," Lucas said.

"Okay. That's okay."

"There's another thing that worries me," Lucas said. "That porn file. There're a lot of photos and most of them have some text. But one of the files seems likely to have come from a police evidence file. From Minneapolis."

"What? Police?"

"I don't know the connection, or how it got in the bigger file," Lucas said. "I suspect it came from the police. The question is, did the Minneapolis cops, or probably one cop, give the file to Tubbs, in an effort to destroy Smalls? If they did, is it possible—"

"That a cop killed Tubbs? So that he wouldn't rat them out if he got caught?"

"Or maybe they realized he wasn't reliable," Lucas said. "The thing is, Smalls and the cops, and Minneapolis in particular, did not get along. Smalls wanted to outlaw public employee unions. The unions saw him as a deadly enemy. When I look into this, that's going to be one aspect of the case," Lucas said.

"Which makes it even a bigger stink bomb," Henderson said.

"It'd be good to keep you out of this . . . in an operative sense," Lucas said.

"Absolutely."

"I might have to perjure myself, but only lightly and not really significantly," Lucas said. "The only two people who'd ever know would be you and me. . . ." *And Kidd and Lauren and Marvel and John, but they should be safe enough,* Lucas thought. He wasn't telling any real lies, he was just warping time a bit.

The governor didn't quail at the idea of perjury, he simply asked, "What are we talking about?"

"I put everything back. The St. Paul cops don't know I've already been to the apartment. I put everything back, and call the lead investigator, and tell him that I've been there for an hour. When they arrive, I'll be sitting there, looking at the paper. . . . I'll insist on taking it to the BCA computer lab. Nobody there knows what I've been up to. They'd find all this stuff, and the porn, Smalls would be cleared, a couple of crooks might go down. I noticed that one of them is a pretty close ally of yours."

"Fuck him," Henderson said. "He's a goddamned criminal, sucking on the public tit. I never saw that in him. But where's the perjury in this?"

"Might not be any. I'd tell them exactly what happened when I entered the apartment, where I looked and what I did, and here's the evidence. I wouldn't have to mention that it was my second trip there . . . that I took the stuff out, copied it, and then put it back. After all, the docs are all in the public record."

Henderson nodded, and closed his eyes. Then he said, "The murder."

"I'd want to stay on that," Lucas said.

"I'd insist. This thing will leak five minutes after you call St. Paul, and there's gonna be a shit storm. I'll be outraged, and you'll be my minister plenipotentiary to the investigation. That'll give us a reason for these . . . conferences."

"That'll work, I think," Lucas said.

They sat there for a minute, then Henderson said, "There's the elephant in the room . . . that we haven't talked about."

Lucas nodded: "Who did it. Who killed Tubbs."

"If he's dead."

"Yeah, if he's dead. But . . . it feels like it."

"*Why* it was done . . . should lead you to who did it," Henderson said. "A lot of people hate Smalls, but the most obvious beneficiary is Taryn Grant."

"But hiring a killer is a problem, no matter how much money you have," Lucas said. "The best model for that is the movie *Fargo*— idiots hiring idiots. From what I've read about her, she's not an idiot."

"She's not," Henderson agreed. "But it could be somebody working on her behalf. Or somebody who *thinks* he's working on her behalf. A psycho."

"I'll talk to her," Lucas said. "As the investigation spreads out, she'd be an obvious person to interview. I'll take a look and see what we can find out about her."

"Another thing: we need to manage the news release. We know it'll leak, we need to be out front on that."

"That's what Mitford's for," Lucas said. "Just make sure he gives me a heads-up before the shit hits the fan."

"I will. Now about your book . . ." Henderson said. He patted the bound printout that Lucas had given him.

"Into the grinder," Lucas said.

AT TEN MINUTES AFTER nine o'clock that night, Roger Morris, the St. Paul homicide detective, wearing a purple velour tracksuit and Nike Air running shoes, stuck his head into Tubbs's apartment and called, "Where are you?"

"In the bathroom," Lucas called back.

Morris found Lucas on his knees, looking at papers he was pulling out of two white plastic sewer pipes. Morris tipped his head back and closed his eyes and said, "Fuck me with a parking meter. We missed it."

"Yeah, well . . . I looked in there and wondered, why would you drain a sewer *up*, in a two-story building?" Lucas said.

"So what is it?"

"Papers, money, and three computer thumb drives," Lucas said. "You can have the money and the papers. The thumb drives . . . finders keepers. I've got a guy waiting for me at the BCA computer lab."

"*We* got a computer lab—"

"Ours is better," Lucas said. "This stuff just might blow the ass off the legislature. . . . These papers, the ones I can read, suggest that some of our beloved politicians are on the take."

"That's a motive on the Tubbs killing," Morris said. "Seriously, man, it's my murder investigation—"

"I want those thumb drives at the BCA," Lucas said. "You'll get the contents—I'll drive you over there, and we'll give you a receipt. I'll tell you what, Roger, I'm only looking at Tubbs for one reason: the kid who found that porn said Tubbs had been hanging around the Smalls campaign, and might have had the opportunity to put it on Smalls's computer. I looked close at the Smalls porn, the stuff from your computer lab, and there's some involvement there that you don't want to deal with. I don't want to deal with it, either, but you *really* don't."

"Like what?"

"Like one of the photos may have come out of the Minneapolis cops," Lucas said. "Maybe the whole file did. Maybe some cops were trying to get rid of Smalls. Maybe Tubbs was killed to seal off the connection."

"No, no," Morris said. A few seconds later, "You don't have to drive me—I'll follow you over. I want that receipt. You can keep the papers and the money, too. But I want copies of every single god-damn document on my computer tomorrow morning."

"Fast as I can get it to you, Roger," Lucas said. "I promise."

CHAPTER 7

L ucas got the contents of Tubbs's hidey-hole into the BCA lab, and the tech there, called in on overtime, loaded up the files and began printing out the documents. When he found the porn file, he asked, "What about this trash?"

"Aw, man," Lucas said. They dialed into the file, and he switched to full drama mode: "Aw, Jesus Christ."

He'd given Morris a receipt for the pile of evidence and Morris had gone home with the promise of complete access in the morning. Now Lucas called him at home and said, "You might want to get over here."

"What happened?"

"We pretty much confirmed that Tubbs–porn connection," Lucas said. "He's got the file on one of these thumb drives."

"I'll be there in ten minutes," Morris said.

WHEN MORRIS ARRIVED, THE first thing he asked Lucas was, "If this file was a setup, if Tubbs did it, and if Tubbs was killed the same day the file was found . . . that night . . . then he'd have had to go to Smalls's office that morning. Right? He couldn't have put it on the day before."

"That's right," Lucas said.

"I'll tell you what: you can check us on this, but we backtracked Tubbs, to see who he'd talked to, and where he'd been, the day he disappeared, and that night. He didn't go to Smalls's campaign office. We've accounted for all his time back a couple of days, and he wasn't there."

"Then . . . he had to have an associate."

"Who might've gotten scared when he saw how crazy this whole thing got," Morris said. "It might've started out as a dirty trick, and all of a sudden, people are talking about multiple felonies and Smalls is going nuts on TV. He figures if it comes out, who put the file on Smalls's computer, he's heading for prison. So he talks to Tubbs, one thing leads to another . . . and *bang.*"

"That seems reasonable," Lucas said, because it was.

They talked about the possibilities as Lucas walked Morris up to the lab, where Lucas said to the lab tech, "You need to call the St. Paul computer lab guy. There's got to be some trigger for the porn file booby trap. Between the two of you, I want you to find it tonight, so Roger and I know what it is when we come in tomorrow."

"That's a tall order," the tech said.

"That's your problem," Lucas said. "It's gotta be there: find it."

To Morris: "I want to show you this one group of photos." He ran through the file, found the pictures of Otis and the others in the group sex, and tapped the caption. "These were the pictures that were presented in court. Unless you believe that the Minneapolis cops are posting this stuff on the Internet, then they had to come out of the Minneapolis computer system. In fact, I was told by this girl"—he tapped Otis's face—"that the photos presented in court were on paper, and were seized when the cops raided the porn operation. I'm thinking . . . this had to come out of Minneapolis's evidence file. I mean, look at the caption: that's cop stuff."

Morris rubbed his forehead: "You're saying somebody in Minneapolis helped Tubbs set up Smalls?"

"It's a possibility," Lucas said.

"Then . . . *that* guy could be the killer," Morris said.

Lucas shrugged.

Morris watched Lucas for a moment, then switched directions: "Have you looked at the document files?"

"I'm getting them printed now," Lucas said. "It looks like it's the same as the other papers—blackmail stuff, cover-your-ass files, whatever. A lot of corrupt bullshit."

Morris considered for a moment, then said, "We need a conference. We need the heavies on this. I'll call you tomorrow at eight o'clock—"

"Nine would be better," Lucas said.

"Nine o'clock, and we'll both have lists of who should be in the conference."

"It's a plan," Lucas said.

He and Morris spent a half hour flicking through the document files, and then through the porn files, looking for any other clue to its origin, but found nothing new. When they were done, Morris said, "Nine o'clock tomorrow."

LUCAS WENT HOME: he'd successfully covered his ass, he thought. Now it should be a straightforward murder investigation, and they already had several pieces of the puzzle.

Morris was a competent investigator, and more than competent:

but he didn't have everything that Lucas had, and Lucas couldn't give him some of it. He really had to stay on the case, Lucas thought. He *wanted* to stay on it. It was getting intense, and he liked intense.

Liked it enough that he got up early to think about it. And at nine o'clock the next morning, in jeans and T-shirt, he'd already finished a Diet Coke and a plate of scrambled eggs, and his list of who should be at the conference. His list: Henry Sands, director of the BCA; Rose Marie Roux, commissioner of public safety; Rick Card, St. Paul chief of police; Morris; and himself. He was trying to remember who would call whom, when his phone rang. He picked it up, looked at the screen.

The governor: "Everything cool?" Henderson asked.

"Yes. We're going bureaucratic, to blur everything over. The St. Paul homicide detective on the Tubbs case, and I, are going to convene a conference with Sands and Rose Marie and the St. Paul chief, lay it all out, and then just start a straight criminal investigation. Maybe parcel some of it out to the attorney general . . . but we'll see what Rose Marie has to say about that. You should stay clear."

"Keep me informed."

MORRIS CALLED A MINUTE LATER, with his list. He had the same list as Lucas, less Rose Marie, and with the addition of the Ramsey County attorney.

He agreed with Lucas on Rose Marie, but Lucas argued against the county attorney: "That guy is owned by Channel Three. If he's in the conference, we might as well put it on television."

"Man, my computer guy printed out those document files and left them for me, and I gotta tell you, it's gonna be political, and it's gonna be ugly. The names in these things . . . they scare the shit out of me. I think we need lawyers. Lots of lawyers. The more the better. These docs aren't for cops."

"I'll take a look as soon as I go in this morning," Lucas said. "But we're cops, so it's okay to have a conference about a possible crime. Nobody can criticize us for that. Then we let Rose Marie and Rick figure out who to bring in, for the political stuff. We can just focus on the murder."

They went back and forth, and eventually Morris said, "I knew you had a sneaky streak, but I didn't know it was this sneaky. But okay, let's do it your way. I'll declare a big-ass emergency and try to get a conference at noon or one o'clock, here in St. Paul."

"Do it," Lucas said.

THE MEETING WAS SET for eleven o'clock, the only mutual time they could all find, in the chief's office in St. Paul. Lucas had a couple of hours, so he called Brittany Hunt, the volunteer who'd discovered the porn file. She was driving to the Mall of America. She was no longer employed, she said, but not too worried about it.

"I talked to my adviser and she said that exposing a criminal like Smalls was a lot more important than my campaign work." She was worried about meeting Lucas without her father present, but he told her that he just had a couple of quick questions that weren't about her at all. "I need to gossip," he said.

She agreed to make a quick detour and meet him at a sandwich shop off Ford Parkway, five minutes from his house. He changed into a suit and tie, then drove over to the sandwich shop, where he found her eating a fried egg sandwich on a buttermilk biscuit. Lucas got a glass of water and sat down across the table from her.

"I was famished," she said.

"So eat." Lucas leaned toward her and pitched his voice down. "Tubbs . . . did he have any special friends in Smalls's campaign?"

She cocked her head and licked a crumb of biscuit off her lower lip, then asked, "You mean, was he sleeping with anybody?"

Lucas said, "Well, any kind of close friend."

She said, "You know . . . I don't know. But I can tell you how to find out. There's a guy there, Cory, mmm, I don't really know his last name, he works in the copy room. He's the biggest gossip in the world. He knows *everything*."

"Cory."

"Yes. He's not really part of the campaign staff, he was hired to do the printing and copying. They do a lot of that. He knows *everything*. Ask Helen Roman. She's the campaign manager, she'll know where to find him."

"Sounds like a good guy to know," Lucas said.

"Yeah. If you like gossip, and we all do." She burped, then looked toward the counter. "I could use another one of those sandwiches. I haven't eaten since the day before yesterday."

SMALLS'S CAMPAIGN OFFICE was off I-94 on the St. Paul side of the Mississippi, ten minutes away. Lucas went there, found Helen Roman, the office manager, who said that Cory Makovsky worked in the distribution center, at the end of the hall. Lucas went there, where he found Makovsky talking excitedly on his cell phone. When Lucas tried to get his attention, Makovsky held up a finger, meaning "Wait one," and gushed a revelation "He'd just seen it online from *People*, there really isn't any doubt that she's pregnant," into the phone.

Lucas looked pointedly at his watch, and Makovsky frowned and said to the phone, "Hang on a sec," and to Lucas, "*What?*"

Lucas said, "I'm an agent with the BCA. Did you murder Bob Tubbs?"

Makovsky took that in for a few seconds, then said hastily into the phone, "I gotta get back to you, Betty."

When Lucas had Makovsky's attention, he asked, "Did you kill him?"

Makovsky, who'd gone a little pale, said, "Of course not. Who told you I did?"

"Nobody. I just wondered," Lucas said. Then: "I was told you might have some information I need. Do you know if Bob Tubbs had a special friend of some kind . . . a lover, maybe . . . in Senator Smalls's campaign office?"

Makovsky's eyes widened, and his voice dropped to a whisper: "Is that the story Smalls is putting out?"

"No—that's the question I'm asking. Did Tubbs have a special friend?"

"I don't know," Makovsky said, with real regret in his voice. "I realize I should know, but I don't. I could ask around."

"Could you do that?" Lucas asked. He dug a card out of his pocket, wrote a number on the back, and said, "If you hear anything, call me."

"I'll do that," Makovsky said, his eyes bright. Lucas believed him; and two minutes after he called Lucas, the word would probably be tweeted, or Twittered, or whatever that was. Probably to *People*.

WHEN HE LEFT the campaign office, Lucas had ten minutes to get down to the St. Paul Police Department, just enough time to re-trieve his car and be marginally late. When he got there, he found he was the first person from outside the department to arrive.

The chief, Morris, and a lab tech were sitting around, drinking coffee, talking about a recent controversial tasing. A Bloomington cop's wife had woken angry in the middle of the night, and had used his duty Taser to tase her sleeping husband in the area sometimes called the *gooch*. He was now claiming a major disability—sexual dysfunction caused by a city-owned instrument—and was seeking to be retired at full pay. He was twenty-seven.

"I'll tell you what," Morris said, holding his coffee cup with his pinkie finger properly out in the air, "That boy won't be sleeping easy with a woman again, no matter who she is."

Commissioner of Public Safety Rose Marie Roux walked in and caught the last of that, and she asked, "Who was that?"

"Talking about the Bloomington tasing," Lucas said.

"Oh, yeah," she said. She took a chair, and plopped her purse on the chief's desk. "The guy who got it in the gooch."

Henry Sands, the BCA director, showed up a minute later, took the last chair, and Rose Marie asked, "So what's up? Or, I sorta know what's up, but what's new, and why is it an emergency?"

Morris said, "Lucas and I found a bunch of stuff in Bob Tubbs's apartment—you all know Tubbs, and know we're investigating his disappearance as a possible murder. Well, the stuff we found suggests that Tubbs planted the kiddie porn on Senator Smalls's computer. There's the theoretical possibility that he found it on Smalls's computer, and was using it to blackmail him, but Lucas and I don't believe that. . . . We think he was killed to eliminate him as a witness to whoever supplied the porn to get Smalls. It's possible that the kiddie porn came through the Minneapolis Police Department, so the killer could be a cop."

"Holy shit," the chief said.

"Plus," Morris continued, "in the same hideout where we found the kiddie porn—the porn was on a thumb drive—we found a bunch of other papers and copies of public documents which pretty much prove that seven serving state senators and representatives have committed a wide range of felonies, along with six former senators and representatives who are no longer in office, and a half-dozen bureaucrats who were paid off for arranging contracts."

There was a long silence while the VIPs looked at the ceiling, sideways, and at the carpet, then, "That's just the fuckin' cherry on the cake, isn't it?" Rose Marie said to everybody, the disgust showing on her face. "That's just the fuckin' cherry."

"What we need from you all," Morris concluded, "is for you to tell us what to do. I mean, we have to continue the Tubbs investigation. We can be pretty sure now that he was murdered—we've got a hell of a pile of motives. But there's a lot of political stuff."

"I need to see copies of everything," Rose Marie said.

"Got it at the BCA," Lucas said. "I can send it over."

Card said, "I need to see it, too."

"I've got a copy for you," Morris said.

Rose Marie held her index finger in the air, asking for silence as she thought for a moment, then: "Here's what I'd suggest. The corruption stuff goes to the attorney general, and he can have some of his under-employed young lawyers look at it. And we need to talk to Senator Smalls's attorneys right away. Smalls may be a suspect in the murder, if the porn was taken *from* him and he was being blackmailed. But if I understand you correctly, you think there's a much greater possibility that Tubbs put the porn on Smalls's computer, in which case, Smalls is being unfairly demonized as a pervert a week before a critical election. We have to tell him what we know, and then let Smalls do what he can with it."

Lucas chipped in: "I don't think the porn was taken from Smalls.

It's a logical possibility, which is why we mention it, but . . . it's like one percent. I think he was framed."

"Okay. More reason to talk to him soon," Rose Marie said.

Sands said to Rose Marie, "You can handle the politics. I think that's proper. But the Tubbs murder . . . and what comes out of it, a definite finding on how the porn got on Smalls's computer . . . is that St. Paul? Or is that us? St. Paul has been handling the case, and Detective Morris seems to have done an excellent job so far."

The chief never tried to catch that hot potato—he just let it fly by.

"It's you," he said. "I'll be goddamned if this department is going to investigate the Minneapolis department. That seems to be one of the critical questions, where the porn came from, and you guys have jurisdiction in Minneapolis. We don't."

"That's true," Sands began. "However—"

Rose Marie jumped in: "Henry, give it to Lucas."

Sands took a deep breath and said, "We've got federal funding being talked about right now. No matter what happens here, whether Smalls or Grant wins the election, we're gonna piss somebody off. The funding comes right through the Senate Office Building."

The chief said, "We got the same problem, big guy."

"Yeah, but it's a few pennies, relatively," Sands said. "I'm talking about another building and putting a major lab out in Worthington."

Rose Marie said again, to both of them, "Lucas has it. Everybody agree? Lucas has it."

The chief sat back and smiled, and Lucas said, *"Okay."*

ROSE MARIE, SANDS, AND LUCAS walked out to the parking lot together, and after Sands took off, Rose Marie said to Lucas, "You should call Elmer and see if he's the one who wants to break the news on Smalls. If he doesn't, I will—but we need to move now. We need to catch the five-o'clocks."

The five-o'clocks—the early-afternoon news.

"I'll call right now," Lucas said. He clicked up the governor's number on his cell phone, and Henderson answered on the third ring. Lucas told him what the group had decided, and Henderson said, "Tell Rose Marie to take the press conference. I'll call Porter now, and tell him what's coming."

He clicked off and Lucas relayed the word to Rose Marie. She said, "I'll set up a press conference for three o'clock. I'll be calling you from my hairdresser's for the background: just e-mail me a few tight paragraphs on the whole thing. Goddamnit, I was hoping Smalls would go down."

"Maybe he still will," Lucas said.

"Maybe," she said. "Taryn is cute, smart, and she's got more money than Elmer."

"Okay . . ."

"So how are you going to handle the investigation? Now that it's public?"

"Don't know yet," Lucas said. "I'm thinking about it."

LUCAS WALKED OVER to his car and climbed in, and his phone went off: Porter Smalls. Lucas answered and Smalls said, "Thank you. I just talked with Elmer. I owe you big-time and I don't forget."

"That makes me a little nervous," Lucas said. "I don't want to be owed: this is my job."

"I don't care. I owe you," Smalls said.

When Smalls got off the phone, Lucas called Kidd: "Did you ever get a chance to look at that list of campaign members?"

"Should be in your e-mail," Kidd said. "There are only a dozen who might be serious contenders. There are two people of particular interest. Daniel MacGuire and Rudy Holly. MacGuire is gay and has run a gay Republicans group, but Smalls has been against gay marriage, so . . . And MacGuire is also a depressive and has anger-management issues, and is taking medication for both. Holly is a conspiracy theory guy, going back to the Clinton years and that whole blow-job business. I've seen some stuff he's put on some conspiracy sites, and the thing is, he's nuts."

"Any lonely middle-aged women in there?" Lucas asked.

"Yes. You're thinking, what?"

"Tubbs wasn't crazy, he was calculating. Somebody had to set the booby trap the morning that the volunteer tripped it—and that wasn't Tubbs, because Tubbs has been backtracked by a pretty good cop: he wasn't at the campaign office that morning. The question is, did he have a lover? Or a very close friend? Somebody he could trust with this?"

After a moment of silence, Kidd said, "Ramona Johnson. She would be your best bet. Divorced four years ago . . . let me see here . . . until about five months ago, she was complaining on Facebook about the lack of eligible men and the problems of middle-aged women. Then she shut up."

"Ramona Johnson."

"Yes. There's one more possibility. A Sally Fey. She's younger, she's thirty-one, and she has a new beau, but she's not talking about it. From what I've seen of her and her e-mails . . ."

"You've got her e-mails?"

"Forget I said that. From what I've seen of her, she's a very shy, quiet type, and she's a little mousy. Doesn't do much with her hair," Kidd said. "But you can see the hope in her eyes."

"You can see her eyes?"

"Try to stay on track," Kidd said. "If the right guy said the right things to her . . ."

"Tubbs could do that. He had a reputation as a ladies' man," Lucas said.

"So put Fey on the list." He spelled her name, and Lucas wrote it down.

WHEN HE GOT OFF the phone with Kidd, Lucas used his cell phone to check his e-mail, looked at the list that Kidd had shipped him. Twelve names, half men, half women. Would it be an ideologue or a lover?

He'd track down as many of the people on the list as he could, and ask them the hard question. Did you set the booby trap? If the answer was no, Lucas would say, "You realize that Tubbs was killed for what he knew. If you're lying, you could be next."

If the answer was still no, the next question would be, "If you didn't set it, who did?"

It *could* work.

CHAPTER 8

Taryn Grant's phone buzzed, a call, not an alarm. She was lying on her bed, waking up from a much-needed afternoon nap. She stretched, yawned, picked up the phone, and said, "Hello?"

"What are you doing?" Her campaign manager, Connie Schiffer.

"Took a nap. I just woke up."

"Good. We need you sharp. You're ready for tonight?" A fundraiser at the Wayzata Country Club. Taryn didn't actually need the funds, but if people gave you money, they tended to support you, to feel a connection.

"Absolutely."

"You're bringing the gorgeous David?" David Wein, a commodities broker who would someday inherit his father's firm. A small firm. David was a corn expert, but was also thoroughly grounded in soybeans, and sometimes dabbled in sugar beets. He looked good, though he was always called David, and never Dave.

"Tonight, anyway," Taryn said.

There was a *tone* in her voice and Connie instantly picked it up: "Ooo, if you're done with him, could I have him for a week or so?"

"Then, when you were done with him, he'd go around comparing our . . . attributes . . . with the boys in the locker room," Taryn said.

After a few seconds of silence, Connie said, "Wait—you're saying that would be a bad thing?"

Taryn laughed and said, "You're *such* a slut. I like that."

"Yeah, well, I'm now walking out to the turbo after spending the last two hours at KeeKee's. I spent four thousand, three hundred and sixty dollars on ridiculously overpriced clothing sewn by poverty-stricken foreigners. I'm all shopped out and we need to talk."

"I have to run through the shower and gel up," Taryn said.

"Fifteen minutes," Connie said.

"If I'm not quite ready, I'll tell Dannon to let you in."

"Mmm . . . Dannon . . ."

Taryn laughed again, pushed *End*. She switched to the walkie-talkie function and was instantly answered by Dannon. She said, "Connie will be here in a few minutes. We've got Push at four o'clock and Borders at five, that'll take another hour. Then back here to dress for the party tonight. David will pick me up."

He said, "I've got the schedule," and "Alice is in the house. Carver will be here at five."

TARYN WENT INTO THE bathroom and examined her eyes for circles, jumped in and out of the shower, then went to work on her face. She used only minimal makeup during the day; her natural Scandinavian complexion was good enough, most of the time.

The problem with politics was that it went on well into the night. The night before, she'd gone to a reception in Sunfish Lake with fifty of the faithful, and it had gone late. When the party ended, a dozen of them had gathered in the homeowner's recreation room and had gotten down to the nut-cutting.

Her lead over Smalls was holding, and the numbers of leaners— people who were not fully committed yet, but who were inclined to vote for her—was increasing. She was going to win, and if she won, if she took off Porter Smalls, she wanted to hit Washington with a bang.

The people in the rec room had had some ideas about how she could do that; two of them were former U.S. senators themselves.

THEN, THAT MORNING, SHE'D been up at five o'clock, and had hit a series of assembly plants at the morning shift changes, and quickly returned to the Twin Cities for the local morning talk shows. She'd done two of them, but one was way the hell out west, and the other was almost downtown. It'd been hectic.

After the talk shows, she spoke to the Optimist Club in Forest Lake, another short out-of-town trip. She could feel a tickle in the back of her throat, and worried that she might be losing her voice. Schiffer had given her some kind of double-secret lozenge used, supposedly, by the president, to keep the voice going. She'd pop one as soon as she was done with her face.

Taryn looked at herself in the mirror: maybe a shadow there in the eyes, from too many twenty-hour days. Maybe from Tubbs? No: that was dwindling in the rearview mirror. She had more important things to worry about.

And nobody had heard a thing from the cops.

She'd been a little surprised by the campaign. She'd known politics was harsh, but had no idea exactly how harsh it was. There seemed to be one polestar, one overriding objective, one singular focus: to win. Nothing else really counted. Just winning.

She liked that. It fit her.

She went back to work on her face.

DANNON HAD JUST FINISHED his backyard checks when Schiffer arrived in her plum-colored Porsche Panamera. He let her in, and she went to the living room, carrying a legal briefcase full of paper, which she began digging through. Dannon asked her if she wanted a drink, and she took a lime-water, which he got for her.

Schiffer was a short, sturdy, dark-eyed woman, twice-divorced, with no regrets about either the marriages or the divorces. She had a degree in mechanical engineering from Duke, but after a month working for a lobbying firm in Washington, D.C., she'd never again looked with desire on an open-channel crimper. One thing led to another, and at forty, she was one of the country's best professional campaign managers.

She was sitting on the soft-as-wool leather couch, looking at a miniature legal pad, when Taryn came down from the bathroom, wearing black slacks and a white angora sweater, with gold earrings and a modest gold necklace.

"Dannon said he'd be in the monitoring room. Alice is outside," Schiffer said.

Taryn nodded and dropped into a chair opposite Schiffer. "So what's up?"

"Things are developing and it's almost all good," Schiffer said. "I talked to Ray Jorgenson, just in passing, and he says that Smalls is toast. That doesn't mean we can let up: we have to go after him even harder. Push his head under. Kick him while he's down."

"I thought we were doing that," Taryn said.

"We are, but we can always do more. Ben Wells is giving a talk to the Minneapolis chamber, and if we could commit to a twenty-five-thousand-dollar donation in two years, and if we can plant a question with somebody, he's willing to go off on Smalls. You know, an unscripted spontaneous statement, spoken in real but slightly saddened anger. He'd call for Porter's withdrawal."

Wells was a Republican congressman, who might like a shot at Smalls's Senate seat someday, after he grew up. Taryn asked, "Would it help twenty-five thousand dollars' worth?"

"Yes. It'd absolutely curdle the Republican vote," Schiffer said. "But Wells wants a call from your father, since you wouldn't be able to make the donation. You know, being . . . a loyal mainstream Democrat."

"I'll talk to Father tonight," Taryn said. "He'll want me to kick the money back to him somehow, but that's not a problem."

"Good. Then let's make it happen." Schiffer drew a line through an item on the yellow pad.

THEY SPENT FORTY-FIVE MINUTES plowing through the minutiae of the campaign. Taryn was running as a law-and-order Democrat, as conservative as she could be and still get the nod from the party. The party understood the problem with taking down Smalls, and hadn't really expected her, or any other Democrat, to win, so it was willing to overlook a little political incorrectness. On the other hand, she couldn't be too incorrect.

Walking the line was both interesting and delicate.

Schiffer said, "About the gorgeous David. If you really are thinking of breaking it off with him—or in him—I'd suggest that you wait for three weeks. Everybody understands that it's a nice, adult relationship, and Smalls has banged enough strange women that he won't mention it, but you probably wouldn't want to call it off right now. It'd make you look flighty. Or unsteady. Or fickle."

"Okay. I've about had it with David's act, but he doesn't know that," Taryn said. "I'll keep him on until the excitement dies down."

"Excellent." Another item checked off on Schiffer's list. "Now, over at Push. We fully support Push and we'll find money for it somewhere. The problem is that the Republicans are unnecessarily locking up money or sending it off to their already-rich friends . . ."

". . . and as a longtime successful businesswoman, I know how that works," Taryn recited, "I adamantly oppose socialism for the rich while the less-well-to-do have their funding cut off . . ."

". . . for important neighborhood programs like Push," Schiffer said, "which keeps the drug dealers out of our neighborhoods . . ."

". . . especially black ones with cornrows, who wear hoodies and those funny low-crotch pants and listen to that awful hopscotch music, or whatever it is."

Schiffer recoiled: "Oh, Jesus Christ, Taryn, don't give me a heart attack," she said, clutching at her chest. "Remember: no sense of humor. How many times do I have to tell you that: *No sense of humor*. Humor can get you in all kinds of shit and we've got this won, if we don't get funny."

"Then we go to Borders," Taryn continued. "I don't drink too much and I tell everybody that I don't want their money but I do want their love, and—"

"*No humor,*" Schiffer said. "You don't want their money, but you do want their respect—"

"I got it, I got it," Taryn said. "You need to take a couple of aspirin, Connie."

Schiffer shook a finger at her: "I lost the first race I ran because I didn't nail down those details. I let my candidate speak honestly. I let him be funny and intelligent: that was the last time I'll make *that* mistake. Now listen to what I'm saying, goddamnit. You want to be a U.S. senator? You want to go higher than that? Then you stay on program."

Taryn nodded: "Yes. I know and I agree. I like to tease you, but I'm on program."

Schiffer relaxed. "I know. You're a natural at this, and with training, you'll get even better. You'll get that big-time polish. Some people spend twenty years in the Senate and *never* get that. You could. You could be a contender."

"If I stay on program."

"Absolutely."

They both knew what they were thinking, though neither said it: Taryn Grant had what it took to be president. She had the business background, she understood economics and finance, she had the money wrapped up, she looked terrific, she had a mind that understood the necessary treacheries: a silken Machiavelli.

THEY DID PUSH at four o'clock, and Borders at five, and Taryn stayed on program. Dannon hovered in the background, with what looked like a G&T in his hand, which was really water with a slice of lemon. Alice Green stayed outside with the cars.

Taryn knew she'd done well with the richie-rich crowd. They were, her involvement with the Democratic Party to one side, her people. She'd known many of the younger ones since childhood, and had slept with two of them.

So she was a little surprised when, after she'd given her talk on shared values, Schiffer had appeared as she began circulating through the Borders living room, and had taken her arm in a nearly painful grip and hustled her out to a hallway.

"We've got a problem," she said.

"What?" Taryn thought, *Murder.*

"Smalls didn't do it. Didn't do the porn," Schiffer said. "One of the governor's people, Rose Marie Roux, has been on television saying that it's possible that he was framed. Smalls had a spontaneous press conference demanding that the people who did this be caught. There's an implication there . . . that it could have been an opposition trick. That would be you."

"When did this happen?" Taryn asked.

"Top of the five-o'clock news. Everybody has it. We need to come up with a reaction and we need it fast."

"Let me finish the hand-shaking," Taryn said. "You go sit in the corner and think."

TARYN WORKED THE CROWD for another half hour, then swirled out of the room, calling out good-byes. Schiffer was waiting at the door with Green. Taryn had four vehicles, the largest and most ungainly and only American one being the large silver GMC Yukon Denali, which she'd acquired the day before she launched her campaign. She didn't want the right-wingers asking why she didn't "Buy American"; and if some leftie asked about the environmental impact, she'd ask, "What, you don't believe in Minnesota's ethanol economy?" In any case, the Porsche, Jag, and M5 stayed under wraps.

Leaving the house, she kissed Ellen Borders on the cheek,

squeezed her husband's biceps, pointed Green, who usually rode with her, at the security car, trading places with Barb Siegel, the media fixer.

Schiffer drove, and Dannon and Green fell in behind, discreet in the gray BMW sport-utility escort vehicle.

In the car with Schiffer and Siegel, Taryn closed her eyes and said, aloud, *"We understand that this news is a preliminary statement, but we certainly hope that Senator Smalls is found not responsible for this distasteful child pornography discovery. But, as long as we have to talk about unpleasant things, let me say that I bitterly resent Porter Smalls's implicit suggestion that his political opponents may be involved with this situation. I'm his only political opponent at the moment, so that was aimed at me. I'll tell Senator Smalls this: I've long been involved in child-care issues, and have devoted quite a lot of my hard-earned money to charities that help children. Need I point out that he has not been? That he should suggest this . . . just totally creeps me out."*

"Not *'hard-earned money,'*" Schiffer said. "You inherited too much, and not everybody knows you founded your own company. Say, *'devoted a lot of my time.'* And get rid of the *'totally creeps me out.'* That sounds Valley girl, and you already look too Valley girl."

Taryn nodded. "Where was I . . . *That he should suggest this, I can only characterize as vicious. As distasteful in the extreme. And, frankly, as creepy. I would remind him that this child pornography was on his personal computer, in his personal campaign office, and if somebody placed this pornography on his computer . . ."*

"Personal computer . . . and 'creepy' is good, because he is a little creepy," Siegel said.

". . . if somebody placed this child pornography on his personal computer, and it wasn't his, then it was one of the people in his campaign

office—the office that he's supposedly running. And I will tell you—I've checked, and none of my people has ever been in Porter Smalls's office. Furthermore, I'd note that what Commissioner Roux said tonight didn't say that Porter Smalls was innocent of the child pornography charge, just that there seem to be other possibilities."

"No. No. Quit after the part where you say, '*the office he's supposedly running,*'" Schiffer said. "When you're done, I'll get some of the TV people together and make the point, off the record, that he's not been shown to be innocent. They'll run with that."

"The more we can hook his name to child porn, the better it'll be for us, even if he's innocent," Siegel said. "If there's a headline every day that says, 'child porn' and 'Porter Smalls,' then that wouldn't be all bad."

"It was better the other way," Schiffer said, "because we had him beat. Now this adds a complication."

"I *will* beat him," Taryn said. "Where are we doing the press conference?"

"I thought the front lawn, inside the gate," Schiffer said. "There's a nice sort of amphitheater thing there on the lawn."

"You think we could get them around by the pool?" Taryn asked.

"Well, we could, but why would we?"

"Because it looks rich. The point is, if this hurts me, I'll be hurt with the more conservative voters out here," Taryn said. "The richer ones. I want to make the point, 'I'm one of you.' I've got the liberals no matter what."

Schiffer thought about that for a moment, and then said, "Yeah. That's good."

Taryn said, "That fuckin' Roux. What the heck was she doing?"

"Didn't even get a heads-up," Schiffer said. "Well, when you get to Washington . . ."

———

THEY WERE ALMOST to the house when Schiffer said, "You know, I read a lot of history. One thing that I've noticed is that people who go a long way in politics seem to have some kind of destiny. Opponents die, seats open up when they need them, they get an appointment that's critical . . . This thing with Smalls. This is a test, but you *will* beat him. It's your destiny. You do ten years, work really hard at it . . . You'd be a hot, smart, rich, law-and-order Democrat, with loads of experience, and still *young*. . . . I mean, who knows where you could go."

Taryn didn't laugh. No false modesty here; just a rich young blond woman with a burning case of narcissistic personality disorder. She did say, "We may be getting ahead of ourselves. Let's get Smalls out of the way first."

"I'm just saying: it's your destiny," Schiffer said, looking across at Taryn in the dark. "You'd be a fool not to ride it hard as you can."

CHAPTER 9

ucas spent the afternoon chasing campaign committee members from Kidd's list. By early evening, he had found and interviewed ten of the twelve.

Two were out of town, one of those two would be back the next day, the other, not for a week and a half, having begun a hunting trip to Northern Ontario. Lucas was curious about that, because the timing seemed odd. He had a conference with Cory Makovsky, the gossip in the distribution center, who said, quietly, "He's being fired."

"Ah. When was he last in here?"

"Couple weeks ago. He was in charge of lawn signs, and the word is, there were a lot fewer lawn signs than the campaign paid for. Of course, it's hard to know for sure, but the rumor is, we're short about ten thousand signs at two dollars each. He went north before Bob Tubbs disappeared."

Lucas crossed the sign guy off his list.

LUCAS ARRANGED THE INTERVIEWS through Helen Roman, the office manager, who also found Lucas a small room with a desk and two chairs. He lined up those people who were working that day, the ten-of-twelve. He asked all of them the same questions, explaining that he was investigating the presumptive murder of Tubbs, but he focused on the four names isolated by Kidd.

MacGuire, a big, square guy with short curly red hair, denied any knowledge of anything that Tubbs had been doing, and was out-front with his gay issues. But, he said, he had no real problem working with Smalls, as conservative as Smalls was. "Senator Smalls is conservative on social issues, and I lean the other way, except on guns—I'm pro-gun, to use the shorthand. But I'm *very* conservative on financial and economic issues. Something has to be done to get the country back on an even economic keel. That's what I work on for the senator. Social issues, I'm not so involved with that. He is against gay marriage, and I'm for it, but we joke about it, you know? He's not really anti-gay, per se—he's got several gays on his staff, men and women both, and when one of them got married to her partner, he sent along a nice wedding present. So . . . it's complicated. But I think of him as a friend. And there are a hell of a lot of worse guys in the Senate than Smalls, and Taryn Grant doesn't seem a hell of a lot more understanding about gay issues than he is."

Lucas dug for opinions about other staffers, and MacGuire shrugged him off.

"This whole thing is a mystery—I have no idea who'd want to set the senator up. I mean, on the staff. Maybe we've got a spy somewhere, I don't know. But it's not me."

"We need to know who it is, if he or she is there," Lucas said. "That person's life could be in danger from the same people who killed Tubbs . . . unless he or she did it. Then, that'd mean you're working with a cold-blooded killer."

"Okay. I'll think about it," MacGuire said. "I'm not lying to you here, I really don't know—but I'll think about it, and ask around."

RUDY HOLLY, the conspiracy theory guy, thought Tubbs had been taken off because he'd been behind the dirty trick involving the porn. "The Republicans in this state rarely do well . . . but now, all of a sudden, they are doing well. The Dems are frantic. I believe that there's a force out there, funded by union money, that is putting pressure on people . . . probably set up the porn thing, then killed Tubbs to cover up. It seems so obvious. . . ."

He went on like that for a while, and before he was done, Lucas had dismissed him as being ineffectually goofy, although his ideas about the killing were roughly the same as Lucas's own. Holly said he had no idea who on the staff might have been involved with Tubbs, or might be working as a spy.

SALLY FEY SHRANK in her office chair when Lucas asked the question, her shoulders turning in, her neck seeming almost to shorten, as though she were trying to pull her head into a turtle shell. She looked up at Lucas and said, "Robert and I had an ambiguous relationship. . . ."

She was twisting her hands, as she spoke. She was a slight woman, who might have been attractive if she'd done anything to make it so. But she didn't: her clothing—she wore dresses—might have come from the 1950s. She wore neither jewelry nor makeup, but did wear square, clunky shoes. She looked at Lucas from under her eyebrows, and at an angle, as though she were worried that he might strike her.

Lucas tried to be as soft as he could be; it wasn't his natural attitude. "Ambiguous . . . how? Was this a sexual relationship?"

"Yes. Twice. I mean, we . . . yes, we slept together twice. When
he went away, wherever he went, it's hard to believe that he might
be dead, because he was so upbeat when I last saw him. . . . Anyway,
I thought maybe the police would ask me about him, but nobody
did, and I didn't know what to do about that. I was scared. . . . I
didn't know what happened to him, and when he didn't call me
Saturday or Sunday, I thought he wasn't interested anymore."

"When was the last time you heard from him?" Lucas asked.

"Friday night, about . . . nine o'clock," she said.

"And when did you last see him?"

"Friday night . . . about nine o'clock. I didn't stay over." Her eyes
roamed the small office, meeting Lucas's eyes only with difficulty.
"I just . . . visited for a while, and went home."

"Then people began looking for him, and you didn't say anything?"

"Well . . . yes. I did think I should," Fey said. "But one day came
and went, and nothing happened, and nobody seemed to really
know where he was, and some people thought he was drinking . . .
and I just . . . let it go. I really didn't have anything to contribute,
and I thought I might get in trouble."

"Did he ever ask you . . . or suggest to you . . . that he might
want to pull some kind of dirty trick on Senator Smalls?"

"Oh, no, he would never have done that," Fey said. "I mean, he
might have tried to pull a dirty trick, but he wouldn't have spoken
to me about it. I *like* Senator Smalls and Robert knew that. The
senator and I have common interests. He likes classical piano and
he likes Postimpressionist art. If Robert had asked me to do a dirty
trick on Senator Smalls, I would have refused and I would have told

Senator Smalls. Robert teased me about that. About me being loyal."

Lucas worked her for a while, but in the end, believed her. "Are you friends with Ramona Johnson?" Lucas asked.

"Ramona? Well, yes, I guess. We don't socialize or anything, but we're friendly."

"What is her attitude toward Senator Smalls?"

"Well . . ." Fey's eyes flew off again. "Oh . . ."

"Nobody will know who said what in here," Lucas said. "Did Ramona have some kind of grudge against Senator Smalls?"

"Oh, no, I wouldn't think so," Fey said. "Just the opposite. I had the impression, mmm . . ." She trailed away.

"You think they had a relationship?"

"I, mmm, I thought it . . . possible," Fey said. "*Please* don't tell her I said that."

JOHNSON WAS THE LAST of the ten people he'd question that day. Before he called her in, he phoned Smalls and said, "I have a somewhat delicate personal question to ask you."

"Ask."

"Ramona Johnson?"

"No. Though the thought has crossed my mind," Smalls said.

"Would she have felt . . . neglected, or spurned?"

"I don't believe so. . . . No. I don't see it. You think she had something to do with the porn?"

"I don't think anything in particular. I'm just trying to get everybody straight, and to cross-check what I can. Looking for motives," Lucas said. "If you wanted to talk to somebody on the committee staff about art or music, who would you have talked to?"

"You've interviewed Sally Fey . . . and she's the one I would have talked to. I didn't sleep with her, either."

"Okay. That's what I needed."

"Wait a minute," Smalls said, "I've got a question for you, before you hang up. Have you heard any rumblings from the AG's office?"

"I haven't heard a thing. Should I have?"

"Mmm. I don't know," Smalls said. "He had that guy over at the St. Paul police when this ICE woman copied the hard drive. Now there's a rumor around that he wants to know what we found that brought about Rose Marie's announcement."

"I think she told him."

"I've heard that he wants it in detail," Smalls said. "He wants to know how it all came about. But all I've got is a rumor."

"I haven't heard a thing," Lucas said.

RAMONA JOHNSON was a fleshy, dark-haired woman with intelligent eyes and a smoldering, resentful aggression that piqued Lucas's curiosity. He began by asking about her career, first as a researcher and then as a senior staffer. She had three degrees, she said, both a B.A. and a master's in political science, and an MBA in business. She'd spent most of her life bumping against various glass ceilings, she said, and was presently planning a number of political initiatives involving Republican women's work issues—glass ceiling issues.

She had nothing to do with Tubbs, she said, and resented the fact that she'd been asked to talk to a police officer investigating his disappearance. "I know you think you're just doing your job, but there are more and more police-state aspects to the way our various security apparati are conducting themselves. Really, your questions are no more than a fishing expedition."

"That's what most investigations *are*," Lucas said. "So, you had nothing to do with Tubbs lately. Have you *ever* had anything to do with Tubbs?"

"No," she said. "I've always been Republican policy, he's always been Democratic operations. We've worked on opposing political campaigns, of course, and we sometimes go to the same parties. I've known him for years, but we've never been . . . intimate. I don't mean that just in a sexual way, either. I mean, we've never really shared confidences."

"You know that possession of that child porn is a crime, and that the use of the child porn in an effort to smear Senator Smalls would be another crime, and that Tubbs, if we could find him, if he's not dead, could be looking at years in prison? As would an accomplice?"

"Is that a threat?" she asked.

Lucas shook his head: "No. I'm telling this to everyone. I want everybody to understand the stakes involved. We're naturally more interested in the possible, the likely, murder of Mr. Tubbs than we are in an accomplice who might not even have understood what he or she was getting into. We'd be interested in discussing a possible immunity, or partial immunity, with that person, if we could find him or her. We'd also want that person to know that if Tubbs was murdered, then he or she might be next in line."

"But that's not me," Johnson said. "Why are you telling me?"

"Because if it's not you, I'd expect you to talk to your friends about this. I want the word to get around. There almost certainly is an accomplice, and we really need to talk to that person . . . for her own protection."

"Well," she said, "not me. Are we done?"

Lucas spread his hands. "If you've got nothing else . . . we're done."

WHEN SHE WAS GONE, Lucas took out his cell phone, went online and looked up the plural of *apparatus*, and found that it was *apparatus*, or *apparatuses*, and not *apparati*. He said, "Huh," turned the phone off and thought about Johnson.

She was the most interesting of the staffers he'd spoken to, because of the underlying self-righteousness, anger, spite . . . whatever. She wore it like a gown. He'd seen it often enough in government work, people who felt that they were better than their job, and better than those around them; a princess kidnapped by gypsies, and raised below her station.

He was still thinking about Johnson, looking at the blank face of his phone, when it lit up and rang at him. Rose Marie calling.

"Yeah?"

"We've got a problem," she said. "That goddamn Lockes is about to serve subpoenas on all of us, to find out what happened that led to the press conference."

"Aw, man . . . Can't you threaten him or something?" Lucas asked.

"Elmer is going to talk with him, but . . . Elmer's going away in two years, one way or another. Lockes wants his job."

"Is he going to subpoena the governor?"

"I don't think so—but he knows you were asked by the governor to look at the case," Rose Marie said. "There's nothing to do but be upfront about it."

"The problem is, I used a couple of personal friends as information sources and computer support," Lucas said, referring to Kidd and ICE. "If I have to name them, they could be pretty goddamn unhappy."

"That will probably come up, but as technical people, they shouldn't have too much of a problem," Rose Marie said. "If they're called, they just tell the truth, and go on their way. They were asked to help out in a law enforcement investigation, and they did."

"Aw, shit," Lucas said.

ICE would not be much of a problem; she'd worked with law enforcement, and had testified in court hearings about her work. But he dreaded calling Kidd, who'd always seemed to Lucas to be a reclusive sort, an artist, a fringe guy who, as it turned out, also knew something about computers. He shouldn't have used him, Lucas thought: Kidd looked and talked tough, but might actually be too brittle for a rough-and-tumble political fight.

He called Kidd, and was surprised by the reaction: "Don't worry about it," Kidd said. "I'm a guy you knew from back when, who's worked in the computer industry, so you got me to take a look. I don't mind showing up to tell him that, as long as I don't have to wear a suit."

"You got a suit?"

"Yeah, but I only wear it when I marry somebody," Kidd said. "Listen, I'm pretty friendly with Jed Cothran and Maury Berkowitz. If you think this guy could cause you some real trouble, I could give them a ring. If they lean on him a little, with the governor, I don't think he'll be inclined to a show trial, or anything. If that's what's worrying you."

Lucas was surprised a second time: Cothran and Berkowitz had been Minnesota U.S. senators, one from each party. "How do you know those guys?"

"Ah, back in the day, I used to sell do-it-yourself political polling kits. This was back before everything was run on polls, and everybody hired a pro. They were customers, young guys on their way up. They sorta became friends."

"I had no idea," Lucas said. "I don't think you need to call them—I was just worried you'd think I sold you out or something. Lockes won't be interested in you. He'll figure you for a technician. He's more interested in the . . . political interplay. You might not even be called. In fact, the governor might be able to head the whole thing off."

LUCAS WENT HOME. Ate dinner, messed around with the kids, told Weather what had happened that day, including the possibility of a subpoena. "Why does everybody seem to think that Lockes is a horse's ass?" she asked.

"Because he's a horse's ass," Lucas said.

A little after nine o'clock, as Lucas was browsing his financial websites, Horse's Ass's minions arrived with a subpoena. There were two of them, one of each gender, and he knew the woman. Sarah Sorensen was a mid-level assistant attorney general, a bland, brown-haired woman who was wearing an animal-rights baseball cap. She gave Lucas the paper and introduced the male half of the delegation, Mark Dunn, who looked around and said, "This is a nice property."

There was a *tone* about the comment that suggested that a cop shouldn't be living quite so well, and Sorensen picked it up and said curtly, "Lucas founded Davenport Simulations. You may have heard of it."

Dunn said, "Of course," and shut up.

Sorensen said to Lucas, "The subpoena is for tomorrow, but

we'd like to have a little pre-interview here, if you have the time. We'd like to get this over with as quickly as possible—tomorrow, if possible. We need to know if we've contacted everybody necessary to get a complete picture."

Sorensen already had the names of all the people in the meeting at the St. Paul Police Department, plus the governor, and Neil Mitford, the governor's weasel, and ICE. Lucas added Kidd's name to the list, feeling guilty about it, even though Kidd hadn't seemed bothered by the prospect.

Sorensen said, "This Ingrid Eccols—ICE, you call her—and Mr. Kidd are essentially computer technicians?"

"That's correct," Lucas said. "We contacted them because we had rather pressing time limitations, with the pornography allegations pushed up against the approaching elections. We got a copy of the hard drive the way we did, through Senator Smalls's attorney, because it was convenient and fast. You understand that we didn't change anything, that we were operating only from a copy of the computer hard drive, that the original was preserved."

"We understand that," Sorensen said.

"We were trying to cover as much ground as quickly as we could, so I called in a couple of personal favors from people I knew to be knowledgeable about computers. And, what popped out, popped out."

Dunn said, "Excuse me, but I don't understand exactly what popped out."

"A kind of booby trap which would reveal the porn to anyone who touched Senator Smalls's keyboard . . . and would allow it to be hidden quickly, should Senator Smalls return before the trap was triggered," Lucas said. "During that investigation, Robert Tubbs's name came up, and further investigation—"

"We have that file," Sorensen said.

"Then you know what I know," Lucas said. "The only thing not in the file is what I was doing today, which was interviewing staff members with Senator Smalls's campaign committee to try to determine whether Tubbs had an accomplice. I interviewed ten members of the campaign, and all of them denied any connection to Tubbs."

Sorensen asked, "And you believe all of them?"

"I don't really believe *any* of them," Lucas said. "I can't afford to—but I think all but one are telling the truth. I just don't know who that one is."

Sorensen said, "Okay. If you can give me the phone number for Mr. Kidd, I think that's all we'll need before tomorrow. Ten a.m., if that's good with you."

AT TEN O'CLOCK the next morning, Lucas showed up at the attorney general's office, wound up waiting until after noon, as Rose Marie Roux, Henry Sands, Neil Mitford, Rick Card, and Roger Morris were called in, one by one, and questioned. The interviews were being done in a conference room with a long table, a dozen chairs, five lawyers including Lockes, the attorney general, Sorensen, and Dunn. A court reporter sat at the far end of the table with a steno machine and a tape recorder.

Lucas was sworn, and told the same story he'd told Sorensen the night before, but in more detail. Lockes, a narrow, dark-haired man who looked like he ran marathons, probed for the reason Lucas had taken the assignment directly from the governor.

"The governor told me that he knew Senator Smalls personally, a lifelong . . . relationship, if not exactly a friendship," Lucas said.

"He said that Senator Smalls swore to him that he was innocent, and had been set up, probably by somebody on the campaign committee staff—possibly a spy working for the Democratic Party. The governor was inclined to believe him, judging from his knowledge of Smalls's character. The governor was then concerned on two fronts: First, one of simple fairness, if Senator Smalls was telling the truth. Second, he worried that if it was, in fact, a dirty trick, it could come back to haunt his party during the elections."

"But why did he come to you, specifically, rather than speak to Rose Marie Roux or Henry Sands?" Lockes asked.

"Because speed was required. Urgently required. The governor was familiar with my work, and once he decided to move, he informed Rose Marie, who informed Henry, and he talked to me, all within a very short period of time. I'm not sure of the exact sequence there."

Dunn asked, "Do you routinely take political assignments directly from the governor?"

"No. And I object to that characterization," Lucas snapped. "The governor realized that a crime had been committed and that an important election could be affected by it."

"He didn't *know* that a crime had been committed," Dunn said.

"Of course he did," Lucas said. "If Senator Smalls was knowingly in possession of child pornography, then he'd committed a crime. If somebody planted the pornography on Senator Smalls, then a different crime had been committed. It had to be one or the other, so the crime was there. As a senior agent of the BCA, he asked me to find out the truth of the matter, and as rapidly as possible, with the least amount of bureaucratic involvement, in an effort to resolve this before the election. I'd emphasize that he was looking for the truth, not just to clear Senator Smalls. It'd be far better for the governor's party if Smalls was guilty: it would give them an extra Senate seat in a very tight political situation."

Lockes said tentatively, "There's been some mention of possible involvement by the Minneapolis Police Department."

Lucas shook his head. "That's purely conjecture at this point." He explained about what appeared to be an evidentiary photograph among the rest of the pornography.

"And this could tie in to the disappearance of Mr. Tubbs," Lockes said.

"Again, conjecture at this point," Lucas said.

"But if there's anything to all of this, if Tubbs doesn't show up somewhere . . . then we're talking about a murder."

Lucas nodded: "Yes. I'm treating it as a murder investigation."

Dunn started to jump in. "If the governor asked—"

Lockes held up a hand to stop him, then said to Lucas: "You're a busy man, with a murder out there. You better get back to it."

Lucas stood and said, "Thanks. I do need to do that."

And was gone.

HE CALLED THE GOVERNOR, outlined his testimony, and Henderson said, "Lockes told me he was going to wind it up today. Your computer pals are testifying later this afternoon, and that should be it. I don't know what he's planning to do, but after talking to me and Smalls, I suspect he smells dogshit on his shoe. If he wants to run for this office in two years, he doesn't need both me and Smalls on his ass. He's gonna have to get through a primary."

"What about Smalls? Could he be a problem?"

"No. He owes us big, and he knows it, and Porter does pay his bills," the governor said. "If it turns out Tubbs did it to him . . . well, Tubbs is probably dead. Not much blood to be wrung out of that stone, even if he wanted to."

"Is he going to win the election?"

"Neil says no—but I'm not sure. Porter's always been pretty resilient. On the other hand, his opponent is pretty hot, has an ocean of money, and a lead, with momentum. Not much time left. So . . . we'll see," Henderson said. "By the way . . . do you know her? Have you interviewed her?"

"No, I've never met her," Lucas said. "Seen her on TV."

"She'd be the main beneficiary, of course, if Smalls went down."

"I'll be talking to her, unless something else breaks before I get there," Lucas said. "Today, I've got one more of Smalls's staff members to interview, and I need to talk to my computer people about their testimony. Make sure everything is okay."

"Stay in touch," Henderson said.

THE AFTERNOON was like walking through tar: Lucas tracked down and interviewed the last of Smalls's volunteer staff, and the interview produced nothing. He talked to ICE and Kidd after their testimony, and learned that it had been perfunctory. He talked again with both Rose Marie and the governor, and updated Morris on the state of his investigation.

"That's not much of a state," Morris said when he was finished. "Investigation-wise, that's like the state of Kazakhstan."

"Tell me about it," Lucas said.

"What's next on the menu?"

"Dinner. It's just nice enough outside to barbecue. The housekeeper's out there now with ten pounds of baby-back ribs, sweet corn from California, honey-coated corn bread, baked potatoes with sour cream and butter, and mushroom gravy."

"You sadistic sonofabitch," Morris said. "I already finished my celery."

CHAPTER 10

Taryn Grant wore cotton pajamas at night, and had just gotten into them, in a dressing room off the hallway in her bedroom suite, a few minutes before midnight, when she heard—or maybe felt—footsteps on the wooden floor coming down to the bedroom. The security people were the only others in the house, and weren't welcome in her bedroom wing.

Something had happened, or was happening. She took down the Japanese kimono that she used as a robe, pulled it over her shoulders, and headed toward the door, just as the doorbell burped discreetly. She pressed an intercom button: "Yes?"

"It's me, Doug. I need to talk with you."

She popped the door and nodded down the hall: "In the sitting room."

"Yes," he said, and led the way.

The sitting room had three big fabric chairs arrayed around a circular table; the walls were in the form of a five-eighths dome—as though a big slice had been taken out of an orange—and kept their voices contained.

"What happened?" she asked, as she settled into a chair facing him.

"I talked with our source at the AG's office. The police unraveled how Tubbs set up the computer, and they've tied his disappearance to the porn. I've got a lot of details, if you want to hear them, but the main thing is, the police will probably want to interview you, since you had the most to gain from the porn attack. You'll need to figure out a response. The guy coming to interview you will probably be this Davenport, who I told you about."

"Give me the details," she said. "All of them. I'll forget them later."

Dannon spent twenty minutes on the briefing, reviewing what had happened that day at the attorney general's office, and the results so far of investigations by Davenport and a St. Paul homicide cop named Morris. "We've had one piece of great good luck: when they found Tubbs's hideout spot, there was no mention of the porn or any dirty tricks, other than the porn file itself. They did find some cash, and it may have been from us, but we were careful there, and it's untraceable."

When he was done, Taryn asked, "The fact that you talked to this guy at the AG's office, could that come back to us?"

"No, I don't think so—not in a way that could hurt us," Dannon said. "I left the impression that we were desperate to work out the political implications of what was going on, this close to the election. Of course, when he took the money, he was technically committing a crime, so he won't be inclined to talk."

"Unless he suddenly starts feeling guilty," Taryn said.

"Not a problem with this guy," Dannon said. "He believes he's on the side of Jesus, helping us beat Smalls. He knows taking the money was a crime of some kind, but he doesn't think he's really done anything wrong. He sees the money more as compensation for his time. A consultation fee."

"Amazing how that works," Taryn said.

"Yeah. Anyway, it all brings up the question about Tubbs's girl," Dannon said. "Davenport is going through the whole campaign committee office, grilling everybody, looking for his accomplice. I don't think she knows anything about us."

"Do you know who she is? What her name is?"

"Yeah, but I'm not going to tell you," Dannon said. "I don't want her name in your head, if you're asked about her."

She looked at him for a moment, thinking about that, then nodded and said, "Okay. I see that. But how could she know about us? Tubbs didn't know for sure. Not until he got here."

"Tubbs *knew*, he just didn't have any proof," Dannon said. "He didn't know my name or anything about me. We made the assumption, incorrect, in retrospect, that if the payoff was big enough, he'd keep his head down, that he wouldn't even want to know where the money came from. But once he started looking, it was just a matter of time before he found us."

Taryn stood and wandered around the sitting area, working it out. "The real problem is, if he mentioned anything to this woman, even his suspicions, those would sort of harden up if she talked with the police. You know what I mean? If Tubbs was alive, but he hadn't gone looking for you, and they found him and put him under oath, he'd have to admit that he couldn't identify the person who paid him. But if this Davenport finds his girl, his accomplice, and she just tells him what Tubbs *thought*, that takes on its own reality. And Tubbs won't be around to cross-examine, to say he didn't know where the money came from."

"That's true," Dannon said. "But: right now, they can't know Tubbs's motive. Not for sure. As far as they know, he might have done it on his own hook. If we *do* something about her, that would confirm to Davenport that there's somebody else operating here. If he finds her and she says she doesn't have any idea why Tubbs planted the porn, then it stops with Tubbs. But if *she* turns up dead, then there's gotta be somebody else. See what I mean?"

"I do," she said. "It's a conundrum."

"I've been thinking about it," Dannon said. "Davenport's already raised the question of whether somebody in the Minneapolis Police Department might have been involved with the porn. Well, there is somebody. When Tubbs first got back in touch with me, with the porn idea, I asked him where he'd get it. He said he knew a vice cop in Minneapolis who had a file of it. I don't know if it's for the cop's own viewing pleasure, or just one of those things that cops do. Anyway, I pushed Tubbs on it, saying I had to vet the guy before Tubbs made an offer. Tubbs told me the guy's name is Ray Quintana. If word ever gets out that he supplied the porn, he's in a world of hurt. So I'm thinking . . . I could call Quintana, mention that Tubbs's girl could be a problem for him, and maybe he could figure out a way to do a little investigating for us. As a vice cop, looking into this porn allegation. Talk to her. Let us know if there's a problem."

"This is turning into a rat's nest," Taryn said. "One complication after another."

"Yes. And maybe the best way out would be to do nothing. Deny, deny. They'll be looking at you for sure, but there's no way to connect us to anything. We've never had any formal contact with Tubbs—you never met him, you don't know him, Connie doesn't know him. . . . We could just sit tight."

"Maybe even put out the word that we suspect Smalls of some

kind of disinformation campaign." Taryn stood and walked a few steps down the hall, then back, and a few steps up the hall, and back.

"I don't know how you'd work that—"

She waved a hand at him: "I do. That's not your concern. The real question mark is Tubbs's girl. If this Davenport cracks her, and she points at us, we can deny . . . but the word'll get out and the implications of it all, like Tubbs's disappearance . . . I'll lose the election."

"But you won't go to prison."

"But I want to win. That's the whole point of the exercise," Taryn said.

They sat in silence for a minute, then Dannon said, "What do you want me to do?"

"Think about it," she said. "You're smart. And I'll think about it overnight. We'll talk tomorrow morning. It's all a balancing of the various risks, and the various goals. It's like a calculus problem: and there is an answer."

THE HOUSE HAD WI-FI throughout, and when Dannon was gone, Taryn fired up her laptop, went online, and looked up Lucas Davenport. Google turned up thousands of entries, most from newspapers and television stations statewide, covering criminal cases on which he'd worked over the past twenty-five years.

There were also what appeared to be several hundred business-oriented entries from his involvement with Davenport Simulations.

Those caught her attention, and she dug deeper. Davenport, it seemed, had been a role-playing game designer as a young man, and then, with the rise of the machines, had created a number of simulations for 911 systems. The simulations were in use nation-wide, and after the World Trade Center attack, Davenport Simulations had moved more extensively into training software for security professionals. By that time, she found, Davenport was out of the business, having sold it to his management group.

The local business magazines estimated that he'd gotten out with around forty million dollars.

So he was smart and rich.

And the first batch of clips demonstrated that he was, without a doubt, a killer.

Somebody, she thought, that she might like.

SHE HAD A RESTLESS NIGHT, working through it all, and in the morning beeped Dannon on the walkie-talkie function and said, "I'm going to get an orange juice. Meet me by the pool in three minutes."

Three minutes later, she was asking, "This Quintana guy, the Minneapolis cop. If we asked him to check around, he wouldn't have any idea where the question was coming from, right?"

"Well, he'd have an idea," Dannon said. "It's possible that he and Tubbs speculated on it, but there's no way he could know for sure."

"Then I think we ask him to look up this woman, Tubbs's girl, and ask the question. He should be able to come up with some kind of legal reason for doing it—that he heard about the attorney general's review and thought he ought to look into the Minneapolis department's exposure, something like that. Some reason that wouldn't implicate him. Just doing his job."

"I thought about that last night—I couldn't decide. I'm about fifty-fifty on it," Dannon said.

"So I've decided," Taryn said. "Do it, but be clever about it. Don't give yourself away. Call from a cold phone."

"I can be careful," Dannon said, "but it's still a little more chum in the water. We could be stirring up the sharks."

"It's a small risk, and we need to take it," she said. "Make the call. Let's see what happens."

CHAPTER 11

A few years earlier, Kidd had become entrapped in his computer sideline when the National Security Agency, working with the FBI, tried to tear up a hacking network to which he supposedly belonged. Kidd's team had managed to fend off the attention, and after several years of quiet, he'd begun to feel safe again.

Part of it, he thought, might be that he and Lauren had finally had to deal with the fact that they loved each other. Then the baby showed up, though not unexpectedly . . .

He *wanted* to be safe. He wanted all that old hacker stuff to be over. If you want something badly enough, he thought, sometimes you began to assume that you had it. He and his network had some serious assets, and hadn't been able to detect any sign that the feds were still looking for them.

Still, he was sure that if the government people thought they could set up an invisible spiderweb, so they'd get the vibration if Kidd touched the web . . . then they'd do that. They'd give it a shot.

So Kidd had had to stay with the computers, watching for trouble, although now, painting six and seven hours a day, he was working so hard that he hadn't time to do anything creative with the machines; and he was making so much money that he didn't have to.

He and the other members of his network understood that even monitoring the feds could be dangerous. Computer systems were totally malleable, changing all the time. Updating access code could lead to serious trouble if it was detected. In addition to that problem, the number of major computer systems was increasing all the time, and security was constantly getting better. So care was needed, and time was on the government's side.

The most powerful aspect of any bureaucracy, in Kidd's eyes, was the same thing that gave cancer its power: it was immortal. If you didn't seek it out and kill it, cell by cell, it'd just keep growing. Bureaucracies could chase you forever. You could defeat them over and over and over again, and the bureaucracy didn't much care, though some individual bureaucrats might.

The bureaucracy, as a whole, just kept coming, as long as the funding lasted.

As PART OF his monitoring efforts, Kidd had long been resident in the Minneapolis Police Department's computer systems, which had useful access to several federal systems. The federal systems had safeguards, of course, but since the basic design of the system had been done to *encourage* access by law enforcement, the safeguards were relatively weak. Once you had unrestricted access to a few big federal systems, you could get to some pretty amazing places.

None of which concerned him when he went out on the network from a Grand Avenue coffee shop eight hours after he'd testified for the attorney general. In his testimony, he'd represented himself as a former computer consultant who was mostly out of the business, and was now concentrating on art. That was true.

Which didn't mean he'd misplaced his brain.

So he got a grande no-foam latte and sat at a round plastic table at the back of the shop and slipped into the Minneapolis Police Department's computer system. Instead of going out to the federal networks, he began probing individual computers on the network. He was looking for a group of numbers—the number of bytes represented by the photo collection.

The collection was a big one, and though there'd be thousands of files in the department's computers, the actual number of bytes would vary wildly from file to file. If he found a matching number, it'd almost certainly be the porn file.

He'd thought he had a good chance to find the file; and he was right.

"THE PROBLEM," he told Lauren later that night, "is that I found four copies of it. I know which computers have accessed the files, but I don't know who runs those computers."

"Sounds like something Lucas should find out for himself," she said.

"Yeah. But how's he going to explain that he knows about the files? Without explaining about me?"

"Maybe that's something you should talk to him about," she said.

Kidd looked at his watch: "You think it's too late to call?"

"He said he stays up late."

Lucas answered on the third ring. "Hey, what's up?"

"I have a certain amount of access to the Minneapolis police computer system," Kidd began.

"I'm shocked," Lucas said. "So . . . what'd you find?"

"I found the porn file. I found it in four different places, but I don't know who controls the files. The files themselves have four different names. The thing is, I don't want to be connected to this one."

"Because then the cops will know you're inside," Lucas said.

"That's right."

"So how'd you do it?" Lucas asked.

Kidd explained, briefly, Lucas thought about it for a moment, then said, "How about this? I get a warrant, or a subpoena, or just an okay, whichever works. I show the file to ICE, and she finds that number. That byte number. We go over to Minneapolis and jack up their systems manager and ICE finds the files, like you did, using that number, all on the up-and-up."

"That would be perfect," Kidd said. "Let me give you the number you're looking for."

"You're not in the BCA system, are you?" Lucas asked.

"Of course not," Kidd said.

"Then how'd you get this phone number?" Lucas asked. "You're calling on my work phone."

"You called *me* on this phone—so your number was on *my* phone," Kidd said. "Jesus, don't you trust anyone?"

Lucas said, "Oh . . . maybe."

Kidd gave Lucas the number he'd be looking for, and hung up. Lauren said, "He suspects you're in the BCA system, huh?"

"Naw, he was just kicking the anthill, to see if anything ran out," Kidd said. "He's got no clue."

"I'd stay out of there for a while, anyway," Lauren said. "Just in case."

"KIDD IS INTO EVERYTHING," Lucas told Weather, as they got in bed. "He's all over Minneapolis and I know damn well he's in the BCA computers, too. He says he's not, but he's lying."

"Don't you trust anyone?" she asked.

"You and Letty," Lucas said. "Most of the time. Of course, I always check back and verify."

THE NEXT MORNING, he called ICE, described the file to her, and asked, "How do I find out how many bytes are in it?"

"Why do you want to know?"

"Because when I was working at the company, the guys there could find specific files by the number of bytes they had in them. I'd like to know how many are in this one, then I can take it over to the Minneapolis cops' system and look for it there."

"That'll work," she said. "Okay, you got the file up? I'll walk you through it."

She did, and eventually had Lucas write down the same number that Kidd had come up with, although he didn't tell her that. When he had the number, she said, "Do you trust the Minneapolis cops?"

"If somebody puts a gun in my ear," he said. "Why?"

"Because what if their systems guy plugs the number into his machine, says, 'Nope, not here.' You're far too ignorant to argue. Then what?"

"I've got that figured out—that was easy," he said.

"Yeah? What're you going to do?"

"I'm gonna take you with me."

———

THERE WAS BUREAUCRACY to be worked through. When Lucas talked to Rose Marie, she was unhappy about the necessity of jacking up the Minneapolis cops, even though she'd known it was coming. "We're doing everything right out in front of the media now, and I'm not going to have you serve a search warrant on Minneapolis," she said. "Talk to Robin and get him straight, we'll bring in their own Internal Affairs unit, and we'll talk about all the cooperation we're getting."

Robin Connolly was the Minneapolis chief of police.

"What if Connolly says no?" Lucas asked.

"He won't. He'll want to be out front on this, he'll want to be informed. If he does say no, I'll call him. I'll tell him that I'll personally stick the search warrant up his ass and then cut him out of the loop on the return."

"You're so grandmotherly sometimes," Lucas said.

Which didn't mean that Connolly didn't throw a fit when Lucas called him and told him what he wanted to do.

"What the hell are you talking about? You think we planted the porn file on Smalls? You're nuts, Davenport. I'm not going to . . ." blah blah blah.

Lucas said, "Rose Marie will be calling you in a minute or so. Maybe she can explain things more clearly than I have."

"Fuck a bunch of Rose Marie," Connolly shouted. "I'll put wheels on that bitch and roll her right into the Mississippi."

Lucas called Rose Marie, who said she'd call Connolly. Connolly called back five minutes later and said, "It might be possible that we can work something out."

"Is Rose Marie in the Mississippi?" Lucas asked.

"Fuck you."

LUCAS CALLED ICE and asked her to gently and with great diplomacy set up an appointment with the Minneapolis systems manager. While he was waiting for ICE to get back to him, he called the duty officer and asked him to get him a good phone number for Taryn Grant. He was sitting in his office, with his feet up on his desk, waiting for callbacks and thinking about how he'd sequence his various visits, when Del stopped in, took a chair, and said, "I bought a Harley."

"Oh, Jesus . . ."

"What? I had one before."

"You were in your twenties," Lucas said. "If you had to lay one down now, they'd be picking you up with a sponge."

"I'm not going on any big rides. . . . It's gonna be a warm-weather bike, just rolling around town on the local streets," Del said. "Besides, most Harley guys are my age. Or older."

"And you know what? They're getting picked up with sponges."

Jenkins came in and when Del told him about the Harley, they slapped hands and Jenkins said, "I'd have one myself, if they weren't such pieces of shit."

"Says the owner of a personal Crown Vic."

Shrake showed up a few minutes later, and they talked about the Harley, and Shrake said, "That fuckin' Flowers used to ride, right after he got out of the army. He had some sorta crotch rocket, though, not a Harley. I remember him showing up at crime scenes on it, when he was working for St. Paul. He had hair down his back, he looked like Wild Bill Hickok."

After another couple of minutes, Jenkins said to Lucas, "I'm hearing rumors that the Geheime Staatspolizei doesn't like the fact that you're working directly for the governor, and bailing out Smalls. I hear you're about to slap a search warrant on the Minneapolis cops, and that's got everybody steppin' and fetchin'."

In Jenkins's personal lexicon, the Geheime Staatspolizei comprised the BCA's top management. It was also the proper name of the German Gestapo, though he probably wasn't pronouncing it correctly—not that Lucas knew for sure.

Lucas explained that a compromise had been worked out with Minneapolis, and that he'd be working in cooperation with the city's Internal Affairs unit.

"That doesn't help much," Del said. "I'll tell you what, my friend. You're not doing yourself a lot of good around here, hanging out with the politicians. The knives are coming out."

"Fuck 'em," Lucas said. "It's a murder case. I'll break it and the tunes will change."

"No, they won't," Shrake said. "Everybody will agree that you did a great job and then they'll stab you in the back. It's the tall poppy syndrome."

"I'll take care," Lucas said.

"You already haven't," Del said.

WHEN THEY'D GONE, Lucas got Taryn Grant's office phone number, called it and spoke to a secretary, who went away for a moment, then came back and said, "Ms. Grant is in her car. I'm forwarding your call directly to her."

When Grant came on—she had the kind of voice he'd always liked, low and husky, like Weather's—he said, "I'm working on the investigation of the child pornography found on Senator Smalls's computer, and also the disappearance of a political operative named Bob Tubbs. I need to talk to you about the situation."

"I've already made a public statement to the media."

"I know, I saw it. But I have a few questions for you, and I also need to brief you on the status of the investigation," Lucas said. "Time is so short, before the election, we want to be sure everybody is informed."

"I'll be home between six and six-forty-five tonight, but then I have campaign visits to make."

"I'll see you then," Lucas said. "If you could give me your address . . ."

ICE CALLED: "I talked to the systems manager over in Minneapolis, and we're on for three o'clock. I'm familiar with their equipment. I didn't tell him exactly what we are going to do, you know . . . just in case they might try to ditch it."

"Good. The chief knows what we're doing, so they might be able to figure it out, but they don't have the number, as far as I know."

WHEN LUCAS got to the Minneapolis Police Department's ugly, obsolete, purple-stone headquarters in downtown Minneapolis, ICE was sitting with her feet up on the systems manager's desk, talking about old times at what was once called the Institute of Technology at the University of Minnesota.

A sergeant named Buck Marion sat in a corner, reading a free newspaper; Marion was with the Minneapolis Internal Affairs unit, and nodded at Lucas. One of Marion's predecessors had gotten Lucas thrown off the Minneapolis police force, for beating up a pimp.

Lucas listened to ICE and the systems manager ramble along, then shook his head, and ICE asked, "What?"

"Nothing like a long, rambling C++ story," Lucas said, not trying to hide a yawn. "Fascinating."

"We're intellectuals," ICE explained. "Anyway, Larry's going to help us look for the files. We were waiting for you." Larry Benson was the systems manager.

"Then let's do it," Lucas said.

ICE explained that they wouldn't be using the specific byte size, but would enter a narrow range that the file should fall into, even if an item or two were missing. ICE leaned over Benson's shoulder and fed him the file size number, and he entered the number range into his system. They all watched as the system thought it over, and then spat out twelve returns. "Twelve returns," ICE said. "Interesting."

Lucas almost blurted out that Kidd had found only four. Before he could, Benson said, "Let's take a look."

He opened them, one by one, on top of each other. Eight of them were irrelevant. Four of them, just as Kidd said, showed an identical opening set of child porn. "Man, I hate to think this shit is floating around in there," Benson said. "One file . . . it's pretty open access, if you know what to look for."

"Any way to tell who has accessed them?" Lucas asked.

"Not really. Well, I can tell you pretty sure in one case, but not the other three. Tom Morgan, Lieutenant Morgan, opened them, let me see, about eight times, all in about a four-day period a little more than three years ago, in August."

Lucas said, "There was a trial right then. Probably for trial purposes. He was one of the people who testified."

Benson said, "The other three sets of files were accessed by three different machines. Each machine accessed only one file, but multiple times."

Marion: "Who's assigned to the machines?"

Benson shook his head. "They're office machines. Maybe somebody uses them most of the time, but the rest of the time, anybody could do it."

ICE reached out and tapped the computer screen. "Look at this: this machine accessed the file four hundred and eighteen times over three years. They never quit looking at it . . . they're *still* looking at it."

ICE AND BENSON STARTED working through it, and Marion said to Lucas, "This is gonna be a disaster. I don't know what's gonna happen if it turns out that a hundred guys were looking at this stuff."

"Maybe it won't be necessary to bring it up," Lucas suggested.

"It'll be necessary," Marion said. "The chief will be inside my shirt, wanting to know what we found. You've probably got to tell your boss. Once that's done, it'll get away from us. If it was only us four . . . but it's not."

Lucas said, "You're probably right. I'm sorry."

ICE said, "All right. Machine One is in Vice, and that machine apparently dealt with the original files, and that's where a variety of files was grouped into one, and that's where the first duplicate was made. The duplicate had the same name as the original, but with a version number, Version Two. That was probably a legit backup. Machine Two is also in Vice, and somebody made a second duplicate on that machine, and saved it under a completely new name. That's the one that has been accessed by Machine Three, the four hundred and eighteen accesses. Machine Three never made a dupe. Machine Four accessed the original file, but only twice. Machine Four is in Vice."

"What's the latest date?" Lucas asked.

"Machine Three has had sixteen accesses in the last month," ICE said. "Both of the Machine Four accesses were last year."

"We've got to nail them all down," Marion said.

Lucas said, "This whole Smalls-porn thing feels improvised to me. It doesn't feel like something that was planned out a year ago. So . . . it probably came off Machine Three. Where's that one?"

Benson said, "It's here, in the building. Down in Domestics."

"How many people in Domestics?"

Benson shrugged, but Marion said, "About twelve or fifteen, counting the shrinks. Seven sworn officers, two or three support people, and the shrinks. Some of the shrinks are part-time, but they'd have access."

"Is there any way to see who signed on the machine and what they did? What they looked at?" Lucas asked.

Benson shook his head. "The only way you could figure that out, would be if Machine Three was in somebody's locked office. But Domestics is an open bay, with people coming and going. The only way to tell would be to observe . . . figure out who was on that machine at what time."

"But all this is in the past," Lucas said. "How would we do that?"

"We can't," Benson said.

"What we can do," Marion said, "is bust some balls."

"Gotta be soon," Lucas said. "Smalls is about halfway off the hook, but the media doesn't like him, so he's only halfway off. They're already saying that Rose Marie never said he was innocent."

"I need to talk to the chief," Marion said to Lucas. "What're you doing this evening?"

"Talking with a really hot chick," Lucas said.

"*Hot chick* . . . that expression is so disco, so 1979," ICE said, with disdain.

Marion, Benson, and Lucas all looked at each other, and then Lucas shrugged and said, "Not for cops."

THEY HAD BENSON SAVE the files and the information they'd turned up to a new, confidential file, and then ICE took off, after Lucas thanked her: "You'll get the bill at your office," she said.

Marion went to see the chief, and Lucas walked down to the training office. Tom Morgan, the lieutenant who'd put together the original file, and had testified in the child porn case, was now the training officer. The new job could either be a matter of grooming a cop for a move upward, or a dead end for a guy who wasn't going anywhere; in Morgan's case, Lucas didn't know which it was.

Morgan was poking at a computer keyboard when Lucas knocked on his doorjamb. He turned in his chair and his face fell, and he said, "Lucas. Goddamnit, I was afraid you'd show up here."

Lucas said, "Really."

"Yeah, everybody in the building is hiding out, afraid you're gonna want to talk to them. The word's all over the place."

"I only talked to the chief . . . and Marion. And Larry Benson . . ."

"Might as well have driven down the hall in a sound truck," Morgan said. He reached back, caught a wheeled guest chair, and shoved it toward Lucas. "Sit down and tell me about it."

Lucas explained the situation, and when he was finished, Morgan said, "Well, that's about what I heard. I'll tell you what, though. When we busted that place, the Pattersons', they weren't putting the files on the Internet. They were too smart to do that. If you wanted pictures from them, you'd get them by FedEx, and they'd be on paper. The Internet was only used for contacts. When we got them, we scanned the paper photos into the system, because that was the only way we had to coordinate them with everything else, for the court case. But they were a separate file. Nobody had access but the people who were working the case. And they should never have been aggregated with other files."

"What are the chances that somebody saw an opportunity for a little private enterprise? Put the files together and then sell them?" Lucas asked.

"I'd say . . . slim to none," Morgan said. "The thing is, the files were down in Vice, and nobody had access to them but us vice guys. And one thing we all knew, and most cops know now, is that cops and snitches are all over the place on kiddie porn. They're everywhere. Guys spend their spare time browsing the 'net, looking for it, looking for a bust. You buy kiddie porn off the 'net, you're gonna lose your job, probably get divorced, and probably go to prison. The vice guys . . . they wouldn't mess with it. It's more dangerous than dealing drugs. Way more. And there's less money in it."

"So you're saying whoever took it wasn't trying to make a buck, and it didn't get loose somehow."

Morgan shook his head: "Nope. Sad as I am to say it, I'd bet those pictures came straight out of here. Straight out of our system."

Lucas asked, "You hear any rumors of guys looking at porn?"

"Lucas, you know how it is. You worked here, for how long? You hear some guys might be looking at porn, some guys might be getting their knobs polished by the street girls, that some guys have a little too much cash, that some cocaine's gone astray . . . you hear all that crap. And most of it's crap. Backbiting bullshit."

That was true enough. The brotherhood of cops was fairly tight from the outside, but from the inside, it was more like a bureaucratic knife fight.

They talked for a while longer, about various possibilities, then Lucas looked at the wall clock and said, "I gotta roll. Thanks for the conversation."

Morgan asked, "Is the stuff gonna hit the fan?"

"Not if Robin handles it right," Lucas said. "What you need is a lot of promises and a big cloud of smoke . . . and then hope something blows up somewhere, and makes the media stampede that way."

CHAPTER 12

Dannon and Taryn were both on their feet, in the library, feeling the stress, and Dannon said, "We don't know anything. We're amazed that people are talking to us. Who *is* Tubbs?"

She nodded. "I worked on it last night before I went to bed. I can do it. But I have to have my head in the right place."

"I'll be outside with Carver. Green will be in the monitor room. We want him to see Green, but not us."

"Yes," she said. She frowned. "What are we talking about, anyway?"

"Exactly." He nodded, and left.

A minute later, her walkie-talkie function buzzed, and Alice Green said, "We've got a Porsche at the gate."

Lucas watched the gate roll back and caught the two clear lenses, and two black glassy spots, one of each on the stone gate pillars, on either side of the driveway. Camera lenses and infrared alarm sensors. The security would be excellent. And the hard drives on the security cameras could be gotten with a search warrant: something to know.

The house was a long and sprawling ranch, built of a yellowish stone and clapboard, with a fieldstone chimney climbing out of one end. The lot itself, just the part he could see, was the size of a football field, dotted with mature oaks, maples, and firs.

The chimney, Lucas thought, would lead down to a really gorgeous wood-burning fireplace, with logs as long as a big man's arm. Lucas liked fireplaces, he just didn't like burning wood—he had few allergies, but burning wood always seemed to set off his nose, and he'd wake in the morning with a sore throat.

He had designed his own house, and had put in a fireplace, though of a fussier, arts-and-crafts style, green tile surround and black steel—and a really, really good set of fake iron logs, which concealed the gas jets. Instant fire, with the push of a button. He'd been told he should feel guilty about that, but he didn't.

Taryn Grant's house was bigger than his, but not enormously so, at least in appearance; nothing like a southern mansion, which was what he'd half expected. Lucas had been all over the contractor on the fine details of his own house, and so he noticed them in Grant's, like the copper flashing on the downspouts, the cabinetry-level detailing in the woodwork around the garage doors. He supposed that in this neighborhood, no house would be worth less than a million and a half; but looking at Grant's house, he suspected that given the size and the detailing, three million might be closer to the mark.

Though if she were as rich as people said she was, that amount would be insignificant to her.

———

HE WALKED UP TO the front door, which opened as he approached it. A slender woman, probably in her mid-thirties, waited behind it. She had dark red hair, high cheekbones, and she wore a delicate turquoise necklace that chimed with her eyes. She looked a little like Kidd's wife, Lauren, Lucas thought.

She smiled and said, "Agent Davenport? I'm Alice Green. Ms. Grant is waiting for you in the library."

Which sounded just slightly snotty. Lucas thought, *I've got a library, too*, and then Green turned away from him and he saw the semiautomatic pistol clipped to the back of her slacks.

Lucas said, "You're security?"

"Yes," she said, looking over her shoulder. "I can stay with Ms. Grant where men can't. Like ladies' rooms."

"Ex-cop or something?"

"Secret Service," she said.

"La-di-da," Lucas said. Green tilted her head back and laughed and said, "Yes," and her reaction made Lucas like her.

GREEN LED THE WAY through the house. Through a side door, Lucas saw a gorgeous brick-floored porch with white-plastered walls and green-glass windows that looked out on a huge enclosed swimming pool. The house didn't look much larger than his from the front, he realized, but was nearly as deep as it was wide.

The library was modest in size, with dark wood shelves filled with books that looked like they'd been read. Grant was sitting on a wine-red couch, and stood up when Lucas stepped into the room, putting aside a magazine. She smiled and said, "Agent Davenport . . ." and put out her hand.

Lucas shook it as he took her in. She was tall and solid, with muscles showing in her neck and forearms; bigger than she'd seemed when he'd seen her on television, but just as pretty. She was wearing a red blouse and black slacks, with a simple gold-chain necklace that looked old.

"Pleased to meet you," Lucas said. "I won't take too much of your time."

"I'd say take as much as you need, but I really am jammed up," she said, as she gestured at an easy chair, and sank back onto the couch.

Lucas took the chair and asked, "Do you know Bob Tubbs?"

"Bob Tubbs? I've heard of him. He works for the party. Has he done something . . . ?"

"You know he disappeared?"

A wrinkle appeared in her forehead. "Disappeared? I'm not tracking this very well . . ."

Lucas decided to slap her: "Basically, I'm wondering if your campaign employed Tubbs to sabotage Senator Smalls's campaign by planting child pornography on his computer," he said.

Another wrinkle in her forehead, and she sat back and said, "Well . . . no."

Lucas had been watching her face for a flinch or any kind of frightened reaction, and what he saw was the beginning of rage. He opened his mouth to ask another question, but before he could, Grant jabbed a finger at him.

"Wait a minute! Wait one fuckin' minute, here, buster," she

said. "Who are you working for? Are you hooked up to Smalls's campaign?"

"I'm hooked up to the Bureau of Criminal Apprehension, Ms. Grant," Lucas said. "We believe that Mr. Tubbs planted the pornography on Senator Smalls's computer. We believe Mr. Tubbs has been murdered to cover up that crime. There's only one reason for him to have planted the porn, and that's to sabotage Senator Smalls's campaign."

"Murdered? Did you say murdered?" The anger faded a bit, overridden by something else. Fear?

Lucas said, "Yes. He's disappeared, and we think there's a reason for it. We think he planted the porn, and then had to be gotten rid of, to cover it up."

"Well, I mean we, I mean . . . We didn't have anything to do with that, if it's even true." Now the anger came clawing back: "And you didn't answer the question. Are you hooked up with Smalls's campaign? Have you ever worked for him? What are your politics? We are less than a week from Election Day, and you come to me with *this*? An accusation I can't refute, because you can't refute a complete negative? When you put this in the paper and on TV—and you will, won't you?—it'll kill me. Sabotage and murder? Are you kidding me?"

The anger was real and was getting hotter and Grant got to her feet and bent toward him: "Answer the question."

She was nearly shouting, and Lucas saw movement at the corner of his eye, and two huge German shepherds ghosted into the room, focused on him.

He said, "The dogs . . ."

She half turned to the dogs and said, "Hansel, Gretel, *easy*," and the dogs' gazes softened.

Green, who'd left the room, stepped in and said, "Ms. Grant . . . can I help?"

Grant said, "No, I'm okay, Alice. Agent Davenport has gotten me a little upset." She sank back on the couch and said, "Well? What contact have you had with the Smalls campaign? Have you taken any money from him?"

Lucas was getting angry himself, and strained to contain it: but some leaked into his voice. "No. I've spoken to Senator Smalls about who had access to his computer, and I've taken information from him. I do not know him, except for the contact involved in this investigation. Personally, I'm a registered Democrat, and my wife has contributed to the campaigns of a number of Democratic candidates, including yours, I believe, though I have not. There's no politics in this, Ms. Grant. What there is, is a vicious sabotage attempt, which would have reduced Senator Smalls's reputation to tatters, and very probably a murder. So, if we could get back to the reason I'm here: you say you knew nothing of the pornography, and you didn't know Bob Tubbs?"

She seemed to go through a brief internal struggle, then controlled it: "As far as I know, I've never met Mr. Tubbs, although it's possible that he was at some of my campaign events—I know he worked for the party, and there've been a lot of people I don't know at my events. So I may have seen him, though I wouldn't recognize him. I have not knowingly spoken a single word with him. I'm not heavily engaged with the party—my candidacy is mostly self-generated. And the pornography, I know nothing about it."

Green had lingered in the doorway, listening, and one of the dogs moved up to Lucas and put its head on his knees, looking straight in at his groin. Lucas said, "Ms. Grant, you wanna move the dog?"

"Make you nervous?"

"Makes me angry," Lucas said. "If this dog bites me, I shoot it. Then I shoot the other one if I have to, then I throw you on the floor, cuff you, and drag your ass down to the Hennepin County jail and charge you with aggravated assault on a police officer. Then you *will* go to jail."

"Gretel won't bite unless I tell her to," Grant said. But she said to the dog, "Gretel, back," and the dog eased away from Lucas.

Green said, "Ms. Grant, I'll be in the nook."

"Thanks, Alice," Grant said, and to Lucas, "I don't like you, and I suspect you don't like me, but try to be fair. Don't stick yourself into this campaign. Don't sabotage me."

"I'm not trying—"

"Whether you're trying or not, that's the effect," Grant said. "Wait a week or ten days, let the election take place, then do your worst. But give me a chance. I've worked very hard for it."

"So has Senator Smalls."

"Smalls should be okay, after Rose Marie Roux's press conference. I'm the one who has the problem now," Grant said. "And listen: even *I* think it's possible that you're right, to some extent. It's possible that somebody who was trying to help me—this Tubbs person—might have put the porn on Smalls's computer. But I know nothing about that. There are dozens of people working in campaigns, all kinds of people who don't like Smalls, and some of those people are a little nuts. So it's possible that somebody went after him, but it's just as likely that they were trying to hurt him, as trying to help me. A lot of union people hate him—especially public employee union people—and the pro-choice people go crazy when they talk about him. Look at them!" She tightened up a fist and smacked it into her thigh, and said it again. "Look at them!"

"We'll look everywhere," Lucas said. "So let me go through this. You didn't know Tubbs, and though you may have shaken hands, or had some slight contact with him, you've never had any kind of substantive talk with him."

"No, I haven't. And let me ask you this—how do you know that Tubbs didn't put the porn on the computer, and then take off? How do you know that he hasn't deliberately put himself out of reach?" she asked. "Win or lose, after the election's over, nobody's going to care much about the porn."

Lucas said, "It's not just that he's gone, it's that he left a lot of cash behind, and he also isn't using his credit cards," Lucas said. "He hasn't used them once since he was last seen on Friday night, and he uses them all the time."

"But you don't *know*," she insisted.

"No, I don't."

"Then don't fuck with me on the basis of guesswork," Grant said. "At least, not until the election is done."

Lucas stared at her for a moment, and she didn't flinch. He asked, "What about your campaign manager? Did she know Tubbs? Who, in your campaign, is in charge of dirty tricks?"

"There are no dirty tricks in this campaign, for the simple reason that anything you can accuse Smalls of doing, he's already admitted. Has he been unfaithful to his wife? Yes. He's talked about it on TV. Made a lot of money as an attorney, screwing over widows? Yes, he's talked about *that* on TV. What kind of dirty trick would work with him?"

"Well, child porn," Lucas said.

"That's absurd," Grant said. "If anybody even hinted at something like that, I'd not only fire him, I'd do everything I could to destroy him."

"I need to talk to your campaign manager," Lucas said.

"I will give you her number, and you can ask her yourself," Grant said. "She wanted to be here today, but I made her go away. I didn't want her . . . using this discussion in some way . . . in the campaign."

Felt like a threat, smelled like a threat, Lucas thought. "Like how?"

"I don't know, but I don't know you, and neither does Connie, and she might have asked a little more about your background to see exactly why . . . you're here."

"I think I've made that clear," Lucas said.

She leaned back on the couch. "Well, you have. But in my position, which is very delicate right now, Connie would say that we couldn't ignore the possibility that you're lying. She'd want some research."

Lucas asked, "How many armed security people do you have? Is Alice Green the only one?"

He saw a quick flash of uncertainty in her eyes, which vanished as quickly as it came; and quite possibly was a trick of his imagination. She said, "Year-round, there are three, working various hours. During the campaign there are eight, because they have to travel with me. This house is extensively wired for security. There are two safe rooms, I can get to them in a few seconds from anywhere in the house, and, of course, Hansel and Gretel are full-time. They're here overnight. If I put them on guard, they stop being dogs and start being leopards."

"Okay," Lucas said. He thought for a moment, and then stood up. "I'm done. I apologize if I upset you, but this is a very serious matter."

She waved a hand at him and said, "Just be fair."

————

THE DOGS TOOK HIM through the door to the living room, where Green was sitting with a magazine that she wasn't reading.

"I'll show you the door," Green said.

On the way, Lucas said, "Chicken."

"I beg your pardon?"

"You didn't want to hear that," Lucas said.

"I'm not paid to hear that," Green said. She hesitated, then said, "Do you have a card?"

Lucas gave her a card, taking a second to scribble his cell phone number on the back. "Call anytime," he said.

"Give me an hour," she said.

ON THE WAY OUT to the highway, Lucas thought about Grant's behavior, and came to a conclusion: she was either totally innocent, or totally nuts. A normal person, guilty, could never have pulled off that performance. But he'd known a number of crazies who could have. . . .

Green called an hour and a half later. Lucas had gone back to the office, having already missed dinner, to check messages and track his agents on their regular assignments. He was most interested in the Ape Man Rapist of Rochester, who was attacking women as often as twice a week, but Flowers reported no progress. Lucas had just turned off his office lights when Green called. He answered: "Yes? Alice?"

Green said, "I don't know where Ms. Grant stands on all of this, but I need to talk to you. We need to keep this private."

"Is she there now?" Lucas asked.

"She's up on a stage. I'm at the back of the room . . . keeping an eye out." Lucas could hear a voice in the background, and then a rumbling sound: applause line, he thought.

Green continued: "I wanted to tell you, she works harder than anyone I've ever met. I find her admirable, if a little chilly. But I don't want to have anything to do with any possible crime, and one of the other security men here . . . his name is Ronald Carver, conventional spelling . . . is pretty rough. I suspect that if you put enough money in front of him, he'd kill somebody for you, and do a thorough job of it. This man Tubbs, the man who disappeared? I'm not saying it's Carver, but if you needed that done, if you needed Tubbs to go away, you'd try to find somebody just like Carver."

"What's his background?" Lucas asked.

"Ex-military special operations of some kind. A master sergeant, which is up there. The head of security, Doug Dannon, is the same kind, ex-military, but much more restrained. His problem is, he's in love with Taryn, so . . . I don't know what he'd do for her. But whatever has been done, I don't know about it, and didn't have anything to do with it. I'm not going to spy on Ms. Grant for you, but I wanted to say this. I hope you keep it under your hat."

"I will. But it's an odd thing to tell a cop you don't know," Lucas said, not quite trusting her. "What if I *was* working for Smalls?"

"I still have friends with the Secret Service," she said. "I had them look you up. I know as much about you as Weather does."

"Well, maybe not," Lucas said, picking up on Green's use of his wife's first name.

"Anyway, you're not working for Smalls," Green said. Longer applause in the background. "I gotta go."

"One more question," Lucas said. "I saw a lot of cameras out there, which must go to what, a hard drive? Or the cloud?"

Long wait, and then Green said, "Oh, God."

"What?"

Another long wait, then Green said, "I wish you hadn't asked that. I wouldn't have called you at all, but . . . Ah, damn. I work in the monitoring room, sometimes. There used to be a monthlong video-record sent out to the cloud. I noticed this morning that the wipe time has been reduced to forty-eight hours."

"Forty-eight hours. Why?"

"I don't know. There's no reason to, and it worries me. The cameras only record when they pick up motion, so it's not that much, and a hundred bucks a month would mean nothing to Ms. Grant. But somebody reduced the wipe time to forty-eight hours, and I was thinking, you know . . . if you were worried that somebody might get the archived recording with a search warrant, and if there was something on it that you didn't want anybody to see . . . I mean, the change was made on Monday—about forty-eight hours after Tubbs disappeared."

Lucas said, "You've got a suspicious mind, Alice."

"Developed by government experts," she said. "I gotta go. Right now. Good-bye."

CHAPTER 13

On the way out the door, Lucas stopped at the BCA men's room, where he found Jenkins, shirtless and shaving. He went to a urinal and over his shoulder asked, "What? You lost all your money gambling and now you're homeless?"

"Got a date," Jenkins said. "She likes it when my cheeks are smooth like a baby's butt."

"So she doesn't get beard burn on her thighs?"

"That's disgusting, but given a person of your ilk, I'm not surprised," Jenkins said.

Lucas finished up at the urinal and walked over to wash his hands and said, "Say you've got a hot, rich politician running for office, but she's losing, then her opponent is hit with a scandal involving child porn on his computers, then the guy you think put it there suddenly disappears and the politician turns out to have armed security people, including a couple of guys with thick necks who were in special operations in the army. What we unsophisticates call 'trained killers.' What do you think?"

Jenkins paused, half of his face covered with shaving cream, the other half bare and shaven; he asked, "You got that much for sure?"

"I'm being told all that," Lucas said.

"Have you hooked Tubbs to Grant?"

"Not yet . . . but Tubbs was probably involved in dirty tricks, and she needed one, bad. And he had a whole bunch of money, cash, in a hideout spot."

"You steal any of it?" Jenkins asked.

"No, no, I didn't."

"Huh," Jenkins said. "Little cold cash is always useful."

"But that would be illegal," Lucas said.

"Oh, yeah, I forgot," Jenkins said. "Listen, we told you, you gotta be careful. Now you gotta be more careful. If Tubbs was found dead with a gunshot wound or his head bashed in, that's one thing. The killer could have been anybody. But if he disappears with no sign . . . then whoever disappeared him knew what he was doing, and that's another thing entirely. You don't find that kind of guy standing around on a street corner—a killer who knows how to organize it, and carries it out clean."

"My very thought."

Jenkins took another thoughtful scrape through the shaving cream, rinsed the blade, then asked, "Would winning the election be worth the risk of murdering somebody? Of getting involved in a conspiracy to murder somebody?"

"That's the problem," Lucas said. "I don't think any rational person would, and Grant seems pretty rational. Either that, or she's crazier than a shithouse mouse. I talked to her today, pushed her a bit, and she pushed back. Never showed a wrinkle of worry, which means she's either innocent or nuts."

"Go for innocent: it cuts down the number of problems," Jenkins said.

"Another thing: I'm told one of these special forces guys is in love with her . . . which creates the question, exactly what would he do to see her win? Would he even tell her what he was planning to do?"

"Remember that guy who went around robbing those ladies' spa places?" Jenkins asked. "You know, manicure stores? Couple years ago?"

"Yeah, but I can't remember why he did it."

"He did it because he figured that there wouldn't be many guys around to deal with. No macho problems. It'd just be a bunch of women, and the places were almost all cash. He was getting a couple thousand bucks a week, paying no taxes, taking it easy," Jenkins said. "Anyway, he was ex–special forces. I tried to get his military records, and couldn't. Never did. We didn't need them, as it turned out, because one of the places he hit made some great movies of him . . . but the point is, I couldn't get the records. That's gonna be a problem, if these guys are really ex-army. Especially if they're former special ops."

"Maybe I won't need them," Lucas said.

"Oh . . . I think you probably will. There's nothing harder to break, IMHO"—he actually said the letters, I-M-H-O—"than a murder done by a guy who's well organized, doesn't feel much guilt, and you can't find the body. I've had two of those, and I'm batting five hundred. The one guy I got, it was luck. This is probably gonna be tougher. So you will need all the background you can get on them. . . . Grant wouldn't hire stupid people."

"I knew that talking to you would cheer me up," Lucas said.

"Yeah, well . . ."

Jenkins went back to shaving, and though it was late, Lucas headed back to his office. He wasn't exactly inspired by Jenkins, but he could make a couple of quick checks.

HE FOUND EMPLOYMENT RECORDS for Carver and Dannon in the quarterly tax reports filed by Grant with the state, which gave him their full names and addresses—they both lived in the same town house complex off I-494 west of the Cities. They didn't show up in the property tax records, so they were probably renting. He couldn't get directly at the income tax records, though he had a friend who could; but he hesitated to use her when he didn't have to, and he didn't really need to know how much they made. The DMV gave him their birth dates, which was what he really needed.

With that, he went out to the National Crime Information Center. Carver had once been arrested, at age eighteen, for fighting, apparently while he was still in high school. The charges had been dismissed without prosecution. Dannon came up clean.

There was almost nothing else, on either of them. Jenkins had been right: he'd need the army records. He picked up the phone and called Kidd.

"I already owe you for the help with the porn and the Minneapolis connection . . . but I've spotted a couple of guys who I'm interested in, and I can't find anything about them in the records that I can get at. Could you get military records?"

After a moment, Kidd said, "I hate to mess with the feds."

"I can understand that," Lucas said. "The thing is . . . these two guys are ex–special operations, apparently, and would have the skills to take out somebody like Tubbs. What I'd like to know is, did they have a record of killing in the military? Did they have a criminal history there? Did they get honorable discharges? I've got no way of getting that."

Kidd said, "I'll tell you what. I'll take a very conservative, safe approach. If I can get the stuff without a problem, without setting anything off, I'll do it. I won't take any risks. But if you use it, how'll you explain it?"

"You could dump it to my e-mail, anonymously. I'll figure out a way to explain it that'll keep you clear."

"I'm already not clear—people already know that I'm involved in this thing," Kidd said.

"What if I put in an official request for the records, with the army?" Lucas suggested. "They'll take it under advisement, but they won't give them to me. If you could find a way to ship the records out of the army's database, like there was a slipup . . ."

"Oh, boy . . ."

"I'll start calling the army the first thing in the morning. If you can help me out, that'd be good. If you can't, you can't."

"Oh, boy . . ."

"And there's another thing," Lucas said. "Something I doubt you could do."

"Lucas, my man, you originally just wanted a little help protecting the American Way . . ."

"I know, I know. But here's the thing. Taryn Grant's got this terrific security system. Cameras all over the place, inside and out. At one time, the photography went out to the cloud, saved for a month. In the last couple of days, somebody cut that to forty-eight hours. They did that about forty-eight hours after Tubbs disappeared. I'm wondering, what if Tubbs showed up at Grant's place, and ran into something with one of these security guys?"

"You want me to find the recordings?" Kidd asked.

"If you can."

"Do you know which cloud?" Kidd asked. "There are lots of clouds."

"I don't know jack shit," Lucas admitted.

"Do you know her cell phone number?"

"Well . . . yeah, I do know that."

"Give it to me," Kidd said. "It's a start, if she monitors the system from her phone."

LUCAS WENT HOME.

Weather and Letty were curious, and Lucas kept them updated on his cases, but he had nothing to tell them. He did describe the meeting with Grant, and Weather said, "She sounds more interesting than I would have expected. Educated."

"She is. And she may have gotten a guy murdered."

"And she may not have," Weather said. "Something for you to think about."

LUCAS SPOKE TO the governor later that evening. The attorney general, the governor said, was all over the papers taken from Tubbs's apartment. "I suggested he investigate them thoroughly, at least until the election was over and done with. That way, he'll have the full attention of the press. He saw the wisdom of that."

"So I don't have to worry about him being in my hair . . ."

"At least not for a week," Henderson said. "What'd you think of Grant?"

"Smart and tough," Lucas said.

"She could be president someday, if you don't drag her down."

"What's that supposed to mean?" Lucas asked.

"I'm just sayin', my friend. Keep me up to date."

―――――

LUCAS GOT TO THE OFFICE early the next morning, conscious of the time difference between Minneapolis and Washington, and began calling the Pentagon. He spent two hours talking to a variety of captains, majors, and colonels—somehow missing lieutenant colonels—and got nothing substantial, except the feeling that everybody dreaded making a mistake. He did get pointed to online request forms, which he dutifully filled out and submitted, and backed those with direct e-mails to the captains, majors, and colonels, reiterating his requests for information.

When he was done, he had no information, but had laid down a solid record of information requests. Now if Kidd came through . . .

Lucas thought about spies, and with no particular place to push, eventually drove over to Smalls's campaign headquarters and talked to Helen Roman, Smalls's campaign secretary, who sent him down the hall to a guy named John Mack, the deputy campaign manager. He was, Roman told him, in charge of operations.

Mack said that he knew Bob Tubbs by sight, and may have said hello at the candy machine, but had never had a real conversation with him. "He's a bit older than I am—we're not contemporaries. I don't know what we'd have in common. We're not even with the same political party."

"Even without knowing him, but just knowing what he did . . . knowing what *you* do . . ."

"Maybe I should take the Fifth," Mack said.

"C'mon, man, gimme a little help . . . Give Smalls a little help."

Mack repeated that he didn't know anything about spying, but just as an intellectual exercise . . .

Tubbs's accomplice would have had one of three motives for

trying to dump Smalls, Mack said: (1) financial—he might have been paid; (2) ideological—he wanted Smalls dumped because he hated his politics; or (3) personal—he (or she) was a close friend or lover of Tubbs; or he (or she) was a personal enemy of Smalls.

If it were (3), it seemed likely that the accomplice would also be older. Perhaps not exactly Tubbs's or Smalls's contemporary, but most of the volunteers were college kids, and unlikely to be close enough to either man to do something as ugly as dropping the child pornography on Smalls, simply at Tubbs's say-so.

Could be (2) ideological, Mack said, although the volunteers were vetted before they were given any real responsibility. "But the thing is, if they planted this thing in Porter's computer, they don't have to have any responsibility. All they need is access," Mack said. "I have no idea how many office keys are floating around, but it's quite a few, and the place is empty late at night."

Or he said, it could be (1) financial . . . though if it were financial, how would Tubbs have made the approach to the accomplice, or spy? He could probably have done it only through personal knowledge of the accomplice, and that would loop right back to (3): a personal relationship.

So Lucas was probably looking for somebody a bit older, Mack said, or a reckless, ideologically driven youngster, whom Tubbs would have to have known. Was it possible that Tubbs had recruited a spy for Taryn Grant's campaign, then enlisted him to do the pornography dump?

"Grant says she didn't know Tubbs, and she seems smart enough that she probably wouldn't lie about it . . . especially if we could find out about it," Lucas told Mack. "Anyway, I believed her. She probably *didn't* know him."

"I'll tell you what—if an operator like Tubbs knew about a spy in our campaign, other Democrats would know about it, too," Mack said. "I think you might be going around threatening the wrong people."

"I wasn't threatening you," Lucas said.

"Then why am I sweating?"

LUCAS WAS MULLING IT all over as he walked out to his car, and as he popped the door lock, took a call from Marion, the Minneapolis internal affairs cop.

"Just an update: I've been tearing up Domestics this morning. I don't have any proof, but I've got a half-dozen names, and whoever copied that porn for Tubbs is probably on the list."

"How'd you get the names?" Lucas asked.

Marion explained that he'd started with the people he'd considered least likely to be involved, and with the threat of felonies hanging over their heads, they'd been cooperative. He'd been looking for people who'd been seen using the Domestics computer at unlikely times, alone or in small groups, or had been unhappy to be seen using it and had quickly signed off when a new face turned up at the office.

"There are five guys and one woman who may—and I say 'may'—have been looking at the porn repeatedly. I think all six probably were . . . kind of like a little club down there that knew about it. Two of the shrinks had heard rumors about child porn on city computers. That's where I got the names."

"What're you doing next?" Lucas asked.

"I've got to talk to the chief about that, but I'm inclined to try to figure out who was the least likely to have dumped the porn to Tubbs, and offer him immunity for information."

"When are you going to do it?"

"After I talk to the chief, I'll have to get with the lawyers . . . I'm thinking it couldn't be any earlier than this evening, and most likely tomorrow."

"Keep talking to me," Lucas said.

ON THE WAY BACK to his office, he called Smalls:

"How's the campaign going?"

"Not well: that bitch has got everybody she knows whispering that the porn was really mine."

"I thought she told the TV people that her campaign wasn't doing that, and she'd fire anybody who did," Lucas said.

"Well, of course she said that," Smalls said. "She's lying through her teeth."

"How do you know that?"

"Because that's what *I'd* do."

Lucas said, "Okay. Listen, we're making more progress, but we need to find Tubbs's accomplice in your office. That'll break the thing wide open. If this was done for ideological reasons, if it was done by a spy, then somebody in your campaign has got to have doubts about that person. It's not that easy to hide your basic beliefs . . . especially if you're a college kid. So, I need somebody, not you but maybe your campaign manager, to talk to everybody about who that might be. We're trying to catch a spy. I'm going to work it from the other end, the Democratic side, see if I can get them to cough somebody up."

Smalls was silent for a moment, then said, "I can do that. In fact, if we leak to the TV people that we're looking for a spy . . . that might help convince them that there really was a dirty trick."

"Whatever," Lucas said. "I'm not really trying to get you re-elected."

Smalls laughed and said, "Gotta be killing a good liberal like you."

"Ah, I'm not that political. Anyway, if you could do that, I'll start on the other side."

"Four days to the election," Smalls said. "If it ain't done by Sunday, I'm screwed."

LUCAS CALLED KIDD: "Anything happening?"

"Not yet. It's delicate."

FROM HIS OFFICE, he called Rose Marie Roux and asked, "What Democratic Party operator would be most likely to know who is spying on who?"

"Well, that'd be Don Schariff, but don't tell him I said so. Why?"

"I'm going to jack him up," Lucas said. "Where can I find him?"

Schariff had an office at the DFL headquarters—Minnesota's Democratic Party was technically called the Democratic-Farmer-Labor Party—and Lucas found him there, by phone, and said he wanted to come over.

"Should I be worried?" Schariff asked.

Lucas said, "I don't know. Should you?"

"I'm wondering if I should have a lawyer sit in?"

Lucas said, "I don't know. Should you?"

The DFL headquarters was a low white-brick building in a St. Paul business park across the Mississippi from downtown that possibly looked hip for fifteen minutes after it was built but no longer did. Lucas talked to a receptionist, who made a call. Schariff came out and got him, and said, "We're down in the conference room."

"Who's we?" Lucas asked.

"Me and Daryl Larson, our attorney," Schariff said. He was a stocky, dark-haired man with a neatly trimmed beard and dark-rimmed glasses. He was wearing a white shirt with a couple of pens in a plastic pocket protector. In any other circumstance, Lucas would have been willing to arrest him on the basis of the pocket protector alone. "I asked, and everybody said when you're talking to a cop . . . especially one investigating the Grant-Smalls fight . . ."

"Okay," Lucas said.

Larson was a tall, thin man whom Lucas knew through Weather's association with the St. Paul Chamber Orchestra. Larson raised money for the orchestra, usually by wheedling rich wives; it'd worked with Weather. When Lucas stepped into the room, Larson put down the paper he'd been reading and stood to shake hands. "Lucas, nice to see you. How's Weather?"

"Broke. She's broke. She's got no money left. She's wondering how we're going to feed the kids."

"Hate to hear that," Larson said, with a toothy smile. "I'll call her with my condolences."

The pleasantries out of the way, they settled into the conference chairs and Lucas outlined some of what he knew and believed about Tubbs's disappearance. He finished by saying, "You guys are probably not going to want to talk about this, because when the media puts Tubbs's disappearance together with the porn trick . . . it's gonna look bad."

"I think we can agree on that," Larson said for Schariff, who'd kept his mouth shut. "But how does this involve Don?"

"I've been told, by somebody who knows these things, that Don knows a lot about the, mmm, tactical maneuverings of the party, and everybody involved in these things."

"I don't do dirty tricks," Schariff said.

Larson put up a finger to shut him up, and said to Lucas, "Go on."

"So the technical fact of the matter is, the booby trap on Smalls's computer had to be set the same morning it went off. Tubbs wasn't there that morning. Hadn't been there for a few days," Lucas said. "So, he had an accomplice. That accomplice might have been acting out of pure greed . . . Tubbs might have paid him. But it's equally likely that it's an ideological thing, that Tubbs knew that there was a spy among the volunteers and got the guy to set the trap. Since Don knows most of the party's operators . . . well, we thought he might also know who the spy is. If there is one."

"Getting information like that isn't a crime," Larson said.

"I didn't say it was—but framing Smalls is. Anybody who helped the spy put that stuff on the computer, or knows about it and doesn't say so, is also in trouble. Conspiracy and all that. Prison time," Lucas said. "I'm not trying to be impolite here, but you see where I'm going."

Schariff said, "Well, I—"

Larson put the finger up again and said, "No." Then to Lucas, "Don and I have to talk. I'll call you later today."

"How about in ten minutes?" Lucas asked. "Things are getting really tight with the election."

"Later today," Larson said. And he wouldn't budge.

OUT ON THE SIDEWALK, Lucas took a phone call from Ruffe Ig-nace, a crime reporter for the *Star Tribune*: "We're getting all kinds of different signals on Smalls. Smalls says he's been cleared by Rose Marie Roux, and she says she's made her statement, which, when you look at it, doesn't quite clear him. In the meantime, people are whispering to our political people that the porn was his. Which way should I lean?"

"I'd have to go off the record on that," Lucas said. "Better yet, why don't you call Rose Marie directly?"

"She tends to blow me off," Ignace said. "Anyway, could we stay a little bit on the record? A highly placed source in the investigation?"

"I'm the only one investigating, so that won't work," Lucas said. "I need to go completely off."

"Shit. All right, we're off the record," Ignace said. "Which way should I lean?"

"Smalls was framed. . . . He's innocent."

"Thanks. We're almost even now. You only owe me a little bit."

"Call me back in one minute," Lucas said. "I might have something else for you."

"You in the can?"

"No, I'm in a parking lot, leaning on my car," Lucas said. "I need to think. One minute."

Lucas leaned against the car and thought about it. One minute later, Ignace called back and Lucas said, "Still off the record, okay?"

"Okay. Against my better judgment. The public's trust in both government and the media would be so much higher if we identified—"

"Yeah, yeah, yeah. We're off the record. Call Don Schariff—S-C-H-A-R-I-F-F—at DFL headquarters. He's got some kind of title there, but I'm not sure what. Anyway, he's involved with DFL intelligence gathering—"

"Spies."

"Yeah. Ask him if Bob Tubbs—"

"The guy who disappeared . . . *Holy shit*, Tubbs? Tubbs dumped the porn on Smalls?"

"I didn't say that," Lucas said. "Schariff might possibly have some information for you. But he'll probably deny any involvement with Tubbs."

"You're saying the Republicans killed Tubbs?"

"Somebody did, but I don't think it was the Republicans," Lucas said. "I think there's a cover-up going on. But it's possible that Tubbs is just lying low, until the election is over."

"Not from what I hear," Ignace said. "I hear the St. Paul cops think he's dead. I hear you do, too."

"Yeah, I guess I do," Lucas said.

"All right, we're more than even. You need anything from me?"

"Not right now. But wait at least an hour before you call Schariff. I just talked to him two minutes ago, and if you call him right now, he'll figure I talked to you. So wait."

"You talking to Channel Three?"

"No. You've got it exclusively. So wait."

"I can do that," Ignace said. "I can probably get one of our political guys to tie Schariff to Tubbs. They must've worked together a hundred times. *Hot dog*. But say it out loud: Tubbs used the porn to frame Smalls."

"I can't say that," Lucas said. "But I can say that you sometimes, against all odds, seem like a very, very smart guy."

"You can kiss my odds," Ignace said. "But no, wait. Thanks, Lucas. I owe you big. If you're ever indicted for anything, I'll take your side."

LUCAS WENT BACK TO his office, called his agents, got updates—still nothing on the Ape Man Rapist of Rochester—and waited for something from the DFL.

Larson, the lawyer, called back two hours later. He was angry: "Lucas, I'd call you a miserable motherfucker if I didn't need Weather's money. You talked to Ignace, over at the *Strib*. You got him on Don's case. He's going to publicly connect Don to Bob Tubbs and Tubbs to the Smalls scandal."

"I'm not talking to anybody," Lucas lied. "I'm just trying to get a little cooperation from people who might know why a guy got murdered."

"You lying motherfucker . . . pardon the language. Don't talk to Ignace again: don't, or I'll find some way to screw you. I promise."

"Do your best, Daryl. But if I find out Don knew something that he's not giving me, he's going to prison," Lucas said. "He'll be part of the conspiracy if he tries to cover it up."

"There's no cover-up," Larson said. "If there's a spy in the Smalls campaign, she was placed by Grant's campaign, not by us."

"You said, 'she,'" Lucas said. "So you know something."

"I'll tell you exactly what we did," Larson said. "We got everybody together, and we tried to figure out who was working for Smalls, all the volunteers, and then we showed the list to Don. He looked it over and said there was one volunteer, a young woman, Bunny Knoedler, who he was surprised to see working for the opposition."

"Bunny?"

"Yes. Knoedler. K-N-O-E-D-L-E-R."

"How surprised was he?" Lucas asked.

"He said she worked on a couple of our campaigns out-state that Tubbs was involved with," Larson said. "Don said she seemed like a pretty dedicated DFLer."

Lucas said, "If this works out, Daryl, I'll send you a hundred dollars myself."

"Fuck you, Lucas . . . but do say hello to Weather for me."

LUCAS LOOKED AT HIS WATCH: getting late. He walked down the hall, saw Shrake on the phone at his desk, went that way. Shrake saw him coming, held up a finger, said, "Uh-huh. Uh-huh. Well, send me the paper. Okay. I gotta go." He hung up and said, "You're quivering."

"You got some time?"

"Ah . . . no. Not if you want me to keep pushing the Jackson thing," Shrake said.

"All right. Where's Jenkins?" Lucas asked.

"He's getting his oil changed," Shrake said.

"He's . . ."

"No, no, not that," Shrake said. "He was going down to a Rapid Oil Change, getting the oil changed in his car."

"Call him, tell him to get back here," Lucas said. "I need to terrorize a young woman, and I want one of you guys to come along."

"Well, hell, that's right up his alley," Shrake said. He picked up his phone and dialed.

With Jenkins on the way back, Lucas called Smalls and asked the question. Smalls made a call and came back immediately: "The girl is working until nine o'clock on the phone bank. Is she the one who did this?"

"Don't know—but we got a tip that made us want to talk with her," Lucas said. "Don't do anything that would let her know we're looking at her."

"In other words, keep my mouth shut."

"I'm far too polite to say that to a U.S. senator."

JENKINS SHOWED UP and said, "I was next in line."

"That piece of shit you drive won't know the difference," Lucas said. "You could fill it up with a water hose. Let's go."

Lucas briefed Jenkins on the way over. They got to Smalls's headquarters a little after four o'clock, and the secretary, Helen, pointed out Bunny Knoedler, a tall, dark-haired, blue-eyed girl with bow-lips, who looked like she might have been Lucas's daughter.

The phone room was just another office, divided up into a half-dozen booths with acoustic tiling on the walls, to hush up the multiple voices. Knoedler was sitting in a booth with two hard-wired phones and a list, and was dialing a number when Lucas leaned over her shoulder and pushed down the hang-up bar on the base set.

She turned and looked up at him and said, "What . . . ?" and he could see in her eyes that she knew who he was.

"We need you to come back into Senator Smalls's office," Lucas said. Jenkins loomed behind him, as though to keep her from running.

"What . . . what?" she asked.

"I think you know what, but we have to talk about it," Lucas said. "Come along."

She put the phone down, and with the other phone-bank people suddenly gone silent, followed them out of the room, sandwiched between Jenkins and Lucas, like a perp walk.

Smalls's office was empty—not even a computer anymore—and Lucas pointed Knoedler at a chair. He and Jenkins remained on their feet, looking down at her. "You're a Democratic spy," Lucas said. "A friend of Bob Tubbs, and you worked with him on out-state campaigns. He planted you here to watch Senator Smalls's campaign."

She was scared, and started to reply. She said, "I—"

Lucas put up a hand to stop her. "We're going to read you your rights. But I want to tell you, in addition to your rights, if you lie to me, that's a crime. You have the right to remain silent, to say nothing at all, but you can't lie to me. At this point, we're looking for information."

Lucas looked at Jenkins and nodded, and Jenkins started the routine. "You have the right to remain silent . . ."

When he was finished, Lucas asked, "Did you understand all of that? That you have a right to an attorney?"

"I haven't done anything illegal," she said, looking at the two of them, looming.

She hadn't asked for a lawyer. This was delicate: Lucas didn't want to talk about illegalities. Instead, he said, "Bob's mother is worried sick about him, but we don't know whether he's just lying low, or if he's been . . . killed. We're afraid that he has been. If he's still around, we desperately need to know that."

"I . . . I . . . I don't know," she said. "I mean, I'm worried, too. He was the guy I was supposed to talk to, if I found anything out. Then he just stopped answering his phone. I was calling him every night, and then . . . he was gone."

She'd just admitted being a spy. "Do you know where he got the pornography?" Jenkins asked. "Did he get it from a police officer?"

"The pornography . . . He didn't have anything to do with that,"
she said. "That's crazy. He didn't do dirty tricks."

"We know you're a little new with this political campaign stuff,"
Lucas said. "But I'm here to tell you, Bob was involved in a few
tricks in the past. And you're sort of a dirty trick, spying on the
Smalls campaign."

"Everybody does it," she said. "Everybody. Smalls has a spy in
the Grant camp, too. Just ask him. Ask him under oath."

"Okay," Lucas said. Smalls had already as much as admitted that.

He looked at Jenkins, who was the asshole. Jenkins said, "I
dunno. I doubt that everybody does it. Gotta be some kind of a
crime. And she's not all that new with this stuff—she's worked
those out-state campaigns."

"It is *not* a crime," she said, showing a little streak of anger. "It's
not illegal. I wouldn't do anything illegal."

"We know that you were close to Bob," Lucas said. "We know
that Bob needed somebody to help set the computer so the pornography would pop up—"

"I had nothing to do with that!" she said, her voice rising. "I
would never do something that dirty. That's rotten. That porn . . .
that belongs to Smalls. Everybody knows about his attitude toward
women, and sex . . ."

"Come on," Jenkins said, the scorn rough in his voice.

"I didn't . . ."

They pushed her for another five minutes, and she claimed that
she worked afternoons and nights, and hadn't been around when
the trap must've been set. They pushed on that, and she eventually
admitted that she thought that Tubbs had been in the office at
night, two days before the trap popped. They pushed on that, and
finally she said the magic words.

"Look," she said. "I want a lawyer. Right fuckin' now."

Jenkins looked at Lucas and lifted his eyebrows. Arrest her? Lucas shook his head; he wasn't ready for that. He said, "We'll want to talk to you again. Do not go away. Do not try to avoid us. I'm tempted to arrest you, and put you in jail overnight, but I'm hoping that you understand that we need to know what happened, more than we need to haul in the small fish. You're a small fish. Do you understand that?"

She nodded, and said, "Lawyer."

Lucas offered to provide one, a public defender, but she said she'd get her own. "Are we done?"

"Yes. But don't run—"

"I'm not going to run, but I want you to take me out of the office," she said. She looked out through the glass window on Smalls's office door. "They're gonna be a little pissed at me."

"That's the least of your problems," Lucas said. "Come on. We'll take you out."

SHE WAS RIGHT: when they walked out of the room, the other volunteers started hissing, and somebody called, "Put her ass in jail." At the door, Knoedler flashed a finger over her shoulder, and Jenkins laughed and said, "That's really classy, sweetheart."

They saw her into her car, and as she backed out of the parking space, Lucas asked Jenkins, "What do you think?"

Jenkins shrugged and said, "Don't think she knew about the porn. But I wouldn't be surprised if she let Tubbs into the office, late one night, after everybody else had gone home."

Lucas nodded. "Maybe. Which would make her a part of it. The thing is, the DFLers swear that they didn't put her on Smalls, and I believe them because if they did, too many people would have to know about it. I'd find out, and they know that. So, they're telling the truth. It had to be Tubbs, working alone, or Tubbs working for Grant. We need to keep going back to her, if nothing else breaks."

"Maybe give Knoedler limited immunity," Jenkins said.

"Don't want to give her immunity, if she set the trap," Lucas said.

Jenkins shook his head: "I gotta tell you: I kinda believed her about that. She got pretty hot about it and that looked real. Besides, she knows we can check."

Lucas rubbed his nose and looked after her taillights, two blocks down the street. "Yeah. It did look kinda real," he said. "Goddamnit."

HE CHECKED ANYWAY, and Roman, the secretary, said that Knoedler hadn't been scheduled to work, because even the volunteers were limited to eight hours a day. "But people, you know, are enthusiastic, and they come and go all the time. She could have been here, and I doubt that anyone would have thought it unusual, or even noticed."

CHAPTER 14

Lauren had put together a munchie plate and Kidd was munching on the last of the celery with pimento cheese as he bypassed the privacy option on Taryn Grant's bedroom security camera.

The camera was inactive, which meant nobody had walked through the bedroom in the past thirty seconds.

He was working off a laptop that was, technically, operating out of a Wi-Fi system in the federal courthouse, which was just up the street. He'd taken the precaution of building a repeater into the building several years earlier.

With nothing moving on the screen, he wandered away from the laptop to look at a landscape he was working on, a view of the Mississippi a few miles above the Coon Rapids Dam. The color of the autumn leaves and the dark river was all accurate enough, he thought, but didn't work for the painting: and accurate color was not a driving aspect of his work.

He pulled on a paint-spattered apron, selected a handful of tubes of oil paint, squeezed some paint onto a glass palette, and began mixing color. An hour later, he was still adjusting the color on the river's surface when the laptop screen flickered to life and Taryn Grant walked into the bedroom.

Kidd stepped over to the laptop as Grant kicked off her shoes, then unzipped the back of her dress, pulled it over her head, and tossed it on the bed. A slip followed, leaving her in her bra, underpants, and genuine nylon stockings held up with a genuine garter belt.

She walked off screen to the left, and Kidd said, aloud, "Come back, come back . . ."

Thirty seconds later, the screen went dead.

She had to come back through the bedroom, though, and Kidd pulled a drawing stool over to the laptop bench, sat and waited. Seven or eight minutes later, naked as the day she was born, fresh out of the shower, Grant walked across the bedroom, wiping down her back with a long white terrycloth towel. She was, Kidd thought, a healthy lass.

As Kidd watched, she tossed the towel on her bed and walked over to a side table, reached behind it, and must have pushed a button or moved a lever—a built-in bookcase on a sidewall smoothly rotated away from the wall. Grant stepped over to the safe and after punching in a string of numbers on the safe's keypad, she pulled open the heavy steel door and started taking out jewelry cases.

Kidd turned to the studio and shouted, "Hey, Lauren. C'mere. Quick."

Lauren popped into the doorway a minute later, said, "I've got to get Jackson . . ." Jackson was at school.

"Look at this," Kidd said, pointing at the monitor.

She looked and a frown line appeared on her forehead and she said, "What is this? Is that Taryn Grant? Kidd, what the heck are you doing?"

"Hey. Look what *she's* doing."

Lauren peered at the monitor. "She's . . . whoa, look at that."

Grant had opened one of a half-dozen jewelry cases she'd put on the bed, and tried on a heavy necklace of knotted gold. She looked at herself in the mirror, then took off the gold, dropped it back next to the case, and opened another case. This necklace was smaller, more demure . . . and sparkled with diamonds.

Kidd tapped a corner of the screen: "She took it out of the safe."

"Can we get a look at it? The safe?"

"I can rewind a bit, look at that corner . . ."

He stepped back through the recording, to the point that the camera had stopped recording. "The camera triggers on movement, and runs for another thirty seconds."

There was a jump, and then the unclothed Grant walked into the screen again, from the left side, and Kidd said, "Yow," and Lauren said, "Yeah, yow. You are in no way qualified to handle something like that."

"*That*, my little pumpkin flower, holds not a candle to your own self," Kidd said.

"Thanks, but to be honest, you're not qualified to handle *me*. I have to tone down my whole . . . Okay, here goes."

Lauren watched as Grant opened the bookcase, and then the safe.

"That's a Robinson Steel-Block," Lauren said, peering at the safe door. "Can we rerun and get closer on the keypad?"

Kidd rattled some keys and the corner of the screen that showed the safe shifted to occupy the entire screen; a few more keystrokes and the recording stepped back and showed the bookcase opening. Grant's hand appeared and she hit the key sequence.

Kidd said, "Jesus, an eight-number code."

"You won't get into a Robinson with a jackknife," Lauren said. "Run that again."

Kidd ran it again and Lauren said, "I think it was 62649628. Or it could have been 95970960. I'll need to look at it some more. Is there an alarm when the safe opens?"

"I'd have to do a little more exploring to figure that out . . . but I doubt it," Kidd said.

"Okay. I want to look at the way she pushed that button again."

They ran the file a dozen times, and Lauren watched Grant's arm and fingers as she pushed the button, or moved the lever, that shifted the bookcase. Eventually, she decided that it was a simple button-push, probably wireless, and that the button was mounted on the back of the side table. "You can see that she feels for it, for a second, and then her middle finger pushes it . . . not a slide motion. It's a button, and she pushes it once: it's not a coded sequence."

Kidd started the live video again, and Grant, now back in her underpants, garter belt straps hanging loose down her legs, hooked her bra and started trying on the jewelry again, including a lot of colored gemstones.

"Look at that, I think that's a ruby," Lauren said. "My God, the thing's the size of a drain stopper."

Eventually, Grant chose what looked like a multiple string of pearls.

"The stuff she looked at, the stuff she rejected—assuming it's all top-of-the-line, and given her money, I'd bet it is—we're looking at a million bucks with just what we saw. There's more in the safe. She was looking for the right necklace. She wouldn't have taken everything out, the rings and bracelets."

"I made a million last year," Kidd said. "We don't need the money."

"That's your money, not mine," Lauren said. "I like to have my own money."

"You can be such a silly shit," Kidd said.

"Whatever. I'm going to want to look at a few key photos," Lauren said.

"Me too," Kidd said. "Like when she puts on her nylons . . ."

"Hey . . ."

". . . my little rutabaga flower."

Lauren patted his chest. "Put that video somewhere safe. I'm late to get Jackson. We'll talk after he's in bed tonight."

KIDD TOLD LUCAS that Lauren had worked as an insurance adjuster, which was true enough: after Lauren called on her rich clients, their insurance needed adjustment. She mostly stole money, for the simple reason that it was . . . money. She'd also steal jewelry, if it was the kind that could be melted or broken down into unidentifiable stones.

Kidd had once needed to get some information on a man who was peddling defense secrets, and had used Lauren to hit his safe, as a cover for his own break-in. The safe couldn't be cracked in place: it was too good. So Lauren had simply used a power jack to rip the safe completely out of the wall, had Kidd throw it out the window of the man's condominium, and had whipped him into carrying the brutally heavy safe, at a fast jog, which was all he could manage, several hundred yards to their car. She'd taken the safe to a machinist friend, who'd cut it open.

Kidd could feel an incipient hernia when he even thought about that night. . . .

She hadn't only stolen for the income, though: she had done it because she liked it, and often because her victims deserved it. The kind of people who were most vulnerable to her were almost always assholes, running some kind of illegal or immoral hustle. She chose them because most would not go to the police. Politicians were a favorite target—no politician had ever called the FBI to report that a hundred thousand dollars in twenty-dollar bills had been taken out of his freezer.

Lauren also had a taste for cocaine and cowboys, both of which she'd given up when she and Kidd had decided a child would be nice. Not that the taste had necessarily gone away.

WHEN JACKSON was put to bed that night, and Kidd was lying on the living room couch reading deep into *George Bellows*, a hefty volume produced by the National Gallery of Art, in conjunction with a retrospective exhibition on the American painter, Lauren came in and said, "Move your feet."

Kidd sat up and Lauren plopped on the couch and asked, "Why'd you show me that?"

"You said last week that you were feeling stale. Then when we were over at the Roosavelts' place, I noticed you casing the place."

"I was looking at the new décor, with Suki," Lauren said.

"Right." The Roosavelts had decorated their new eight-thousand-square-foot penthouse with, among other things, a big Kidd landscape, and Kidd and Lauren had gone over to see what the installation looked like.

"Hey . . ."

"I need to know what's going on in your head," Kidd said.

"A lot of stuff," Lauren said. "But to get back to Taryn . . . You think I should crack her house?"

"No. I want you to think about it," Kidd said. "All about it. About what would happen if you were caught, about the effect it would have on Jackson and me, and what would happen if you weren't caught. How would that change things? Or would it change anything?"

Lauren said, "I don't know. I don't know what would happen. But ever since you showed me the video . . . it's like I've got a fever."

"You had the fever before then. I could see it. If you hadn't, I wouldn't have shown you Grant's bedroom."

"Yeah . . ." She stood up and wandered over to the window and looked out at the river, where it disappeared around the bend and rolled off to the Gulf of Mexico. "Yeah, you're right. I've been looking at places."

"I was afraid of that," Kidd said.

"I've never been caught," Lauren said, turning back. "I've never been printed."

"You didn't have that much riding on it before," Kidd said.

"You're right. I didn't."

"I quit," Kidd said. "As much as I could, anyway."

"You could quit because you never wanted to do it that much—industrial espionage, sneaking around in factories . . . it all seemed so weird," Lauren said. "You didn't need it, because you're basically a painter, not a thief. But I'm basically a thief. That's what I do. That's my painting. I'm not basically a housewife."

"But nobody's going to put me in jail for painting . . ."

"That *Times* critic might," Lauren said. "He said you were a throwback to a bygone era and that your prices were absurd for something as old-fashioned as paintings."

"I'm trying to be serious," Kidd said. "About everything. That's why I showed you the video. I want you to think about your life."

She turned away from him and bobbed her head. "All right. I'll do that. I *will* do that, Kidd."

THEY TALKED for two hours. Lauren was mostly right—Kidd was basically a painter, but there was one spot in his heart that would never go away, reserved for the beauty of computers and their languages.

Much later that night, Kidd was back in the studio when a computer chirped at him. He went over and looked at it. Military records depository. He touched a key and the computer on the other end hesitated. "Open sesame," Kidd said, feeling the rush.

The army's computer opened up.

CHAPTER 15

Lucas was lying on a couch reading the Steve Jobs biography, which he'd been meaning to do for a long time, when his cell phone rang. He looked at the screen, which said it was two minutes after eleven o'clock, and "Caller Unknown."

"Hello?"

"Don't say anything. This is a wrong number. Look at your e-mail. Don't call me back before tomorrow night."

Click. Kidd was gone; the call had lasted six seconds.

LUCAS GOT OFF the couch and padded back to his study, sat down at the computer, and brought up his e-mail. He had incoming mail from the military records depository.

He clicked on it, and found two PDF documents. He clicked on the first and found a thirty-page document on Ronald L. Carver, Sgt. E-8 U.S. Army, marked "Secret." Lucas had never been in the army, and thought E-8 was a rank, but wasn't sure. He went out on Google to check: E-8 was a master sergeant.

The document was a mass of acronyms and it took him an hour

to work through the thirty pages, going back and forth to Google, searching for definitions, making notes on a yellow legal pad.

Weather stuck her head in and said, "You're not coming to bed?"

"Not for a while." She was up late; not working in the morning. "Something came up."

"Don't drink any more Diet Coke or you'll be up all night."

She went away and Lucas went back to Carver. Scanning the document, he'd figured that Carver had spent three years in Iraq and two more in Afghanistan. He had a Silver Star and a Bronze Star for bravery under fire, and had been wounded at least twice, with two Purple Hearts. Neither wound had been serious. Both had been treated in-country, and he'd returned to active duty in less than a month, in each case.

Then something happened, but Lucas couldn't tell what it was. Carver had been reprimanded—exact circumstances unspecified— and very shortly afterward had been honorably discharged.

Reading through the document a second time, he determined that Carver had been through a number of high-level training courses: he was a Ranger, he was parachute qualified, he'd taken a half-dozen courses in anti-insurgency warfare, and had spent a lot of time on "detached duty" in both Iraq and Afghanistan.

Working through military sites he found through Google, he determined that Carver had made the master sergeant rank about as quickly as was possible. Then he was out.

Lucas leaned back in his chair and processed it. He thought Carver had probably been some sort of enlisted-ranks combat specialist, what the Internet military sites called an "operator." Lucas suspected that he'd killed a lot of people—his training all pointed in that direction.

But the reprimand could cover a lot of territory. Carver, he thought, might very well have killed either the wrong person, or too many of them. With Carver's medals, experience, and training, Lucas thought it unlikely that he'd been kicked out for rolling a joint.

IN A LOT OF WAYS, the records for Douglas Damien Dannon were parallel to Carver's. Dannon had been in the military for six years, leaving as a captain, honorably discharged. There was nothing in the records to indicate that he'd been pushed out.

Like Carver, he'd spent most of his service time in either Iraq or Afghanistan. He'd won the Bronze Star for bravery under fire, had been wounded by a roadside bomb during the initial invasion of Iraq. After a couple of years as an infantry lieutenant, he'd been assigned to a mobile intelligence unit, and then later, to an intelligence unit at a battalion headquarters. Lucas wasn't sure exactly what that meant, and spent some time looking up words like *battalion*, *company*, *brigade*, and *division*.

A battalion was apparently a mid-level unit, in size, and his particular battalion had apparently been deeply enmeshed in combat in Iraq. Dannon had gotten good efficiency marks, but Lucas wasn't sure how exactly to evaluate them. In his own bureaucracy, good efficiency marks were subject to interpretation by insiders, and could damn with praise a little too faint.

BY THE TIME LUCAS went to bed, a little after two in the morning, he'd learned enough to know that Grant's security detail could plan and carry out a murder with calculated precision and had no large problem with qualms. They would have the means, the training, the personalities that would allow them to get it done.

If they were responsible for Tubbs's murder, catching them would be the next thing to impossible.

Next to impossible, he thought, as he drifted away to sleep. *Next to . . .*

He opened his eyes, listened to Weather breathing beside him, then crept out of bed again, taking his phone with him, into the study, where he called Virgil Flowers. Flowers answered on the third ring and asked, "What happened?"

"I need you up here tomorrow, early. Ten o'clock or so."

Flowers groaned. "You had to call me in the middle of the night to tell me that? I thought the Ape Man was out again."

"Sorry. I was afraid you'd be out of there at five o'clock, in your boat," Lucas said. "I'm running out of time up here, and I need you to look at some paper. You're the only guy I know who could do it."

"What?"

"You were an army cop," Lucas said. "See you up here."

Lucas hung up, went back to bed, and slept soundly.

THE NEXT MORNING, Weather dropped a newspaper on his back and said, "Ruffe."

"What'd he say?"

"He said that the state—meaning you, though he doesn't use your name—is investigating the possibility that Tubbs was killed to cover up the dirty trick on Smalls. The Democrats are furious, while the Republicans are outraged."

"So . . . no change," Lucas said.

"Watch your ass, Lucas," Weather said. "The whole thing is about to lurch into the ditch."

A COUPLE OF HOURS later, Virgil Flowers, a lanky man with long blond hair, put the heels of his cowboy boots on Lucas's desk and turned over the last page of the two documents, which Lucas had printed for him. Flowers said, "You're right. These are two goddamned dangerous guys. Carver, especially, but this Dannon wouldn't be a pushover, either. He'd be the brains behind the operation."

Lucas had called Flowers in for two reasons: he was smart, and he'd been an MP captain in the army, before joining the St. Paul Police Department, and then the BCA. He normally worked the southern third of the state, except when Lucas needed him to do something else.

"I was struggling with the gobbledygook," Lucas said, tossing the papers on the desk. "I figured as a famous former warlord, you'd know what it was all about."

"I met a few of these guys in the Balkans," Flowers said. "They're scary. Smart, tough. Not like movie stars, not all muscled up with torn shirts. A lot of them are really pretty small guys, neat, quiet— you'd think you could throw them out the window, but you'd be wrong. Some trouble would start up, you know, and they'd get assigned a mission, they'd be really, really calm. Sit around eating crackers and checking their weapons. Contained. The army cuts them a lot of slack, because they're very good at what they do . . . which, basically, is killing and kidnapping people."

"An uncommon skill set," Lucas said.

"Yeah. I didn't have a lot of contact with them," Flowers said.

"They had their own compounds. They're secretive, a lot of them get killed—they have an unbelievable mortality rate. Even with that, they stay in the military. Some of them call the army 'Mother.' I think they get hooked on the stress and the camaraderie. Or maybe the sense that they're doing something really important, which they are. If they leave the military, they tend to get in trouble as civilians. Some of them, after they leave, wind up as military contractors, or working for military contractors, right back where they started. Roaming around the world, with a gun in their back pocket."

Lucas said, "Bob Tubbs, if he was working for the Grant campaign, might have posed some kind of danger to them. Maybe he wanted more money. Maybe he couldn't keep his mouth shut, maybe he wanted credit for taking down a senator. Who knows?—but he may have represented some kind of danger. And you've got these guys right there—"

"You don't have a fuckin' thing on them, do you?" Flowers asked.

"Not a fuckin' thing," Lucas said. "Which is why I brought you in. I want you to tell me: if a guy disappears without a trace, and you have these two guys hanging around . . . what are the chances?"

"You don't need me to figure that out. You already have," Flowers said, kicking his feet off the desk. "You just want me to say you're right."

"Am I right?"

"Probably. What are you going to do about it?"

"Will I ever get any evidence against them?"

"Not unless something weird happens," Flowers said. "Listen, let me tell you. Strange things happen in combat areas. Unpleasant things have to be done . . . and somebody has to do them. But those things can't be pulled out in the open. The do-gooders would be screaming to high heaven and careers would be wrecked. You know, 'That's not how we do things in America.' Well, you know, sometimes it is. Look at bin Laden: he was executed, not killed in a gunfight. Everybody knows that, but he was so big, there's a national collective agreement not to mention it. When something like that happens, people like Carver are holding the gun. There was no way to hide the bin Laden thing, but in other cases . . . they have to hide what they did. The army *knows*, but it doesn't know. Even the do-gooders in the Congress *know*, but they don't want to hear it. It's like the guys in Vice, or Narcotics. They're like *you*, really. Sometimes, strange things need to get done."

"Okay."

"Now, I don't know what Carver did that got him kicked out, but it was serious, and he was lucky," Flowers said. "I'd say it's about ninety–ten that if he'd done the same thing as a cop, whatever it was, he'd have gone to prison. Whatever he did, he had to go—but at the same time, the army took care of him."

"What if I subpoenaed some colonel in here to get specific about what he did?"

Flowers snorted. "Never happen."

Lucas said, "We go to federal court—"

"It would take you ten years before you saw the guy's face, and then he wouldn't be able to remember anything specific," Flowers said. "I'm not kidding you, Lucas. It wouldn't happen."

"So what do I do?" Lucas asked.

Flowers stood up and yawned and stretched. "I don't know. Sneak around. Plot. Manipulate. Lie, cheat, and steal. Do what the army did—settle it off the record. Or, forget it."

"I got one senator, one governor, and one would-be senator pointing guns at my head."

"If they take you down, can I have your job?" Flowers asked.

Lucas didn't smile. He said, "Careful what you wish for, Virg."

Virgil: "Hey. I wasn't serious."

"I am," Lucas said.

Lucas took Flowers to lunch, and they talked about it some more, and about life in general. Flowers had recently come off a case where he'd run down four out of five murderers. Three of them had been killed—none of them by Flowers—one was in Stillwater for thirty years, and one was walking around free. Flowers had been unhappy about the one who walked—and Lucas had argued that he'd done as much as he could, and that overall, justice had been served, even if the law hadn't gotten every possible ounce of flesh.

Now Flowers was arguing the same thing back to him. If Dannon and Carver had killed Tubbs, Lucas wouldn't find out about it except by accident. If justice were to be done, it would have to be extrajudicial.

"You think I should push them into a gunfight?" Lucas asked, only half-jokingly.

"Oh, Jesus, no. It'd be fifty-fifty that you'd lose," Flowers said. "If you took on both of them, it'd be seventy-thirty."

Lucas said nothing.

"Of course, if you *did* lose, at least you'd die knowing that I'd be here to take care of Weather," Flowers said.

"It's good to know you have friends," Lucas said.

WHEN FLOWERS LEFT—he said he was headed for the St. Croix River to check out possible environmental crimes, which meant that he was going fishing—Lucas went back to the BCA and shut his office door, sat in the chair where Flowers had been sitting, and put his feet up in the same spot.

If Dannon and Carver had been involved in the murder of Tubbs (if Tubbs *had* been murdered—the small possibility that he hadn't been wriggled away at the back of his thoughts), there were two possibilities: that one of them had done it on his own, and the other didn't know about it; or, more likely, that both of them were involved.

What about Grant? Did she know? He considered that for a while, and finally concluded that there was no way to tell. If she did know, or if she suspected, she'd be the weak link. He'd be tempted to go after her under any normal circumstances, but the circumstances were anything but normal. With a razor's-edge election coming up, any suggestion by a police official that she might know about a murder could tip the balance. And with no evidence on which to base the probe, that police officer could be in a lot of trouble if his suggestion didn't pan out.

For practical purposes, he'd have to confine his investigation to Dannon and Carver.

He thought about them for a while—about what Flowers had seen in their records—and then picked up his phone. The woman on the other end said, "It's been a while."

"You got time for tea?" Lucas asked.

"A social occasion? Trading information about old friends, and who's been up to what?"

"We can do that, too."

They took tea at a Thai place on Grand Avenue. Sister Mary Joseph was exactly Lucas's age; they'd walked hand in hand to kindergarten, when she was simply Elle. She might well have been, Lucas thought, when he thought about it, the first female he'd loved, though they'd gone through life on radically different paths. She'd chosen the nunnery and he'd chosen the craziest possible contact with the world.

But their paths had continued to cross: she'd become a professor of psychology at the University of St. Patrick and the College of St. Anne, and because of Lucas, had taken an interest in criminal pathology. She'd worked in most of the state's prisons, including those for the criminally insane.

Lucas got to the Thai place first, and she came in ten minutes later. In the early years she'd worn a full habit, and had persisted for years after most nuns had gone to modern dress. She'd finally changed over, and now wore what Lucas called "the drabs": brown or gray dresses and long stockings with a little brown coif stuck on top of her head like the vanilla twist on a Dairy Queen cone.

She slid into the booth opposite him and asked, "What's the problem?"

"How you doing, Elle?"

"I'm doing fine, but I'm running a little late."

Lucas told her about Dannon, Carver, and Grant, about what he thought and what Flowers thought. He paused while she ordered a cup of chai, and he got a second Diet Coke, and then continued. When he finished, she took a sip of tea, then said, "You know there are no guarantees."

"Of course."

"Go after Dannon," she said. "Dannon is the thinker and probably a manipulator. He'll try to figure a way out. Carver would consider that unmanly. He'd clam up, and if necessary, take one for the team. He'd sit there and say, 'Prove it.' Dannon might *say* the same thing, but he'd be looking for a way out."

"Dannon wouldn't take one for the team."

She made a moue, then said, "There's one exception. If he is, in fact, in love with Ms. Grant, he might take one for her . . . if she's involved. If he thinks Carver acted alone, he might also turn on Carver. Not because he wanted to, but to protect Ms. Grant."

Lucas said, "A hero."

"Yes. In his own eyes. Have you considered the possibility that Ms. Grant was involved in the killing?"

"I have, but there's no way to know. I can see Dannon or Carver doing it, but Grant, with all that she's got going for her, and the campaign . . . it seems nuts."

"Yes, but step back," Elle said. "Consider that fact that if they were going to take the risk of playing this dirty trick on Senator Smalls, she almost had to know about it—that something was up. Maybe not the details. When Tubbs disappeared, she most likely would make an . . . assumption. She probably would have asked some questions. Whether anybody would answer her, I don't know. That depends on all the different personalities involved."

Lucas explained that he didn't feel that he could go directly after her: that it would be unfair if she was innocent, and that too much was on the line.

"So go after Dannon . . . but ask that she be there when you question him. He might not give up much, but keep an eye on her. On her reaction. Is she astonished that anyone would think that Dannon could do it? Or is she worried? Does she try to protect him, or does she throw him under the bus? Does she feel like she can't throw him under the bus? That could tell you a lot, and it'd be a private session. Nothing leaking to the press."

ELLE WAS ON HER WAY to a piano recital, so Lucas walked her back to her car, and they agreed she'd come over to Lucas's house the following week for dinner. When she was gone, he wandered along the street, looking into windows, thinking about the possibilities, and a couple of blocks down the street took a call from the governor: "I saw the piece in the paper this morning," Henderson said. "Was that you, trying to break something loose?"

"Not necessarily," Lucas said. "Listen, what would you think about the idea of suspending the investigation until after the election? If Grant is involved, we could take her down even if she got elected. But I'm starting to worry about the fairness of it all."

"Let me worry about that," the governor said. "Do you have any indication that the Grant campaign was involved in . . . Tubbs's disappearance?"

"No proof. But Grant has a couple of killers working for her." Lucas filled him in on Dannon and Carver.

"Okay. You keep pushing, but no more press," Henderson said. "No more talking with Ruffe. No comments to anyone. I will have a press conference, and I will tell everybody that I spoke to the lead investigator in the case—that would be you—and that while you have established that the child porn was an attack on Senator Smalls, and that he almost certainly is innocent, that there is, at this point, no indication that the Grant campaign was involved. I will say that it appears likely that Tubbs was working alone, out of a personal animus toward Smalls. I'll ask Porter to back me up. He'll do that."

"Why do you think he'd do that? He's pretty goddamn angry," Lucas said.

"Because I'll call him before the press conference, and I'll tell him what I propose to say, and tell him if he doesn't back me up, I won't have the press conference," Henderson said. "The press conference will get him in the clear in tomorrow morning's papers and TV, which he desperately needs."

"All right. I'll keep it quiet."

"Attaboy. This thing is going to work out, Lucas. For us. It really shouldn't matter whether we get the killer this week or in two weeks. What matters right now is to try to square up this election. Let's focus on that: you do what you do, and let me try to get things straight with the voters."

"That sounded like something your weasel wrote," Lucas said.

"Who do you think taught him his stuff? If anything new erupts, call me, first."

A LITTLE LATER, as he was driving back to his house, he took another call, this one from Kidd. "I'm not too far from your place. You got time for a walk?"

"I'm on my way there, now," Lucas said. "What's up?"

"Let's talk about it when I get there. Radios make me nervous."

Lucas realized he was talking about cell phones, and said, "See you there."

Lucas had just pulled into his garage when Kidd showed up, driving a Mercedes SUV. Lucas said, "Fat ride. That's spelled P-H-A-T."

Kidd: "Wrong century, pal. Phat was about 1990."

"That's the second time one of you computer people told me I was outdated."

"Well, you gotta keep up," Kidd said. He paused, looked up at the sky, then said, "You know, I take that back. Really, maybe you don't need to keep up. Maybe keeping up is for idiots."

"Let's take that walk," Lucas said.

They strolled up Mississippi River Boulevard, taking their time. Kidd asked, "You get anything out of those army docs?"

"I had one of my guys look at them—he's ex-army, an MP captain. He said Dannon and Carver are dangerous guys."

"He's right," Kidd said. He had his hands in his pockets and half turned to Lucas. "I want to tell you some stuff, but I don't want it coming back to me, or showing up in court. It's for your information—and I'm giving it to you because I trust you, and because you may need it."

"You didn't stick up a 7-Eleven store?"

"Worse," Kidd said. "I stole military secrets."

"I got no problem with that," Lucas said. "What'd they say?"

"After I pulled those docs out of the record center, I did some more digging around," Kidd said. "It turns out, there's a classified report on what happened with Carver. There was no way I could get it to you by 'mistake.' "

"Okay."

"The short version of it is, he and a squad of special operations troops flew into a village in southern Afghanistan in two Blackhawks, with a gunship flying support. They were targeting a house where two Taliban leadership guys were hiding out with their bodyguards. They landed, hit the house, there was a short fight there, they killed one man, but they'd caught the Taliban guys while they were sleeping. They controlled and handcuffed the guys they were looking for, and had five of their bodyguards on the floor. Then the village came down on them like a ton of bricks. Instead of just being the two guys with their bodyguards, there were like fifty or sixty Taliban in there. There was no way to haul out the guys they'd arrested—there was nothing they could do but run. They got out by the skin of their teeth."

"What about Carver?" Lucas asked.

"Carver was the last guy out of the house. Turns out, the Taliban guys they'd handcuffed were executed. So were the bodyguards, and two of them were kids. Eleven or twelve years old. Armed, you know, but . . . kids."

"Yeah."

"An army investigator recommended that Carver be charged with murder, but it was quashed by the command in Afghanistan— deaths in the course of combat," Kidd said. "The investigator protested, but he was a career guy, a major, and eventually he shut up."

"Would he talk now? I need something that would open Carver up."

"I don't think so," Kidd said. "He's just made lieutenant colonel. He's never going to get a star, but if he behaves, he could get his birds before he retires."

"Birds?"

"Eagles. He could be promoted to colonel. That's a nice retirement bump for guys who behave. But, there's another guy. The second-to-the-last guy out. He's apparently the one who saw the executions and made the initial report. He's out of the army now. He lives down in Albuquerque."

"I've got no time to go to Albuquerque," Lucas said.

Kidd shrugged: "That's your problem. I'm passing along the information. He's there, he apparently had some pretty strong feelings about what he saw. They might even have pushed him out of the army. Up until then, he looked like he'd probably be a lifer. Same general profile as Carver's, but a few years younger. He was an E-6, a staff sergeant."

"You got a name and address?"

"Yeah, I do. Dale Rodriguez is the name." Kidd dug into

his hip pocket, pulled out a sheet of white paper. "Here's the address."

Lucas took the paper, stuck it in his own pocket. "How do I explain finding this?"

"On those docs you got from the army records center, Carver's last unit is listed. If you search for the unit on Facebook, you'll find a half-dozen different guys listing it as part of their biographies. Rodriguez is one of them."

"Ah. I've got a researcher who is good with Facebook and all that."

"You might have to get in touch with all of them as a cover for contacting Rodriguez."

"That can be done," Lucas said.

"And keep me out of it."

"You're gonna have to tell me someday how you come to have access to all this information. Government secrets. It can't be legal," Lucas said.

"Probably not entirely legal," Kidd said, scuffing along the street. "I've been doing this forever, from before there was an Internet. My access just grew. From the early hacking days, fooling around, back in the eighties. Now . . . I do databases. When I do computers at all, which isn't that often anymore."

"With a specialty in revealing secrets."

"Not really," Kidd said. "Sometimes I go looking for information, and I stumble over stuff that should be out there, in public. Secrets that shouldn't be secrets. Some stuff *should* be secret—I'm not going to give away any biowarfare docs—but a lot of other stuff is criminal and gets covered up."

"I'm seeing some of that right now, on the local level," Lucas said.

"Yeah. Embezzlement gets covered up, nepotism, favors for special groups or corporations that can run into billions of dollars . . . special access. At the federal level, a lot of it gets classified one way or the other. I see no reason to honor that. It's crime, plain and simple."

CHAPTER 16

Dannon was waiting by the door when Taryn got back, late, from a campaign rally. She was getting beat up: she'd been to East Grand Forks, on the North Dakota border, early that morning, had flown to International Falls, on the Canadian border, in the afternoon, and in the evening, had been in Duluth, on the Wisconsin border, where the cars met her and brought her back home.

The campaign had been shifting: it was all TV, and appearances that were sure to make TV, especially in those cities where they could still move votes. No more one-on-one talks, no more gatherings of the influential money men. It was too late for that. Now, it was all the downhill rush to Election Day, three days out.

When Taryn came in the house, trailed by Carver, Alice Green, and Connie Schiffer, the campaign manager, Carver peered at Taryn, hard, and she gave a terse nod and said to Green, "We're all done, Alice. You can take off. Six o'clock tomorrow morning."

Green said, "Thank you, ma'am. Six a.m. You try to get some sleep." Green turned and left.

"Good advice," said Schiffer to Taryn. "My butt is worn-out. And that goddamn Henderson."

"At least he gave us a little break," Taryn said. The governor had emphasized, at his press conference, that Tubbs had probably been working alone. Smalls, at a later press conference, hadn't challenged that assessment, and had said that it was time to get the election back on track. "Henderson seemed like he was trying to get everything back to neutral."

"I'd prefer a neutral in our favor," Schiffer said. "But you've got to be ready for the questions, tomorrow, about this Knoedler girl."

"Yeah, yeah . . ." Taryn waved her off: they'd talked about it in the car. "If you think of anything else, call me on the way home: I'll be up for another half hour."

"No Ambien," Schiffer said. "We don't need you stoned or sleep-walking if we wind up on one of the earlier shows."

Taryn nodded and said, "Take off." And to Carver and Dannon, "Set up the security. I'm going to look at the schedule and think in bed for a while."

Schiffer left, pausing to say, "We're still good. We've got four points, but we can't take any more erosion. Two points and we're tied and we lose control."

"Gotcha."

As Schiffer was leaving, Dannon asked Carver to do a serious look around the yard. One of the radar buzzers had been going off, Dannon said, and he hadn't been able to isolate why.

"Probably another goddamn skunk," Carver said. He pulled his jacket back on and went to look.

When he was gone, Taryn turned to Dannon and asked, "What?"

"I talked to Quintana," Dannon said. "He says that Davenport somehow figured out where the porn came from. He and the internal affairs officer at the Minneapolis Police Department are digging around, and Quintana says his name is going to come up. He thinks he can stay clear—but before he knew that Davenport was digging around, he went over to the Smalls campaign headquarters and talked to . . . the woman who set up the trap."

"Not this Knoedler girl?"

"No."

"That's a relief," Taryn said. "Might as well tell me the name of the real one."

Dannon shook his head. "Not yet. Really, it's a psychological issue—it's hard to fake surprise or confusion if you're not surprised or confused. Anyway, Quintana is afraid that if Davenport finds the source, she'll tell him that Quintana already talked to her. And there's no good reason he should have . . . or that he should have talked to her specifically. So if she mentions Quintana, they'll know he was likely the source of the porn, and he's in very deep shit. Like, going-to-prison deep shit. At that point, we don't know what happens. He didn't make any threats, but I gotta believe that he'll cooperate if he's given a break. Quintana doesn't know who I am, but he's a cop, and if I'm dragged into this, he might recognize my voice."

"What are you saying?" Taryn asked, one hand on her hip, her fist clenched.

Dannon hesitated, then said, "I think this woman . . . has to go away. If she goes away, she can't give up Quintana."

"Oh, Jesus Christ."

She stared at him for a moment, and he said hastily, "Don't worry about it. Don't think about it."

"One question. Why not Quintana himself?"

"Harder target. He might already be on edge, he carries a gun, he's been in a couple of shootings. If something went wrong . . . Anyway, I've been out scouting around. The woman is easy, and it'll be clean."

She continued to stare at him, he didn't flinch, but felt it, and then she said, "I have a personal question for you. I . . . it seems like I've seen certain things in you. Do you . . . have some feelings for me? Something I should know about?"

He shrugged again, and then said, as though he didn't want to, "Well . . . sure. For quite a while."

"I've had some of that myself," Taryn said. "There's nothing I can do about it right now—I have to be steady with David, for appearances' sake. I can't seem like I might be flighty, or that I play around. I wanted you to know that David is on his way out. He doesn't know, I'll wait until after the election to tell him. But then, you and I . . . we'll talk."

"Only talk?"

She gave him her best smile. "I don't know what will happen. But I need somebody like you . . . and for more than a bodyguard." She looked at her watch. "We'll talk about this. . . . Right now, I need some sleep."

Dannon was left standing in the living room; as she turned into the hallway to the bedroom wing, she flashed another bright smile at him. He'd never expected that. And he never expected the result: his heart was singing. He'd heard about that happening, but he'd never before felt it.

He walked around for a while, enjoying the glow. The glow never really faded, but he moved on to thinking a little wider, a little broader . . . and after a while, he made an executive decision.

LATE THAT NIGHT:

Dannon walked down the street, moving carefully, watching the car lights. Cop cars had a peculiar look to them: if they weren't going fast, they were going slow. They were big, and they were sedans. He didn't want to be seen anywhere near this particular house.

He was nearly invisible in a black cotton jacket and black slacks; there were almost no lights around, and lots of little clumps of hedge and old trees and crumbling concrete pillars that had once been decorative.

He was told that it was a bad neighborhood, though he'd been in much worse; in fact, he'd been in a dive an hour before that he thought he might have to shoot his way out of. Still, this wasn't exactly a well-lit park: he had yet to see a single soul on the street.

Though wickedly aware of his surroundings, he didn't look around; looking around attracted the eye. People who saw him would ask themselves, "Why's that guy looking around like that?" He'd learned not to do it.

He came up to the house—he'd passed it a few minutes earlier, moving much faster, checking it out—but now he crossed the woman's lawn, avoiding the concrete steps that led up the front bank. The storm door was unlatched, which made things that much easier. He opened it, quietly, quietly, took off one glove, slipped the lock-pick into the lock on the main door, worked the pins, kept the tensioner tight, felt it click once, twice and then turn. He put the glove back on.

He opened the inner door, slowly, slowly, and stepped inside, leaving the door cracked open. He took the pistol out of his pocket, waited for his eyes to fully adjust, saw a movement at the corner of his eye. A cat slipped away into the dark hallway, looking back at him.

When he was sure that nothing was moving, he took a telephone from his pocket, selected a quiet old song, "Heart of Glass" by Blondie, and turned it on. The music tinkled out into the dark, quiet, pretty . . . disturbing.

A woman's voice: "Hello? Is there somebody there? I'm calling the police."

He thought, *No, she isn't*.

"Hello?"

The hallway light clicked on, and the music played on.

He heard her footfalls in the hallway, and then she appeared, wearing a cotton nightgown.

Dannon shot her in the heart.

For Taryn.

He didn't look at the woman's face as she stepped back, stricken, put her hand to her chest, and said, "Awwww . . ." He reached out with his plastic-gloved hand, hit her in the face with the barrel of the pistol and she went down. Her feet thrashed, and he waited, and waited, and she went still. He stepped over her, walked down the hall to the bedroom, turned on the light, and took her purse, and tipped over a small jewelry case, took her cell phone, which was on the bed stand.

He'd been inside for about a minute, and the clock in his head said he should leave. He went back through the hall, checked the woman's still body.

She was gone, no question of it. He fished a plastic bag out of his jacket pocket, shook out a glove, carefully rolled her body back, slipped the glove beneath it, and then let the body roll back in place. Okay. This was all right.

Ninety seconds after he entered the house, he was out. He walked two blocks to his car, started up, then cruised as quietly as he could past the woman's house. As he passed by, he picked up a cigarette lighter and a cherry bomb from the passenger seat, lit the cherry bomb, and dropped it out the window. He was a hundred yards up the street when he heard it go off.

He did that because, at that moment, Carver was at Dannon's town house, sending an e-mail to Grant, under Dannon's name. When he'd done that, Carver would go back to his own town house, wait a few minutes, then make a phone call to a Duluth hotel, to see if they'd found a Mont Blanc pen. Then he'd go browse pens on Amazon and eBay. There'd be time stamps on all of that, if the cops came looking.

Two minutes after that, he dropped the thoroughly clean gun into a nearly full trash dumpster behind a restaurant. It would be at the landfill the next day. He took the money and credit cards out of the purse and threw the purse into a patch of weeds.

The plastic bag went in another dumpster, a mile from his apartment. The credit cards went down a sewer, the cash in his pocket.

Clean hit.

CHAPTER 17

Lucas was up early the next morning, went for a run, got home and called his part-time researcher, a woman named Sandy. He told her that he needed her to work on a semi-emergency basis. He wanted all the names she could find for Carver's last military unit, and said he was especially interested in people who were no longer with the military. "Check the social media—all your usual sources. If you find anybody, I want to know what they're doing."

He'd just gotten out of the post-run shower when Turk Cochran called from Minneapolis Homicide.

Cochran said, "Hey, big guy. The word is, you've been snooping around city hall, trying to figure out if somebody over here supplied Porter Smalls's kiddie porn."

"You calling to confess?"

"Yeah, I did it with my little laptop. No wait, I meant my little lap dance, not laptop. Is this call being recorded?"

"What's up, Turk?" Cochran hadn't called simply to crack wise.

"What I meant to say is, some really bad person broke into Helen Roman's house last night and shot her to death. I was told that this particular murder might be of interest to yourself."

"Helen Roman?" For a moment, Lucas drew a blank. He *knew*

that name. . . . "*Helen Roman?* Smalls's secretary? Somebody killed her?"

"That's what I'm saying. Looks sorta like a robbery, but sorta not like a robbery. You want to take a look?"

"Tell me where. I'll be there." Lucas had taken any number of calls about murders: this one had his heart thumping.

HELEN ROMAN'S SMALL HOUSE was on the outskirts of what the Minneapolis media called "North Minneapolis." That was the approved code designation for "black people," usually referred to, further down in the story, as the "community," as in "community leaders asked, 'How come you crackers never talk about white junkies getting aced in East Minneapolis?' "

Lucas left the Porsche at the curb, said hello to a patrol sergeant he'd known for twenty years or so, and crossed the lawn to the small front porch, where Cochran was sitting in an aluminum lawn chair. Cochran was a big man, fleshy-faced with a gut, and the lawn chair was his, kept in the trunk of his car, so he'd have somewhere to sit when he was working around a crime scene.

"Why's it *not* like a robbery?" Lucas asked.

"Didn't take enough stuff," Cochran said. He was wearing gray flannel slacks, a red tie, and a blue blazer; he looked like a New York doorman. "She had quite a bit of takable stuff, lying around loose. The thing is, when something like this happens, either the shooter runs, instantly, or he stays around long enough to accomplish the mission. It's not very often that they stay around for fifteen seconds. It's either nothing, or five minutes. But why am I telling *you* that?"

"I would not be confident in that generalization when applied to a specific case," Lucas said.

"Jeez, you know a lot of big words," Cochran said. "If I understood them all, I agree—*somebody* might stay around for fifteen seconds, like this guy did, but not often."

"You got a time for it?"

"Right around one in the morning. Actually, since you ask, about five after one. A guy was watching TV up the street, heard a shot. If that was *the* shot. The thing is, he said it sounded like a shotgun: a big BOOM. I asked him if he knew what a shotgun sounded like, and he said yeah, he's a turkey hunter. But: the medical examiner's guy tells me that it looks like Roman was shot by a small-caliber weapon, probably a .22. Inside the house. Windows and doors all closed. I'm not even sure that could be heard, five houses away."

Lucas said, "Huh." And, "So you haven't figured out the *boom*."

"No, but who knows? Maybe that *was* the shot. The ME's guy says it looks pretty consistent with a one-o'clock shooting, the condition of the blood and the body temp."

"Who found the body?"

"A woman named Carmen West," Cochran said. "She puts up lawn signs for Smalls around the north end."

"Sounds like dangerous work," Lucas said.

"You mean because Smalls is a right-wing devil, and right-wing devils are not liked on the north side?"

"Something like that. Anyway . . ."

"Roman was supposed to be at work at six o'clock this morning," Cochran said. "Last days of the campaign, and all that. When she didn't show by eight, somebody at the office phoned West and asked her to knock on Roman's door. West said the door was open. . . . She looked in, and saw Roman in the hallway. Called 911."

"All that seems legit?"

"Yeah, it does." Cochran pushed himself out of his chair. "Come on in, I'll show you around."

Lucas followed him up to the porch and Cochran said, "Notice the door."

"Nothing there," Lucas said, checking out the door.

"It wasn't forced," Cochran said. "We can't find *anything* forced. Either the door was unlocked, which seems unlikely for a single woman, or the guy had a key. We talked to the neighbors, who said she didn't have a housekeeper, and her only relative—an heir—is her daughter, who lives in Austin, Texas, and was there this morning and took our call."

"Roman didn't have a boyfriend?"

"Daughter says no. She said they talked once or twice a week."

LUCAS HAD BEEN TO all kinds of murder scenes in his career, and this was like most of them: that is, like nothing in particular. Another house with a worn couch and a newer TV and personal photos on the wall. A kitchen smelling of last night's single-serving pepperoni pizza, dishes in the kitchen sink, waiting to be washed, but now with nobody to wash them.

And, of course, a dead body in the hallway.

Roman was flat on her back, her hands crossed on her chest. She had a slash across her face, which Cochran thought might have come from a gun sight. Her eyes were closed, which was better than open, for the cops, anyway; for Roman, it made no difference. "It looks like the shooter encountered her in the hallway, hit her with the gun, then shot her," Cochran said.

"Or vice versa."

"Could be. Can't tell her posture when she was hit, because the bullet's still inside. No exit, no trajectory." As he spoke, Lucas heard a gust of laughter, from somewhere behind the house: children playing.

"Goddamnit. I need to talk with her," Lucas said, looking down at the body. "I mean, we could have either a multiple murderer, or a freakin' weird coincidence."

"I might be able to help you with that, with the one-or-the-other," Cochran said. He squatted, carefully, dug inside his jacket for a pencil, and pointed the pencil at a patch of black fabric under one of her arms. "See that? That's a man's glove. It's pinned under her. There's only one glove, nothing else like it in the house. We're thinking . . ."

"Could be the killer's."

"Yeah. Either pulled off, or dropped out of a pocket," Cochran said. "Anyway, there's gonna be all kinds of DNA in it. If we get lucky . . ."

If they got lucky, they'd get a cold hit from the Minnesota DNA bank. All felons in Minnesota were DNA-typed.

"How soon?"

"Tomorrow morning. It'll be our top priority," Cochran said.

"I may send you a couple of swabs."

"Yeah?"

"Maybe," Lucas said.

LUCAS SAW A TOTE BAG sitting by the corner of the bed, and what appeared to be the silvery corner of a laptop poking out of it. "Would you mind taking the laptop out and turning it on?"

Cochran said, "No, I don't mind. . . . It doesn't seem too connected to the shooting scene. But it should have been stolen." He slipped the laptop out and said, "This isn't good."

"What?"

"It's a Mac PowerBook, like mine. The first screen you come to is gonna want a password."

"Let's give it a try," Lucas said. Cochran didn't want to put it down on anything the killer might have touched, so they carried it back outside, and he handed the laptop to Lucas and sat down in his lawn chair. Lucas sat on the stoop below him and turned it on. When they got to the password, Lucas asked, "What was the daughter's name?"

"Callie . . . Roman."

Lucas typed "Callie" into the password slot, and the computer opened up.

"Christ, it's like you're a detective," Cochran said.

Lucas went to the e-mail and started scrolling backwards. He found a BLTUBBS on the second page down, turned to Cochran and said, "It's not a robbery."

"Do tell?"

"Well, maybe not. But if it is, we really are ass-deep in coincidence."

He found a half-dozen messages from Tubbs in the past three weeks. Tubbs and Roman had been talking about something, but the messages were never specific. "Call you this evening . . ." and "Where will you be tonight?"

The replies were as short and nonspecific as the questions. The only thing that might mean something was a note from Tubbs that said: "Got the package. Talk to you tonight. Call me when you get home." The message was sent four days before the porn popped up on Smalls's computer. The last access of the pornography on the Minneapolis police computers had been five days before.

Lucas asked Cochran, "Cell phone?"

He shook his head. "No cell phone, but she didn't have a land-line, either. The killer took the cell. Like he should have taken the computer," Cochran said. "You want to give me the whole run-down on this?"

LUCAS SHUT DOWN the computer and handed it back to Coch-ran, stood up, dusted off the seat of his pants, leaned against the porch banister, and told him about the investigation, leaving out only what was necessary. When he was done, Cochran said, "You never talked to her? I mean, you talked to her, but you didn't inter-view her?"

Lucas rubbed his face and said, "Man, it's like the old joke. Ex-cept the joke's on me."

"What joke?"

"The one about the guy who rolls a wheelbarrow full of saw-dust out of a construction site every night."

"I don't know that one," Cochran said.

Lucas said, "The security guy keeps checking and checking and checking the wheelbarrow, thinking the guy had to be stealing something. Never found anything hidden in the sawdust, and no-body cared about the sawdust. Couple of years later, they bump into each other, and the security guy says, 'Look, it's all in the past, you can tell me now. I know you were stealing something. What was it?' And the guy says, 'Wheelbarrows.'"

Lucas continued, "I was convinced that the person who set the trap had to have been planted on the Smalls campaign, which meant somebody new—a volunteer, or a new hire. I interviewed all the likely suspects. But she's one of his oldest employees. I talked to her every time I went there, and it never occurred to me to question *her*."

"She was the wheelbarrow."

"Yeah. She was the fuckin' wheelbarrow. Right there in front of my eyes."

"Fuckin's right," Cochran said. "C'mere. I got a special surprise."

He heaved himself out of his chair and Lucas followed him back into the house and into the bedroom. Cochran took a plastic glove out of his jacket pocket, pulled it on, and opened the bottom drawer on the bedside table. He took out a framed photograph and turned it in his gloved hand so Lucas could see it in the light from the bedroom window.

Helen Roman, at least ten years younger, sitting on Porter Smalls's lap in a poolside chaise, somewhere with palm trees. Drinks on the deck below the chair.

Lucas looked at Cochran, who nodded: "Jilted lover?"

"At least. Several times by now," Lucas said. He looked around the bedroom, and out the door into the lonely little dilapidated house, and thought about Smalls's resort out on the lake. "She must have been pissed. You know what I'm sayin'?"

WORD OF ROMAN'S DEATH was going to get out soon enough, but Cochran hadn't begun any notifications, other than the daughter. The woman who found the body had been sequestered, and hadn't called the campaign or anyone else.

Lucas told Cochran that he was going to talk to Smalls, and Cochran nodded, but when Lucas called, Smalls's phone clicked over to the answering service, as Smalls had warned him it often might. He turned it off when he was speaking, and he'd said he'd be speaking almost constantly in the week before the election. Lucas phoned Smalls's headquarters and was told that the senator was, at that moment, appearing at a Baptist megachurch in Bloomington, on the south side of the metro area.

Lucas got the address, plugged it into his nav, and took off. On the way, he called Grant, and was again forwarded to the answering service. He'd gotten Grant's campaign manager's number, called that, and got Schiffer. "Where's Ms. Grant?" he asked, after identifying himself.

"Is there a problem?"

"You might say so. I need to meet with Ms. Grant and her security people, especially Douglas Dannon and Ronald Carver. I assume Ms. Green will be there as well?"

"Well, Carver isn't with us. . . . I suppose we can call him, if it's urgent."

"It's urgent. Where are you?"

"I'm in Afton. We're setting up for a rally in the park and a luncheon. Taryn's in Stillwater right now, she'll be going to Bayport in, mmm, fifteen minutes, and Lakeland at eleven-fifteen and Afton at noon."

"How about Afton at eleven-thirty?"

"I'll tell her to push everything up a bit, if it's really urgent. We'll be in the park. Look for the TV trucks."

"It's urgent. I'll see you at eleven-thirty in the park."

He made one more call, to the governor, who answered with a "What now?"

"Somebody murdered Porter Smalls's secretary last night," Lucas said. "Smalls had a sexual relationship with her and broke it off. Years ago, though. She was probably the one who set up the trigger on the computer."

Long silence. Then, "Jesus, Lucas, who killed her?"

"I have some ideas . . . but now I don't know what's going to happen," Lucas said. "I wanted to let you know, though: the whole thing might be headed over the cliff, again."

"Think I'll go to North Dakota. There are some border issues to deal with."

"Not a bad idea," Lucas said.

THE MEGACHURCH HAD PARKING for perhaps a thousand cars, and on this Sunday morning, there were probably twelve hundred jammed into the lot. Lucas walked into the entry and saw Smalls standing at a rostrum at the front of the church.

He'd apparently finished his talk and was answering questions. Lucas threaded his way through the crowded pews to the front, and stood waiting until Smalls saw him. When Smalls turned his way, Lucas tipped his head toward the back, and Smalls nodded at him and then said, "You know, folks, I could stand here and talk all day, but I've got another rally I've got to go to. You can reach me online with any more questions, and I can promise, you'll get an answer. Let's take two more questions. The lady in front, with the green blouse . . ."

Five minutes later, led by a security man, with another one trailing behind, and his campaign manager walking beside him, Smalls headed for a side door. Lucas walked that way. Smalls waited at the door until he caught up, and then led the way into a back hallway.

Lucas said, "We need to talk privately."

Smalls said, "It can't be good news."

"No . . ."

Smalls said, "Hang on," and walked back to the people who'd come through the door behind them, spoke to one, who pointed down the hall. Smalls walked back to Lucas and said, "Come on. I'd like Ralph to come along."

Ralph Cox was his campaign manager. He was a tall, ruddy-faced man with curly black hair and overlong sideburns. Lucas nodded to Smalls and said, "That's up to you," and followed Smalls down the hall to an office. Smalls opened the door, and the three of them stepped inside.

Lucas pushed the door shut and asked, "You had an affair with Helen Roman?"

After a long pause, Smalls said, "Years ago."

"Did she think that it might lead to something permanent?" Lucas asked.

"What's going on? Is she the one who pushed the porn?"

"Would she have reason to?" Lucas asked.

Smalls wet his lower lip with his tongue, then said, "She was . . . disappointed when I broke it off. Pretty unhappy. I tried to make it up to her by overpaying her on the secretary's job. There might have been some bad feeling at the time, but . . . that was years ago."

Cox asked, "What happened? Have you arrested her?"

"She was murdered last night," Lucas said.

Smalls staggered, as though he'd been struck. He reached behind himself, found an office chair, and sank into it. "My God. Helen?"

"She was struck in the head, the face, then shot with a small-caliber pistol," Lucas said. "It looks at least superficially like a robbery, but I think . . . it's related. I opened her computer and found notes from Tubbs. They're cryptic—follow-ups on personal conversations. They don't mention porn. They don't even mention you. But Tubbs mentions that he's got some kind of package, and that's just a couple of days before somebody dropped the porn into your computer. Anyway, they had some kind of relationship. . . . I mean, maybe not sexual, but at least conversational. And it seemed like, conspiratorial."

Cox said to Smalls, "We've got to get on top of this, and *right now*. We've got to give it a direction. There are two possibilities— that Tubbs and the Democrats led her into it, for purely political reasons, and that she was killed by a coconspirator, or that she dumped the porn to ruin you, because she was bitter about the broken relationship. We've got to hit the Tubbs angle hard. We've got to steer it—"

"Shut up for a minute. You can talk about that later," Lucas said to him. Back to Smalls: "You said she was disappointed. How disappointed? You think she might have done the porn?"

"I don't know . . . maybe. Maybe she was a little resentful. I didn't think so for a long time, but in the last couple of years, she's been getting more and more distant."

"Ah, Jesus Christ on a crutch," Cox said.

Smalls: "Watch your mouth, Ralph. We're in a church. If they heard you . . ."

"Sorry. But for God's sakes, Porter, if this comes out the wrong way, the TV people will dig up every woman you've ever slept with, and from what I understand, there's a lot of them."

Lucas said, "Could we—"

Cox jumped in again. "I'm gonna leave you guys to talk. I gotta call Marianne and get something going. We got no time for this, no time."

And he was out the door.

"Who's Marianne?" Lucas asked.

"Media," Smalls said. He pushed himself out of his chair. "I'll tell you, Lucas, this is pretty much the end, for me. Ralph can do all the media twisting he wants, but it ain't gonna work."

"There's something else going on," Lucas said. He hesitated, thinking that he might be about to make a mistake. "It's possible that if Tubbs was working for the Grant campaign that he was killed to break the connection between the porn and the Grant campaign. And that the same people who killed him, killed Roman."

Smalls waved him off, with a hand that looked weary. "Yeah, yeah, but I'll tell you what, Lucas. Political campaigns don't have killers on their staffs. End of story."

Lucas looked at him, didn't say a word.

Smalls peered back, then said, "What?"

Lucas shrugged.

"What, goddamnit? Are you . . . Grant doesn't have a killer . . . ?" He was reading Lucas's face, as a politician can, and he said, "Jesus Christ, what'd you find out?"

"Watch the language," Lucas said. "This is a church."

"Don't hassle me, Lucas. This is my life we're talking about."

"Grant has these two bodyguards," Lucas said. "They were involved in some very rough stuff in Iraq and Afghanistan. One of them was pushed out of the army for something he did there. He killed a bunch of people he shouldn't have—executed them. Including a couple of kids. I talked to an ex-army guy, a BCA guy now, who understands these things, and he said these guys essentially specialized in killing and kidnapping."

Smalls took off his glasses, rubbed his face with his hands. "I . . . This is really hard to believe."

"I know. I'll tell you what, when you spend your life doing investigations, you become wary of coincidences. Because they happen. It's possible that there was a dirty trick, followed by two killings, at a critical moment in a political campaign, and it's all purely a coincidence that the person who most benefits had two killers standing around. I personally am not ready to believe that."

"What're you gonna do?"

"I'm gonna go jack them up. But they're smart, and I have no evidence. None. If they tell me to blow it out my ass, well . . ."

"Killers," Smalls said. "I tell you, politics has gotten rougher and rougher, but I never thought it could come to this. Never. But maybe . . . Now that I think about it, maybe it was inevitable."

LUCAS TOOK OFF FOR AFTON. Afton was a small town, one of the oldest in Minnesota, built on the wild and scenic river that separated Minnesota from Wisconsin. The river was gorgeous in the summer and early fall and at mid-winter, after the freeze; less so in the cold patch of November or the early rains of March. But this day, though November, was particularly fine.

Lucas went to the University of Minnesota on a hockey scholarship, but since you couldn't major in hockey—and his mother peed all over the idea, suggested by the coaches, that he major in physical education—he wound up in American studies, a combination of American literature, history, and politics. He did well in it, enjoyed it, and since it was commonly used as a pre-law major, he thought about becoming a lawyer like a number of his classmates.

After all the bullshit was sorted through, a levelheaded professor suggested that he try police work for a year or so. He could always go back to law school, or even go to law night school, if he didn't like the cops—and the time on the street would be invaluable for certain kinds of law practice.

Lucas joined the Minneapolis cops, and never looked back: but the four years in American studies stuck with him, especially the literature. He thought Emily Dickinson was perhaps the best writer America had ever produced; but on this day, heading east out of the Cities, then south down the river, he thought of how some of the writers, Poe and Hemingway in particular, used the weather to create the mood and reflect the meanings of their stories.

Poe in particular.

Lucas could still quote from memory the first few lines of "The Fall of the House of Usher": *During the whole of a dull, dark and soundless day in the autumn of the year, when the clouds hung oppressively low in the heavens, I had been passing alone, on horseback, through a singularly dreary tract of country, and at length found myself, as the shades of the evening drew on, within view of the melancholy House of Usher. . . .*

And Lucas thought what a literary conceit that all was: he'd gone to a murder scene on a beautiful fall day, and heard children laughing outside. And why not? The murder had nothing to do with them, and old people died all the time.

Now he, the hunter, was headed south to tackle a couple of probable killers, a fairly grim task; but over here, to the right of the highway as he went by, a man was washing down his fishing boat, preparing it for winter storage; and coming down the road toward him, a half-dozen old Corvettes, all in a line, tops down on a fine blue-sky day, the women in the passenger seats all older blondes, one after the other.

And why not? Life doesn't have to be a long patch of misery.

There was plenty of room for blondes of a certain age, to ride around in seventies Corvettes, like they'd done when they were girls; a few beers at Lerk's Bar, and then a dark side street with a hand up their skirts. That was still welcome, wasn't it?

He'd made himself smile with all the rumination. He really ought to lighten up more, Lucas thought, as the last of the Corvettes went past. Hell, what are a couple more killers in a lifetime full of them? And he liked hunting, and what better day to do it than a fine blue day in the autumn of the year, with not a cloud in the heavens, when riding through a singularly beautiful tract of country, in a Porsche with the top down?

Fuck a bunch of E. A. Poe.

And his Raven.

THE GRANT CARAVAN had pulled to the side of the street in what passed for downtown Afton. A small crowd was hanging around in the park across the street, and a cable TV station was setting up a small video camera in front of a bandstand. Grant and her people were apparently in an ice cream parlor.

Lucas dumped the Porsche and started across the street to the parlor. As he did, Alice Green came out the front door and moved to one side, and nodded toward Lucas; then Grant came out the door holding an ice cream cone, squinted at him in the sunlight, and licked the cone as he came up.

Lucas thought, Some women shouldn't be allowed to lick ice cream cones, because it threw men into a whole different mental state. . . .

Schiffer came out of the ice cream parlor, also licking an ice cream cone, with markedly less effect; she was followed by a tall, bullet-headed man with fast eyes who Lucas suspected was one of the bodyguards; his eyes locked on Lucas. Then another man came out, smaller than the first, but with the same fast eyes, and the same quick fix on Lucas. Lucas wanted to put a hand on his .45, but instead, called, "Ms. Grant—glad you had the time."

"What's so urgent?" she asked.

"These two gentlemen," Lucas said, flicking a finger at Carver and Dannon. "Are they Misters Carver and Dannon?"

Grant turned, as if checking, then turned back and said, "Yeah," and nibbled on the cone, which looked like a cherry-nut, one of Lucas's favorites.

"Then let's find a place where we can talk," Lucas said.

"Courtyard," Green said, nodding toward an empty outdoor dining space to the left of the ice cream parlor. "You don't want to talk to me?"

"Not at the moment," Lucas said. "You might keep people away? Even other staffers. This is sort of private."

Green nodded; Schiffer said, "I'm going to listen in."

They moved over to the empty space, Green hovering on the periphery, listening. Lucas said, "One of Porter Smalls's secretaries was murdered last night. Shot to death in her house, in Minneapolis. I went through her laptop and she'd been corresponding in a fairly cryptic way with Bob Tubbs before he disappeared, and just before the pornography popped up on Smalls's computer."

He'd been watching Carver and Dannon, and nothing moved in their eyes, which Lucas thought interesting, because he thought something should have.

Grant said, "Well, that's awful, but what does it have to do with us?"

"Tubbs is dead, I'm almost certain of it, at this point, and now

Helen Roman has been murdered. It was all done very well, from a professional-killing standpoint. Most people who kill for money are fools and idiots and misfits. This doesn't appear to be the work of fools."

Grant said, "Yeah, yeah," and made a rolling motion with one forefinger—*moving right along*—as she simultaneously took another nibble of the cherry-nut.

"Well, it's possible that she put the porn on Smalls's computer to get revenge on him," Lucas said. "They'd had some personal disagreements, apparently. But if that was what it was, a personal matter, why would anybody kill her? Or Tubbs?"

"Well, I don't know," Grant said. "Are you sure she was killed for that reason? Because it had something to do with Smalls?"

Lucas was forced to admit it: "No. Not absolutely sure. But pretty sure. The other possibility is that the people who paid for the porn to be dumped on Porter Smalls, knowing that doing so involves a number of felonies, are breaking the link between themselves and the pornography. Breaking the link very professionally. I did the obvious: I looked for professional killers. The only ones I could find"—Lucas nodded at Carver and Dannon—"are employed by you."

"What!" Schiffer blurted, not a question.

Lucas had been watching Carver and Dannon again, and again, their eyes were blank; if they'd been lizards, Lucas thought, a nictitating membrane might have dropped slowly across them.

"That . . ." Grant waved her arms dismissively. "I really do have to talk to somebody about you. Professional killers? They're decorated war veterans. Were you in the military? Did you—"

Dannon interrupted her, and said to Lucas, "We had nothing to do with anything like that. We're professional security guys, end of story. If you have any evidence of any sort, bring it out: we'll re-fute it."

"I want to have a crime-scene guy take DNA samples from you," Lucas said. "Doesn't hurt, nothing invasive—"

"DNA?" Grant sputtered. "You know what—"

"It's okay with us," Dannon said, and now there was something in his eye, a little spark of pleasure, a job well done. Lucas thought, *This isn't good.*

Grant snapped at Dannon: "Don't interrupt. I know that you had nothing to do with this, I know the DNA will come back nega-tive, but don't you see what he's doing? When the word gets out that my bodyguards have been DNA-typed in a murder case? This guy is working for Smalls—"

"No. I'm not," Lucas said. "I guarantee that nothing about the DNA samples will get out before the election. I'll get one guy to take the samples and I'll read him the riot act. He will not say a word, and neither will I. If word gets out, I'll track it, and if it's my guy, I'll see that he's fired and I'll try to put him in jail."

Grant, Schiffer, Carver, and Dannon exchanged glances, and then Grant said to Dannon, "You've got no problem with this?"

"No. It's probably what I'd do in his place." He showed a thin white smile: "Because, you know, he's right. We *are* trained killers."

He poked Carver in the ribs with an elbow, and Carver let out a long, low, rambling laugh, one of genuine amusement, and . . . smugness. Lucas thought, *They know something.*

WITH THEIR CASUAL ACQUIESCENCE to the DNA tests, Lucas was left stranded. He asked some perfunctory questions—where were you last night at one o'clock? (At our apartments.) Did anyone see you there? (No.) Any proof that you were there? (Made some phone calls, moved some documents on e-mail.) Can we see those? (Of course.) Did you know either Tubbs or Roman? (No.)

Lucas walked away and made a call, asking them to wait, got hold of a crime-scene specialist, and made arrangements for Carver and Dannon to be DNA-typed.

He went back to them and said, "We'd like you to stop in at BCA headquarters on your way back through St. Paul, anytime before five o'clock. You'll see a duty officer, tell him that you're Ronald and Douglas—you won't have to give your last name or any other identifier—and that you're there at my request, Lucas Davenport's request, to be DNA-typed. A guy will come down to do the swabs. This will take one minute, and then you can take off. The swabs will be marked Ronald and Douglas, no other identifiers."

Carver and Dannon nodded, and Grant said, "What a crock," and tossed the remains of her ice cream cone into a trash can. "If you're done with us, I'm going to go shake some hands. I'll tell you what—nothing about this better get out."

"It won't," Lucas said. To Carver and Dannon: "Don't go anywhere."

Grant led her entourage across the street, with Green lingering behind. She said to Lucas, "Interesting."

"They did it," Lucas said. "You take care, Alice."

"I can handle it," she said.

"You sure? You ever shot anyone?"

"No, but I could."

Lucas looked after Dannon and Carver: "If it should come to that—and it could, if they think you might have figured something out—don't give them a chance. If you do, they'll kill you."

CHAPTER 18

Ray Quintana was a fifty-one-year-old Minneapolis vice cop, a detective sergeant, and having thought about it, he figured that he'd thoroughly screwed the pooch, also known as having poked the pup or fucked the dog. He didn't know who'd been calling him about Helen Roman, but he suspected that who-ever it was had gone over to Roman's house the night before and killed her.

Quintana wasn't a bad cop; okay, not a terrible one. He might have picked up a roll of fifties off a floor in a crack house that didn't make it back to the evidence room; he might have found a few nice guns that the jerkwads didn't need anymore, that made their way to gun shows in Wisconsin; he might have done a little toot from time to time, the random scatterings of the local dope dealers.

But he'd put a lot of bad people in jail, and overall, given the op-portunities, and the stresses, not a bad guy.

When Tubbs had come to him, he'd put it out there as a straight business deal: Tubbs had heard from somewhere unknown that the Minneapolis Police Department had an outrageous file of kiddie porn. Quintana had known Tubbs since high school; Tubbs had been one of the slightly nerdy intellectuals on the edge of the popular clique, while Quintana had been metal shop and a football lineman.

Tubbs had said, "I'll give you five thousand dollars for that file. Nobody'll ever know, because hell, if I admit it went through my hands, I'd be in a lot more trouble than you."

Quintana had asked him what he was going to do with it, and Tubbs had told him: "I'm gonna use it to screw Porter Smalls. I'm gonna get Taryn Grant elected to the U.S. Senate. When that happens, I'll be fixed for life. I'll remember you, too."

Had Grant hired him?

"I don't know—I'm being funded anonymously," Tubbs said. "But that's obviously where it comes from. I got the cash, and enough to split off five thousand for you."

How much had Tubbs gotten?

"That's between me and Jesus," Tubbs said. "I'm taking all the risk. You get more than it's worth, and if you don't want the money—well, I'll get another file. I know they're floating around out there."

Quintana wanted the five grand. Hadn't really needed it, but he *wanted* it.

Quintana's problem now was that Marion from Internal Affairs was on the trail, as was Davenport. Quintana knew Davenport, had worked with him, both on patrol and as detectives; Davenport scared him. Eventually, he thought, they'd get to him. Tubbs hadn't exactly snuck into city hall. They might even have been seen talking together.

Quintana was thinking all of this at his desk, on a Sunday morning, staring at the wall behind it, over all the usual detective litter. He was so focused that his next-door desk neighbor asked, "You in there, Ray?"

"What?"

"I thought you were having a stroke or something."

Quintana shook his head. "Just tired."

"Then what are you doing in here? It's Sunday."

"I was thinking I shoulda gone to Hollywood and become an actor. I could have made the big time."

"Man, you *have* had a stroke."

He went back to staring.

His delivery of the porn file could get him jail time. Worse, he suspected that whoever was calling him had killed Roman. Even worse than that, he'd talked casually with Turk Cochran when he'd come in from Roman's place, and Cochran said that Davenport thought it might be a pro job.

Even worse than that . . . Quintana suspected the same pro might be coming to shut *him* up.

If Quintana kept his mouth shut, he might be killed as a clean-up measure. If he kept his mouth shut, Davenport could plausibly come after him as an accessory to murder, especially if word got out that he'd interviewed Roman, or had been seen with Tubbs.

That all looked really bad.

There was a bright side: Tubbs was presumably dead, and Roman certainly was. That meant that any story that he made up couldn't really be challenged. If he could just come up with something good enough, he would probably stay out of jail, and might even hang on to his pension. At least, the half that his ex-wife wasn't going to get.

But what was the story? How could he possibly justify handing the file over to Tubbs? He thought and thought, and finally concluded that he couldn't.

So he thought some more, and at one o'clock in the afternoon, picked up the phone and called the union rep at home, and said he needed to talk to the lawyer, right then, Sunday or not.

The union guy wanted to know what for, and Quintana said he really didn't want to know what for. At two o'clock, he was talking to the lawyer, and at two-thirty, they called Marion. The lawyer, whose name was James Meers, said Quintana needed to talk with Marion and probably with Davenport, as soon as possible. Immediately, if possible.

Lucas took the call from Marion, who said, "We got a break."

He'd set up the meeting for four o'clock.

LUCAS PARKED HIS PORSCHE in one of the cop-only slots next to city hall and threw his BCA card on the dash, which usually managed to piss somebody off; but they'd never towed him. The attorney's office, where the meeting would be held, was a block or so away, in the Pillsbury building. As he walked along, he spotted Marion, whistled, and Marion turned, saw him, and waited.

"I thought somebody liked my ass," Marion said.

"Probably not," Lucas said. "You know what Quintana's going to say?"

"Well, since it's you and me . . . I suspect it might have something to do with the porn. We've been looking at possibilities, and his name's on the list. He had access to the relevant computers both in Vice and Domestics."

"Ah, boy. I've known him for a long time," Lucas said. "Not a bad cop—give or take a little."

"You know something about the take?" Marion asked.

"No, no. If he's taken anything, he's smart enough that nobody would know," Lucas said. "That's what's odd about this deal—why in God's name would he give a porn file to anyone? Especially when it was going to be used like this? You know, a public hurricane. That doesn't sound like the Ray Quintana we know and love. He's always been a pretty cautious guy."

"Mmm. Got a pretty clean jacket, too," Marion said. He looked up at the Pillsbury building. "I guess we'll find out."

QUINTANA AND MEERS were waiting, Quintana was in a sweat, and showing it. Meers was a soft-faced blond with gold-rimmed glasses in his mid-thirties, who looked like a British movie star, but Lucas couldn't think which one. A guy who'd been in a tennis movie. When Lucas and Marion were seated, he said, "Ray's got a problem. I don't think it has to go any further than this . . . it's not criminal, or anything, but he sorta screwed up."

Marion looked skeptical, lifted his hands, and looked at Quintana. "So what is it?"

Before Quintana could say anything, Meers added: "He also has some valuable information for you, he thinks. The fact is, he didn't have to do this—he's doing it voluntarily, this meeting, and he's not even going to try to deal on the information. He's just going to give it to you, because he's a good cop. I hope you keep that in mind."

Marion looked at his watch: "Are we done with the introductions?"

Lucas was the good guy: he looked at Quintana and asked, "How you doin', Ray?"

"Ah, man, I messed up," Quintana said.

"What happened?"

Quintana leaned forward in his chair, his hands clenched in his lap, and spoke mostly to Lucas. "About two weeks ago, Bob Tubbs came to see me. I knew him all the way back in high school, and we'd bump into each other from time to time. We weren't friends, but you know, we were friendly. So, he comes to see me in the office. He sits down and says he's got a big problem."

Quintana told it this way:

Tubbs said, "You guys have an extensive file of kiddie porn somewhere in your computers. Here in Vice, and down in Domestics. I don't care about that, but there's one picture in there that I need to see. I need to see it off the record."

Quintana: "What's this all about?"

Tubbs: "A very large person in the state legislature is banging a girl on the side. Young, but not too young. But now it turns out that she might have been involved in some kind of porn ring and probably prostitution, and was busted by you guys. I need to look at her picture. I can't get at it through regular sources, because she was underage when she was busted, and the file is sealed."

Quintana: "Why do you need to look at it?"

Tubbs: "Because this guy is in a pretty tender spot. He's in the process of getting a divorce. His wife's lawyer is a wolverine, and if she gets a sniff of this chick—and maybe she already did—they're going to make an issue of it. Then, it's all gonna come out. He needs to know if this girl's the one involved in porn and prostitution and all that. I've seen his girlfriend. Now I need to look at the file."

Quintana: "Even if she was, what would he do about it?"

Tubbs: "Put her ass on a plane to Austin, Texas. He's got a buddy in the Texas legislature who'll give her a job, and his old lady won't be able to find her."

Quintana: "Why doesn't he do that anyway?"

Tubbs: "Because it'll cost an arm and a leg. If she's not the one, he won't do it. The other thing is, he doesn't want to ask the girl, because he's afraid it'll change things. And she might decide to ask for a little cash herself. If she's the one. All he wants to do is *know*."

Lucas asked, "You gave him the file?"

Quintana shook his head. "No. All I did was sit at the computer and call up the file. I knew what he was talking about, the girl, because it went back to Tom Morgan's case three years ago.

"I showed him the picture, and he asked me to enlarge it, the best shot of her face. He looked at it and then he said, "Close, but no cigar. She's not the one."

Marion: "Then what?"

"I closed the file and he said thanks, and he went away."

Marion: "Didn't give you a little schmear?"

"No, no. Nothing like that," Quintana said. "Look, this was a fast favor for a guy. Didn't look at the porn, didn't do any of that. A favor for a guy big in the legislature. You know how that works."

"You believed all that bullshit?" Marion asked.

Quintana shook his head: "It looks bad now, but yeah, I believed him. Like I said, I knew him forever."

Lucas said, "If you didn't give him the file, how'd he get it?"

Quintana shook his head. "I don't know for sure. But I've got my suspicions."

"Like what?"

"He was standing behind me when I signed on," Quintana said. "He might have seen my password . . . it's . . . this sounds even stupider . . . it's 'yquintz.' And I mean, he was right there. Once you've got the password, you can get in even from outside, if you need to. After I signed on, I looked up the file. He saw that, too."

Marion said, "Unbelievable."

Quintana ran his hands through his hair. "Yeah, I know. Oldest goddamn trick in the book," Quintana said. "I never saw it. I mean, all he wanted to do was look at one face."

Lucas mostly didn't believe it, but was willing to buy it if he got anything that would aim him at Carver and Dannon. He asked, "What was this information you got?"

"Yesterday I was working over on Upton—we think there might be a high-ticket whorehouse over there, don't tell anybody. Anyway, I was sitting in my car taking down tag numbers and taking pictures of these girls coming and going, and I get this phone call. The guy says that he bought the pornography file from Tubbs and Tubbs said he got it from me. I say, 'That's bullshit, I didn't give him anything.'

"The guy says, 'Well, he said he got it from you, and I think he might have told a woman over in Smalls's office. And he might've told her about me, too. She's the one who put the porn in. Nobody knows who I am, but somebody needs to go over and talk to this woman, this Helen Roman. Like a cop. Needs to ask her where the porn came from, and where it went.'

"I said, 'I didn't give anybody any porn. Who is this, anyway?'

"He said, 'A guy who doesn't like Porter Smalls.'

"I said, 'I don't like Porter Smalls either, but I didn't give a thing to Tubbs.'

"The guy says, 'Look, all you have to do is check with her.'

"I say, 'Not me.'

"Then the guy hangs up," Quintana said.

"And you've got the phone number," Lucas said.

Quintana nodded: "I do." He dug in his pocket and handed Lucas a slip of notepaper, with a phone number on it.

Lucas took the paper, and Marion said, "I'm gonna need that."

Lucas nodded, took out a pen and a pocket notebook, and wrote the number down, and passed the original slip back to Marion. "I'm going to run down the number and look at the activity on that phone," Lucas said. "If this is real, it could be a serious break."

"I just hope I get credit for it," Quintana said.

Meers said, "That's pretty much the story. A simple request from a friend, to help out a guy in the legislature. If you go after a guy for that, we wouldn't have a police department left."

Marion said, "You know the problem, though: it's not important unless it becomes important. Ray's now all tangled up in what could be a double murder case. One way or another . . ."

Quintana said, "Come on. If I hadn't told you, you'd never have found out. I could've lied. Instead, I came right in, as soon as I worked it out. I even gave you what Lucas said could be a break. A *serious* break."

Marion looked at Lucas and asked, "What's the BCA think?"

Lucas said, "This is all on you guys. Do what's best: I don't care. I just want the phone number." He looked at Quintana: "Where's the phone they called you on?"

"In my pocket." He fished it out: an iPhone.

"I'm going to need to take it with me. I need to take it to our lab, we'll get in touch with your . . . Who's your service provider?"

"Verizon."

"We'll get in touch with Verizon, and when we know where our targets are, we're going to want you to call them," Lucas said.

Quintana shook his head. "You can take my phone, but these

guys are way too smart to be using their own phone. I'd give you ten to one that it's a disposable."

"That's why we need to catch them with it. We'll be monitoring the call and the location it comes from," Lucas said. "I'll probably get back to you tonight. Where you gonna be?"

"Without my cell . . . I'll probably go home if Buck is done talking to me. I've got a landline there."

"Okay. You sit there, wait for my call," Lucas said. "You go along with all of this, I'll testify on your side in any kind of proceedings."

Quintana nodded. "I'll do that."

He passed Lucas his cell phone, and Lucas said, "If you'll all excuse me . . . I gotta run."

As he headed for the door, Quintana called, "You believe me, right?"

Lucas paused at the door, then said, "No, not the whole story. Not even very much of it. But I believe the phone number."

THEN HE HAD a lot to do. From his car, as he headed back across town to the BCA, he called Jenkins and told him to find Shrake: "I know it's Sunday, but I need you to babysit some people for me. Only until tonight. I need to know where they are, all the time."

"How complicated is this going to be?"

"Not complicated. You have to tag a campaign caravan." He told Jenkins to find out where Taryn Grant was going to be, described Dannon and Carver. "It's those two guys you've got to stay with. I want you to go separately so if they split up, you can follow both of them. But they should stick pretty close to Grant for as long as I need you to watch them."

"Good enough," Jenkins said.

———

LUCAS HAD TO MAKE some calls, first to the director, and then the deputy director, and between them they found a technician who was willing to come in and set up the phone monitoring system. When he got there, the tech came up to Lucas's office and said, "We don't usually need a subpoena for Verizon, if we just want a location, but I'll check with them first. That's not usually a problem, though."

"Then get it going," Lucas said.

He was a little cranked: if this worked out, there'd be somebody in the bag by midnight. He called Jenkins: "Where are you guys?"

"Grant's up in Anoka. We're on the way. Then she's going to St. Cloud for an eight-o'clock appearance and then back home. Probably back in the Cities between ten and midnight."

"Keep me up to date," Lucas said.

Lucas called Quintana: "It'll be late—I'll probably come get you around nine or ten o'clock."

Lucas needed something to eat. He called Weather to find out what the food situation was, and was told that the housekeeper was making her patented mac & cheese & pepperoni. "I'll be there," he said.

He was pulling his jacket on when Virgil Flowers called: "I was talking to Barney and he didn't know what you were up to, but he said you might use my help. I'm down in Shakopee. I can either go home, or head your way."

"My house," Lucas said. "Helen's making her mac and cheese and pepperoni."

"What happened to that vegetarian thing you guys were doing?"

"Ah, that only lasted a month or two. Besides, pepperoni isn't meat—it's cheese made by pigs," Lucas said. "Anyway, we'll be going out later. I'll tell you about it when you get there."

He called Weather and told her that Flowers was coming to dinner, and she said, "We got plenty."

Which was true: the mac and cheese and pepperoni usually went on for the best part of a week.

LUCAS GOT HOME, changed into jeans, a wool vest over a white dress shirt, and an Italian cotton sport coat, blue-black in color that would be excellent, he thought, for nighttime shoot-outs. It hadn't yet been tested for that. When he got back downstairs, Flowers had come in, wearing a barn coat, jeans, and carrying a felt cowboy hat. His high-heeled cowboy boots made him an inch taller than Lucas.

"There better not be a fuckin' horse in my driveway," Lucas said.

A bit later, Lucas took a call from the BCA tech, who said they were set with Verizon, and they could give him a real-time location as soon as Lucas called the other phone, which, as it happened, also used Verizon. There'd been no calls on the phone for two days; the last call had been to Quintana's number.

They all ate together at a long oblong dinner table, Flowers and Letty happily gabbing away—Flowers, a part-time writer with a developing reputation, had done a biographical piece about Letty that had been published in *Vanity Fair*, with photographs by Annie Leibovitz. They were all now dear friends, Annie and Letty and Virgie.

Leibovitz had taken a bunch of pictures of Lucas, too, but the magazine had used only one. Lucas thought it made him look like a midwestern prairie preacher from the nineteenth century. As for the friendship, he thought Letty and Virgie were getting a little too dear. The issue came up before dinner, and Weather told him he was losing it if he thought Flowers had untoward ideas about Letty.

"When it comes to being around women, I wouldn't trust that guy further than I could spit a Norwegian rat," Lucas had grumbled.

"Why? Because he reminds you so much of your younger self?" she'd asked.

"Maybe," Lucas had said. "But not that much younger."

"He's not interested in Letty," Weather had declared.

"Okay," Lucas said. "How about in you?"

"Don't be absurd," she'd said, ostentatiously checking her hair in the mirror.

AFTER DINNER, Lucas and Virgil went to Lucas's study, with Letty perching on a side chair, and Lucas briefed him about the situation. "Basically," Flowers summed up, "we've got nothing, but if their phone's GPS says that they're in a certain spot, you think that's good enough for a search and seizure."

"I know it is, because there's been another case just like it," Lucas said. "It was in LA, but the federal court refused to order the evidence set aside."

"And so this could prove that these two highly trained killers were involved with the porn, and we know for sure that they've got guns."

"Uh-huh."

Virgil thought about that and said, "Okay."

They'd sat down to eat at seven, had finished with the food and talk at eight, and at eight-thirty, sitting in the den, Lucas took a call from Jenkins. "This is going to wind up sooner than I thought," Jenkins said. "She finished talking, the TV is pulling out, now she's going around mixing with the kids, but that's not going to last long, once the TV is gone. I think we'll be out of here in fifteen minutes, and then it's an hour back to her place."

He said to Flowers, "Let's go. Excuse me—I meant, 'Saddle up.'"

"Yeah," Virgil said, getting his hat.

"Don't let him push you around," Letty told Virgil. "That hat looks good on you. Not everybody could pull it off, but you can."

"Thank you, sweetheart," Flowers said, and he and Lucas were out the door.

They took Flowers's truck, and as they backed out of the driveway, Lucas noticed that Flowers was smiling.

"What's the shit-eating grin about?" Lucas asked.

"Ah, I love pimping you about Letty. And Weather, for that matter."

"I don't mind, as long as you keep your hands off Helen and that mac and cheese and pepperoni," Lucas said.

JENKINS CALLED TO SAY that Taryn Grant's caravan consisted of three cars. The first carried what appeared to be three lower-ranking campaign people, one of whom was probably the media liaison. The second car was a big American SUV, and carried Grant, a short, heavyset woman, and one of the bodyguards; from Lucas's description, he thought it was probably Carver. The third car carried the other bodyguard, Dannon, and a thin woman who was apparently also security.

"Alice Green, ex–Secret Service," Lucas said. "Where are you guys?"

"Shrake is out front, I'm a quarter mile back, with four cars between us."

"Stay in touch," Lucas said. "Let me know for sure when they hit 494."

Quintana lived in Golden Valley, a first-ring suburb west of Minneapolis. He was standing on his front porch when Lucas and Virgil arrived. He got in the backseat, and Lucas introduced Flowers. Quintana said, "I appreciate the chance."

"Like I said, it's up to Minneapolis what they do about this," Lucas said. "But you kinda blew it, Ray."

"I know that," Quintana said. "But tell me you don't do a little off-the-record relationship stuff. I thought Tubbs might be something for me: a guy to know."

"I understand that," Lucas said. "I don't buy all that other stuff."

"Ahhh . . ." Quintana shut up and looked out the side window.

After a couple minutes of silence, Virgil said to Lucas, "At least we know he's not lying to us now."

"How's that?" Lucas asked.

"His lips aren't moving."

Quintana began laughing in the backseat, and then Lucas and Virgil started.

THEY PULLED INTO a mostly empty strip mall parking lot a mile from Grant's house. The streets were good between the mall and her house, and they could be there in a couple of minutes. They talked about Tubbs and Roman, but not about Quintana's problem.

"I wish that motherfucker Tubbs wasn't dead," Quintana said. "Then I could kill him myself."

Lucas asked Flowers how his most recent romance had been going.

"I think it's gone," Flowers said. "We're apparently friends, now."

"That's not necessarily the kiss of death," Quintana said from the backseat, and they talked about that for a while.

Jenkins called when the caravan got off I-94 and headed south on I-494, and then when it got off I-494 and headed west. Lucas called the tech and said, "I'm making the call."

And at that moment, as he hung up on the tech and prepared to call the unknown phone, another call from Jenkins came in. "Man, we got a problem. We got a problem."

"What?"

"I got a cop car on my ass, and so does Shrake. The caravan has pulled over ahead of us. Shit! They made us. I gotta talk to this cop."

"Goddamnit, where are you?" Lucas asked.

He got the location, and told Flowers to go that way, and then made the call on Quintana's phone and handed it to Quintana. It rang, and rang, and rang, with no answer. The tech called and said, "We've got a location for you. The phone's at Hampshire Avenue North and Thirtieth."

"What?"

"It's at Hampshire Avenue North and Thirtieth. There's a park there."

Lucas asked, "Where in the hell is that?"

"Well, if you're at Grant's house, it's about eight miles east. As the crow flies."

"Sonofabitch," Lucas said.

"What're we doing?" Flowers asked.

"Got no choice, now. We'll try to shake them, see if anything comes loose," Lucas said.

He turned around in his seat and said to Quintana, "I'm going to point out these guys and tell you to look at them. Like you'd seen them before. I want you to take a long look, then come over and mutter at me. Don't let them hear what you're saying."

"I never saw them," Quintana said.

"Ray, for Christ's sakes, I'm trying to shake 'em. We're doing a pageant."

Quintana cracked a smile. "All right."

"What do you want me to do?" Flowers asked, as they turned a corner and saw the lights on the squad cars.

"Well, given the way you're dressed, you could ask me if I want them hog-tied," Lucas said.

"Don't take it out on me," Flowers said. "I'm not the one who . . ."

". . . poked the pup," Quintana said.

"Shut up," Lucas snarled, no longer in the mood for humor.

WHEN THEY CAME UP on the lights, the street was full of cops and politicians. Flowers turned on his own flashers, and a cop who started toward them stopped and put his hands on his hips. Lucas, Flowers, and Quintana got out, and the cop waited for them to walk up, and then asked, "Any chance you're the BCA?"

"BCA and Minneapolis police," Lucas said.

At that moment, Taryn Grant, who was in the street with a half-dozen campaign workers and her security people, came steaming toward them and shrieked, "I knew it was you. I knew it."

"Shut up," Lucas said, but without much snap.

"This is the last straw." She was wildly angry; her blond hair had come loose from whatever kind of spray had been keeping it neat, and was fluttering over her forehead. Her campaign manager, Schiffer, took her arm and tried to pull her back, and Grant pulled free.

Dannon, Carver, and Green had come up behind Grant. Lucas turned to Quintana and said, "Take a look."

Quintana, with the unpleasant grittiness of a vice cop, stepped up close to Carver and looked him straight in the face for a long beat; then stepped over to Dannon and did the same thing. Neither man turned away, but they didn't like it.

"Who's this guy, and what does he want?" Dannon asked.

"I'm a cop," Quintana said. "You got a problem with that?"

"I don't like somebody standing two inches in front of my face breathing onions on me," Dannon said. "So back off."

Quintana did. Carver nodded at Flowers and asked, "Why's there a cowboy with you?"

"Lucas might've wanted you hog-tied," Flowers said. "He thought I'd be the guy to do it."

Carver stared at Flowers for a minute, then asked, "You in the military?"

"Yeah, for a while."

"Officer?"

"Yeah."

"MP?"

"Yeah."

"I thought so," Carver said.

Quintana had stepped over to Lucas and said, in a low tone, "I can't hardly believe it, but I think it really is that second guy I talked to." He looked back over his shoulder at Dannon and Carver and said, "The smaller one. He's got that funny accent—Texas. Like George Bush."

Dannon stepped toward them and said, "We gave you those DNA samples."

Lucas nodded and squared off with Grant. "We've got two days before the election and this whole thing is coming to a boil. We're watching everybody, because we don't want anybody else to show up dead: there have been two murders so far. We don't need a third."

"We don't have anything to do with any murders," she shouted, and Lucas could see little atoms of saliva spray in the headlights of Flowers's truck.

"We can't take any chances—*you* could be a target," Lucas said. "We had no plans to stop you. We were making sure that everybody got home all right."

"Fuck you," she shouted.

Lucas told Shrake and Jenkins to go home, and back in Flowers's truck, Lucas asked Quintana, "How sure are you?"

Quintana shrugged. "Hell, Lucas—he *sounded* like the guy. It's not like he's some random asshole and I'm trying to pick him out of a hundred people by the tone of his voice. He's your suspect, and I can tell you he's got that accent, and that was right, and his tone was right, and the way the words came out, that's exactly right. He sounded exactly like the guy on the phone. You say you're looking for professional killers and you find two professional killers, and then I listen to one of them . . . what are the chances that it's not him?"

"Slim and none, and slim is outta town," Lucas said. "I want you to go back to the office and write this down. A standard incident report and e-mail it to me. I'll talk to Marion and tell him you're working with me."

"I appreciate it," Quintana said, and he looked like he did. "In the meantime, I might move out to a motel for a couple of weeks."

"Stay in touch," Lucas said to Quintana, as Flowers pulled away from the curb. "I don't want to wonder what the hell happened to you."

Flowers asked, "We're going to Hampshire and Thirtieth?"

"Yeah, if we can find it."

Lucas called up the Google Maps app on his iPhone, and fifteen minutes later they pulled to the side of the road, houses on one side, a park on the other. Dark as tar on the park side.

Flowers got a flash and Lucas dialed the phone. They walked up and down the road, and then Virgil heard it buzzing down in the weeds. It took a minute or so and a couple of calls to find it. Flowers bagged it and handed it to Lucas.

"Have them check the battery," Flowers said. "They probably had to pull an insulating tab off. Maybe they forgot to wipe it."

"Fat chance," Lucas said. "But I'll do it anyway. I'm pulling on threads, 'cause threads are all I've got."

CHAPTER 19

Taryn fixed herself a lemon drop, with a little extra vodka, as soon as she was back in the house; Dannon helped himself to a bottle of beer, Schiffer had a Diet Pepsi, Carver poured a glass of bourbon, Green got a bottle of Evian water. Schiffer said to Taryn, "All right, enough is enough, if you want to call the governor in the morning, go ahead and do it. But right now we've got more important stuff on the table."

"He thinks we killed somebody," Taryn shouted at her. "He thinks—"

"You know you didn't, so he's got no proof. You gotta keep your eye on the ball," Schiffer shouted back, the two women face-to-face. "We've got one more day of campaigning. We can still lose it."

Taryn looked at her over the glass, then asked, "Where are we?"

The media woman, whose name was Mary Booth, stepped up: "While you were up north, we're seeing a new Smalls ad. It ran prime time, Channel Three at seven o'clock, it's been on 'CCO and KSTP. We'd bought out the KARE slots so it wasn't there."

"Yeah, yeah, yeah, what is it?" Taryn asked.

"Well, all that neutrality thing is done with. He knows there's no time left, so he dropped the bomb—he says you planted the porn on him," Booth said. "He doesn't come right out and say the words, but he talks about the Democrats and opposition dirty tricks, and he gets angry. I'd say it's quite effective."

"Let's see it," Schiffer said.

They gathered around the living room TV and the media woman plugged a thumb drive into the digital port and brought the advertisement up: Smalls was dressed in a gray pin-striped suit, bankerish, but with a pale blue shirt open at the collar. He was in his Minnesota Senate office, with a hint of the American flag to his right, a couple of red and white stripes—not enough of a flag display to invite sarcasm, but it was there.

He faced the camera head-on and apparently had been whipped into a bit of a frenzy before they started rolling, because it was right there on his face: ". . . spent my entire life without committing an offense any worse than speeding, and now the Democrats and the opposition plant this dreadful, disgusting pornography on me, and yes, my fellow Minnesotans, they *still* think they're going to get away with it. They're still pretending to think that I might have collected this . . . crap, even though they know the name of the man who did it, a longtime Democrat dirty trickster named Bob Tubbs. They're laughing up their sleeves at all of us! Don't let them get away with it! This is not the way we do these things in Minnesota."

When he finished, Schiffer said, "Not bad."

Taryn was on her second drink: "What do we do?"

"We bought a lot of time tomorrow afternoon and evening. We can pretty much blanket the state. Mary, Sandy, and Carl will write a new advertisement overnight in which you are warm and understanding—but also a little angry. Maybe we'll say something about how we have to be rational and careful . . . hint that he's a little nuts. I'll call you in the morning about wardrobe. I'm thinking maybe something cowgirl, maybe . . . what's the name of that stables you ride at?"

"Birchmont," Taryn said.

"Get you out there in jeans and a barn coat, the one you wore out to Windom, and a jean jacket, cowboy boots . . . let your hair frizz out a little . . . and we do something along the lines of, 'We don't know where the porn came from, and if we find out, no matter who put it out there, we will support any prosecution. In the meantime, let's turn back to the serious issues in this campaign. . . .'"

As she was talking, outlining a possible quick advertising shoot, Booth's phone rang and she pulled it out and looked at it, while still listening to Schiffer. She saw who was calling and declined the call, but then a second later, a message came in, and she looked at it, and interrupted Schiffer to say, "I gotta take this," and stepped away.

Taryn was saying . . . "You don't think they'll mock me for the cowboy outfit?"

"They won't have time to, and it'll look really down-home and honest," Schiffer was replying . . .

. . . When Booth came back and said, "Oh my God, the *Pioneer Press* is on the street with a front-page story that says this dead woman, the woman that got murdered, had a long affair with Smalls and that the police are investigating a possible domestic motive for her murder."

They were all struck silent for a moment, then Taryn said, "Davenport said they had a personal conflict. He didn't say they had an affair."

Schiffer said, "Whatever, this could do it for us. It'll play right through Election Day. I still think the horse thing will work for us. Maybe we're a little more sympathetic about Smalls's problems."

Taryn finished the second drink and said, "While still hinting that he's nuts . . . let's do it. This is all so ludicrous that we shouldn't let anything go."

Schiffer raised her voice and said, "All right, everybody, let's clear out. Mary, you get the guys and get going on the ad. You can sleep tomorrow night. Everybody else . . . Taryn, I'll call you at nine o'clock. I'll cancel the Channel Three thing, that was the only morning show . . ."

As SCHIFFER WAS PUSHING everybody out, Taryn tipped her head at Dannon, saying, "Follow me," and drifted back to the bar. Dannon followed and she said, quietly, "Who's got the overnight?"

"Barry."

"Send him home. You and I need to talk. Carver's going to be a problem."

Dannon sighed, pulled a bottle of lemon water out of the refrigerator and poured his second drink over a couple of ice cubes. "Did he say something to you?"

"Yeah. When people clear out . . ."

"Okay," Dannon said.

He started back toward the group in the hallway, and she caught his sleeve and said, "One other thing. I'm so . . . angry, confused, cranked up . . ."

"It's been unreal . . ." Dannon began.

"And I really need something that David doesn't have, to mellow me out. . . . I'd like to see you back in the bedroom. You know. Send Barry home."

———

DANNON HAD UNUSUAL SKILLS in the area of death and dismemberment, but he was like anyone else when it came to sex. He'd slept with twenty women in the past twenty years, but had never really desired one. He'd wanted the sex, but hadn't been particularly interested in the package that it came in.

Taryn was an entirely different thing. He'd wanted her from the first week he'd known her. He'd seen her naked or semi-naked two hundred times, out in the pool, so that was no big thing, but seeing her naked when he was finally going to consummate that years-long desire was an entirely different thing.

As soon as the words "bedroom" came out of her mouth, he began to sweat: you know, would everything work? He kicked Barry out, made himself do all the checks, and had another beer, thinking that the alcohol might lubricate the equipment.

He needn't have worried: he walked back to the bedroom with the fourth drink in his hand, and as he walked in, she was coming out of the bathroom, naked except for her underpants, which were no more than a negligible gossamer swatch the size of a folded hankie, and she said, almost shyly, "I've been waiting . . ."

And then he was on her, like a mountain lion, and the equipment was no problem at all. He couldn't remember getting out of his clothes, didn't remember anything until she screamed, or moaned, or made some kind of sound that seemed ripped out of her, and she began patting his back and saying, "Okay / okay / okay / okay."

And it was okay for about ten minutes of stroking her pelvis, stomach, breasts, rolling her over, stroking her back and butt, and rolling her again and then they were going once more and he blacked out until he heard once more that scream/moan and "Okay/okay/okay . . ."

He collapsed on top of her, lying there sweaty and hot, until she said, "Whew," and "We should have done this years ago."

THEY TALKED FOR A WHILE, this and that, the campaign and Schiffer and Carver and Alice Green . . . Dannon told her for the first time why he and Carver were so casual about the DNA check: there was no DNA from Tubbs, because the cops didn't know where to look for it, and there was none with Helen Roman, either, because great care had been taken. "Besides, our DNA profiles are already in the army and FBI files. When there's a chance that some suicide bomber is going to blow you into hamburger, the army wants to be able to identify the scrap meat. We've all got DNA profiles."

Taryn said, "Ah: so it didn't make any difference."

Taryn rolled out of bed and went to a side bar, pulled open the top drawer, and took out a bottle of vodka, two or three drinks down from full. She asked, "You want more water?"

He said, "Sure."

She got some ice from the bar's refrigerator and poured the water over it, and made another lemon drop for herself, with enough lemon to bite, brought the drinks back to the bed and put his cold glass on his belly below his navel. He said, "Jesus, cold," and picked it up, and she laughed, almost girlishly, rolled onto the bed next to him, careful with the drink, and said, "Carver."

"What'd he say to you?" Dannon asked.

Taryn rolled toward him, one of her breasts pressing against his biceps; she wetted a finger and circled one of his nipples in a distracted way, and said, "This afternoon, before we went over to that school, he said that he hadn't signed up for all this. That's what he said, 'signed up.' I asked what that meant, and he said that he hoped I'd be more grateful than I had been so far. I said that I would be, that if he'd hold on until I was in the Senate, I could take care of him in a lot of ways: money, another army job, get his record wiped out, whatever he needed. He said, 'Money's good,' and said we could talk about the other stuff, then he asked when he'd get a down payment."

"What'd you say to that?"

"I said too much stuff was coming down right now: that I assumed he'd want a big brick of cash that he wouldn't have to pay taxes on, but even for me, it takes a while to get cash together. Almost nobody uses it anymore, except dope dealers, I guess."

Dannon said, "Got that right. I can't remember the last time I saw somebody buying groceries for cash, except me."

"He said, 'Well, better get on that. I'm gonna need a big chunk pretty soon. I got a feeling that when everything settles down . . . my services might not be needed.' I said, 'You've got a job as long as you want it, and you'll get paid as much as you need.' He laughed and said, 'I kinda don't think you know how much I need.'"

Dannon said, "That's the problem with Ron. He's hungry all the time—more pussy, more dope, more money. There won't be an end to it."

"I know, but I don't know what to do about it."

Dannon said, "Ron and I . . . he was enlisted, I was an officer. We're not natural friends. I'm not being arrogant here, lots of the enlisted guys are sharp as razors: but that's the way it is. He doesn't think, except tactically. How exactly to do one thing or another. He thinks three days down the road, but not three months or three years. He'll get us in trouble, sooner or later."

Taryn said nothing, waiting, watching Dannon think.

He said, finally, "There's something else."

"What?"

"I'm kinda worried that from Ron's perspective, *I'm* the problem," Dannon said. "He'll figure he can handle you. But you and me together . . ."

"You actually think . . . he might come after you?"

"I think it's inevitable," Dannon said. "It'll occur to him pretty soon. After it does, he won't wait. That's the three-days-thinking problem again. He'll think about it, then he'll move."

"Oh, dear."

"I think he has to go away," Dannon said.

"You mean . . . someday?"

"No. I mean right away. I know it'll be a political problem, but . . . I know this guy down in Houston. For ten thousand dollars, he'll fly Carver's passport to Kuwait. He's got a deal with one of the border people there."

"I don't understand," Taryn said, though she had an idea about it.

"Simple enough. Ron goes away. I FedEx his passport and ten grand—I've actually got the cash in my safe-deposit box—"

"I'll pay you back."

"I got this. My guy in Houston flies the passport to Kuwait and walks it across the border into Iraq. We call up this Davenport guy, say that we're worried because Ron didn't show up for work on Wednesday and he doesn't answer his phone. We don't know where he's gone."

"And Davenport thinks it's possible that he's run for it."

"Yeah, because they send out a stop order on him, and because of his background, and what they think—that he killed Tubbs and Roman—they include the border people and the airport security, and *they* report back that his passport left the country, and then crossed the border into Kuwait and then out of Kuwait and into Iraq."

"Don't they take pictures, you know, video cameras of everybody going through the airport?"

"Sure. But IDs aren't synced with pictures. They ask for your passport when you check in, but going through security, they only ask for a government ID. This Houston guy shows Ron's passport to the airlines and the security people, who check him through. The cops look at the security video, and they never see Ron, so they figure he ran some kind of dodge, and got through behind security. It's easy enough to do. Listen, all kinds of people from this country are carrying all kinds of stuff into Kuwait and then across the border into Iraq. This is a very *established* deal. . . . This Houston guy, it's his thing. It can be done."

"If you're sure . . ."

"It'll hurt, politically, but once it's done, we're really secure," Dannon said. "We'll be the only two who know the story. You're already a senator before the shit hits the fan, another guy goes missing . . . but, if Ron's passport goes into Iraq, what's Davenport going to do?"

"How soon?"

"Tomorrow," Dannon said. "We can't afford to wait. I can't give Ron a chance to move on me." He was on his back and Taryn snuggled her head down onto his chest and he stroked her hair. Without Ron, he thought, the future had no horizon. . . .

———

TARYN WAS PRETTY TIRED of the sex by the time Dannon went to sleep. She listened to him breathe, then slipped out of bed, pulled on a robe, and padded through to the living room, closing the bedroom door behind her, poured some vodka over a couple of ice cubes, sat on the couch, and thought about it.

Dannon, once he'd gotten rid of Carver, was going to be a problem. She could see it already: he was looking at a permanent relationship. He was looking at love. When she got to Washington, an heiress and businesswoman already worth a billion dollars or so, a U.S. senator . . . any permanent relationship wouldn't be with an ex–army captain who carried a switchblade in his pocket.

That their relationship wasn't going to be permanent would quickly become obvious. Then what? What do jilted lovers do, when they're men? What do jilted alcoholics with switchblades do?

Something to think about. Dannon, like Carver, would have to go away. But how? She sat on the couch for another hour, and another two vodkas, thinking about it: and what she thought was, *Best to wait until we get to Washington.*

THE NEIGHBORHOOD AROUND TARYN'S was quiet and dark and gently rolling. The highest nearby spot was between two pillared faux-plantation manors on five-acre lots, screened from the street by elaborate hedges. From the top of that low hill, any approaching cars could be seen three blocks away.

Lauren was behind the wheel of Kidd's Mercedes GL550, a large luxury vehicle and one that fit well in rich neighborhoods. Kidd sat in the passenger seat, looking at a hooded laptop that was plugged into an antenna and amplifier focused on one of the manors. Kidd was riding on the manor's Wi-Fi; and Lauren, looking over his shoulder, said, "We're not Peeping Toms."

"I'm not peeping, I'm trying to figure out who in the hell that is," he said, watching the scene in Taryn Grant's bedroom. "I think it's her security guy. The only security guy, if we counted right. I can't find anyone else."

"It's perfect," Lauren said. "They're both fully occupied."

"You're scaring the shit out of me," Kidd said.

"I'm so excited I'm gonna have an orgasm myself in the next two minutes," Lauren said. "Trade places. I'm going."

Kidd didn't bother to argue. He got out of the car—no interior lights, they had custom switches, and the switches were off—and walked around to the driver's side, as Lauren clambered into the passenger seat.

She was wearing trim, soft black cotton slacks, a silky white blouse, a red nylon runner's jacket with reflective strips front and back, and black running shoes. She had a thin black nylon ski mask in her pocket. The ski mask could be instantly buried; and no burglar in his or her right mind would be out with a red jacket, a shiny white blouse, and all those reflective strips.

Kidd started the SUV and they eased on down the hill toward Grant's house. As they rolled along, Lauren turned the jacket inside out: the lining, now the outer shell, was jet black. She pulled it back on, and was now dressed head to toe in black. A hundred yards out, Lauren said, "I'll call." Kidd tapped the brakes—no red flash on the custom-switched brake lights—and when they were stopped, Lauren dropped out and quietly closed the car door.

Five seconds later, with the hood over her head, she vanished into the woods between Grant's house and the neighbor's.

———

THE GROUNDS WERE PROTECTED by both radar and infrared installations, but Kidd had switched off the alarms on the rear approach, and had fixed the software so that they couldn't be turned back on without his permission. Lauren had one major worry: that the dogs would be turned loose. If that happened, she was in trouble. She had a can of bear spray, which should shut them down, but she had no idea how effective that would be.

For the time being, the dogs were in the house—one of them in the living room, where it could see the front hallway and the hall coming in from the garage; and the other outside the bedroom door.

Inside the tree line, she pulled a pair of starlight goggles over her head. They were military issue, and she'd had to pay nine thousand dollars for them six years before. With the goggles over her eyes, the world turned green and speckled: but she could see.

She began moving forward, like a still-hunter, placing each foot carefully, feeling for branches and twigs before she put weight down. Long pauses to listen. Fifty yards in, she crossed a nearly useless wrought iron fence. Any reasonably athletic human could slip right over it; Grant's dogs could jump it with three feet to spare, and a deer would hardly notice it. Once over the fence, she took nearly fifteen minutes to cross the hundred yards to the edge of Grant's back lawn. By that time, she knew she was alone. She took out her phone, a throwaway, and messaged Kidd, one word: "There."

One word came back. "Go."

Kidd was back on top of the hill, back on the manor's Wi-Fi. Nothing inside the house had changed. Grant's lawn was dotted with oak trees and shrubs, and Lauren stuck close to them as she closed in on the bedroom. There were motion and sonic alarms outside the bedroom windows, but Kidd had them handled. When she was below the windows, she took out a taped flashlight with a pinprick opening in the tape. She turned it on, and with the tiny speck of light, looked at the windows. Triple glazed, wired, with lever latches. Fully open, there'd be a space three feet long and a foot high that she'd have to get her body through. She could do that. . . .

She pulled back, listened, crept down the side of the house. A light came on in the living room and she froze. Nothing more happened and she felt her phone buzz. She risked a look: *Grant moving.* She listened, then began to back away from the house, heard a crunch when she stepped in some gravel, froze. Moved again ten seconds later, backing toward the woods.

From her new position, she could see the lighted living room, and Taryn Grant looking out the window. She was wearing a robe and had what looked like a drink in her hand. A dog moved by her hip, and Lauren thought, *Bigger than a wolf.*

The phone vibrated. She was into the tree line, and stopped to looked again: "Dogs may know . . . dogs may be coming."

She thought, *Damnit,* and texted, "Come now," and began moving more quickly. She crossed the fence, which should give her some protection from the dogs, and made the hundred yards out quickly, but not entirely silently. At the street-side tree line, she knelt, stripped the goggles and mask off, stuffed them in her pockets, and then Kidd was there in the car.

She was inside and pulled the door closed and they were rolling and Lauren looked out the window, toward Grant's house, but saw no dogs. "She let them out?"

"I think so—into the backyard, anyway. Didn't seem like there was any big rush. Maybe she was letting them out to pee."

"That's probably it," Lauren said. "I never saw them. They didn't bark."

"They don't bark, not those dogs," Kidd said.

"I know." She took a breath, squeezed Kidd's thigh. "I haven't felt like this in years. Six years."

They came out of the darkened neighborhood to a bigger street, and Kidd went left. They could see a traffic light at the end of the street, where the bigger street intersected with an even bigger avenue.

Kidd asked, "What do you think?"

"Piece of cake," Lauren said.

CHAPTER 20

The next step was not obvious. Lucas had Quintana's belief that he'd spoken to Dannon on the phone, but that was not proof. Nor would it convince a jury to believe that a crime had been committed, not beyond a reasonable doubt. He needed a scrap of serious evidence, something that he could use as a crowbar to pry Grant, Dannon, and Carver apart.

He was also bothered by the sporadic thought: What if Tubbs showed up? In most killings, there was some physical indication that violence had been done. With Tubbs, there was nothing.

THE NEXT MORNING he did what he usually did when he was stuck, and needed to think about it: he went shopping. Nothing was so likely to clear the mind as spending money. He idled over to the Mall of America and poked around the Nordstrom store, looking for a good fall dog-walking jacket.

He didn't have a dog, but a good dog-walking jacket was useful for a lot of other things. He had the exact specification: light, water-resistant, knit cuffs and waistband, modern high-tech insulation, warm enough for late fall and early winter days. And, of course, it had to look good.

He'd drifted from jackets to cashmere socks, especially a pair in an attractive dark raspberry color, when his phone rang: Cochran, from Minneapolis Homicide. Both Dannon and Carver had shown up to give DNA samples, and Lucas had sent the samples to Minneapolis.

"Turk, tell me we got them," Lucas said.

"No, we don't. We got James Clay," Cochran said. "We got a cold hit from your DNA bank."

James Clay? "Who the hell is James Clay?"

"Dickwad from Chicago. Small-time dealer," Cochran said. "Moved up here five years ago when he got tired of the Chicago cops busting him for dope. We've been chasing him around for the same thing. We got him on felony possession of cocaine, got DNA on that case, he went away for a year. Since then, we've caught him holding twice, and both times, it was small amounts of marijuana, so he was cut loose."

"Jesus Christ, that can't be right," Lucas said. "Roman wasn't killed by any small-time dope dealer."

"Sort of looks that way—of course, it's possible he was paid to do it, though I doubt anyone would hire him," Cochran said. "I'll tell you, the dope guys say he's exactly the kind of punk you'd want for a killing like this. He thinks the house is empty, goes in, she surprises him, he freaks out, whacks her with his gun, then shoots her, with some piece-of-crap .22."

"Aw, man . . . Turk . . ."

Cochran said, "Listen, Lucas: he's an old gang member, probably done two hundred nickel-dime burglaries, funding his habit, been shot at least once himself. He'll steal anything that's not nailed down. If all this election stuff hadn't been going on, it'd be exactly who you'd have been looking for."

"Is Clay still alive?"

"Far as we know. He was last night. He was hanging out at Smackie's," Cochran said.

"If he was paid to kill Roman, he'd be dead himself, and we wouldn't be finding the body," Lucas said. "He sure as hell wouldn't be hanging around Smackie's."

"Lucas, what it is, is what it is," Cochran said.

"You gonna find him?" Lucas asked.

"Sooner or later. Sooner, if he goes back to Smackie's."

"We need him right now," Lucas said. "You know Del?"

"Sure."

"Del knows all those guys. If you don't mind, I'm gonna go get him and look around town."

"Hey, that's fine with me. If you find him first, give me a call— I'll do the same, if we find him."

Lucas walked out to his car, calling Del as he went. Del picked up and Lucas asked, "Where are you?"

"In my backyard, looking at a tree," Del said.

"Why?"

"We got oak wilt," Del said. "We're gonna lose it."

"Look, I'm sorry about your tree, but I need help finding a guy. Right now. I'm going to get some paper on him. Meet me at my place."

"Half hour?"

"See you then."

LUCAS WAS TEN MINUTES from his house, driving fast. On the way, he called his office, talked to his secretary, told her to call Turk, get the specifics on James Clay, including any photos, and e-mail them to him. "I'll be home in ten minutes. I need it then," he said.

The house was quiet when he got home. Letty was in school, Sam in preschool, the baby out for a stroll with the housekeeper.

He went into the study, brought up the computer, checked his e-mail, found a bunch of political letters pleading for money, and a file from his secretary. He opened it, found four photos of James Clay along with Minneapolis arrest records and a compilation of Chicago-area arrests from the National Crime Information Center.

Clay had somehow managed to make it to thirty-one, despite a life of gang shootings, street riots, drugs, knife fights, beatings, burglaries, and strong-arm robberies. His last parole officer wrote that there was no chance of rehabilitation, and that the best thing anyone could hope for was that Clay would OD. He sounded pissed.

The photos showed a light-complexioned black man with cornrows, a prison tattoo around his neck—ragged dashes and a caption that said, "Fill to dotted line"—and three or four facial scars, along with a nasty jagged scar on his scalp. A photo taken from his right side demonstrated the effects of being shot in the ear with a handgun with no medical insurance. Some intern had sewn him up and sent him on his way, and now his ear looked like a pork rind.

Lucas was reading down the rap sheet when Del knocked on the door. He walked through the living room to the front door and let him in: "What kind of shape are you in at Smackie's?"

"They won't buy me a free beer, but they know me," Del said. He was dressed in jeans, a dark blue hoodie, and running shoes. "Is that where we're going?"

"Yeah. To start with." He picked up all the paper on Clay and thrust it at Del. "I'll drive. You read."

They took Lucas's Lexus SUV, which had gotten a little battered during the last trip to his Wisconsin cabin, when a tree branch
fell on the hood. Lucas couldn't decide whether to get it fixed, or
wait until he was closer to trading it in. Something else to think
about.

On the way up Mississippi River Road, headed to Minneapolis,
Lucas filled Del in on the problem. Del was reading Clay's sheet,
and said, "The name sounds familiar, but I don't know the guy.
Any reason to think that he might be holed up somewhere, with
a gun?"

"Turk apparently went in to Smackie's looking for him, so if he
had any friends there, somebody might have told him to start running. If he gets down to Chicago, it could be a while before we
find him."

"I see his mother lives here," Del said. "There's a note on the
probation report."

"I hate that. The mothers always turn out to be worse than the
children," Lucas said. "You remember that one mother, those two
brothers—"

"I heard about it. Shrake thought it was fun."

"Sort of was, I guess," Lucas said. "Especially when he fell off
the roof into that thornbush. He was crying like a Packers fan at
the Metrodome."

They crossed the Marshall/Lake Bridge into south Minneapolis,
and four minutes later left the car on the broken tarmac of the Pleasure Palace Bar & Grill parking lot. An "A" had fallen off the sign
over the bar's door, so it now said "Ple sure Palace," but it didn't
make any difference, because everybody who was nobody called it
Smackie's.

The bar was painted Halloween colors of black and orange, supposedly because it was once all black, and when the new owner decided to paint over the flaking black concrete blocks, he ran out of orange halfway through; either that, or got tired of doing the work. The bar had two long, low, nearly opaque windows decorated with neon beer signs and stickers from various police and fire charitable organizations.

Del led the way inside. Smackie's was dark, and smelled like boiled eggs floating in vinegar, and maybe a pickled pig's foot. Fifteen men, and four women, half of them black, half white, were scattered down a dozen booths, looking at beers or the TV set mounted in a corner or nothing at all. A bartender was leaning on the back of the bar, eating an egg-salad sandwich. As they came up to the bar, he swallowed and said, "Del." Nobody else looked at them, because Lucas was so obviously a cop.

Del said, "I didn't know you were back."

"Almost a month," the bartender said.

Del said to Lucas, "He had a hernia operation."

"Fascinating," Lucas said. He pulled out a picture of Clay. "You seen this guy?"

The bartender took another bite of the sandwich, chewed, then said, through the masticated bread and egg, "Yeah, the Minneapolis cops already been here. They're looking for him, too. He was here last night, pretty late, then he went away. Haven't seen him since."

"Does he live around here?" Lucas asked.

"Every time I've seen him, he was walking, so probably around here somewhere. The Minneapolis cops were asking if his mother comes in here."

"Does she?" Del asked.

The bartender shrugged. "I don't know. I never seen him with any old ladies, and we don't get many old ladies in here."

"Is he in here pretty regular?" Del asked.

"Yeah, most days."

Lucas tipped his head toward the people in the booths: "Any of these people know him?"

The bartender looked past him, then shook his head. "I wouldn't say so. I don't pay that much attention to who sits with who. We got a waitress comes in later this afternoon, she'd know better than me."

"But you think he comes from around here."

"Yeah, unless he takes a bus. I seen him coming from the direction of the bus stop."

Del looked at Lucas and shook his head. Not that many people would take a bus to a dive like Smackie's. It wouldn't be worth the money, since almost any other place would be better.

Del said, "We'll check back," and he and Lucas started for the door. They were almost there when the bartender called, "Hey, guys. C'mere."

They walked back to the bar and the bartender flicked a finger at the window on the left side of the bar. The glass was dark green and dirty, not easily seen through, but they could see a very short man walking down a street toward the bar. The bartender said, "You owe me."

Del: "That's him?"

"Uh-huh."

THEY WATCHED THE SHORT MAN until he crossed the street and started toward the bar entrance. Lucas looked around and said, "Better take him outside," and Del said, "Yeah," and they went to the door, waited for a few seconds, then pushed through into the daylight. Clay was only fifteen feet away. He saw Lucas, and quick as a rat, turned and started running.

His feet were churning like a machine, Lucas noticed as he took off after the other man, but his legs were so short that he was only making about two feet per churn; Lucas caught him in a hundred feet. He didn't want to make the mistake of having a knife or gun pulled on him, so when he was close behind, and Clay turned to look at him, he hit Clay on the back of the neck and sent him sprawling, hands first, into the street.

Clay rolled over and looked up the muzzle of Del's pistol. "How you doin', James," Del said. "You're under arrest for murder."

"They're lying to you," Clay said. He was very short, maybe five-two, and thin.

"Who's lying to us?" Lucas asked.

"The Chicago cops. I had not a single fuckin' thing to do with any of that."

"Tell the Chicago cops that," Lucas said. "Roll over on your face, keep your arms out . . . you know the routine."

Lucas patted him down, took a short folding knife out of Clay's back pocket, handed it to Del. Del cuffed him, and they stood him up and Lucas held on to the cuff link while Del gave him a more thorough pat-down.

A young white kid, maybe ten, rode up on a fenderless half-sized bicycle, an unlit cigarette dangling from his lower lip. He stopped and asked, "You guys cops?"

"Yes," Del said. "You go on home, son."

"Blow me," the kid said, and rode away.

"That's righteous, that's righteous," Clay shouted after the kid, who gave him the finger.

"I guess he doesn't like any of us," Del said.

They put Clay up against Lucas's Lexus, and Lucas called Cochran. Cochran came up and Lucas said, "We got Clay for you."

"What? How'd you do that?"

"By accident, mostly." He explained about Smackie's.

Cochran said, "All right. I'll come down there myself and pick him up."

"Good. Because I hate to write reports," Lucas said. "He's your guy."

LUCAS HAD BEEN BOTHERED by Clay's reaction to the arrest. He told him, "You stand right there. If I've got to chase you down again, it won't be any patty-cake slap on the neck like last time. You understand that?"

Clay said, "Hey, man, you gotta listen to this. I never—"

"Shut up," Lucas said.

He and Del moved off ten steps, and Lucas said, "If he killed Roman . . ."

"I know," Del said. "He's been around. If he killed her, it should have been nothing but, 'I wanna lawyer.'"

"Maybe he's stupid," Lucas said, glancing at Clay.

"He *is* stupid, but not *that* stupid," Del said. "Doesn't take that much firepower to remember 'I wanna lawyer.'"

"Yeah." Lucas scratched his chin. "I'd like to ask him something . . . see his reaction."

"You give away too much, you're going to piss off Turk."

"Little rain falls in everybody's life," Lucas said.

Lucas ambled back to Clay and said, "You're toast. We got the

DNA. Why'd you do it? You get paid? Or was it because it looked easy?"

"What'd I do?" Clay asked, and Lucas got the impression that he really was confused.

"Gimme a break," Lucas said. "You been around. You know what the deal is. You're a smart guy—you killed that old lady and you took her purse and her other stuff. What'd you do with the gun?"

Clay's eyes had widened, and he shook his head. "What are you talking about, man? I never killed no old lady. What the fuck you talking about?"

"Up on the north side? Middle of the night? This coming back to you, now? One shot, right in the heart? Did you think she was like, attacking you? That she had a gun?"

"What? I never killed nobody. Nobody." He looked from Lucas to Del and shook his head.

"Where you living, James?" Del asked. "You living with your mom?"

"I gotta place. Look, I'm doing all right. I got a part-time gig with this guy. . . . I didn't kill nobody. I don't got a gun."

Lucas pushed him, and Clay said he took messages around town for some guy, whose name he didn't know. Translated, that meant that he was delivering dope; in any case, he had a job.

"When we go up to your place, we're going to find the other glove, won't we?" Del asked.

"Other glove? Hey . . . you got my glove?"

"You're missing one, right?" Del asked.

"Yeah, I missing one. How'd you know that?"

"A little birdie whispered it to me."

"Somebody took my glove. Or maybe I dropped it," Clay protested. "I was wearing it up to Smackie's. I was walking home, it gotten cold, I takes my gloves out, and I only got one. I say, 'What's this shit?' I go back to Smackie's, but there's no glove, and nobody saw it. . . . You saying you found my glove?"

"Yes. Under the old lady's body," Del said.

"Man, you're crazy. You're fuckin' insane, man." He looked at the two of them, then said the magic words: "I wanna lawyer."

Del looked at Lucas and said, "Turk's gonna be pissed."

COCHRAN WASN'T COMPLETELY UPSET with the preemptive interrogation for the simple reason that he had the glove with the DNA, and a glove with DNA was about all a jury required. He and another cop picked up Clay, listened to Lucas's unformed doubts, said "Thank you," and headed off to the Hennepin County jail.

"What're you going to do?" Del asked.

"Probably piss off Turk some more. I'm going to talk to Jamie Moore, see if he'll get Clay to talk to me again."

When Turk was gone, Del started back to Smackie's.

"Where're you going?" Lucas asked.

"See if the bartender knows about that glove," Del said.

"Good." Lucas went along.

The bartender, however, didn't know about the glove. "But I'm behind the bar. You have to ask Irma."

"The waitress?"

"Yeah, the waitress."

"You got a phone number?" Del asked.

He did, and they got it, and went outside to make the call.

Irma was on a bus, on the way to work. Lucas put her on the

cell-phone speaker, identified himself, and said, "We just arrested one of your customers, a guy named James Clay," Lucas said.

"I don't know that name," she said.

"He's a short guy with some scars on his face, tattoo around his neck, deals a little dope," Lucas said.

"Colored guy?"

"Yeah. Got cornrows," Lucas said.

"Okay, yeah, I know who he is."

"He says the other night, he was in your place, and he lost a glove in there, and didn't find out until after he left, but then he went back to look for it. You remember anything like that?"

"Well, yeah. He asked me if I seen a glove on the floor, but I didn't."

"Okay. How about this? Was there a guy in there, maybe five-ten, six-foot tall, sort of blond, blond mustache?"

"Oh, yeah. All the time."

Lucas's heart jumped. But: "All the time?"

"Hey, this is Minneapolis. I see about thirty guys like that. All the time."

That wasn't good. Irma said she'd be at work in forty-five minutes, and Lucas said he might stop by with a photograph.

ON THE WAY BACK to Lucas's house, he told Del what he'd learned about Grant's bodyguards, and explained why he hadn't involved Del from the start: the danger of messing with politicians.

"I appreciate the thought, but I can take care of myself," Del grumped.

"No, you can't, not anymore," Lucas said. "If I get fired, I'm okay. Even with this depression, or whatever you want to call it, I make more off my investments than I earn from the BCA. If you get fired, what're you gonna do? Get a job as a bank guard? Stick up liquor stores? There aren't a hell of a lot of openings for guys with your job description: 'Hang around bars and bullshit people and sometimes arrest them.'"

"It's a little more complicated than that," Del said.

"Del . . ."

"Yeah, yeah. You're right," Del said. "I'd probably wind up running a bar and hating it. Or be a repo man for somebody."

"Repo? You'd wind up hanging yourself off your kid's swing set."

SANDY, THE RESEARCHER, called as they were pulling into Lucas's driveway: "I found a half-dozen men from Carver's former unit. . . . One guy, down in Albuquerque, says he was with Ron Carver on the night he got in trouble. His name is Dale Rodriguez. He's willing to talk about it."

Lucas looked at his watch: one o'clock in the afternoon. "Check on flights to Albuquerque, e-mail me when you find out when they are."

"For today?"

"Yeah. And write up your notes on the Albuquerque guy, and e-mail those, too."

He rang off and punched up Flowers. "Where are you?"

"Home." Home was in Mankato, ninety miles south of the Twin Cities.

"Start up this way. Bring gear for an overnight," Lucas said. "You may be flying, but you won't need a weapon."

"Where am I going?" Flowers asked.

"Albuquerque, if we can get you a flight."

"You gonna brief me?"

"If we have time. Otherwise, take your laptop and I'll send you a long note when you're in the air."

"You want me to hang around?" Del asked after Lucas rang off.

"Unless you need to deal with that tree."

"The old lady's got that covered," Del said. "Tell you what: print out a picture of this Dannon and Carver, and I'll run them up and show Irma."

LUCAS DID THAT.

Del left, and Lucas checked his e-mail, found the airline schedule from Sandy, and called Flowers. "There's a four-twenty flight. Can you make that?"

"Yes. I took my grab-bag and I'm on my way," Flowers said. "Probably won't have time to swing by your place, though."

"That's okay. It's an interview with a friendly," Lucas said. "Be good if you could do it tonight. I'll try to set it up."

He called Sandy: "Do you have phone numbers for the Albuquerque guy, this Rodriguez guy?"

"Yes, I do. When I talked to him, he said he was going off to class at a tech school there. He said he'd be back late in the afternoon. They're an hour earlier than us."

"Good. We're gonna need a ticket for Flowers on the four-twenty. Tell Cheryl to fix that, will you?"

"Okay, and I'm sending my notes on Rodriguez . . . now."

Lucas rang off and three seconds later, his e-mail pinged at him, and Sandy's file came in. It was short: name, address, cell-phone number. She'd asked Rodriguez about Carver and he'd wanted to know why, and she'd said that there was a murder investigation going on, and that Carver was a "person of interest." Rodriguez said that Carver "oughta be in jail," and when Sandy asked why, Rodriguez said he'd shot some people in Afghanistan and shouldn't have. Sandy had said that might be relevant, and asked Rodriguez if he'd talk to an investigator. He'd said he would. Sandy noted, "He didn't seem all that reluctant. He sounded angry."

Which was all good, in Lucas's view. The army had buried the file, and Carver might have felt safe, but if Lucas threatened to revive it, he might be able to drive a wedge between Carver and Dannon.

HE CALLED JAMIE MOORE, the public defender, and said, "You're gonna get a client named James Clay, who is being checked into the Hennepin County jail about now. Turk Cochran's got him on a murder charge."

"That's profoundly interesting," Moore said in a dead voice.

"I need to talk to him," Lucas said. "Off the record."

"What's in it for him?" Moore asked.

"They got him on that Helen Roman killing, Porter Smalls's secretary. I don't think he did it. I want him to detail where he was when the murder happened, and then I'm going to backtrack him, see if his story holds up."

"What does Turk have on him?"

"Cold hit on DNA. Found a glove under the victim's body," Lucas said. "Pretty conveniently under the victim's body. But unless James gets a break, he's done. You know what it's like to argue with DNA."

"Let me check around," Moore said. "Unless you're telling me a big fat one, I'll get Dan to go over there and sit in with you."

"Aw, not Dan, for Christ's sakes, I hate that little snake," Lucas said.

"Really? All right, let me look around. . . . I got Nancy Bennett. How about Nancy?"

"She's fine. Also a snake, but a much better-looking one."

"Give her an hour. She'll have to do a little pre-interview, find out what's what."

"He's already asked for an attorney."

"Give us an hour."

Lucas spent forty-five minutes writing a long memo to Flowers, who'd get it either in the airport lounge or in the air. He sent along Sandy's memo on Rodriguez, and asked Flowers to get anything on the type and level of violence in which Carver had been involved, and what had happened on the last mission. He wanted details.

Forty minutes after he'd called the public defender, Moore called back and said, "Nancy's at the jail. She'll wait for you."

Del called: "Irma says she doesn't know if they were in there. She doesn't think Carver, she's not sure about Dannon, because she says there's a lot of guys who look like him. In fact, there's one sitting here right now."

"Okay. It was worth the try. Listen. Meet me at the Hennepin jail."

BENNETT AND CLAY were waiting in an interview room when Lucas and Del walked in. Bennett was a tall, thin, dark-haired woman wearing a jacket-and-pants combination that wouldn't show dirt. Clay saw Lucas and said, "This is the sucker who hit me."

"Is that right?" Bennett asked.

"Yeah. He was running. I used just enough violence to restrain him," Lucas said. "He got an owie on his wrist."

"Coulda got hurt," Clay said.

Bennett ignored that and said to Lucas, "I don't want to hear any bullshit about who did what to whom. Listen to what he has to say and take off. I got other things to do."

"We'll listen, anyway," Lucas said.

She nodded at Lucas, then said to Del, "Those look like last month's jeans, Del. You forget to change on the first?"

Del said, "Don't be a twit."

"A what?"

"A twit."

She showed a sliver of a smile. "Well played."

CLAY, ACCORDING TO CLAY, had spent Saturday evening, from around eight o'clock until the next morning, at a recreational facility called Joan What's-Her-Name's, and Del asked, "The red house?"

"That's it."

"How many people were there?"

"You know . . . coming and going," Clay said.

"How many were staying?"

"The usual ones. The one called Mike, and Larry. Larry was there, lost his shoes somewhere, spent the whole time walking around in his socks. Chuck. This really, really white guy named Joe. He was so white it hurt my eyes to look at him. . . . A guy named Dave went through, he was a white guy, too, another guy named Bill was passed out on the couch the whole time. A couple of chicks . . ."

They were playing cards, he said. They tried to get the chicks to play strip poker. "She strips and then you poke her, heh-heh."

Nobody else laughed, so he shrugged and said, "They didn't play, they just wanted to, you know, get high."

He'd been there all night, he said. He'd gotten high with what he brought with him, because he didn't have any money, and then went to sleep on the floor in a back room. There was somebody else in there with him, but he didn't know who. "All I know is, I was sleeping under a window with a crack at the bottom and when I got up in the morning, I was freezing and it felt like my bones was breaking."

Larry was still there when he woke up, still high; Bill was still passed out, and might have been dead. Somebody should check. Chuck was lifting a weight in the kitchen: it was a dumbbell, and there was only one, so he was changing hands with it, and was drinking Campbell's Tomato Soup straight out of the can.

They pulled as many details as they could from him, and when they were done, Lucas turned to Bennett and said, "We're going to check on this. See if the deputies will put him in the drunk tank by himself, at least until we go into this place. Tell Jamie we'll send him a note."

"You believe him?"

"He's pretty obviously a miserable dirtbag liar and a piece of low-life scum, but, he had a lot of detail," Lucas said.

Clay said, "Hey, I'm sitting right here."

Lucas said, "Just kiddin'."

BACK OUTSIDE, Del called a friend on the Minneapolis narcotics squad and asked about the chance of a raid that evening on Joan What's-Her-Name's, and was told that it'd be a problem: too many people were off, and overtime and everything. Del asked if Minneapolis would mind a BCA raid, and after a little talk, everybody agreed that it would be okay. One of the Minneapolis guys, who was working anyway, would ride along.

Lucas told Del, "Set it up. Late as you can—we'd like to get the same cast of characters, if we can."

"Probably go for eleven o'clock," Del said.

Lucas went home for supper and found Virgil Flowers sitting at his kitchen table, a black felt cowboy hat to one side; he was drinking a Leinie's.

"How was Albuquerque?" Lucas asked. Flowers should have been arriving there in an hour.

"You got me a ticket on Delta," Flowers said. "What do you *think* happened?"

"The plane broke?"

"Exactly. They're bringing another one in from Chicago. Revised departure time is ten o'clock, assuming that the replacement plane makes it this far. They're probably bringing it in on a truck. Anyway, I won't be interviewing anybody tonight. Since your house was close by . . . and I hadn't had dinner . . ."

"We're having meat loaf," Weather said.

Flowers said, "Mmmm, mmm."

AT DINNER, Weather asked Lucas for a summary of the case. He put his fork down and said, "Nothing's clear. One of Grant's bodyguards, or both of them working together, probably killed Tubbs and probably killed Helen Roman."

"Are you going to clear it up tomorrow?"

"No. I might *know* something tomorrow, but whether I'll have a court case . . . whether I'll *ever* have a court case . . . that, I can't say."

"If you find out tomorrow before four o'clock, call me," Weather said. "Otherwise, I'm going to vote for Taryn Grant."

"I already did," Flowers said. "I mailed in my ballot last week."

Lucas said, "The thing that plagues me is, she might *know* something. She might even be involved."

"Do you care that much? You're as cynical about government as anyone I've ever known," Weather said.

"I'm not *that* cynical," Lucas said. "I'm cynical about the fact that there are so many little payoffs going around all the time, so many little deals, that the legislature is greased by corruption."

"I think you overstate the problem."

"No, he doesn't," Flowers said. "The legislature runs on corruption. But a killer in the U.S. Senate . . . an actual murderer? The prospect is the tiniest bit disturbing."

CHAPTER 21

Flowers went to Albuquerque, and Lucas went on the raid, which wasn't that much of a raid, as raids went.

The target house, the "red house," halfway down Minneapolis's south side, was owned by an obscure real estate investment group and rented to a thirty-one-year-old woman named Joan Busch, who was known by half the Minneapolis cops who worked the neighborhood. She'd once been a minor terror in the clubs, according to the Minneapolis vice cop who rode with them, but had gotten older and given up fighting.

She sold dope when she had it—marijuana—but more often, simply provided people with a warm place to party, as long as she could party along. She had a fifteen-year-old daughter who lived with a guy allegedly named Crown Royal, but, more importantly, brought in a child-support check.

"Nasty woman. Nasty," the vice cop said. "But, she won't let guns in her place, because she's afraid somebody'll shoot her nasty ass."

Lucas and Del were in Lucas's Lexus, with the vice cop, driving circles around the neighborhood, waiting. Lucas had supplied the BCA's SWAT team, which had scouted the location. The raid was supposed to go at eleven o'clock, but, as usual, things came up, and people ran late, and when Lucas turned the corner at eleven-forty, he saw the first of the SWAT guys go through the front door.

"There we go," he said.

"That door's been busted down so many times, you could open it by breathing on it," the vice cop said.

They parked directly in front of the house, behind a SWAT van, and Lucas, Del, and the vice cop ambled across the lawn and up the porch steps. Joan Busch was sitting on a ratty brown couch, looking both high and discouraged. Five men and a woman were facing a couple of different walls, hands on the walls, and had already been patted down. One man lay behind a couch, unmoving. The whole place smelled like weed, like an old motel room might smell of cigarette smoke.

"What happened to him?" Del asked, nodding at the unconscious man.

"He was like that when we came in," the SWAT leader said. "He's breathing, but he's not waking up. We've got an ambulance on the way."

"Must be Bill," Lucas said.

All seven of the house's inhabitants were stoned to some degree; when Lucas checked IDs, he found a Michael and a very, very white guy named Joe. The other woman, whose name was Charlotte Brown, said that she lived upstairs. Lucas told her to sit on the couch next to Busch, and then, after talking to the vice guy, they cut loose everybody except the two women, and Michael and Joe.

The freed men were taken outside one at a time by the vice guy, so that he could tell them that they were being released on his say-so, and that they owed him big time. A few minutes later, an ambulance showed up, and the unconscious guy was trundled out.

When that was done, Lucas and Del took the other four into the kitchen, one at a time, for questioning.

Michael and Busch were confused about the night that Clay was supposed to be in the house. They thought they might remember him, but were not sure exactly of the when: "That sucker comes and goes," Busch said. "In and out all the time."

He'd never come in the house with a gun, Busch said, "Because he knows if he do, that's the end of him. I throw his ass out and never let him come back. Cops don't mind a little weed, but they death on guns."

Brown, though, remembered something about Clay trying to start a game of strip poker. "I said, 'You so short, why'd I play strip poker with you?' and he said, 'Only my body short, 'cause all my growth went somewhere else.' Made me laugh, but I said, 'I ain't playin' strip poker with *nobody* in this house.'"

She said he was still there when she went upstairs, sometime well after midnight, but was gone when she came back down about noon.

Joe remembered him, too. "He was sleepin' on the floor when I got up. He was snorin' like a chain saw, you could hear him out in the street."

That was at six o'clock in the morning, or thereabouts. "I got to be to work at eight o'clock so I set my phone at six o'clock so I could go home and get washed up. The phone went off and he never moved, he snored right through it."

How high had Clay been the night before?

"He had this piece of hash he wanted to trade for a couple rocks, but nobody would trade him—I didn't have any myself—so he took out his pipe and smoked it," Joe said. "He was pretty high, best as I remember, but I don't remember too clear."

Was it possible that he could have gone away during the night and come back?

"Well, it's possible, but I don't know why he would," Joe said. "He didn't have any money to buy anything. All he had was that little piece of hash, wasn't bigger than about a nickel."

"How do you know he didn't have any money?" Del asked.

"'Cause somebody had one little rock and wanted twelve dollars for it, and he said he could only pay later and they said, 'Bullshit,' and he turned his pockets out, and he didn't have but eighty cents or something. And that little piece of hash."

"He have a gun?"

"Not that I seen."

WHEN THEY WERE FINISHED with them, they got their names, addresses, cell phone numbers—they all had phones—and told them not to leave town for a while. "Be the first chance you have to get a guy out of trouble, instead of in," Del said.

Out on the sidewalk, Lucas said, "Turk *will* be pissed. Clay's stoned on hash at two o'clock in the morning, and he's sound asleep at six. He's got no gun, and he doesn't have enough money even to catch a bus, so how does he get to North Minneapolis from way down here?"

"That's if everybody's remembering the right night," Del said. "Between the four of them, they couldn't *count* to four."

"I promise you something, Del," Lucas said. "Helen Roman wasn't killed by that dumbass. She was done by a pro. A guy who isn't a small-time burglar, and who never had to make a killing look like a burglary. She was killed by Carver or Dannon."

"Hey, I believe you," Del said. "But a jury would have its doubts. Especially when the defense attorneys start rolling out the military hero stuff, and they will."

"Yeah," Lucas said. "They will. We need somebody who's inside it."

"Dannon or Carver."

"Or Grant," Lucas said.

LYING IN BED THAT NIGHT, Lucas realized that it wouldn't be Grant. Grant was either completely innocent, or completely guilty. For her, there could be no middle ground.

As a rich woman, with her potential election to the Senate, she couldn't admit to the slightest knowledge of anything, without losing everything. A criminal trial would be brutal, and if she were convicted, she'd be looking at life in prison—thirty years in Minnesota. Even if she were acquitted in a criminal trial, the civil trials by the murder victims' relatives might still effectively destroy her, as O.J. Simpson had found out.

Logically, if she were guilty, nothing that Lucas could do would pry her open. And if she were innocent, she wouldn't know anything.

Therefore, Dannon or Carver.

With Dannon, he had Quintana's belief that Dannon was the man behind the phone call. The phone call indicated knowledge of at least the planting of the pornography on Smalls's computer, and from there, inductively, the murders of Tubbs and Roman.

With Carver, he had nothing about the specific case, but he did have the army records that suggested that Carver could kill, and in a cold way: the army case involved the execution of bound prisoners. On the other hand, the army killings involved levels of stress and circumstance about which Lucas knew nothing. Might those killings have been somehow justified? That was, he thought, possible.

Sister Mary Joseph—Elle—thought he should go after Dannon, because he was the thinker, and if you convinced him he was in trouble, he might decide to negotiate. On the other hand, she thought, Carver would simply stonewall.

But the army records, and the possibility that publicity might force the army to reopen the case, were a powerful pry-bar. In a sense, Carver had already been found to have murdered people, and if that were pushed into the open, he might already be eligible for a long, unpleasant prison term.

He rolled around, thinking about it, and rolled some more, got up, drank some milk, sat in his underwear in the living room, and finally went back to bed.

Pry-bar. Carver.

ELECTION DAY.

In the dawn's early light, he rolled out of bed when he felt Weather moving, and she said, "You had a bad night."

"Push coming to shove," Lucas said.

"When are you going to push?" she asked.

"Today, I think. There's no time left."

"Take your gun with you," she said. And, "God, I hate it when I think things like that. Take your gun with you, because somebody might try to kill you and you might have to kill them."

"Yeah. Well." He had nothing to say; and he would take his gun. He always did.

"How're you going to start?"

"By trusting somebody I have no really good reason to trust," he said.

WHILE WEATHER WENT IN the bathroom, Lucas walked downstairs to his study and called Alice Green. She came up on the second ring, sounding a little sleepy:

"Yes?"

"Lucas Davenport, the much-loved cop."

"I think Taryn talked to the governor about you," Green said. "Tried to get you fired."

"Yeah? What'd he say?"

"Not to be vulgar, but the phrase 'Go shit in your hat' comes to mind."

"With a person of the governor's refinement, I'm sure that phrase never occurred to him," Lucas said.

"This is probably not the time to discuss it, but I wouldn't mind being on his security detail," Green said. "I understand he doesn't have female security at the moment."

"I could ask him, Alice, but I don't think it's extremely likely," Lucas said.

"He's got something against women?"

"No, but his wife does," Lucas said. "You're far too good-looking to pass the test."

"Nothing to be done about that, I guess, unless you want to come over and punch me in the face," Green said.

"What I'd like to do," Lucas said, "is meet you somewhere to talk, before you go on the job today."

"Will this get me fired?" she asked.

"Maybe. I'd try to keep you out of it, but if it's a murder . . ."

"The thing is, disloyalty in one job might keep me from getting *any* other job."

"I'm trying to tell you the truth," Lucas said. "I can't absolutely guarantee that it wouldn't get out."

After a moment, she said, "There's a Caribou Coffee halfway between my place and Taryn's. I could meet you there at seven-fifteen. I'm on the job at eight."

"I'll see you then," Lucas said.

ALICE GREEN WAS DRESSED in green when Lucas arrived: a green blouse the color of her eyes, a much darker green jacket in a kind of knobby fabric, and black slacks that appeared to be form-fitting until you looked closely. She was paying for a cup of coffee, and Lucas looked closely, and realized that everything she wore was functional, nice-looking but tough, rather than luxurious, and well suited to a fight; the jacket was long enough and loose enough to conceal a pistol.

She paid, walked toward a far corner; saw him, nodded, but kept going. Lucas got a Diet Coke and checked the other customers before he walked over to her table, where she was blowing on a paper cup full of dark coffee. She said, "If anybody I know comes in, I'll have to shoot you."

Lucas sat down: "I need to talk to Carver, alone, I think. I've found a lever that might convince him to talk with me. I'll call him unless you think it would be a terrible idea."

She considered for a moment and then said, "Well, it would be a terrible idea, but talking to either one of them, Dannon or Carver, would be a terrible idea. I assume you've got your back against the wall."

"It's my last shot," Lucas said. "I'm almost certain that Dannon was involved in placing the porn on Smalls's computer. If Tubbs and Roman were killed to cover that up, then it's at least possible that he was acting alone and Carver could give me some insight into how to get him. Or, it's possible that Carver cooperated, but would take a plea. Also, I've got something on Carver that might convince him to cooperate. So, I'm looking at Carver."

"I doubt that he'll crack," Green said. "He'll stonewall. So will Dannon, for that matter. There's not much choice there."

Stonewall. She picked the same word as Elle had. "If you *had* to make a choice . . . which one would you choose?" Lucas asked.

She thought for a moment, sipping at the coffee, and finally said, "If I had to choose, I guess I'd have to agree with you: I'd go with Carver, if you've got some leverage. He's not as smart as Dannon. It's barely possible that you might confuse him enough to get something. I don't think that would be the case with Dannon. Also, Dannon's got another reason to stonewall: Taryn has started sleeping with him. If you take him down, she'd go down, too. At least, he'll see it that way. So he'll stonewall."

"It'll be tough either way," Lucas agreed.

"I'd say you've got no chance with Dannon, no matter how involved he is, and you've got a five percent chance with Carver. Or two percent."

"Off the top of your head . . . what are the chances that Grant knows what they did? That she's involved, that she directed it or approved it?"

Green shook her head: "She's a smart woman. I'd be surprised if she was involved. But . . . and I say *but* . . . she's obviously a sociopath. It wouldn't bother her that people died to get her into the Senate. It *would* bother her that she could go to prison for it. She's made that calculation, too. That's why she gets so angry when she sees you."

Lucas nodded, and said, "Okay," then leaned forward, his forearms on the table. "If I drive a wedge between Dannon and Carver, what would happen?"

"I don't know. They're colleagues, but not exactly friends," Green said. "Dannon is somewhat . . . disparaging . . . when it comes to Carver, because Carver was a sergeant, an enlisted man, and Dannon was an officer. He treats me more as an equal because I was with the Secret Service. Carver feels it. It pisses him off."

"What's Carver's relationship with Grant?"

"He's become . . . overly familiar. I don't know what happened, but yesterday I heard him call her 'honey,' when he thought they were alone. I pretended not to hear."

"She's not sleeping with him, too?"

"Oh, no. She's definitely the officer type. In fact, I'm a little surprised by the thing with Dannon. When I say 'officer type,' I'm talking generals, not captains. But, maybe it's just sex."

"All right," Lucas said. "Do you have a phone number for Carver?"

"Yes. He's already at the house, by the way. He'll be with Taryn until three o'clock, when he gets a couple hours off, to get ready for tonight. If you need to meet with him privately, you could call him while she's speaking. She has four brief appearances today, mostly for the television cameras, and for a couple of blogs. Then they'll head back and watch the results come in."

"Any idea about times?"

She took a piece of paper out of her bag and pushed it across the table. "I made a copy of her schedule. I'd call at one of the first two events—the schedule there is pretty hard. Later in the day, the time-table tends to slip."

"All right," Lucas said. "Thank you. Uh, do you have Carver's double-secret cell-phone number?"

"I do." She pulled back the paper with the schedule on it, took a pen out of her bag, and wrote the number on the paper. "Don't tell him where you got it."

"I won't," Lucas said.

"Did you find out what Carver did in the army? Is that what you've got on him?"

Lucas's eyebrows went up. "You know about that?"

"I don't know what it is, but I know something bad happened," Green said. "I suspect people wound up dead. I tried to find out, but I'm told it's all very classified."

"How about that," Lucas said.

She gazed at him for a moment, then said, "But you know?"

He smiled: "That's classified."

She smiled back. "You're a piece of work, Davenport. If it weren't for Weather, I'd take you to bed."

"If it weren't for Weather, I'd go," Lucas said.

THE EXCHANGE KEPT LUCAS warm all the way out to the car. He'd jump off a high building before he betrayed Weather, but a little extracurricular flirtation kept the blood circulating; not that all of it went to the brain.

Green asked Lucas not to call Carver until at least Grant's first appearance of the day. "I want it to be in Carver's head that I was around when you called. A little psychological insurance that he doesn't think of me, when he wonders how you got the number for his phone. He's a scary guy."

"I can do that," Lucas said. "And you lay low. It should be over in another day or two, one way or another."

She said, "I feel like it's gotta happen today. Everything is coming down to today. Taryn's snap polls say she's up, but it's really, really close, and Smalls may be narrowing the lead. It feels to me like everything's going to end tonight, when the votes come in."

CHAPTER 22

After leaving Green, Lucas went back to BCA headquarters in St. Paul and rounded up Del, Shrake, and Jenkins. After talking with Henry Sands, the director, he got the green light to borrow four more male and two female agents from other sections. They'd work in two shifts; he would have preferred to use Virgil Flowers to lead the second shift, but Flowers was still in New Mexico. Instead, he assigned the second shift to Bob Shaffer, a lead investigator with whom he'd worked on other cases.

He got the working group together in a classroom and briefed all nine of them on the entire Smalls/Tubbs investigation, and told them about his planned approach to Carver.

"One of the problems we're facing is that these two guys are probably tougher than any of us, and very experienced in killing, very cool about it," Lucas said. "What I'm going to do is try to drive a wedge between them, which could create an explosive situation. *Could* create an explosive situation—but it might not do anything at all. There's no way to tell what will happen. We're going to spend today, tonight, and tomorrow monitoring Carver, and Dannon, too. If nothing happens before then, it's probably a bust."

When he was done, one of the agents, Sarah Bradley, raised a hand and asked, "If you really get Carver jammed up with this army case, and if he's armed, what happens if he goes off on you?"

"He's too experienced to go off on me, I think," Lucas said. "If we hook up at a restaurant or coffee shop—that's what I'm thinking—it'd be too public. He might leave ahead of me, go storming out of the place, and then try to back-shoot me, I suppose, but I don't see that, either. He'll want to think about it."

"But this army thing—it sounds impulsive, like he cracked," Bradley said. "If he cracked then, he could crack again."

Lucas said, "That's not the feeling I got. I got the feeling that the army was talking about a cold series of executions. He thought he could get away with it. Either that nobody would know, or that none of his platoon would tell, or that if somebody did, he'd be covered. He was partly right—they kicked him out but didn't prosecute. The point is, it seems to me that he . . . thought about it. At least a bit."

"That's what you *think*, but not what you *know*," Bradley said. "I'm not so much worried about *you*. If he shoots you in the coffee shop . . . then he'd have to kill the witnesses. And he could do that. He's essentially already done it once."

Lucas hadn't considered that, and said, "Huh."

"You'd be better off with a couple more guns in the shop," Bradley said. "Probably Jane and me. He doesn't sound like the type to be looking at women as potential combatants: he'd be too macho for that."

Jane was the other female agent, Jane Stack.

Lucas said, "Let me think about it."

Shrake said, "Sarah's exactly right. The rest of us look too much like cops, except Del, and he'd recognize Del. Let's put Sarah and Jane in."

Lucas eventually agreed, and divided the group in two. "I don't know when I'll be talking to him, but I expect it'll be late afternoon or evening. As soon as I find out, the first shift sets up. We'll monitor the meeting—I'll be wearing a wire—and then we'll take him all the way through the day, until he goes to bed. This could be a very long night, with the election. As soon as we're sure that the night's over, Bob and his guys will pick him up, take him all day tomorrow, and then the first shift picks him up again tomorrow evening. We're all clear on overtime. As soon as we leave here, the first shift should go on home, or wherever, get your shopping done, get something to eat . . ."

When the bureaucratic details were handled, they broke up. Del, Shrake, and Jenkins followed him back to his office, where they talked some more about the surveillance aspects. A tech would put a tracking bug on Carver's vehicle, and Del would try to get one on Dannon's, if he could do it without being seen.

"The big question is: Is he gonna talk, or is he gonna stonewall, or is he gonna shoot, or is he gonna run?" Jenkins said.

"That's four questions," Shrake said. "It irritates me that you can't count."

THEY WERE STILL AT IT when Flowers called from Albuquerque. Lucas put him on the speaker phone.

"I talked to Rodriguez, and he seems like a pretty straight guy. He's going to school here, he's got a wife and a couple of kids. He's willing to make a formal statement if we need it. It's about what we thought, with a couple of other things . . ."

"Do tell," Jenkins said.

Rodriguez told Flowers that military intelligence sources had pinpointed what they thought would be a meeting between two rival Taliban chieftains in a border village. How that intelligence was developed, Rodriguez didn't know for sure, but he suspected the original tip came from a paid Afghani source in the village, and that had been backed up by electronic intelligence—the army had been monitoring the relevant Taliban cell phones.

In any case, Carver's unit, which included Rodriguez, and was basically made up of a couple of officers and a bunch of NCOs, had been dropped five kilometers from the meeting site. The soldiers had followed a little-used ridge path into the village. The house where the meeting was to take place had been spotted by the informant, who'd placed a tiny multi-mirrored reflector, similar to those used on golf course pins, on the roof of the place.

When the attack team had gotten close enough, they'd illuminated the village—which was made up of forty or so houses built on the edge of an intermittent stream—with infrared light, and had spotted the sparkle of the reflector.

They'd entered the house at three o'clock in the morning, in a raid pretty much like any police raid. They'd found the Taliban asleep on an assortment of beds and air mattresses and on the floor.

One of the men had tried to resist and was shot and killed. The others had not resisted and were frisked and cuffed at both the hands and the feet and made to lie facedown on the floor, Rodriguez said.

When they'd launched the raid, they'd simultaneously called for helicopter support, which was waiting. But within minutes after the men in the house had been subdued, the raiders began taking heavy fire from neighboring houses.

"The choppers included a gunship, and Rodriguez said that from the air, they could see what looked like muzzle flashes from dozens of weapons," Flowers said. "That was not supposed to happen. They realized pretty quickly that they weren't going to be able to haul a bunch of bound prisoners out of there, so they decided to run for it."

The attacking team did a hopscotch retreat back along the ridge, to where they could be picked up by the Blackhawk transport helicopters, with the gunships keeping the Taliban shooters out of their hair.

"Rodriguez and Carver were supposed to be the last men out of the house," Flowers said. "Carver carried a SAW—that's a light machine gun—and he went last because he could really lay down a big volume of covering fire. Rodriguez went, but then he heard smaller-arms firing from the house, and ran back because he thought some of the Taliban had gotten inside and Carver would need help. What he found was, Carver had executed the prisoners, shooting them in the head with his personal sidearm, a nine-millimeter Beretta. Rodriguez didn't have time to investigate, or anything, this all happened in a few seconds, and then they were running for their lives. When they got back to their base, he reported what he'd seen. He was kinda freaked out. Carver denied it, said that some Taliban had broken through the back of the house, and if any prisoners were dead, they were killed in the firefight. Rodriguez said that the gunships had video, and the video didn't show an attack on the back of the house, but it could have happened. Eventually . . . well, you know what happened. The army got rid of Carver and Rodriguez both."

Rodriguez could have stayed in, Flowers said, but after reporting Carver's action, thought he'd never be trusted again by the special ops people. "That's all Rodriguez was interested in—special ops. He didn't want to be in a regular outfit. But he said that he'd heard other things about Carver—that Carver had always been the first to shoot, that there was at least one other incident—Rodriguez called it an incident—in which civilians had been killed, and nobody had done anything about it. Rodriguez says that Carver was a killer, and that a lot of other people knew it, and that quite a few of them didn't like it. So, they got rid of him."

"Covered it up," Lucas said.

"Yeah, that's what it amounted to, although I don't know what kind of investigation could have been done, given the situation," Flowers said. "Still, I think you might be able to threaten Carver with exposure, tell him that he'll wind up in Leavenworth, and he might believe you. I'm not sure that there's any possibility of a real follow-through on that. At least, not in time to do any good in your case."

"All right," Lucas said. "You recorded all of this?"

"Yeah, of course. If you want me to, I could stay here, transcribe it, and get Rodriguez to sign it."

"Do that," Lucas said. "But try to get back tonight or tomorrow morning. We might need to stick the document up Carver's nose."

"Probably gonna be tomorrow morning," Flowers said. "I don't think I'll get the docs done in time to catch the afternoon plane."

"Then get the docs," Lucas said. "I'll see you tomorrow."

DEL, SHRAKE, AND JENKINS watched Lucas make notes, and five minutes later call Carver. Carver came up on the phone almost instantly. He said, "Yeah."

"This is Davenport, the cop that's been following you around."

"How'd you get this number?"

"I'm a cop," Lucas said. "I need to talk to you. I need to talk to you right away, and somewhere private, where Dannon and Grant aren't around."

"I don't think I want to do that," Carver said, and the line went dead.

"Well, shit," Lucas said.

"You're a smooth talker," Del said.

"I wonder if he's got a smartphone," Lucas said. He sent a text: "Six executed in Afghanistan. Want to hear the governor talking about it on TV? Take the call."

He sent it, and got back "delivered" a second later. Ten seconds after that, Carver took the second voice call and said, "What kind of bullshit is this?"

"You know what kind of bullshit it is. It's Leavenworth bullshit," Lucas said. "Now, you need to take a little time off this afternoon, go out for a cup of coffee. There's an obscure Caribou Coffee a couple miles from Grant's house. Give me a time."

After a moment of silence, Carver said, "Three o'clock."

"Good. And I'll tell you, Ron, we are going to put some serious shit on you. We're also going to give you a way out. All of that gets canceled if you talk to Dannon or Grant. They're the targets in this. We've already got a guy willing to swear that Dannon set up the porn deal for Grant. You can walk, or you can get added to the list. I'll see you at three, and we'll decide which it is."

Lucas clicked off without giving him a chance to answer.

THEY HAD TIME to kill, and with one thing and another, killed it. The two women were going in with briefcases and spiral binders and carefully coordinated suits: real estate agents. Lucas would be wearing a wire, monitored from a van with a plumber's logo on the side, and a real phone number for anyone who needed plumbing services. Jenkins and Shrake would be nearby, but out of sight in separate cars, listening to the conversation on their own radios.

When Carver arrived, a tech who was riding in the plumbing van would try to place a battery-powered GPS tracker on Carver's car, if he could do it without being seen. When Carver left, he'd be tracked by Jenkins and Shrake, who would be well out of sight, running on parallel roads where they could. Lucas and the two women would follow in separate cars.

Del would watch Dannon. If he had an opportunity, he'd place another GPS tracker on Dannon's vehicle.

Since Lucas had been in the same coffee shop that morning, talking to Green, he knew the layout of the place. He told the two women agents, Stack and Bradley, to park as close as they could to the coffee shop's door, hoping that would push Carver away from a parking place that he could see from the shop, and give the technician a good chance to install the tracking bug.

The women were to take a table on the left end of the semicircular seating area, out of sight from where Lucas would take a table, on the far right end.

AND THAT'S WHAT they all did.

The two women went in at ten minutes of three, ordered a Northern Lite Salted Caramel Mocha and a large Americano, and two cranberry scones, put their briefcases on the floor by their ankles, tops open, guns right there, and opened a notebook full of pictures of houses.

Lucas arrived five minutes later, and as he did, Shrake called: "He's here, across the street behind the BP station. He's watching you."

"All right. I'm going in. If he pulls out a deer rifle, shoot him," Lucas said.

"Will do."

Lucas went in, saw the two women at the table on the right, got a Diet Coke and another scone, and walked down to the left, an empty table near the restroom door. His phone rang and Shrake said, "He's coming," and a second later, "He's parking on the side."

Carver slouched along the outside walk, pushed through the door. He was wearing a dark blue nylon shell over a cotton sweater, black slacks, and boots. He looked around the room, his gaze pausing on each of the people at the tables, on the servers, and finally to Lucas. Lucas nodded. Carver turned away, stepped up to the counter, got a large cup of black coffee, and Lucas thought, *Scalding hot coffee.*

Carver was a big guy, thick through the chest, but moved easily, comfortable with his size. Lucas wondered, if it came to a fistfight, if he could take him; and he decided he could. Lucas watched as Carver got his coffee and crossed to Lucas's table, put the coffee on the table, and sat down and asked, "What is this bullshit?"

Lucas said, "I know goddamned well that either you or Dannon killed Tubbs and Roman. I thought about it for a while, and decided that it'd be either Dannon by himself, or both of you together. I don't know where Grant comes in, if she's even aware of it. I need somebody to talk to me about it. I picked you."

"I have no idea of what you're talking about—"

"I hope that's not true, because whether or not it is, I'm going to hurt you. I got the records from the investigation into the shootings in Afghanistan, and I've got a guy who can put them on the political agenda. I think I can get the army to pull you back in—they can do that, for crimes committed under their jurisdiction—and I think I can get you sent to Leavenworth. I'm not sure I can do all that, but I think I can. And I will, unless you talk to me."

"There's nothing to talk about," Carver said. "The army cleared me. Those people were killed by Taliban firing through the windows, blind firing—"

"The report says there are witnesses who say otherwise. We've got video shot from an Apache . . . is that right? An Apache? A helicopter gunship? They have night-camera video from every angle on that house you raided, and nobody's shooting into it, not in a way that would hit people lying on the floor."

"It's that fuckin' Rodriguez, isn't it?" Carver said. "Listen, I gave him a down-check on an evaluation, stalled him out at E-6, and he never got over it. Said he was going to get me. Now he's talking to you, right?"

Lucas spoke right past him: "I can offer you a deal. You give me anything that points at Dannon, or Grant, for that matter, and we'll let sleeping dogs lie. Nobody will mention the word 'Afghanistan.' I can't offer you immunity for anything you've done here in Minnesota, only a prosecutor can set that up, but I can offer to testify in your behalf, in any court case that comes up, to say that you cooperated and aided the investigation."

Carver looked at Lucas over the coffee, which he hadn't touched, and finally said, "That's it? That's all you got?"

"I can't tell you what else we have—but one reason we came to you, is that we can hang the child porn thing on Dannon, and the two killings that follow the child porn. All by itself, the porn will get him twenty years. We need one more little thing to get him for the whole works—we're still processing the Roman scene, and we've got quite a bit of DNA. That takes a while to come back. If it comes back Dannon, he's done. If it comes back Carver, and you've been stonewalling us . . . then that's done. No deal. No way."

Carver shook his head: "First of all, as a suck-ass small-town cop, you got no idea of what you're getting into with the army. They cleared me, and if you try to prove otherwise, they'll hand you your ass. And I don't give a shit about any governor. The army's bigger than any governor, and they'll hand him *his* ass, too. Not because they're protecting me. Because those generals, they'll be protecting themselves."

"I'm willing to find out," Lucas said.

"Then you're gonna have to," Carver said. "Second of all, even if I knew something, I wouldn't tell you, because you can't even give me immunity. The best I could hope for, if I knew about these killings, would be what? Life with parole? Twenty years? Say I keep my mouth shut, and you're right about the governor and all that, and the army pulls me back . . . nothing they do could be worse than what you're talking about. To tell you the truth, given what happened that whole night . . . *heroes in a firefight* . . . I don't see any way they convict me of anything."

"So."

"So, you can take your deal and stick it up your ass," Carver said. He leaned back in his chair, as though satisfied with his decision.

"From what the army investigators say about what happened in Afghanistan, I don't suppose the murders of a couple more people would bother you—nothing for me to work with, there," Lucas said.

Carver rolled his eyes up and sideways, as if to say, *Please*, the way New Yorkers say it. As if to say, *Now you're wasting our time.*

"That's like asking me if I feel bad when somebody gets killed in a car accident. I mean, I gotta tell you, if I don't know them, I don't feel bad. It's like that with this Tubbs guy. Don't know him, never saw him. If I could snap my fingers and he'd come walking through the door, I'd do it. But feel bad, if he's dead? No. Sorry."

"All right. I got nothing more," Lucas said.

Carver looked at him for a moment, then pushed his chair back and stood up. As he turned, Lucas said, "I might have a deal for Dannon, too. If he takes it, I'll put you away forever. Thirty years, no parole. You'll be an old man when you get out."

"Fuck you."

"Whatever," Lucas said. "You got my phone number. The deal is open until Dannon talks to me. At that point, you're done."

"Double fuck you," Carver said.

"Keep your eye on the TV. You could be a star," Lucas said.

Carver walked away.

CHAPTER 23

Kidd finally boiled it down to a single line: he said, "I think it's moronic."

"I know what I'm doing," Lauren said.

"I'm not sure of that. As far as you know, they'll have a dozen extra guards around the place to keep the starfuckers away," Kidd said.

"They'd be out front. I'll be going in from the dark side, right down the neighbor's tree line," Lauren said. She'd been studying satellite pictures all day, including several taken within the past week, with resolution good enough to see the hubcaps on cars. "I'll have my starlights. The security alarms will be off, the dogs will be locked up, all kinds of people will be walking around the place, and most of them will be either rich or important, so nobody will be inclined to question them."

"Jesus." Kidd dragged his fingertips through his eye sockets.

"One last time," Lauren said. "I swear to God, I do this, and I'm done. I'll go back to being the little housewife."

"You're not a little housewife."

"Yes, I am. I'm not a famous painter. I'm not a famous computer hacker," Lauren said. "People say, 'You're *that* Kidd's wife? You lucky woman.' You know—get your cookies in the oven and your buns in the bed, while Kidd takes care of the important stuff."

Kidd had to laugh, and she said, "Now you're laughing."

"I'm laughing because it's so fucking stupid. Why can't you be a rock climber or something? A scuba diver? You're smart—go to college, get a degree, become a famous . . . whatever."

"Right. Whatever. Even the Famous Kidd can't think exactly what that might be."

They were in the living room, in a couple of easy chairs overlooking the Mississippi. The weather was changing: not only from one day to the next, but from autumn to winter. The sky was gray, overcast, with thick clouds the color of aluminum, not a hint of the sun. Cold. On really bad days, Kidd sat in front of the window and drew the scene, with a pencil or a crayon and a sketchbook, and the scene changed every time. Lauren pushed herself out of her chair and walked to the window, pressed her forehead against the cool glass.

After a moment, Kidd walked up behind her and draped an arm over her shoulder. "All right. Let's do it."

"Thank you. You can't tell me this doesn't light you up, at least a little bit," Lauren said.

"The biggest problem is Jackson," Kidd said. "We can't both get caught. If they grab you . . ."

"You have to run," Lauren said. "But they won't grab me. . . . I absolutely will not push. I'll go in with my finger on the abort switch. The first second that trouble shows up, I'll go right back down the tree line. You get me, and we roll."

"One last time," Kidd said.

She turned back to him, her face bright. "I'm really stoked, Kidd. I'm high as a kite."

DANNON WAS DRIVING, TARYN was in the backseat. Schiffer, the campaign manager, was in the front passenger seat with two cell phones, three ballpoint pens, one red, one green, and one black, and a blue-cloth three-ring binder. Inside the binder was an inch-thick stack of paper, much of it given over to a listing of every voting precinct in Minnesota, all 4,130 of them, with the results of the last Senate campaign, which had been won by Porter Smalls.

Thirty precincts had been designated as critical signposts. For those precincts, the far right column was kept in red, green, or black ink; red for those precincts where exit polls suggested Smalls would exceed his total in the last campaign, green for those in which he was running behind, and black for those in which there was no discernible change.

Of the thirty, as of three o'clock in the afternoon, he was running behind his previous total in seventeen of the twenty-six where they had been able to gather enough responses to report. In the other nine, there was no discernible change. He was running ahead in none of them. All by itself, that would have been good; but what was happening was actually better than good. People who voted before five o'clock tended to be more conservative than those who voted after five o'clock.

Taryn had been scheduled to make four appearances during the day, set up to capture the noon and early evening news: going in, they'd thought they might need the small extra boost from those television appearances. Porter Smalls had ended his campaign with a breakfast at the St. Paul Hotel in St. Paul, so wouldn't be much of a factor on the news. Besides, the news departments at TV stations in Minneapolis were generally liberal, and would give Taryn a publicity break if they could get away with it.

In the front seat, Schiffer said into one of her phones, "I don't want to know about helium. I want some of the balloons to go down, instead of up. Is that too much to ask? Get it done."

On her second phone she said, "Well?" She listened for a moment, then grunted and wrote a number in the right column in green ink. She said, "Keep it going," and hung up and turned to Taryn.

"Eighteen of twenty-seven, and we're running stronger in our precincts than Sterling did last time."

"You want to make a call?" Taryn asked.

"I never believe it until I see the actual numbers . . . but yeah. You got it. You're the new senator from Minnesota."

Taryn said, "Yes!" and Dannon slapped the steering wheel and cried, "Oh, my God, it makes my dick hard!"

Taryn said, "Douglas . . ."

"I'm sorry, it's . . ."

Schiffer: "Don't worry about it. Makes my dick hard, too."

AT FOUR-FIFTEEN THEY ARRIVED at St. Mary's Park for a rally timed to the evening news. Del was there, too, wearing a navy blue suit that was a couple sizes too big for him, with a wrinkled white shirt and a blue-white-and-chocolate-striped nylon tie whose wideness would have made him proud in 1972. His hat had a snap brim and a feather. He looked like a flake and nobody paid any attention to him.

He got on his cell phone and told Lucas, "Dannon's still with her. Man, I think she's gonna win. She's not saying so, but it's coming through."

"Carver's still sitting there, I don't know what he's doing, but it's something," Lucas said. Carver had gone from the Caribou Coffee to a Starbucks, not far away.

"I'll call you back if anything happens," Del said. "It looks like they're gonna be here for a while. A couple of TV trucks just came in. I'm gonna stick that bug on their truck."

"Make sure you can do it clean."

"Do that," Del said.

LUCAS WAS ON THE STREET, ten miles away, in a parallel parking spot, ready to roll out in front of Carver, if he came that way. He couldn't actually see Carver, but Jenkins could, from a dry-cleaning shop across from the Starbucks. From his vantage point, Jenkins said it looked like Carver had gotten two or three cups of coffee at twenty-minute intervals and spent the rest of the time crouched over an iPad.

"I don't think he's reading the Bible," Jenkins said, on his handset. "But whatever it is, he's all over it."

"Maybe he's buying plane tickets," suggested Shrake, who was on the same net. Shrake was a half-mile up the street, ready to follow if Carver broke that way.

"That worries me," Lucas said. "We don't have enough to pull him in. If he gets on a plane, all we could do is wave good-bye."

"I haven't seen him take out a credit card," Jenkins said. "I'm more worried that he's waiting for his dry cleaning."

"This guy isn't dry cleaning, he's strictly wash-and-wear,"

Shrake said. "He's all Under Armour and nylon shells and combat boots."

"Sounds like you," Jenkins said. Then: "Hey. He's up. Looks . . . He's headed out." A minute later, "He's turning your way, Lucas. You better move."

"Got him on the monitor," Shrake said.

Lucas rolled away and said, "I'm gonna jump on 94, bet he's headed back to Grant's."

CARVER HAD SPENT an hour with his iPad, part of the time doing what Lucas had feared: checking planes from Minneapolis to the East Coast—New York, New Jersey, Philadelphia, Miami. He'd also checked in with old acquaintances working with contractors who supplied private security personnel in Afghanistan and several other nations in the Middle East and Africa; he asked about job openings.

Time, he thought, *to get out of Minneapolis.*

He spent the last minute or two on his cell phone. He was in-house for the party that evening, which Schiffer had said would go until ten-thirty or so, and then they'd head downtown to the Radisson Hotel for the victory party, if there was a victory party. The house party was reserved for political big shots and large donors.

He punched Dannon's number, and Dannon came up: "Yes."

"Is she winning?"

"Yes. Looks like it's in the bag. You at the house?"

"No, but I'm heading that way now," Carver said. "I need to talk to you. Privately. Right now. I got hit hard by Davenport."

Dannon said, "We're doing the last show. We'll be back there by five-thirty."

"I'll be waiting," Carver said.

———

KIDD AND LAUREN HAD a bad moment when they turned Jackson over to the babysitter. The babysitter was a middle-aged nurse who was grateful for the extra under-the-table cash money from Kidd; five hundred a month, with babysitting services on a moment's notice. She worked the day shift, and was available anytime after three o'clock in the afternoon, seven days a week. She adored Jackson, and Jackson liked her back.

But leaving Jackson, a thin child, tall for his age, strong, with a happy smile morning to night . . . Kidd got desperately tight in the throat, and Lauren said, "I know: but we're doing it. I need this, Kidd."

So they left him.

AT 45 DEGREES NORTH, the night comes early in November. They rolled out a few minutes after seven-thirty into the kind of autumn darkness that comes only with a thick cloud layer, no hint of starlight or moonlight, and no prospect of any. Lauren drove.

She was already dressed in her black brushed-cotton suit. Her hood, and her equipment, were locked in a concealed box behind the second row of seats. They chitchatted on the way across town, through enough traffic to keep things slow; Jackson wasn't mentioned.

They were a mile from Grant's place at eight-fifteen. The day before, they'd spotted a diner with a strong and reliable Wi-Fi and no protection, with parking on the side and in back, out of sight from the street. Kidd signed on from a laptop and dialed up another laptop, which was hooked into his cell phone, back at the condo.

His phone made a call to a friend who, at that moment, was playing a violin in a chamber quartet at the birthday party for a St. Paul surgeon's wife. Kidd let the call ring through to the answering service, left a message that suggested handball on Friday.

"Done," he said, when he'd hung up. An alibi. Both of their desktop computers would be roaming websites all through the evening, and they'd send out a couple of e-mails.

"Let's see what's going on."

Kidd signed on to Taryn's security system. All the cameras were operating, the interior cameras showing perhaps two or three dozen people in suits and dresses with cocktails, all apparently talking at full speed. The bedroom was dark, which was perfect. If it hadn't been, Lauren would have had to come in through a dead-ended hallway, at a seating area, that would have been more exposed to a visitor, but was free of cameras. This way, she could go in through the en suite bathroom. Outside, the cameras showed several uniformed men behind the fence along the line of the street, and a few people standing in the street, looking at the house.

"The uninvited," Lauren said. "Check the backyard."

Kidd cycled to the backyard cameras. They saw one guard, moving along the perimeter of the huge lot. A side camera showed the dog kennel, with both dogs sitting inside, alert, apparently watching the guard.

"There's the competition," Kidd said.

"Not if they're penned up," Lauren said. "They can't see my entry point. As long as they're not set loose . . ."

"They've got noses like radar," Kidd said.

"Yes. Keep an eye on them. If they turn them loose, I'll call it off."

They watched for fifteen minutes, until Lauren said, "Okay, we've got it."

Just before Kidd killed the image from the cameras, they saw a security man in a coat walk through the picture. "Mean-looking guy," Kidd said. "I think that's Carver."

"I'll stay away from him," Lauren said.

"Yeah. Far away." He reached out, put his hand on top of her head and turned her face toward his, and kissed her and said, "Let's call it off."

"No. I'm going in," Lauren said. "Tomorrow, I'm back to little housewifey."

"Fuck me," Kidd said, as he started the car. "Fuck me."

DANNON AND CARVER got together before dark, and Carver laid it out, exactly as it had happened: Davenport was blackmailing him for information.

"He's gonna get me, man," Carver said. He didn't seem scared, Dannon thought: he looked wired, like he might before a bad-odds mission. "He says that the governor will go on TV and talk about what happened in the 'stan. He says they can force the army to take me back and put me on trial. He said it was a massacre like that one in Vietnam, and there's no way that Obama could let it go."

"That's bullshit, man," Dannon said. "That whole thing is buried so deep, and the guys who buried it all have stars now. They'd never get you."

"That's what I told him," Carver said. "I think he's going to do it anyway. I'm telling you, he's a crazy mean cocksucker. He's got nothing unless I talk, except the 'stan, and he'll use it to bust my balls."

"If you talk, he'll bust more than your balls. He'll put you in the penitentiary forever," Dannon said.

Carver said, "I know. I been thinking about it ever since I talked to him. He can't do anything fast enough to keep me off a plane. I'm thinking I fly to Paris, take the train to Madrid, and fly out to Panama. Confuse the trail. I got a buddy there, runs a fishing place over on the Pacific side. By the time they get to Panama, if they even bother to chase me, I'll be deep in-country. I'll be wearing a sombrero and talking taco."

"Ah, man . . ."

"You got something better?" Carver asked.

"I need to think about it," Dannon said.

"Listen. I know you're sleeping with Taryn, so you can talk to her. You put this on her, right now. Tonight. I need cash. A lot of it. I got the passport, I know how to travel, there's nothing I want in the apartment that I can't get in a duffel bag or two. Maybe you could clean the rest of it out for me later. But I need cash."

"How much? You mean, traveling money?"

"I mean traveling money, and hiding money," Carver said. "Living money."

"What are we talking about, Ron?"

Carver hesitated, then said, "It's like Tubbs said. If you want to retire . . . I need a million."

"Jesus Christ, man, she can't come up with a million overnight."

"Sure she can. I've seen her wearing a half-million in diamonds. They're right there in her safe," Carver said. "I'll take diamonds. What's that one, that big green one? The Star of Kandiyohi? That's probably another half-million—I've heard people talk. And I know she keeps cash around. I need enough cash to get to a place where I could sell the diamonds or whatever else she wants to unload. And then I'm gone. . . . I want to be in Paris tomorrow night."

"I don't know," Dannon said. "I'll talk to her, maybe figure something out. A million is pretty goddamn rich, though. Pretty goddamn rich, man."

"How many millions has she got?" Carver asked. "A thousand millions? Isn't that right? I've heard people say that, that she's a billionaire. It takes one one-thousandth of what she's got to get me out of the way, stashed down south? She'll never hear from me again, she can go be a senator or a president or whatever."

Dannon nodded. "Okay. I'll talk to her. *I'll talk to her.* You gotta take off for the hotel pretty soon. Get us set up there. I'll try to get an answer tonight, and I'll talk to you at the hotel."

"Good. I appreciate it, man." Carver ran his hands through his thick hair, then shook it out. "Isn't this a bunch of shit? That guy, Davenport, you watch out for him. Maybe you ought to come with me. I mean, Paris. We could be in Paris tomorrow night."

"City of Light," Dannon said.

"What?"

"City of Light. That's what they call Paris."

"City of Cheese. That's what they oughta call it," Carver said. "I never noticed the light, but they sure got a shitload of cheese."

CHAPTER 24

L ucas drove past Grant's house with the driver's-side window down, along the street lined with towering pines and blue spruces. He could hear, distantly but clearly, Aretha Franklin singing "Think."

From the street, he could see that the front door was open, and he could see people inside; and he could see guards along the front lot line. Another dozen people were milling outside the front fence, one of them with a large handwritten sign that said, "Yay for the New Senator." As Lucas continued down the street, he saw, in his rearview mirror, a TV truck turning the corner.

She won, he thought. The TV people would be looking at exit polls, and would know which way the wind was blowing, even if they wouldn't say so until the polls closed. He continued around a curve, turned into an intersecting street, followed it down its twisting length to a slightly larger street, took a right, and followed the new street out to an even larger, straight street. Just around the corner, he pulled up behind Del, got out, and walked to the passenger side.

Del popped the door and Lucas got in. Del was eating a cheese and bratwurst sandwich, with onions, and Lucas said, "Maybe we oughta talk outside."

"Gotta man up," Del said. "Besides, only two more bites, and it's cold out there."

"Nothing's happening," Lucas said.

"Well, they're in there together. I wonder if Carver said anything?"

"I gotta believe he did, 'cause if he didn't, this is a huge waste of time," Lucas said.

"Yeah, and it's your fault," Del said. He finished the sandwich, dug a napkin out of a brown paper bag, burped, wiped his fingers and chin. "Goddamn, that was good."

"I thought Cheryl had you off that crap. Had to be ninety percent cholesterol."

"Ah, we compromised. I can have one a week. Gotta make it count."

Shrake called on the handset: "You hear the one about the guy walking around with his dog at night, and runs into his old pal with *his* dog?"

"Big waste of time," Lucas said. "But, no, I haven't."

"I'll tell it to you sometime," Shrake said. "Right now, I should probably mention that I went by Grant's place, and Carver was walking out to his truck. He was talking to Dannon. I think he's moving."

Lucas said, "I'm on it," said good-bye to Del, who was monitoring the main vehicle, the one Dannon had been driving, and walked back to his truck. Carver started moving two minutes later, and Lucas and Shrake and Jenkins and Bradley and Stack followed him downtown, and watched him turn into a parking ramp that fed the Radisson Hotel, where the victory party would be held.

BRADLEY AND STACK FOLLOWED him in. They were dressed for the party, Bradley with a big pin that said "Taryn" and Stack with a bunch of credentials around her neck that looked like news credentials. They'd both changed their hair a bit and Bradley had gotten a pair of black-rimmed glasses. Neither looked like the real estate ladies from that morning. The three men waited in the street, and five minutes after Carver drove into the garage, Bradley called on her cell phone and said, "He's in the ballroom, he's talking to security. Looks like they're setting up for tonight."

"Has he looked at you?" Lucas asked.

"No."

"Good. Stay out of sight," Lucas said. "You don't want him to see you more than a couple of times."

Annoyed, she said, "Yeah, I've done this before."

"I know you have . . . but I worry."

IN WHAT WOULD HAVE BEEN an expansive family room, if Taryn had had a family, all the white folks and the necessary number of blacks and browns were cuttin' a rug, if a lot of really stiff heirs and fund managers and entrepreneurs and politicians could, in fact, cut a rug.

Taryn had had a few drinks and was dancing with everyone, lit up like a Christmas tree, feeling the rush. Dannon had tried to catch her eye, but she'd resolutely moved on to the next Important Person.

———

KIDD COULD SEE HOW pumped Lauren was, so he didn't bother to argue any further, though he drove slowly. Eventually, however, they'd arrived at Grant's house, and there was no way to put it off. He hit the switch that killed the taillights, let the car roll to a stop, said, "Luck," and Lauren slipped out the door and into the night.

Lauren had always had a taste for cocaine, given up only when pregnancy was a prospect, and not touched since then; but now, as she slipped out of the car, over the curb and into the trees that marked the edge of the neighbor's lot, she felt as high as she ever had on coke, with the same preternatural awareness, her senses reaching out through the trees to the political party three hundred yards away.

Lauren was in her black suit, with a black nylon backpack. She'd opened a pair of sterile surgical gloves in the SUV, before getting out, and Kidd had helped her get into them as a surgeon would, with no contact on the outer surface that would spread germs . . . or DNA.

Once back in the trees, she pulled on her starlights and moved slowly toward Grant's place. There was a lot of light from that direction, and none from the house to the other side. The light threw India-ink shadows behind each tree. Ten feet from Grant's property line, she found a particularly deep shadow and lay down in it for five minutes, without moving; watching and listening.

She saw a guard moving across the yard, away from her; he apparently had been assigned to the backyard. She decided she needed to time him. She took out the cold phone and called Kidd. She said, "I'm at Target. I'll be a while. Call you when I'm ready to go."

"Okay. Everything's fine, here."

Target was the edge of the yard, where she lay. Cell phones are radios, and hobbyists listen to the calls. . . .

She hung up and lay back in the weeds. Three minutes, four minutes. The backyard guard had disappeared around the corner of the house, where the dog kennel was, and now reappeared, having walked all the way around the house. He was an older guy, hands in his pockets, peering here and there, but not obviously ready to act.

When he'd gone halfway around the house again, Lauren took a breath, punched in Kidd's number, said, "I'm gone." She crossed the four-foot-high wrought iron fence that marked the property line, and, keeping a tree trunk between herself and the house, crossed halfway to the house. At the tree, she paused again, watching and listening, and saw nothing.

Ten seconds, and she moved again, paused at another tree, then ran lightly across the yard to the house and lay down in a spreading arborvitae shrub at the house's foundation. She pushed the starlights up and off, and stowed them in her pack. She smiled at a thought: the thought that the guard would hear her heart pounding in the bush.

A minute passed, then another, and she lay completely covered and unmoving, on her stomach, so she could make a fast dash for the side tree line if she had to, like a sprinter coming out of the blocks. The target window was straight above her head.

She hadn't felt like this in six years, and she nearly giggled.

A minute later, the guard ambled by, his head turned away from the house. When he was out of sight, she started counting seconds under her breath. At the same time, moving automatically, she stood up, looked through the window into a darkened bathroom. Kidd was watching the security cameras, and hadn't seen anything, so she stuck a couple of suction cups to the window, pulled a glass cutter from her leg pocket, and putting a lot of weight behind it, scored the first layer of glass. At "forty" she hit the glass with the back end of the cutter, and heard it crack along the score line. She pulled on the suction cups, but the glass was stubborn, and she hit it again. This time, it came free, and she lowered it to the ground. She was at sixty.

At one hundred twenty, she hit the second layer of glass twice, and pulled it free. The noise—a series of sharp but not particularly loud cracks—was unavoidable. The last sheet of the triple-pane glass would have to be done more carefully, because it had a foil alarm strip around the perimeter. Kidd thought all the alarms were off, but it would be best not to break it. She wasn't sure she had time, so she lay back in the bush, and at the count of two-twenty, the guard came past the house again.

When he was gone, she stood up again, and carefully cutting inside the foil strips, she yanked the last pane of glass off, and lay down again. She dialed Kidd and said, "Let's get coffee." He said, "I'll see you there."

He knew she was ready to enter; and she knew that there'd been no alarm yet.

Yet. Big word.

SHE PULLED A SHORT strip of thick, soft plastic tarp out of her pack, and waited again for the guard to pass. When he did, she put the tarp over the edges of the cut window glass and carefully boosted herself through the window. She stepped on a toilet seat, moved quickly to the water-closet door, into the main bathroom and to the bathroom door. She opened it, just a crack.

The bedroom was dark. She could hear the distant vibration of voices and the deeper thump of rock music, but nothing from the bedroom. She dialed Kidd and said, "In." He made no reply, but he was there, live, and if something broke, he'd start screaming.

She took a moment to remove the tarp from the window, then moved quickly through the bedroom, groped for the button that would open the bookcase panel, found it, opened it, put the phone to her ear. Was the bookcase button booby-trapped? Kidd said nothing, issued no warning. The safe was there, in the dark: she felt for the keypad, found it, tried a combination, turned the lock handle. It didn't budge. No panic: she had a sequence to run through, one of four possibilities. She hit it on the second one.

There must have been twenty small jewelry cases in the safe. She threw them in the pack, felt deeper into the safe, picked up something heavy and cylindrical . . . a roll of coins. Heavy: gold. She felt around, found a dozen more rolls. And cash: stacks of currency. Christ, this was good. She threw everything into her bag, and then closed the safe, and pushed the bookcase button . . .

And Kidd started screaming: "Hide hide hide . . ."

She punched off the phone and at the same moment, she heard them: somebody coming down the hall, arguing, coming fast. No time, not time even to get to the bathroom . . .

The bookcase was sliding back in place as she bounced once across the bed to the far side, pulling the pack along, hit the floor, then slipped under the bedskirt and pulled the pack with her, under the bed. At the same moment, the bedroom door opened, and a streak of light cut across the carpet.

DANNON FINALLY GOT TARYN out of the crowd. She was about two-thirds drunk, he thought, as he hustled her along by her arm, all the way to the bedroom, a few curious partiers looking after them. They pushed through the door, but didn't bother with the light: they needed privacy, not illumination.

"What is it?" Taryn snarled. "This is my night, you can't—"

"Shut up and listen, goddamnit, this is more important than any of that political bullshit," Dannon said, shaking her. "Carver got hit by that goddamn Davenport. Davenport found out what Carver did in Afghanistan, and supposedly is going to get the governor to say something about it, on a talk show or something—that Carver massacred some people."

"Did he?"

"Well, that depends on how you look at it," Dannon said.

"So he *did*," Taryn said.

"*Listen*. Davenport is trying to get Carver to turn on us. Offering him immunity. Carver's freaking out. He wants you to give him a million dollars in diamonds and cash, tonight. He's going to run for it. He thinks he can hide out in Panama."

"That sounds crazy," Taryn said.

"It's not entirely crazy, except that he won't stop with a million. He'll spend it in six months. He'll buy a goddamn fishing trawler or something, something that won't work out, and he'll keep coming back. Or he'll get in trouble and he'll tell everybody that a U.S. senator is a pal of his, and he'll be coming to you for a little influence peddling . . . and more money. It's the same deal as with Tubbs."

"Is there any chance that Davenport would give him immunity?" Taryn asked.

"Oh, hell, yes. If he could bag you and me? Hell, yes."

"So . . ."

"I'm gonna take Ron out tonight. I'll work out some kind of excuse to get him down to his vehicle, and I'll hit him—"

"The car will be full of blood—"

"No-no. I can do this. There won't be a speck of blood. We've already got the perfect graveyard. I'll get my pal to carry his passport across the border into Iraq . . . and we're good. Good forever."

A PHONE RANG; for a freaking split second, Lauren thought it was hers and she slid her hand down her leg to the side pocket, but then heard Taryn say, "Wait . . ." and then, as the phone continued to ring, Taryn said, "Damn it, where is it? Okay."

She'd been rummaging through her purse, Lauren thought. Then Taryn answered the phone and said, "We're in the back . . . probably pretty soon. Yeah, I've stopped, don't worry about it. Okay, we're coming out."

Lauren heard what sounded like a woman dropping a purse on a tabletop, and the door swung open.

Taryn's voice: "Do it. Do it."

Then they were gone, still talking, their voices diminishing as they went down the hall. Lauren started breathing again, slipped out from under the bed. The room was no longer entirely dark. She could be seen by the monitors if she stood up. She crawled across the carpet, pulling the pack, to the bathroom, which wasn't covered by the cameras. At the bathroom, she slipped inside, and as she was closing the door, saw Taryn's purse on the dresser on the opposite wall.

Thought about it, then went to the window, looked and listened, and satisfied that the guard wasn't right there, dropped the pack into the arborvitae. Then she went back to the bathroom door, got down on her knees, and then on her stomach, and slipped across the floor, staying close to the wall where the camera wouldn't see her. It would see her if she stood up at the dresser.

She stayed on the floor to the outer door, reached out and slowly, slowly closed the door. As soon as it was dark, she stood, went straight to the purse, dipped inside, found Taryn's iPhone, then hurried back across to the bathroom. She peered out the window, then pulled back: the guard was right there, on the lawn, still looking away from the house, toward the trees.

He went on by, slowly, and as soon as he was out of sight, she dropped the tarp across the cut edges of glass, pushed through the window, dropped behind the bush, on top of her pack. She stuffed the tarp into it, took the starlights out and put them on. She wouldn't wait now: she called Kidd, said, "Running," and took off, zigzagging between trees, into the tree line, then through the trees toward the street.

At the tree line, she knelt, pulled off her starlights, and stuffed them in her pack, and then the darkened car rolled up. She was inside then, and Kidd did a U-turn and asked, his voice tight, "How'd it go?"

"Pretty routine," she said. "Hey, slow down. I've got to text a guy."

"What?"

"Give me Lucas's cell phone number."

LUCAS WAS IN HIS LEXUS, alone, waiting for Carver to move again, when his phone burped at him.

Thinking Weather or Letty, he pulled it out and found a message from an unknown number:

Dannon will kill Carver tonight at the hotel and bury him in the perfect graveyard. Best wishes, Taryn.

Lucas said, "What?"

CHAPTER 25

Lucas sat for a minute looking at the message, didn't understand how it could possibly be right, then called the BCA duty officer on his own phone and asked him to do a look-up on the number: he came back a minute later and said, "Billed to Taryn Grant."

Lucas said, "Sonofabitch," to nobody. He couldn't think what he had to lose, so he redialed the number, and was instantly switched to an answering service, which meant that the phone had been turned off. He said, "Davenport . . . you sent me a message. Call me back."

He waited four or five minutes, then his phone burped: Del.

"Grant and Dannon and the campaign manager just came out of the house, and it looks like they're putting a caravan together," Del said. "I guess they're headed downtown. I've been monitoring Channel Three, and they are leaning pretty hard on her winning. They haven't called it yet, but they will before midnight."

"Last time I saw, it was pretty close," Lucas said.

"Yeah, but the suburbs are in, and the Iron Range isn't—she'll be two-to-one, up there."

"Okay. Listen—are you sure Dannon is with the convoy?"

"Pretty sure. I saw him getting in the truck, he's driving. That Green chick is in the second truck, and there are a couple more . . ."

"Okay. I'm gonna want you to buzz Grant's truck once it gets on I-94. I need to confirm that Dannon's in the truck. When you're sure, get your ass down here as fast as you can."

"I can do that."

Lucas rang off, waited for another call from Grant. Nobody called, until Del came back again and said, "I ran their convoy. Dannon's driving."

"Get down here. I'm outside the Radisson parking garage. Drop your car, and hook up with me."

DEL ARRIVED TWENTY MINUTES later, walking up the street in a gray hoodie, hands in the front pocket, looking a little like a monk. Lucas popped the lock on the passenger side, and Del climbed inside. "You sounded stressed," he said.

Lucas called up the message from Grant and passed the phone over to him. Del read it and said, "This don't compute."

"I had Dave look up the number. It's hers."

"Did you . . ."

"I called her back," Lucas said. "She'd turned off the phone."

"This is messed up. This isn't right," Del said. "I mean, even if it's true . . . she wouldn't send this message."

"That's what I can't figure out," Lucas said.

"What're you going to do?"

"Get past the first flush of the party . . . have Sarah and Jane keep an eye on Dannon and Carver . . . and maybe when things have settled down a little, I'll go in and get Taryn alone and brace her."

"You've been friendly with Green. Is there any possibility . . . ?"

Lucas groaned: "I should have thought of that. Maybe they're all using phones paid for by Grant."

"But why did she sign it 'Taryn' instead of leaving it alone?"

"Dunno." Lucas took his cell back and messaged Green: "Did you send me a note about C&D a few minutes ago?"

Del said, "She's driving, it might take a while for her to get back."

"She's a woman, it won't take—" Lucas's phone chirped, and he looked at the message screen. It said, "No," and the incoming phone number was wrong.

He texted back, "Are all your phones billed to Grant?"

Another ten seconds. "No."

"Any new info on C&D?"

"No."

Del said, "Something's happening, and we don't know what it is."

They thought about it, and then Del said, "You gotta make a call, here. Do we take it in and show it to Carver?"

"There's no way he'd believe it: he'd figure we're trying to ramp up the pressure," Lucas said. "It'd completely blow the fact that we're watching them full-time."

"But if he gets killed . . ."

"Yeah."

"I'm not worried about him, man, I'm worried about *you*," Del said. "If it got out that you got this message, and then didn't do anything about it . . ."

Lucas thought about that, then got on the radio to Bradley and Stack. He had to wait until the women got out of sight, where they could use their handsets. When they were both up, he said, "We've got a problem, and I can't really explain it. But: we need to be all over Carver and Dannon. I need to come and talk with Taryn as soon as possible."

Bradley said, "Wait, wait . . . you won't be able to talk to her for a while. Channel Three and Eleven called it for her. It's a mob scene in here. . . . She'll be up on the stage, making a speech . . ."

Lucas could hear a wall of noise in the background, and he said, "Okay. Call me as soon as she gets offstage. But you and Jane *must* keep track of Dannon and Carver."

"That's almost impossible, Lucas," Stack said. "We can keep track of them, kinda, but they keep going backstage with these politicians, these out-of-bounds areas, and then they'll pop out somewhere else. If we stay right on them, they'll spot us for sure."

"Do what you can. Call me when Taryn gets offstage. The minute she gets off."

The party rocked on.

Lucas rang off and Del said, "Maybe you ought to have them identify themselves, and tell Carver and Dannon that they're bodyguards and they aren't going away."

"Then we're right back to where we started," Lucas said. "With nothing—and with them knowing that we're on them like a cheap suit. If we go to them directly, we'll lose it all."

"Is that better or worse than somebody getting killed?"

Lucas had to think about that, and finally said, "I want them."

They sat in the street for an hour, talking to Stack and Bradley, and were finally told that the noise and tumult were beginning to wind down. Most of the good food and booze was gone, and the less needy of the party faithful were beginning to leak out the doors, Bradley said. Taryn was thanking some fourth-level party worker and his big-hair wife, a guy who'd raised a quarter million or something.

DANNON WAVED CARVER into the back where the food service people were working, where the hotel functionaries were counting bottles and security guards were taking breaks, got him back to a side room with the soft-drink and candy machines and said, "She can't get you all of it, not right now. She can get you a good part of it, if you'll take gold."

Carver was truculent: "What's a good part of it?"

"Quarter million, give or take, in cash," Dannon said. "She's not sure of the exact amount, but it started at a half million that she stacked up over the last six years, for the campaign. As it turned out, she only needed about half the cash. The good thing is, it's all cold, in case we had to make some payoffs. Then there are two hundred gold Eagles, no serial numbers or anything else. Right now gold is selling for seventeen hundred an ounce, which is another three hundred and forty grand. That's close to six hundred thousand that we can get our hands on tonight. The diamonds . . . She won't give up the diamonds. They've all got sentimental value for her. She says that as soon as we get clear of the campaign, she'll put another four hundred thousand on you, in Panama. You might have to make some arrangements—"

"Like what kind of arrangements?" Carver asked, but he'd brightened considerably.

"You might have to get a piece of land down there with your own money. Like, pay a hundred grand for a piece of oceanfront, or whatever, under a different name. She pays you half a million for it.

That keeps things straight with the tax people. It'll all be handled through front companies."

"Well, shit, we can do that," Carver said.

"Sure. It's not rocket science," Dannon said.

"When do I get it?" Carver asked.

"When do you want it?"

"Tonight, if we can do it," Carver said. "I can be on a six o'clock plane for New York."

"There are going to be people around the house, people coming back with Taryn," Dannon said. "I've got the numbers for the safe. We could do it right now—take your truck, you can drop it at Hertz on your way out of town. We were going to turn it back in tomorrow anyway."

"Good. Good. Can we go now?"

"Let me talk to Schiffer."

LUCAS AND DEL were still sitting in the street. Everything was running behind schedule; Taryn had been expected to speak at 11:30, but that got pushed to 11:45. She was supposed to talk for ten or fifteen minutes, but the thank-yous went on and on. Finally, at 12:30, Stack called Lucas and said, "It's winding down. She won't be here long after she finishes speaking."

"When was the last time you saw Carver and Dannon?"

"They've been going in and out of the back," Bradley said. "But Dannon's here right now, he's talking to Schiffer."

"Carver's right at the edge of the stage," Stack said. "He's talking to some guy in a suit. . . . Wait, he's going into the back again."

"I'm coming in," Lucas said.

Lucas took the stairs to the ballroom where the party was; people were going out through multiple folding doors, most of them with yellow credential tags around their necks that said, "Taryn VIP"—party invitees. There were guards at the door doing perfunctory credential checks, but there were more people leaving than arriving. A TV guy carrying a light stand hustled by, and a guard put a finger out to Lucas, a gesture asking for a credential, and Lucas showed him his BCA identification. The guard's eyebrows went up and he waved Lucas through.

Inside, a few hundred balloons, red, white, and blue, were scattered around the floor and floating around the ceiling, and a drunk young man was popping them with what looked like an Italian switchblade while his friends laughed at him. The carpet smelled like spilled champagne.

Taryn seemed to be getting ready to leave the stage, waving fairly randomly at the crowd, laughing; strobes popped in her face and her teeth flashed in the brilliant white pops.

Four sixty-inch TV screens were sitting on high stands at the edges of the ballroom, and Lucas paused to check the numbers: Taryn was up more than sixty thousand votes and the Iron Range was still coming in large; there were a few Republican counties yet to report out west, but they'd make little difference. It wasn't a huge victory, but a clear one: Smalls was toast.

CARVER AND DANNON took the back stairs to the parking ramp. Carver said, "Man, I wasn't sure she'd go for it. You gotta get in on this, dude. She's not gonna fuck you forever, and money is definitely better than pussy."

"Shut up," Dannon said.

"True love, huh?" Carver said, and he laughed.

Dannon was checking the garage. An older couple was getting into a Prius a hundred feet away, and a Chevy Tahoe was rolling toward the exit. He could see a man standing in the elevator lobby, apparently waiting to go up. They got to Carver's truck and Carver went to the driver's side, got inside, and Dannon took the pistol from his waistband and held it in his right hand, waited as Carver unlocked his door.

When the locks clicked, he opened the door with his left hand and then climbed inside, keeping his right hand out of sight. Carver looked at the dash as he started the car, and Dannon pulled the door shut with his left hand, and Carver shifted into reverse to back out, looked over his left shoulder, checking for traffic . . .

Dannon brought the .22 up and shot him in the temple. Carver's head bounced off the side window and Dannon shot him again, the .22 shots deafening inside the truck, but hardly audible outside. Carver slumped, his face not even looking surprised. Dannon pushed the gear shift back into Park, took a plastic bag out of his jacket pocket and pulled it over Carver's head, and cinched it around his neck. If Carver weren't quite dead, the plastic bag would do the job; and it would keep blood out of the car, though there shouldn't be too much in the way of blood, with the small-caliber bullets going straight into the brain.

That done—it took fifteen seconds—he got out, climbed in the backseat, and pulled Carver into the back, and tried to wedge him down onto the floor. Carver was too big for that, so he got out again, moved the passenger seat fully forward, and pushed Carver's head and chest down on that side, folding his legs onto the other side.

The back windows were darkened, but Dannon walked around to the back of the truck, took out one of the blankets they kept there, for when passengers wanted to sleep on trips, and spread it over Carver's body.

He closed the door and walked back to the driver's side, looking in the side windows as he went: Carver was invisible.

Two minutes after the shooting, he backed the truck out of the parking slot and started toward the exit. He was forty-five minutes from the perfect graveyard.

LUCAS WORKED HIS WAY to the front of the ballroom. Taryn was still talking to people on the stage, but Schiffer had a hand on her back and was moving her toward the stairs. Lucas moved close, where Schiffer could see him, and fixed his eyes on her face and sent her a telepathic message to look at him, and, as usually happened, a few seconds later she glanced his way, recognized him, and frowned. He jabbed a finger at Taryn, and then did it again.

She turned away, but he knew she'd seen him, and as they got closer to the edge of the stage, she said something sharp in Taryn's ear, and Taryn frowned and looked down and saw Lucas, turned and said something to Schiffer that he couldn't hear.

Lucas kept working toward the end of the stage where a crowd was waiting to talk to and touch Taryn as she came off. She moved slowly down the stairs, then through the crowd, shaking hands and patting shoulders. Lucas kept moving to stay directly in front of her, and eventually she got to him and she said, to the side of his face, so only he could hear, "Now you're in real trouble, governor or no governor."

"Why did you send me that message about Dannon and Carver?" Lucas asked.

She pulled her head back and said, "What?"

She didn't send it, Lucas thought. It was right there on her face.

"Do you have your cell phone? You sent me an urgent message from your phone."

She said, "What? Why would I . . ." She turned to look behind her and called, "Marjorie . . . Marjorie."

One of her campaign people, a short woman in a blue dress, shouldered her way through the crowd; she was carrying a clipboard, a huge tote bag, and two purses.

Taryn said to her, "Give me my purse."

The woman handed the purse over. Someone in the crowd tugged on Lucas's jacket, and he half turned and saw Bradley there. She put a hand to her ear, miming a handset, and mouthed, "Right now." Bradley eased back into the crowd and Taryn was saying, "Where's my phone? Marjorie, where's my phone?"

"I . . . I . . . I don't know." Marjorie looked frantic. "I never saw a phone."

"It was in there," Taryn said. "I put it there."

"You did not send me a text message?" Lucas asked her, virtually speaking into her ear. They looked like they were dancing.

She said, "No, no . . ."

Lucas backed away, and Taryn looked after him, puzzled, then dug through her purse again, while talking to Marjorie, and Schiffer began to urge her through the crowd. Lucas got to the edge of the ballroom and stepped behind one of the TV-set stands, put the handset to his face and said, "This is Lucas: What's up?"

Shrake came back instantly: "Carver's truck is moving, it's leaving downtown. Jenkins and I are on it, but we're gonna need help."

Jenkins said, "I was parked in the bottom of the garage, near the exit. I don't think it's Carver in the truck: I think it's Dannon."

"Where's Carver?"

"Don't know."

Del came up: "Dannon's truck is still in the garage. Maybe they switched vehicles."

"Okay," Lucas said. "Jane, Sarah, have you seen Carver?"

Stack came back. "I haven't, not since before you came up. He went in the back . . ."

Bradley said, "I saw Dannon maybe ten minutes ago, going into the back."

Lucas said, "Okay, you guys take off, help Shrake and Jenkins. Chase them down. Lights and sirens until you get close, then hang back and follow, okay?"

"Gotcha," Stack said.

Lucas asked, "Del, you're pretty sure Dannon's truck is still in the garage?"

"Yeah," Del said.

"Okay. Work your way up the parking ramp, see if you can spot him or Carver or the truck. I'm going into the back, see if I can chase them down."

"What's going on?" Del asked.

"I don't know—but Shrake, Jenkins, don't lose that car. Don't let it get too far ahead of you, either. I want you to be able to see it, if it stops."

"That's a risk," Shrake said. "He could spot us."

"I trust your professionalism that that won't happen," Lucas said.

"Thanks a lot," Jenkins said. "Shrake, I'm right behind you. Take a right."

"Taking a right," Shrake said.

"We need to get those goddamn women up here," Jenkins said.

"We're coming, we're coming," Bradley said.

————

LUCAS BADGED HIS WAY into the back. Taryn and her closest campaign people, including Green, were going through in a cluster, heading for a back elevator that would take them to the parking ramp. Taryn never looked back but Green did; she nodded and went on. Lucas hurriedly checked the back area—no Carver—and then took the stairs down to the parking ramp.

He arrived just as the elevator did. Green took the lead, and they walked over to the truck that Dannon had been driving, and Green took the wheel. Schiffer got in the passenger side and Taryn in the back, and the rest of the crew broke for different vehicles, and Lucas, still not seeing Carver, ran toward the truck carrying Green.

As he did that, Del pulled onto the floor and paused. Lucas ran up to Green's window and she rolled it down and Lucas asked, "Where's Carver?"

Green said, "He and Dannon headed back to the house. We're having an after-party, they're setting up there."

Lucas was unhappy about that, but nodded, and Taryn called, "Where's my phone?"

"Don't know," Lucas said, and he turned and walked down the ramp toward Del's car, putting the handset to his head: "Jenkins . . . I've been told that Carver and Dannon were going together out to Grant's house. Are you sure they weren't both in the car?"

"Man, they had to stop at the pay booth, and I was right there. There was a lot of light behind them, coming through the windows. There was only one guy in the car, and that was Dannon. Unless Carver was on the floor or something."

"Goddamnit," Lucas said. "You think you could buzz him?"

"Yeah. Once."

"Is Shrake close enough to pick him up after you buzz him?"

Shrake: "We're on 94 North, I'm about a quarter mile behind Jenkins. I could do it for a while, but he's driving right at fifty-five. If I hang back here, he could get suspicious. We need Jane and Sarah right now."

Bradley: "We're getting on the ramp now. . . . We're coming."

Lucas said, "Jenkins, go ahead and buzz him. We need to know if both of them are in there."

Lucas walked down to Del's car and Del opened the passenger-side door and asked, "What are we doing?"

"I can't find Carver. Nobody's waiting for him, because they think he already went."

"Is it possible he split?"

"You mean, called a cab or took a bus?"

"Okay, that doesn't seem likely," Del said.

Lucas looked at the phone message again: *Dannon will kill Carver tonight at the hotel and bury him in the perfect graveyard. Best wishes, Taryn.*

"He could be dead," Lucas said.

"That would take balls the size of the Goodyear blimp," Del said.

"I might have put Carver in the shit," Lucas said. "I was trying to drive a wedge between them, but what if he said something, or made some kind of threat, and they decided they needed to get rid of him immediately? What if he tried to blackmail them? What if he gave them a deadline?"

"Then . . ." Del said.

Lucas said, "Let's go back to my car."

"You're going after them?"

"We're both going," Lucas said. "We don't need to track Green.

But if Dannon killed Carver, he's going to dump him. We need to be there—we need everybody to be there."

"I could drive," Del said.

"They're too far ahead of us," Lucas said. "I need to drive."

"Goddamnit. I hate it when you drive," Del said. "I get so puckered up that I've got to pull my asshole back out with a nut pick."

"Thanks for the image," Lucas said. "Let's go."

CHAPTER 26

hey left Del's car in the garage and took off in Lucas's Lexus, lights and siren, Lucas turning the corner and busting the red light and then off through traffic to I-94, Del braced against collision, hanging on to his seat-belt strap with one hand, the other hand braced against the dashboard.

"Ask them where Dannon is at," Lucas said, as they rolled onto the interstate.

Del got on the handset, and Shrake came back with a mileage marker and Del said, "They've got seventeen miles on us."

"But they're going fifty-five and we're going ninety-five." Lucas did some math in his head and said, "We'll be catching up two-thirds of a mile every minute, so we'll catch them in more or less twenty-five minutes. That's not fast enough."

He dropped the hammer and the big Lexus groaned as it edged past a hundred miles an hour, then to a hundred and five.

"How do you do that?" Del asked.

"Do what?"

"That math?"

"The same way you would have done it, if you'd had nuns

beating fractions into your head in third, fourth, and fifth grades," Lucas said.

"How fast will it take us to catch them at a hundred and five?"

"Uh, about . . . five-sixths of a mile every minute . . . we're about sixteen miles behind them now . . . you take sixteen divided by five and multiplied by six . . . about nineteen and one-fifth minutes . . . more or less."

"How do you know it's five-sixths of a mile every minute?"

"Because sixty miles an hour is a mile a minute. We're going fifty miles an hour faster than they are, and that's five-sixths of sixty . . . so we catch up five-sixths of a mile every minute."

"Well, hell, even I could do that."

"Yeah, if you knew how."

JENKINS CALLED. "There's one guy in the truck. I came up fast with my high lights on and illuminated the truck, then passed him in a hurry, like I was an asshole. There's only one guy in the truck."

Lucas took the handset from Del: "Get as far out in front of him as you have to, to lose his headlights. Then find a side road and dodge off on it, until he passes. Then get behind again. Where in the hell are Jane and Sarah?"

"Jane is a mile behind Shrake, and I'm right behind her," Bradley said. "I'm going to start falling back in case she has to pass Dannon."

Shrake said, "I'm gonna have to pass in the next couple of minutes. I'm coming up on him."

Stack: "I'll tell you what—he's not going to Taryn Grant's place. Not unless he's taking the way-scenic route."

———

THAT'S THE WAY IT went for sixteen minutes. At four minutes, Shrake had to pass. He also reported one person at the wheel, and that he was sure it was Dannon. Stack moved up until she was running a half-mile behind Dannon, and Jenkins, coming off a side road, fell in behind Stack and ahead of Bradley. Bradley passed him, so that Jenkins could hang back longer. By then they were well up I-94, running parallel to the Mississippi River.

At sixteen minutes, Jenkins called to say that he could see Lucas's flashers. Lucas turned off the lights and eased off the gas. They passed Monticello, the city lights spreading off to the right, toward the Mississippi, and then plunged back into the dark. Five minutes later, he came up behind Jenkins and dropped his speed to fifty-five. They ran like that for another fifteen minutes, and as Stack was coming up on Dannon, she called and said, "I think he's getting off at the exit. . . . He's getting off. I'm going straight."

Lucas: "Jenkins, pull off and kill your lights. Sarah, keep going behind Jane, turn around as soon as you can."

As Jenkins moved to the shoulder, Lucas pulled over behind him, then fished an iPad out of the seat pocket behind Del.

Jenkins, looking at the GPS tracker, called: "He's gone right, he's headed down toward the river."

Lucas thought, *Perfect graveyard*. He called back, "Wait one," brought the iPad up, went to Google Earth, got a satellite view of the area and said, "There's no bridge down there. It's not a dead end, just a bunch of back roads."

Jenkins: "Let's go to the top of the overpass."

"Go," Lucas said, and they waited until a couple of cars passed, then ran dark to the overpass and up the exit ramp, and pulled off at the top. In the distance, probably a mile away, they could still see Dannon's taillights. He seemed to be moving slowly, tentatively. Lucas went back to Google Earth, pulled up a measuring stick. He hopped out of the Lexus and carried the iPad to Jenkins's car, and stood by the driver's-side window.

"He's about one-point-two miles in," Jenkins said, looking at the monitor for the GPS bug.

Lucas enlarged the satellite view, then stretched the measuring tape down the map. There was nothing on the map at 1.2 miles, but at 1.4, there was a minor track going off to the left, probably gravel or dirt, along the river.

They watched the monitor and the iPad, and at 1.4, the taillights disappeared, but they could see the faint streak of headlights, now running parallel to both the highway and the river. Two-tenths of a mile down the side road, Dannon stopped. Below them, on the highway, Shrake did an illegal U-turn across the interstate median, and came up the ramp; a minute later, he was followed by both Bradley and Stack.

When they were up, they got out of their cars and gathered around Lucas, who said, "We're going to head down to that intersection. About one-point-four miles. No lights. When we're there, we'll go in on foot. He's about two-tenths of a mile in, probably three or four hundred yards. I want Sarah and Jane to stay with the cars."

"I want to go in," Stack said.

And Bradley: "I do, too."

"I don't have time to argue," Lucas said. "The fact is, we'll be on foot, and you don't have the shoes for it. If he sees us coming, he could come busting out of there in that truck, and we'll be in trouble. We need somebody in the cars who can take him, if it comes to that. Jenkins, Shrake, Del, and I have all done this before, and we've all been in gunfights. You two haven't. So, you stay with the cars. End of story. Let's load up and go."

THE TWO WOMEN WEREN'T happy about it, but they did it.

Jenkins had a pair of night-vision goggles, and the most experience with them. He'd lead. All six of the cops had LED flashlights, big 135-Lumen Streamlights. They all loaded up and started down the side road, running dark, except for taillights, following Jenkins.

The countryside was densely wooded, with breaks for the occasional farmstead and backwoods house; and with the clouds, black as a coal mine. Lucas could barely see the road in front of him, and took it slowly, at twenty miles an hour, watching Jenkins's taillights, feeling for the right edge of the tarmac with his tires.

"At twenty miles an hour, how long does it take to go one-point-four miles?" Del asked.

"You'd go a mile in three minutes," Lucas said. "You'd go the rest of the way in four-tenths of three minutes. Three minutes is one hundred and eighty seconds, and one-tenth of that is eighteen seconds. Four-tenths would be seventy-two seconds. So, four minutes and twelve seconds."

"How big a grave can you dig in four minutes and twelve seconds?"

"Don't have the math on that one," Lucas said.

AT A LITTLE MORE than 1.3 miles on Lucas's odometer, they saw the road going left, which looked like a darker tunnel on a black sheet. Jenkins pulled off to the left side of the road, Lucas edged off behind him, and the others followed. They all climbed out into the cold night, and Lucas whispered, "No talking. This guy might have experience night-fighting. Spread out, don't shoot each other. Stay on the road. No noise."

The four men moved off, spread across the road like gunfighters in an old spaghetti western; and, Lucas thought, they *were* gunfighters, every one of them. Jenkins was the lead man, with two to his left, one to his right, in a V, like a bunch of Canada geese headed south.

Lucas was counting steps. Two hundred and eighty slow steps down the road, and they could hear Dannon working, the rhythmic *chh! chh! chh! chh!* of a spade digging into damp earth, but they couldn't see him.

WHEN DANNON WAS IN the army, he'd served as company level and battalion level intelligence officer. In the latter job, in Afghanistan, he'd serviced a dozen sources in villages scattered around the forward operating base. They would call into the cell number and leave messages, which the native translator would render into English. Most of it was inconsequential—this guy or that guy had come or gone, and he was Taliban or an Arab or whatever. Arabs were always interesting, because they were rare and sometimes important. Most times, they were kids from Saudi or Jordan looking to make their bones, wandering across the landscape like itinerant skateboarders; but sometimes interesting. The Americans usually tried to pick up the Arabs.

The actual pickups were done by special ops people. Dannon had gone along on a number of the operations, when there was space available—the commander encouraged staff people to get out in the weeds—and had twice been involved in firefights with the targets. Both times, they'd been kids, and both times, killed.

But.

Except for the fights themselves, it had always been high-tech: sources fingering the targets, live calls when a target was leaving a village, tracking them from gunships, then closing them down.

He'd never used a GPS tracker, and it never occurred to him that there might be one on his truck. He'd never been tailed, and though he'd watched his rearview mirror, looking for cars that were pacing him, it never occurred to him that cars that overtook him and disappeared in the distance were the watchers. He'd never thought that night-vision goggles could be used against him.

He'd never been snuck up on in the dark.

But.

He'd sat on nighttime ambushes, every sense digging into the dark, and as he dug Carver's grave, that was operating on some level. At one point, a few minutes after he started digging into the reeds in the swampland, he picked up what seemed to be a vibration. He stopped digging and walked out to the road, and peered in the dark toward the turnoff. Nothing but darkness.

He turned back, navigating with a taped flashlight, a thin needle of light showing him the path.

He worked for another five minutes, and then felt another chill. What *was* that?

There was no specific noise, other than the engines from the interstate, a mile away, but there was something under that . . . an unidentifiable pattern . . .

He didn't feel foolish at all: the special ops people always had said that when you had a feeling, pay attention to it; most times, it was nothing. The other time, if you hadn't paid attention, it would kill you. So he paid attention, sitting, no longer digging. The burial site, near where they'd put Tubbs down, was off a gravel track, down a path that led to the river, and then off the path fifteen yards.

Lots of zigs and zags.

He was invisible, he thought. He sat, listening, listening . . .

And heard the crunch of gravel.

No. Imagined he heard the crunch of gravel? He wasn't sure. He slipped his gun out of its holster, pressed the safety forward.

Duckwalked out to the path to the river.

A MINUTE OFF THE TRACK, Lucas felt Del's arm slow him down, and pull him in. They bunched up and Jenkins whispered, "His truck is twenty-five or thirty feet in front of us. I think he's off to the right, right by the truck."

Lucas said, "Keep the lights handy. Light him up if you see him."

They moved on, up to the truck; and then a few steps beyond. Lucas heard the crunch of gravel and put out a hand to Del, who was to his left, stopping him in his tracks. Del did the same, to Jenkins, and Jenkins to Shrake. They all froze, and listened, peering into the blackness.

Three of them could see nothing; but there was some kind of faint, faint noise coming from the front. Jenkins saw Dannon edge into the path, a gun in his hand.

Jenkins had his flashlight in his left hand. He pointed it at Dannon's eyes, pointed his pistol, and without warning, turned it on.

Dannon was there, thirty feet away, pinned by the dazzling light like a frog on a tenth-grader's dissection tray. Unlike those frogs . . .

Jenkins shouted, "Freeze, freeze or we'll shoot."

. . . Unlike those frogs, Dannon leaped sideways back into the swamp reeds and then, scrambling on his hands and knees, still clinging to his pistol, began running mindlessly through the brush.

The cops all turned on their lights and played them through the brush, and caught flashes of Dannon, the movement of the swamp weeds and brush as he tore through them, and Lucas shouted, "Jenkins, Shrake, Del, go after him, take care, take care . . ."

Lucas turned and in the light of his own flash, ran back up the dirt track toward the gravel road, pulled his handset and said, "Sarah, Jane, he's coming right at you. Watch out, watch out, he's on foot, I think he's coming for the road. . . ."

NOTHING AT ALL WENT through Dannon's head. He'd had some escape and evasion classes, and one of the basics was simply to put distance between yourself and your pursuer. Distance was always good; distance gave you options. He didn't think about it, though, he just ran, fast and as hard as he could, and he was in good shape.

Good shape or not, he fell three or four times—he wasn't counting—and the small shrub and grasses tore at him and tried to catch his feet; he went knee-deep into a watery hole, pulled free, and ran on, looking back once. He was out of the light, now, he was gaining on them, he was almost there . . .

And he broke free into the road. He couldn't see it, except as a kind of dark channel in front of him. The lights were now a hundred yards back, but still coming, and he ran down the dark channel. When he got far enough out front, he'd cut across country again, and then maybe turn down toward the river. . . .

He ran a hundred yards down the channel, heedless of the sounds of his footfalls, breathing hard. . . .

———

LUCAS WAS ON THE ROAD, moving faster than Dannon, but at the wrong angle—Dannon, though in the swamp, was cutting diagonally across the right angle of the gravel road and the dirt track. Lucas could tell more or less where he was because of the brilliant lights of the cops behind him, and the sound of Dannon's thrashing in the brush. Then the thrashing stopped, and Lucas stopped, trying to figure out where he'd gone.

BRADLEY AND STACK HEARD him coming. Stack whispered, "I'm going to hit the car lights."

"Okay."

Stack reached to the light switch, to the left of the steering wheel, and waited, waited, trying to judge the distance, and when it seemed that he might be close enough,

Flipped the switch.

And Dannon was there, covered with mud, clothes hanging wet from his body, a bloody patch on his head, mouth hanging open. He had a gun in his hand and as Stack stepped to the left of Bradley, he brought it up and Bradley screamed, "Drop the gun," and he didn't, he brought it higher . . .

The women shot him.

Later, it would turn out that they'd each fired four times, though neither was counting, and of the eight shots, had hit him five times.

Two of the shots would have been wounding; two of the shots would have killed him in seconds or minutes; one of them went through his throat and severed his spinal cord, and Dannon went down like Raggedy Andy.

CHAPTER 27

Lucas not only heard the gunfire, but saw it. He was at right angles to the confrontation, running back to the cars, saw the lights go on, and then behind the lights, the sound of the gunfire and the flicker of the muzzle flashes. The women were both shooting 9mm weapons, and the flashes were small, even in the dark night. He shouted, "Davenport coming in . . ."

Running as hard as he could, he was there in fifteen seconds. The two women were still by the cars, guns pointed at Dannon's body. Lucas came up, and Bradley said, her voice cool, "He had a gun, he pointed it at us."

Lucas nodded once, said into his handset, "You guys get to the closest road, he's down."

He did that as he stepped over to Dannon's body and checked it. He was on his side; blood pooling around him, his gun still gripped in his hand.

Lucas backed away, and Jenkins ran up and looked at the body.

He said, "Who . . . ?"

Bradley said, "We did."

"Jesus," Jenkins said.

Del and Shrake came up and stopped beside Jenkins; all three of them were covered with mud, their trousers wet above the knees. Del had a scrape above one eye. Lucas said to Jenkins, "Get your flashers on, block the road. Figure out what county we're in, and call the sheriff's office and get some deputies down here."

To Shrake: "Call the duty officer and get a crime-scene crew on the way. Tell them to bring lights—lots of lights. Tell them to hurry."

And to Bradley and Stack: "You two put your guns away. Decock them but leave them in the same condition, don't reload them. Stay around the car, don't approach the body."

To Del: "Come on. We've got to check on Carver."

"Hope to hell Carver's down there," Del said. "Be a hell of a note if Dannon was out digging black dirt for his flower garden."

THEY HURRIED ALONG THROUGH the night, turned the corner down the dirt track, to Dannon's truck. They shone lights in the window, without touching the truck, but it was empty. They then stepped carefully through the brush back to the spot where they'd heard Dannon digging. There was a hole in the ground, and beside it, a bulky body with a plastic bag on the head. "That's him," Lucas said. "I'm not gonna touch the bag."

"You think Tubbs is out here?" Del asked.

"I'd bet on it, but I'm not looking around here now," Lucas said, shining the light down on his shoes. The ground was damp, but not actually swampy where he was standing.

"One thing about November," Del said, shining his flash up into the sky. "No bugs."

"Yeah, that's one thing about it," Lucas said. "Let's go back and wait for the crime-scene people."

————————

THEY HAD THREE SHERIFF'S cars at the scene in twenty minutes, one blocking the road, the other down by the mouth of the dirt track, one with the BCA group. The crime-scene truck arrived a few minutes after three-thirty, and took charge of the scene, along with the sheriff's deputies. They also took charge of the women's pistols.

After they'd walked the crime-scene crew through the entire action, and marked the critical bits, Lucas ordered the two women and Shrake and Jenkins back to BCA headquarters: "I want full preliminary reports from everyone, start to finish, with timelines. Right now, tonight. When you're done, cross-check them, then get some sleep. We'll meet tomorrow at one o'clock in the afternoon and figure out the bureaucratics. Jane and Sarah, you did good. The guy murdered at least three people in cold blood, and if you hadn't shot him, he'd have killed you and taken one of the cars. Nobody could have asked for more."

Lucas called the BCA duty officer and asked him to send another crew to cover Dannon's and Carver's apartments. "Seal them off at a minimum."

The four of them coughed and shuffled their feet and talked for a minute or two, before going to their vehicles, to trundle back up the road. By that time, both the area around Dannon and the area around Carver were bathed in work light, and one of the crime-scene people was making a movie of the shooting area.

Del asked, "We're staying?"

"We might have to come back, but right now, we're going to talk to Taryn Grant."

"You think she knew about this?"

"I . . ." Lucas had to stop and think. "I'd give you six-to-five that she did. No better than that. We have nothing with her name on it. If she's involved, we'll have to find something in Dannon's apartment. Probably not Carver's."

BY THE TIME THEY got back to town, it was after five o'clock, not even a hint of the dawn. They dropped off I-94 onto I-494 at the western edge of the metro area, then turned off and headed deeper west, into the lake neighborhoods. When they got to Grant's house, they found the street deserted; no well-wishers, no TV trucks. There were a few lights in the house, and two security guards at the driveway.

Lucas and Del got out of Lucas's truck and walked up the driveway. The guards moved down to block them, and Lucas pulled out his ID and said, "We're with the Bureau of Criminal Apprehension. We need to wake Ms. Grant. Now."

One of the guards looked at the ID with his flashlight and said, "You got it . . . but I think she's still awake. There are still some people here."

Del asked, "Any more of you guys around?"

"Yeah, one guy behind the house, he moves back and forth across the yard."

THEY WALKED UP TO the front door, rang the bell. Del scratched his neck and looked at the yellow bug light and said, "I *feel* like a bug."

"You look like a bug. You fall down out there?"

"About four times. We weren't running so much as staggering

around. Potholes full of water . . . I see you kept your French shoes nice and dry."

"English. English shoes . . . French shirts. Italian suits. Try to remember that."

"Makes my nose bleed," Del said.

The door opened, and Green looked out: she was still fully dressed, including the jacket that covered her gun and the fashionable shoes that she could run in.

She took a long look at Del, and asked, "Where're Dannon and Carver?"

"Dead," Lucas said. "Where's Grant?"

"In the living room."

"You want to invite us in?"

She opened the door, and they stepped inside, and followed her to the living room.

Grant was there, still dressed as she had been on the stage; she was curled in an easy chair, with a drink in her hand, high heels on the floor beside her. Schiffer was lying on a couch, barefoot; a couple of Taryn's staff people, a young woman and a young man, were sitting on the floor, making a circle. Another man, heavier and older, was sitting in a leather chair facing Grant. Lucas didn't recognize him, but recognized the type: a guy who knew where all the notional bodies were buried, a guy who could get the vice president on the telephone.

When Lucas came in, behind Green, Grant stood up, putting her drink aside, and asked, "What? What now?"

"Your pal Dannon murdered your pal Carver and took his body out in the countryside to bury it. We were tracking him, and when we approached him at the grave he was digging, he tried to shoot it out. He's dead."

There was a moment of utter silence: Schiffer seemed to be the most affected, as she got to her feet, her face gone white, a hand at her throat.

Grant recovered first, and asked, "What . . . does that mean?"

"We were hoping you could help us with that," Lucas said.

"I don't know what that means," Grant said.

"You sent me a message earlier tonight . . ." Lucas began.

Grant put up a hand: "No. No, I didn't. I already told you that."

Lucas took his phone out of his pocket, called up the message, stepped up to her and said, "Here's the message. Is this your phone number?"

She looked at the message and the number, and said, "That's not right. That's crazy."

"Is that your phone number?"

"Yes, but my phone, I can't find my phone. It's gone. Somebody took it out of my purse. Marjorie had my purse . . ."

She looked at the woman on the floor, who said, "I was really careful with the purse. It was zipped up."

Lucas said, "The call came in at ten-oh-six. You were still here at ten-oh-six, weren't you?"

Grant looked at Schiffer, who said, "Yes . . . we were still here. We left for the hotel around ten-fifteen."

Grant said, "Then the phone call came from here. My purse was back in the bedroom. In fact . . ." She looked at Schiffer. "In fact, you called me while I was back there."

They stared at each other for a moment, then Schiffer said, "That's right," dug around in her bag, pulled out her phone, and said, "I made that call at nine-fifty-eight. What's that . . . eight minutes before you got the message?"

"There was nobody in the bedroom but me. I went back there

to get ready to go," Grant said. To Schiffer: "I got the call from you . . . I put my phone back in my bag. My bag was on the chest of drawers."

Green stepped over to Grant and took her by the arm and said, "One second . . ." She pulled Grant off to one side, twenty feet away, stood with her back to Lucas and the rest of the group, and whispered directly into Grant's ear. Grant looked at her, then nodded, came back and said, "I'd like to alter that statement a bit. Doug Dannon escorted me back there. We didn't talk, I just wanted some privacy to pee. I was alone when Connie called, and I dropped my phone back in my purse and came straight out here. Then when we were ready to go, I went back and got my purse."

"Can we look at the bedroom?" Lucas asked.

Schiffer said, "Maybe we ought to have a lawyer."

Lucas: "There's a very good chance . . . actually, it's not a chance, it's a certainty, that this is a crime scene. Somebody called me on Ms. Grant's phone, who had knowledge that Dannon was planning to kill Carver. As he did. A lawyer might tell you not to talk, but he can't keep us away from a crime scene."

Schiffer shrugged, and Grant said, "I don't care, anyway. This is . . . awful. Awful! This is insane! The bedroom . . ."

She walked back toward the bedroom wing, and Lucas, Del, Schiffer, Green, and the others followed. Halfway down the hall, Lucas looked back and said, "I don't want anyone here except Ms. Grant."

Grant said to Lucas, "I want witnesses. You have lied to me and worked for Smalls since the beginning of this thing, and I wouldn't put it past you to frame me. I want witnesses. I want Connie and Alice with me."

Lucas said, "I did not . . ." Then he stopped and nodded. "Ms.

Green and Ms. Schiffer. Nobody else. Do not touch a thing. Stand in the doorway where you can see and hear, but do not touch anything. Do not touch the door or the doorknobs or anything else."

They stepped inside the bedroom and Grant pointed to her left and said, "I went in there to use the bathroom. My purse was right here, on the dresser." She pointed at the dresser. "Doug was out in the hall. Nobody could have gotten past him, without him knowing. And I don't know why a, a . . . confederate . . . of his would call to say he was planning to kill Ron. Anyway, I used the bathroom, and came out, and as I came out, the phone rang, and I talked to Connie, and then put the phone back in the purse and went out. With Doug . . ."

When they'd entered the bedroom, Del had slid off to the left to clear the bathroom. He came back and listened to Grant's narration. When she finished, he asked, "When you were in the bathroom, did you notice anything unusual? Did you look out the window?"

"Out the window? No, I didn't look out . . . Why?"

"Because the window seems to be missing," Del said.

LUCAS HAD BEEN INVOLVED in any number of clusterfucks in his working life, but the one at Grant's house was notable. They all went to look at the window, which was, without a doubt, missing. Then they trooped around to the backyard, where they found three separate sheets of glass lying under an arborvitae.

Lucas said, "Why would—"

Taryn put a hand to her lips and said, "Could they get in the safe?"

"What safe?" Del asked.

They trooped back inside, and Taryn reached behind a side table and did something, and a bookcase rotated out from the wall. They all looked at the safe, which was closed. She said, "Would you turn away for a minute?" and they did, and turned back when she said, "Okay," and turned the heavy handle that worked the safe locks.

She pulled the door open and looked into a safe that was completely empty.

In the silence, she stumbled backward, staring at the empty steel hole in the wall, and screamed, "No! No! No!"

Lucas was looking at her face when she opened the safe, and in his estimation, there was no chance that she was faking the reaction. Not even if she was crazy; not even if she'd known the safe was empty, and had rehearsed.

No chance.

LUCAS MOVED EVERYBODY out to the living room, and sat them down, and called the BCA duty officer again, and told him what had happened. He said, "You've got people spread all over the metro area."

"Leave the Dannon and Carver apartments. Seal them up—we can get to them later. Right now, I need a crew here. Get them moving."

Grant was pacing the living room, hands to her face. Everybody else sat without talking. Green went into the kitchen to get something to drink, and Lucas followed her. She handed him a personal-sized bottle of orange juice, opened one for herself, and asked, "Is there any possible way to keep me out of this? As an informant? I need the work."

"If you don't have a problem with the possibility of a little perjury," Lucas said.

"I don't, because I never told you anything meaningful," she said.

"I keep thinking, the one person who may have had access to that phone, and who might have been aware of the whole Dannon-Carver situation, and who might have been willing to warn me . . . was you."

"But I didn't. And when we give our statements, you'll find that I was right on the door when Taryn went back to the bedroom with Doug. I was monitoring the door, and the comings and goings, every minute. I couldn't have made that phone call: and I didn't."

"So you're out, if that's what the statements show," Lucas said. "I'm leaving my ass in your hands. I won't mention you, and you don't mention me, except when we spoke in public."

"Thank you."

They carried the bottles of juice back into the living room, where Grant looked at them, and muttered, almost to herself, "Almost four million."

Lucas: "What?"

"That's what they got—whoever it was. Four million. Cash, gold coins, and mostly a lot of jewelry. Diamonds, gold. The Star of Kandiyohi, which is a diamond as big as a robin's egg, a Patek Philippe watch that I got from my grandfather, worth a quarter million dollars all by itself. . . ."

Schiffer looked at her and said, "Okay. Agent Davenport has his crime scene. But you are a United States Senator-elect, and we have important issues to deal with. We need legal advice. Now."

Schiffer looked around: "Not another word, anybody. Not another word to Agent Davenport or other police officers, not until the lawyers get here."

CHAPTER 28

Weather usually slept hard from ten o'clock at night until six in the morning. Lucas came to bed at all kinds of times, usually between midnight and three, so when he didn't come to bed on election night, she didn't miss him until she woke up at six. Then she got on the phone, a cold clutch in the stomach, and when he answered, she said, "You're not shot."

"No," he said. "But there was some shooting."

He spent five minutes telling her about it, in detail, and at the end of it, she said, "I'm revising a rhino in two hours and I'm shaking like a leaf." Translated: She was fixing a nose job that some other surgeon had messed up.

"Stop shaking," Lucas said. "I'm fine, Jenkins and Shrake are fine, Bradley and Stack are a little screwed up, but they'll be okay, and Del is good, except that he looks like a bug."

Then he had to explain that.

THE LAWYERS ARRIVED, and officially informed Lucas that there would be no further statements from the principals, until there had been extensive consultations. They said it in a long-winded way, and Lucas had to take a break from it, when a crime-scene supervisor called.

"We've been out here walking the area and we've found what looks a lot like another grave. It's about a hundred and fifty feet from the grave Dannon was digging, on the same track, on the same side of the road. We'll document it and open it."

"Do that," Lucas said. "It's Tubbs."

THE CRIME-SCENE CREW ARRIVED in force, and started by processing the window in Taryn's bathroom and the ground outside. They would get to the safe, but the supervisor complained to Lucas, "Why'd you let her open the safe? There might have been prints on the keypad."

"Given the look of the rest of it, do you really think so?" Lucas asked.

"Well, no. But . . ."

"No buts. If this was a real robbery, it was a pro. Like, a top pro," Lucas said.

"You think it wasn't real?"

"I'm not sure of anything," Lucas said. He looked at his watch: "Gotta make a call. I'll talk to you again before I leave."

THE SUN WAS UP, somewhere behind the clouds, but exactly where was hard to tell. In any case, it was light outside when Lucas wandered down to the end of the driveway and called the governor.

The governor's phone rang four times, then Henderson said, "This time of the morning, it can't be good."

"About your party's senator-elect: her top security guy murdered another one of her security people and tried to bury him by the Mississippi halfway to St. Cloud. We interrupted that and there was a shoot-out and he was killed. The crime scene has found another dug-up area nearby. I think they'll be pulling Tubbs out of there, in the next couple of hours."

After a moment, the governor laughed and said, "You are a piece of work, Lucas. You and that fuckin' Flowers, both of you. I really get my entertainment dollar's worth."

"The last person who said I was a piece of work, offered to take me to bed," Lucas said.

"Well, I'll pass on that," Henderson said. Then, after a moment of silence, the governor said, "I'll have to mediate this. I'll have to confer with other Important People. Porter, of course, is going to lay an ostrich-sized egg. I don't see how Grant can stay on as a senator, and frankly, that's about the best possible outcome I could have imagined."

"How's that?" Lucas asked.

"Guess who would appoint her replacement?" Henderson said. "I'd have Porter Smalls out of my hair and a new senator who would be wildly happy about supporting me for a better job .... if somebody goes looking for, say, a vice president."

"That hadn't occurred to me," Lucas said.

"Because you're not a natural politician," the governor said. He laughed again. "This is the kind of thing that makes life interesting."

"Unless you're Dannon. Or Carver."

"Well, yeah, I suppose," the governor said. "I'll assign somebody to say a prayer for them."

———

AFTER THAT, IT WAS a lot of crime-scene stuff, lawyers and political wrangling. Tubbs was dug up and after a nasty autopsy, he was reburied. He'd been hit on the head with a heavy, rounded object like a baseball bat. Death had not been quick.

They found the smear of blood that Tubbs had left in Dannon's car. Unfortunately, the crime-scene tech who found it, and sampled it, unknowingly destroyed the scrawled TG—for Taryn Grant— that Tubbs had hoped they'd see. DNA proved that Tubbs had been in Dannon's car, but they already knew that Dannon or Carver had killed him. So Tubbs's last, fading, flickering effort came to nothing.

LUCAS GOT STATEMENTS from everybody and Alice Green had been telling the truth: at the time Grant went to the bedroom with Dannon, Green had been assigned to the door, and could be seen doing that on the security tapes. Connie Schiffer, in particular, had been curious about Grant and Dannon leaving the party, heading back to the bedroom, and had exchanged looks with Green.

One other politician, arriving late to congratulate the new senator, spoke to Green at the door, and remembered that Grant had not been in the room when he got there. He asked for her, and a moment later she reappeared from the direction of the bedroom, to give him a hug.

The tapes of the bedroom showed nothing, because the room started out dark. Then there was a flicker of light, apparently when Grant walked into the room, and she'd reached out (automatically, she said) and hit the privacy switch, which turned the cameras off. A minute later, she hit the privacy switch again (again, she said, an automatic reflex) and turned the cameras back on as she left. She left the door open, so there was a bit of light, and then a short time later, the door mysteriously closed again, killing the light. There was nothing more on the tape for several hours, when Grant got back from the hotel and hit the privacy switch on the way to the bathroom.

The next people on the tape were Grant, Lucas, Del, and the others, going down to investigate the bedroom.

All of that supported what both Grant and Green had said, except on one point: Grant hadn't been in the bedroom long enough to get to the bathroom and pee, not unless she'd set the women's North American land-speed record for micturition. Nor had she reported the cut-out windows, which seemed impossible to miss. The toilet was in a separate booth, and the window was right overhead. But she was sticking to her story, saying that she hadn't bothered to turn the light on in the bathroom and was in a hurry and simply hadn't noticed the windows. In reality, Lucas suspected she'd gone back to talk with Dannon, but didn't want to admit it, because the next thing Dannon did was kill Carver.

He also suspected the robbery had taken place when the door mysteriously closed, because that must have been when the phone was stolen; and after the party had gone to the hotel for the victory celebration, the house had been closed and the dogs turned loose.

He further suspected that Green, or possibly Carver, could have had something to do with the robbery: probably through an accomplice. He thought that because they monitored the security cameras, and if Grant had ever forgotten to turn the cameras off, could have seen her opening the safe; they probably knew something about the contents of the safe, and that it would be well worth hitting; and they knew about the security measures outside. Also, both Green and Carver had his phone number.

He still didn't understand why either one would call him with the message from "Taryn."

That made no sense at all.

ONE OF THE CRIME-SCENE crew had found what appeared to be two small imprints under the arborvitae bush below the bathroom window. One looked like an impression from the outer edge of a hand; the other just a little curve in the dirt, possibly the impression of a heel. He'd taken photos of both.

When he showed the photos to Lucas, he said, "We're not sure that they are what I think they are. I couldn't testify to it . . . I mean, I could say what I think, but any good defense attorney would tear my ass off."

"Cut the crap: What do you think?"

"The curves are small . . . like a small hand and a small heel. Like they were made by a woman."

Somebody with large balls, like an ex–Secret Service woman, Lucas thought. Could Green have cut the windows out earlier in the day, to make way for an accomplice? But that seemed unlikely. Why would she think that Grant wouldn't be going back to pee, and wouldn't notice the cut-out windows?

THE POLITICAL WRANGLING WAS more amusing than anything. The governor called, laughing again, a week after the murders hit the newspapers, and said, "Well, I called and told our senator-elect what all the Important People said, and she said I should write it all down on a piece of paper, roll it into a sharp little cone, and shove it where the sun don't shine. She's not quitting."

"Jesus, I thought she *had* to, from what I've been reading," Lucas said.

"With a billion dollars, you don't have to do much of anything you don't want to, and she doesn't want to quit," the governor said. "If she does a few million in political advertising over the next six years, nobody'll even remember this little dustup. So, we're moving right along to the important stuff, like revising the estate tax."

"That's the end of it?"

"Not quite. I've invited Grant to a little confab in my office tomorrow, with Porter Smalls. Mitford will be there, and her campaign manager, and I'd like you to sit in. And I'll get Rose Marie to come along."

"Why is that?"

"Because I want everybody clear on what happened here, and why everybody did what they did—including you and me," the governor said.

THE NEXT AFTERNOON, they all got together at the Capitol, in the governor's conference room: Henderson, Grant, Smalls, Mitford, Rose Marie, Lucas, Connie Schiffer, and Alice Green, still working as Taryn's security.

For a political gathering, there was a remarkable lack of even symbolic amity. The governor shook hands with everybody, but nobody shook hands with anybody else.

The governor sat at the head of the conference table, cleared his throat, and said, "I don't expect all of us to be pals after this, but I'd at least like to get things clear for everybody. Senator-elect Grant has, of course, made it clear that she didn't have anything to do with the rogue security people on her campaign staff, and in fact feels that she was being set up for long-term blackmail by those same people. In any case, she will not resign and will take her seat in the Senate in January."

Smalls said, "I think that—"

The governor: "Shut up for a minute, will you, Porter? Let me finish."

"I just—"

"You'll have your chance," Henderson said. He looked at Taryn Grant and asked, "Setting aside all the BS aimed at the media, am I correct that this is your position?"

Grant nodded: "Yes."

Connie Schiffer started to say, "I think we all know that Senator Smalls—"

The governor interrupted: "No. Be quiet. We don't want any of that. So we know that Senator-elect Grant will take her seat in the Senate. I'll now turn to Lucas Davenport, the lead investigator in this case. Lucas, do you have any issues that you will continue to pursue?"

Lucas said, "There are several small mysteries about the whole case that I'd like to resolve, and some minor entanglements—for example, Minneapolis still has to decide what to do about the files that were used to frame Senator Smalls. But at this moment, I see no further possibility for arrests or prosecutions involving anyone in this room. I will tell you that I suspect that Senator-elect Grant is not telling us all that we need to know to effectively close out this case. I have no proof of that, and I see no way to get any proof, unless it turns out that either Douglas Dannon or Ronald Carver has somewhere left behind some evidence of her involvement. We have been through both of their town houses, and through Dannon's safe-deposit box at Wells Fargo. We found considerable cash, but we found nothing that would implicate Senator-elect Grant in any wrongdoing."

"So you're at the end of that road," Henderson said.

"Yes, unless something extraordinary turns up, but I don't think that will happen."

Henderson said, "Okay. I want to tell everybody that I asked that Lucas be assigned to this case, because I trust him absolutely. And now I am ordering him not to speak to any media or to anyone else regarding his suspicions about anybody in this case, unless or until he has absolute proof of wrongdoing. Is that clear to everybody? Lucas?"

"That's clear," Lucas said.

Henderson turned to Smalls: "Porter."

Smalls said, "This is one of the most disgraceful moments in the history of American politics and I'm a student of that history, so I know. I was the victim of the most brutal character assassination ever carried out against an American politician, and the main financial sponsor of that assassination actually benefits, and goes to the Senate. Well, I'll tell you—there are people on both sides of the Senate aisle who are frightened by what was done here. I will go to Washington for the lame-duck session, and I will talk to my friends there."

He looked directly at Grant: "I will tell them that I think you are guilty of the murder of three people and that you were the sponsor of the child-pornography smear, and that I think a person of your brand of social pathology—I believe you are a psychopath, and I will tell them that—has no place in the Senate. And I will continue to argue that here in Minnesota for the full six years of your term, and do everything I can to wreck any possible political career that you might otherwise have had."

Grant smiled at him and said, "Fuck you."

The governor said, "Okay, okay, Porter. Now, Taryn, do you have anything for us?"

"No, not really. I'll be the best senator I can be, I reject any notion that I was involved in this craziness." She looked at Smalls: "As for you, bring it on. If you want to spend six years fighting over this, by the time we're done, you'll be unemployable and broke. I would have no problem setting aside, say, a hundred million dollars for a media campaign to defend myself."

"Fuck *you*," Smalls said. And, "By the way, I'd like to thank Agent Davenport for his work on this. I thought he did a brilliant job, even if I wound up losing."

Grant jumped in: "And I'd like to say that I think Davenport created the conditions that unnecessarily led to the deaths in this case, that if he'd been a little more circumspect, we might still have Helen Roman and Carver and Dannon alive, and might be able to actually prove what happened, so that I'd be definitively cleared."

Smalls made a noise that sounded like a fart, and Henderson said, "Thank you for that comment, Porter."

After some more back-and-forth, Henderson declared the meeting over. "We all need to go back and think about what we've heard here today, think really hard about it. We need to start winding down the war. We don't need anything like this to ever happen again."

The people at the meeting flowed out of the conference room, into the outer office, but then stopped to talk: Grant with Schiffer and Rose Marie, Smalls with Mitford. Henderson pulled Lucas aside and said, "Let's keep the rest of the investigation very quiet. Back to quiet mode."

"Not much left to do," Lucas said. "I'll let you know if anything else serious comes up, but I think it's over."

"Good job," Henderson said. "But goddamn bloody. *Goddamn bloody.*"

Lucas saw Green hovering on the edge of the gathering and waved her over. She came, looking a little nervously over at Grant, who was talking with Rose Marie and paying no attention to Green.

Lucas said, "Governor, this is Alice Green, a former Secret Service agent and Ms. Grant's security person. I think she's a woman of integrity, and if you someday have an opening on your staff for a personal security aide . . . she's quite effective."

Henderson smiled and took her hand and didn't immediately let it go. He said, "Well, my goodness, as we wind up for this upcoming presidential season, I might very well have an opening . . ."

Lucas drifted away, and let them talk.

OTHER BITS OF THE CASE fell to the roadside, one piece after another.

The Minneapolis Police Department showed little appetite for investigating itself concerning the possibility that dozens of its personnel had been viewing child porn as a form of recreation. A few scraps of the story got out, and there were solemn assurances that a complete investigation would be done, even as the administration was shoveling dirt on it. Quintana, no dummy, apologized to everybody, while hinting that he'd have to drag it all out in the open if anything untoward happened to him. He took a reprimand and a three-day suspension without pay, and went back on the job.

Knoedler, the Democratic spy, got lawyered up, and the lawyers quickly realized that everything could be explained by the Bob Tubbs–Helen Roman connection, and there were no witnesses to the contrary. They put a "Just Politics" label on it, and it stuck.

Clay, the suspect in the Roman murder, was freed, and Turk Cochran, the Minneapolis homicide detective, mildly pissed about that, gave Lucas's cell phone number to Clay and told him to check in at least once a week and tell Lucas what he was up to. Clay started doing that, leaving long messages on Lucas's answering service when the call didn't go through, which threatened to drive Lucas over the edge.

Two weeks after the shootings, a few days after the meeting in the governor's office, Dannon's aunt came from Wichita, Kansas, to Minneapolis, to sign papers that would transfer Dannon's worldly goods to her. She was his closest relative, as his parents had died twenty years earlier in a rural car accident, and he'd left no will that anybody could find.

The crime-scene people told Lucas that she would be at his apartment to examine it and to sign an inventory, and Lucas stopped by for one last look. A BCA clerk was there, with the inventory, and Lucas found nothing new to look at. The aunt, after signing the inventory, gave him a box covered with birthday-style wrapping paper; the box had been unwrapped, and opened.

"I think you should give this to that woman, the senator," the aunt said. Her name was Harriet Dannon.

Lucas took out a sterling silver frame. Inside was a news-style photo of Grant on the campaign, shaking hands with some young girls, with Dannon looming in the background. The frame was inscribed, "I'll always have your back. Love, Doug."

"I never thought he was a bad man," Harriet Dannon said. "But I mostly knew him as a boy. He was a Boy Scout. . . . I never thought . . ."

LUCAS DIDN'T QUITE KNOW why Harriet Dannon thought *he* should give the picture to Grant, but he took it, and back outside, thought, *Might as well.* He was not far from her house, and he drove over, pulled into the driveway, pushed the call button.

A full minute later—there may have been some discussion, he thought—the gate swung back. He got out, walked to the front door, which opened as he approached. Alice Green was there: "What's up?"

"Closing out Dannon's town house. Is Senator Grant in?"

"She's waiting in the library. With the dogs."

Lucas reached inside his sport coat and touched his .45, and Green grinned at him. "Won't be necessary," she said. And very quietly: "Thanks for the governor. That's going to work out."

"Careful," he said.

GRANT WAS IN THE LIBRARY, sitting in the middle of the couch with the two dogs at her feet, one on either side of her; like Cleopatra and a couple of sphinxes, Lucas thought.

He walked in and she asked, "What do you want?"

"I was over at Dannon's apartment, we're closing it out. He left this: I guess he never had a chance to give it to you."

She looked at the photo, and then the inscription, then tossed it aside on the couch. "That's it?"

Very cold, Lucas thought. "I guess," he said. He turned to walk away, and at the edge of the room, turned back to say, "I know god-damn well that you were involved."

She said not a word, but smiled at him, one long arm along the top of the couch, a new gold chain glowing from her neck. If a jury had seen the smile, they would have convicted her: it was both a deliberate confession and a smile of triumph.

But there was no jury in the room. Lucas shook his head and walked away.

IN THE CAR, backing out of the driveway, he had two thoughts.

The first was that Porter Smalls, in vowing to smear Grant with other members of Congress, was pissing into the wind. He could go to the lame-duck session and complain all he wanted about Taryn Grant, but nothing would be done, because Grant was a win-ner. In Lucas's opinion, a good part of the Congress seemed to suffer from the same psychological defects that afflicted Taryn Grant—or that Taryn Grant enjoyed, depending on your point of view. Their bloated self-importance, their disregard of anything but their own goals, their preoccupation with power . . .

Not only would Taryn Grant fit right in, she'd be admired.

The second thought: He was convinced that Grant was involved in the killings—not necessarily carrying them out, but in directing them, or approving of them. Once a psychopathic personality had gotten that kind of rush, the kind you got from murder, he or she often needed another fix.

So: he might be seeing Taryn Grant again.

He would find that interesting.

A COUPLE MORE WEEKS slipped by.

A mass shooting in Ohio wiped everything else out of the news, and the whole election war began to slip into the rearview mirror.

Flowers arrested the Ape Man Rapist of Rochester, a former cable installation technician, at the Mayo Clinic's emergency room. He'd tangled with the wrong woman, one who had a hammer on the side table next to her bed. And though the rapist was wearing his Planet of the Apes Halloween monkey head, it was no match for her Craftsman sixteen-ounce claw. After she'd coldcocked him, she made sure he couldn't run by methodically breaking his foot bones, as well as his fibulas, tibias, patellas, and femurs. Flowers estimated he'd be sitting trial in three months, because he sure wouldn't be standing.

Lucas would sit in his office chair for a while every day, and stare out his window, which overlooked a parking lot and an evidence-deposit container, and run his mind over the Grant case. He didn't really care about Grant's jewelry, but the phone call plagued him.

He kept going over it and over it and over it, how somebody else could have worked it, and then one day he thought, *Kidd could monitor the security cameras.* And he thought, *No way Kidd could get his shoulders through that bedroom window.* And Lucas thought, *Had there been a twinkle in Kidd's eye when, speaking of Lauren's previous career, he'd said, "Insurance adjuster"?*

He thought about Lauren, and he thought she was far more interesting than an insurance adjuster. She *seemed* more interesting than that. . . .

He looked up her driver's license and found she'd taken Kidd's name when they married. Without any real idea of where he was going, he idly looked up their marriage license, and found that her maiden name had been Lauren Watley.

Then he checked her employment records. . . .

And there, back, way back, he found that she'd worked as a waitress at the Wee Blue Inn in Duluth, where the owner was a guy named Weenie.

LUCAS KNEW ALL ABOUT Weenie. He was, at one time, Minnesota's leading fence and criminal facilitator. Everybody knew that, but he'd never been convicted of a crime after an arrest for a string of burglaries as a teenager, and a short spell in the youth-offender facility.

Never arrested because he only dealt with high-end stuff, the stuff taken by the top pros; he didn't deal with guns or anyone who routinely used violence. Just the good stuff. If you needed to change two pounds of gold jewelry into a stack of hundred-dollar bills, Weenie could do it for you, for twenty percent. If you needed to cut open a safe, he knew a machinist who could do that for you.

And Lauren had worked as a waitress for . . . fifteen years, sometimes, it seemed, under the name LuEllen. *Fifteen years?* Lucas laughed: that was not possible.

Not possible. He knew her *that* well.

What *was* possible was that Weenie provided her with an employment record, wrote off her salary while sticking the money in his pocket. In the meantime, she was off doing whatever she did. . . .

Lucas wasn't exactly sure what that was, but he now had an idea . . . an itch that needed to be further scratched.

A MONTH AFTER the shoot-out with Dannon, on a crisp, bright, dry December day, Lucas got in his 911 and aimed it north on I-35, and let it out a little. He went through Duluth at noon, stopped at the Pickwick on the main drag, ate meat loaf and mashed potatoes, and then cruised on up to Iron Bay, a tiny town off Lake Superior.

Iron Bay had once been the home for workers at a taconite plant, and when the plant went down, so did the town. At one time, a house could be bought for ten thousand dollars, and many had been abandoned. The town had seen better days since, but it was not yet a garden spot.

Lucas threaded his way through a battered working-class neighborhood, and finally pulled into the driveway of a small ranch-style house. A heavy old man named James Corcoran came to the door, sucking on a cigarette, and said, "That car is a waste of money, in my opinion. You shoulda gone for the Boxster. All the ride, half the price."

"Got hooked on the looks," Lucas said, checking out his car. "A Boxster is nice, but you know . . . a 911 is a 911."

"Come on in," the old man said. "You want a beer?"

"Sure."

THEY SAT IN THE living room and Corcoran, who'd once been the town's only cop, said, "So, Lauren Watley. I do remember that girl and I hope she's all right."

"Married to a millionaire artist," Lucas said.

"Good for her, good for her," the old man said. "Her dad was one of the bigger jerks in town. Smart guy, engineer at the factory, but when he lost his job, he packed up, put it all in the car, and took off. Never looked back, as far as I know. Took every last cent, too. Janice Watley woke up one morning and didn't have enough cash to buy cat food."

"How old was Lauren at the time?"

"Don't really know," Corcoran said. "Junior high school, I guess. After her old man took off, the family went on welfare, and child support, but hell, that was nothing. Then, we started having some break-ins around town. Whoever was doing it knew what was going on, who had what, and where it was. For a long time, it was only money. But then, there was a guy here who ran the only thing in town that was worth a damn, a payday loan company. He had a coin collection, and it disappeared. Probably worth fifty grand."

"You thought Lauren was doing it?"

"You know, it was one of those small-town things," Corcoran said. "Everybody knew what their situation was over there. They had *no* money. Janice couldn't find a job . . . hell, nobody could find a job after the plant went down. So they were hurting. But they weren't hurting enough. They found the money for a used car. They paid cash for things . . . and the feeling was, money was coming from somewhere."

"But there was no proof."

"No proof. Lauren got to be in high school, and then this coin collection disappeared. The owner's name was Roger Van Vechten. He sued the insurance company, because they only wanted to give him thirty thousand, and he wanted fifty. But that was later. Right after the coins disappeared, I happened to be in Duluth, for something else entirely, buying something, I can't remember what . . . anyway, I see little Lauren coming out of the Wee Blue Inn. You know the guy there . . ."

"Weenie . . ."

"Yeah. Dead now," Corcoran said. "He was the biggest fence in the Upper Midwest. Everybody knew it. The question was, what was Lauren doing coming out of the Wee Blue Inn? I thought I knew the answer to that and followed her back to Iron Bay, and we got to her house and I braced her. Made her turn her pockets out. She had two dollars and some change. I checked the car . . ."

"You had a warrant?"

Corcoran laughed, and then started coughing. When he recovered, he said, "Oh, hell, no. That was a different time, up here. I just did what needed to be done. Anyway, I checked her, and she was pissed, but she didn't have a thing. Said she went down there to apply for a waitress job. I said, 'Lauren, you ain't no waitress.' And she said, 'Jim, you never been poor.' She called me 'Jim,' when everybody else her age would have been calling me 'Mr. Corcoran.' She was fifteen and all grown up."

"I've known women like that, girls like that," Lucas said, thinking of his Letty.

"But that wasn't the kicker," Corcoran said. "The kicker was, we had some rednecks out here who made a connection down in the Cities, and got the local cocaine franchise. One day, I borrowed a couple deputies from the sheriff and we raided them, and we got a half-kilo of coke and eight thousand dollars in cash. I locked it up in the evidence cage at the police department, which was on the side of city hall. That night, somebody cracked the back door on city hall, slick as you please, broke through the drywall into the police annex, cut the lock on the cage, and took the cash and the coke. I know goddamned well it was Lauren and I didn't have one speck of evidence. I just looked at her and I could see it in the way she looked back at me: she thought it was funny. She was getting back at me for bracing her."

Lucas smiled, and said, "Yeah, I can see her doing that."

"You got something on her?" Corcoran asked.

"Exactly what you got," Lucas said. "A belief."

"And not a speck of evidence."

"Not a speck," Lucas said.

"Well, good for her," Corcoran said. "I always liked that girl."

On the way out of town, Lucas stopped at the only gas station to get a Diet Coke and whatever kind of Hostess Sno Ball imitation they had, and found himself looking at a rack of postcards.

A COUPLE OF DAYS later, Lauren and Kidd were going out for a late lunch, and they stopped in the bottom hallway to check the mail. Lauren took a postcard out of the mailbox and Kidd asked, "Anything good?"

"It's a postcard from Lucas. . . . It says, 'Glad you're not here.'" With a puzzled look on her face, she turned it over and found a photo looking out over Iron Bay and Lake Superior.

"Oh, shit," she said, stricken.

"What?"

"Lucas knows."

FIFTEEN MINUTES LATER, wrapped in warm winter jackets, she and Kidd stood side by side on the Robert Street bridge, looking down at the dark waters of the Mississippi.

Kidd said, "This is the only time since I knew you, all those years, that you ever kept anything that they could stick you with."

"Because it's gorgeous," she said. A gold watch dangled from her fingers. "It's a Patek Philippe, from 1918. I've looked it up—it could be worth anything up to a quarter million."

"And it would hang you, if anybody ever saw it," Kidd said.

"I know," she said. "But I refuse to give it back to a killer."

"It's a shame, though," Kidd said.

"Would you do it if it was a Monet?"

"Jesus Christ, no," Kidd said. "If it was a Monet . . . I'd . . . I'd . . ."

"You'd never drop it in the river," Lauren said. She relaxed her fingers, and the watch dropped like a golden streak through the gray light of winter, and a quarter million dollars disappeared into the black water below the bridge.

"That's it," Lauren said, dusting her hands off. "Not a speck of evidence, now."

"Not a speck," Kidd said, hooking an arm through hers. "C'mon, little housewifey. Let's go get a cheeseburger."